CORRESPONDENTS

Also by Tim Murphy

Christodora
The Breeders Box
Getting Off Clean

TIM MURPHY

CORRESPONDENTS

A NOVEL

Grove Press
New York

FIRST EDITION

Published simultaneously in Canada
Printed in the United States of America

First Grove Atlantic hardcover edition: May 2019

This book was set in 11-pt. Janson Text
by Alpha Design & Composition of Pittsfield, NH.

Library of Congress Cataloging-in-Publication data is available for this title.

ISBN 978-0-8021-2937-6
eISBN 978-0-8021-4704-2

Grove Press
an imprint of Grove Atlantic
154 West 14th Street
New York, NY 10011

Distributed by Publishers Group West

groveatlantic.com

19 20 21 22   10 9 8 7 6 5 4 3 2 1

To the Ackareys

A fish said to another fish, "Above this sea of ours,
there is another sea, with creatures swimming in it—
and they live there, even as we live here."

The fish replied, "Pure fancy! Pure fancy!
When you know that everything that leaves our sea
by even an inch, and stays out of it, dies.
What proof have you of other lives in other seas?"

—Kahlil Gibran, *The Forerunner*

PROLOGUE

MAHRAJAN

LABOR DAY WEEKEND, 2008

Before everything changed that afternoon, Rita Khoury had been so happy that she'd finally stopped thinking about unhappy people elsewhere. The night before, in a mid-priced chain hotel off I-84 in central Connecticut, she and Jonah Gross had had incredibly gratifying sex before falling asleep in each other's arms on cool sheets as the A/C lowed. The next morning, after showers and coffee, Rita felt a warm buzz of contentment while sitting in the passenger seat of Jonah's Mini Cooper on the Mass Pike heading east. At a certain point after Worcester, she realized that not once that morning had she observed a stray object aside the road and tensed, thinking it was perhaps an IED or the charred corpse of a dog, goat, or child. She understood this to mean that she was unusually relaxed, Jonah's right hand in hers on her knee as his left maneuvered the wheel.

She was both eager and anxious to go the mahrajan, to reintroduce Jonah to her sister and present him for the first time to her mother, her nephew and niece, and, of course, to Bobby and the high-tech leg that had replaced his real one. She hadn't been to a mahrajan in nine years, and while one part of her thrilled to join the line of dancers—something that had filled her childhood heart with a sense of the exotic world that awaited her beyond Massachusetts—another part was reminded of the constraining flatness of childhood, the tyranny of day trips in the back seat of the car (relieved only by a book), the feeling that provincial adolescence would never end and that the big, dazzling universe would never, ever unfold before her.

Funny, she considered, she'd always thought that the first boyfriend she'd bring to the mahrajan one day would be Sami. There would be a comforting sense that the dancing, the food, the old ladies gossiping in Arabic with their startling glottal stops every few syllables wouldn't be strange and new to him, that she wouldn't have to do much cultural translating. *You're about to see Arabic culture distilled through a hundred years of a Boston accent and mostly Republican politics*, she'd have told Sami, and he'd have said, *Well, fair enough, you've seen your share of Arabic culture distilled through a bunch of French bourgeois snobs*, and they would have both laughed and had a wonderful time dancing dabke and drinking arak with her relatives, who—that one prior time they had met Sami, the Christmas of 2002, before the invasion—had found him handsome and impossibly sophisticated, with his French accent and all the places he'd lived.

But, of course, all that had been before she'd sabotaged herself. And it so happened that the first boyfriend she was bringing to this festival that figured so strongly in her earliest memories was, like her, an American and, unlike her, Jewish.

And now Jonah squeezed her hand twice and said, "So, hey. Tell me more about your people you're about to drag me into."

How to explain the Lebanese Maronites of Boston's North Shore? When she thought of her father's people en masse, she always thought first of their eyes, dark and soft and kind and looking a bit heartbroken, even if the person in question was not, with inky smudges beneath them, suggesting fatigue and defeat, even if, again, such was not the case. Then pair those eyes, those supple olive faces, with a Boston accent, full of dropped *R*s and that adenoidal flatness, as though invisible fingers were pinching the nose shut.

To her, such faces had always signified family and home, security and prosperity. But seeing similar faces in Iraq had provoked other feelings in her. How could a face look so familiar yet also be a portal to poverty, displacement, terror, despair, bottomless depression, trauma, rage—and, finally, empty resignation? How often she had watched the warmth, the hospitality in such faces at war with the suspicion, the bone-deep anger, the spiritual exhaustion.

So now, to Jonah, she merely said, "Lebanese Maronites were mountain peasants a hundred years ago, totally looked down on by the Beirut elite, who were Sunni or Orthodox. But here in the U.S. they've all become doctors and lawyers and bankers and business owners. So they made out okay."

Jonah laughed. "They sound pretty much like the Jews of northern Westchester County."

"They are basically Jews," she said. "They love Israel."

"They do?"

"Of course," she said sharply. "But since 9/11, all they want is to fit in and not have Americans think of them as Arabs or Muslims."

Jonah gave her the side-eye. "Your voice is escalating."

She laughed. "I know. But I get annoyed at Arab Americans who try to fly under the radar."

"You mean literally? Going through security at the airport?"

She laughed and brushed away his hand on her knee. She loved his dry, fucking-with-you sense of humor. "Just drive," she commanded.

They'd been on a rather desolate industrial strip off the highway, but now they found themselves in downtown Lawton, driving through the grid of what could be so many Northeastern former factory towns, an array of peeling, triple-decker homes, late-Victorian dark-brick hulks of churches and schools, storefronts with grand old engraved signage reading Woolworth or Feinstein's Apparel, then, in their windows, plywood or tin placards reading COMIDA LATINA or ABOGADO Y AGENTE DE BIENES RAÍCES. A few buildings, like a library and a municipal office, were clad in early-1970s Brutalist concrete, gray facades scarred now with graffiti and grime.

They passed under an archway sign, slightly the worse for wear, reading LAWTON: IMMIGRANT CITY & BIRTHPLACE OF LABOR RIGHTS.

Jonah read the sign aloud. "Really?"

"It's true," Rita said, shaking her head and smiling. "Well, I don't know about *birthplace*. But one of the greatest mill-worker strikes in the world happened here in 1912 when the workers' hours were cut. About twenty thousand workers from countries all over Europe walked out." Rita got emotional and proprietary when talking about this strike, as she had since she was eleven, when, obsessed with it, she'd written a history paper on it.

"But then," she continued, "the textile industry here dried up, right around when Puerto Ricans moved here, and the long-timers blamed the Puerto Ricans for ruining the city and moved out, and then the Dominicans and the Southeast Asians moved here, and with no jobs anymore it became the drug capital of northern New England. And now it's the poorest city in Massachusetts, and the schools are in receivership, and families like mine will only come here once in a blue moon for something like the mahrajan, and they're scared their cars will be stolen. And voilà, that's what you're seeing around you now. The once great and mighty Lawton."

"It's like an old Hudson River town," Jonah commented.

"Except without the trendy hipster renaissance."

"Mm."

"But it is where I'm from," Rita said. "I mean *really* from. My family. Much more than the suburbs." She pointed up ahead to the left. "That's the church." She rolled down the car windows. "Listen, you can hear the music."

Jonah nodded appreciatively. "I feel like we're going to a souk."

They pulled into the parking lot of a sandstone church with an asymmetrically peaked roof and an air of having been built during the Nixon administration. The facade bore an enormous mosaic of a black-haired, large-nosed Jesus, arms outstretched, two-dimensional and with a stylized nimbus around his head, in a Byzantine style, mountains in the distance.

Jonah laughed. "Now that's a Jewy-looking Jesus! Oh yes! I'm gonna like this."

"That's the genuine Sephardic Jesus," Rita noted. "And you're right," she added, kissing Jonah on the nose. "He does look a bit like you."

On the far side of the parking lot was a very large tent, crowded with people, from which wafted the scent of grilled meat and spices. Live music throbbed, all hand drums and synthesizer keyboards meant to sound like an oud. A man's voice wailed in Arabic over the instrumentation.

Rita's face lit up in recognition. "Oh, listen! This is a very famous song. It's called 'Ana Wel Habib.' *Me and my love.*"

"Anna well habib," Jonah parroted her.

"Just give me a sec." She pulled down the mirror over the passenger seat in the car, extracted lipstick and eyeliner from her bag. She'd never much cared about her looks or fashion, but over the years she'd learned to make at least half an effort, certainly in group settings, and particularly when with her mother. She'd started coloring over the wiry gray strands that had begun popping out of her dark curly hair, watched what she ate and how much wine she drank, managed to exercise every few days, bought a few fashionable new things to wear every season. Most nights she moisturized half-heartedly. That was about the length to which she went in terms of self-presentation. When they first met her, most people thought she was black Irish, half-Italian perhaps, and couldn't account for a certain deep-set intensity in her eyes and a modest but noticeable bridge in her nose. Arabs however, often asked, *Inti Arabi?* and she'd smile and answer, *Nus*, half. Certain half-Arab women, like Ally, her beloved princess of an older sister, were preposterously beautiful, dark chocolate hair and enormous brown eyes popping off creamy skin, but Rita didn't think she'd gotten that particular deal of the cards. She thought she was okay looking, not stunning but not unsightly, even if her eyes' relation to her nose vaguely evoked a Picasso. And that had always suited her just fine, to the very minimal extent she'd ever cared about such things—far, far less than Ally, she was sure of that.

She and Jonah walked, arm in arm, toward the tent, where a large circle of people, hand in hand, moved rightward in increments to the music, *step-step-kick-and-stomp*, the basic components of the dabke, which she'd been dancing at weddings since she was four years old.

"You *are* getting on that dance floor with me, you know," she said.

Jonah was squinting toward the tent. "It looks like the hora," he said.

"It's not that different. You cross your left leg in the front, though, not the back, before you kick. It's easy. If the Irish side of my family can learn to do it, you can. Come on, you're a Semite. It's in your genes."

"This Semite needs a beer first."

Before they entered the tent, her nephew Charlie, six, and niece Leila, eight, bounded out of the crowd toward them, tackling her. "Auntie Rita, Auntie Rita!" they shouted.

"Oh my God!" Rita laughed, kneeling down to hug them. "Hi, guys! It's so good to see you!"

Leila hopped on one foot before her. "Look, look, I got a tattoo on my face. Do you know what it is?"

"It's a monkey!"

"It's a *chimpanzee!* The girls at the table over there did it."

Rita kissed her niece. "It's *so cool*, Lei-lei."

Charlie hopped up and down before her, too. "What's mine? Can you tell?"

"It's an alligator."

He frowned. "It's a croco*dile!*"

"Ohhh, it's a *crocodile!* How can you tell the difference?"

Charlie's frown deepened. "Auntie Rita, you should be able to tell!"

"Yeah." It was Jonah, who squeezed her shoulder from above. "Auntie Rita, you should *really* be able to tell."

"I know, I should," said Rita, game. "Lei-lei and Charlie, this is my boyfriend, Jonah."

Charlie looked up at him. "Are you gonna dance dubbie?" he asked.

Leila frowned at her younger brother. "It's dub-*kee*. With a *k*."

Jonah shrugged. "Who knows? Maybe I'll dance dubbie, too."

This cracked up Charlie, though Leila continued to frown skeptically.

Ally stepped out of the tent, striding purposefully toward them in khaki capri pants and a French sailor's top. She'd dialed up her smile, as ready to charm as when she was five and had campaigned, successfully, to be the snow queen in the school holiday pageant. Rita, who had not seen her in three months, rose and hugged her older sister and only sibling, feeling, as she had felt since they were little girls, that when she was with Ally nothing could go wrong, or that even if anything did, it didn't matter much because Ally—crisp, capable, diplomatic, and kind—would fix it.

"You guys are attacking Auntie Rita already and she's not even in the tent!" Ally exclaimed, one hand still loosely holding her sister's.

"We're not *attacking* her, we're showing her our tattoos," Charlie corrected.

Ally leveled her eyes at Rita and Jonah. "They're *temporary* tattoos, thank God." She then regarded Rita keenly. "You look *amazing*."

You say "amazing" as though it's some dramatic improvement from the last time you saw me, Rita wanted to tease. But instead she said, "Thank you! So do you! I love your hair."

Ally's face darkened. "Do you really?" She'd had her long curls cropped into something short and even a bit playful and edgy. "You don't think it makes me look too—" She faltered for the word.

"Butch?" Rita offered.

"Well, no, not *butch*. I don't care about that. Just too . . . severe?"

"You mean butch?"

"No!"

"You don't look butch. It's perfectly adorable. Very chic."

Ally—for whom looks had always been a central concern, even if both humility and feminism had forever admonished her for this—seemed to slacken with genuine relief. "Well, thank you. Gary said that I looked ready for the women's softball team."

"No!" exclaimed Rita. Gary was her brother-in-law, a human resources executive for a biotech firm on Route 128, whom she found impenetrably dull at best and reliably offensive at worst. She felt the pang of inflamed sisterly loyalty she often felt toward Ally in relation to Gary's jabs, which Ally strove to find funny. But then again, Rita always had to remind herself, Ally had made her choices. And so had she.

Ally then hugged Jonah. "Well, hello again!" They'd met a month before in D.C., when Ally had come down alone for a work conference and stayed overnight with Rita. Later, Ally had texted Rita: *He's a keeper.*

Daddy will love him. And Rita had texted back: *And mom?* And Ally had texted back: *Does mom love anyone? lol.* And then Rita: *Mom loved Seamus.* That had been the family dog back in their elementary school years.

Now Ally asked Jonah: "Are you ready for Middle Eastern exotica?"

Jonah pointed to Rita. "What do you think I have right here?"

Ally laughed. "You should've heard her growing up when she had a Massachusetts accent. *Very* exotic."

"Hmm," said Jonah, turning to Rita. "I bet that was sexy."

Rita blushed. "We need to terminate this line of conversation right now." She could joke about her childhood Boston accent, which was still unfortunately preserved on some old cassettes and VHS tapes that she knew her sister held on to, probably for blackmail purposes someday.

Ally herded everyone toward the tent. "Come in, come in! Everyone wants to meet you, Jonah. They might let you eat and drink something before they pull you onto the dance floor."

They slipped inside. Rita tensed involuntarily. Suddenly, she was surrounded by Arabs—talking, laughing, eating, drinking, dancing, gambling, crowding together to take pictures, chasing children, gesticulating, throwing dollar bills at the belly dancer. She scanned a sea of dark hair, save the rare visiting non-Arab, somebody's friend or relative by marriage, and of course save certain women who, in time-honored Lebanese style, insisted on living as brassy blondes.

And she spotted the old ladies, the taytahs and sittus and the tantes, hunched over in their chairs and clucking together, their hair rigidly set, their giant black patent-leather purses upended from their laps by adoring grandchildren who climbed all over them. They reminded Rita of her own late sittu, the formidable Marguerite Daou Khoury, who in the 1970s and '80s held court at the mahrajan in grand fashion, loudly discoursing on whether Irish or Italian men made better husbands for Lebanese women or correcting the other sittus on the proper way to roll a stuffed grape leaf.

They were winding their way through tables, Rita scanning faces left and right that all felt vaguely familiar yet were mostly unplaceable, until the face she sought came into focus. Her Irish mother, Mary Jo

Khoury (née Coughlin), unsmiling, her white, crinkly skin like phyllo dough, with her sensible auburn wash-and-wear hairdo, poking judgmentally at a plate of hummus with a bit of pita bread.

"Look at Ma," Rita whispered to Ally as they approached the table. "Still looking at the food like it's alien even though she's been eating it half her life."

Ally laughed. "So true! You know that after all these years, she still thinks the whole thing is a little bit Ali Baba magic carpet."

"Ha!" said Rita. "But I'm still happy to see the crabby old gal."

And also: Hadn't she heard that cousin Bobby would be here? Where was he?

"Hiiiii!" She beamed toward the table, forcing sunshine out of herself. Dutifully, she went to her mother first. "Don't get up," Rita said, embracing her and pecking her cheek. "Ma," she pulled Jonah forward, "this is the guy I've been talking about."

Jonah thrust forth a hand. "It's very nice to finally meet you, Mrs. Khoury."

Mary Jo grabbed his arm, pulled him down toward her, and planted a dry, dutiful kiss on his cheek. "Don't make me feel old," she said. "Just call me Mary Jo. It's nice to finally meet you, too. I've gotten an earful about you."

"A good earful, I hope."

Mary Jo cocked her head at her younger daughter. "She's crazy about you. You must be smart. She doesn't have any patience with dummies."

Rita shaded her face with her brow and shook her head. "Ma, you are mortifying me already."

But her mother waved her off. "Why are you so late? We thought you'd be here an hour ago." She delivered this in her Merrimack Valley accent, nasal and underwhelmed. "I didn't know it took so long to get up here from Connecticut."

"We left early, but we got hungry and stopped for breakfast in Worcester," Rita said.

Her mother shook her head. "You probably don't have any appetite now for all the nice things here."

"Believe me," said Jonah, "I have an appetite."

Rita pulled her mother's paper plate of hummus and tabooleh close, tearing off a piece of bread for Jonah. "Why isn't Dad here yet?" she asked.

"He's in surgeries until four," Ally supplied.

Rita turned to Jonah. "Story of our childhood," she groaned.

"Hey!" Mary Jo pointed an indignant finger her way. "You think he put you through Harvard on peanuts?"

But Rita just snatched more pita from her mother's plate and passed it to Jonah. "You've always loved that peanuts line, Ma. Anyway, listen. I thought you said you were bringing Bobby today."

At this, everyone laughed, including Mary Jo. "Oh, your cousin's here, don't worry," she said. "Go take a look on the dance floor."

"Oh yeah?"

"Go see."

Rita wove her way through a few tables to get closer to the dance floor in the center, where a large circle of people were stepping in unison a few paces to the right, then, with a kick, bobbing upward a moment before moving on. And there, with his high-tech prosthetic leg with a Nike at the end of it, his arm on the shoulder of the man to his left, his Red Sox cap askew on his head, was Bobby, his face aglow with joy, stepping and kicking along with the rest.

Rita gasped, delighted. "Oh, Bobby!" she cried, to no one in particular. But an older woman to her right heard her.

"You know him?" she asked Rita.

Rita, still smiling and shaking her head, her eyes fixed on Bobby, grateful that her first sight of him in so long had been a happy one, said, "It's my baby cousin."

"God bless him," the woman said.

Rita laughed. "That's for sure."

When the song ended, everyone clapped, and several of the dancers, especially the children, crowded around Bobby to hug and kiss him and take pictures with him. Rita laughed out loud again.

She hung back off the dance floor and waited until Bobby, his fans dispersed, spotted her and walked toward her, with a far more fluid gait now than when she'd last seen him, when he was still acclimating himself to the prosthesis.

She held open her arms. "The star of the mahrajan is an Irishman!" she said, as they hugged.

"Look who's here!" he said. "Lovely Rita, meetah maid." He'd been calling her that since he first heard that song when he was six years old. Bobby was one of the only ones in the family who made no effort whatever to suppress his Boston accent. It had been a mark of regional pride among him and the other Massholes when he was in Iraq.

"Look at you," she said. "You look great!" And, truly, he did. He was part of a network of Iraq and Afghanistan vets from north of Boston and southern New Hampshire who met informally throughout the week at various gyms and worked out together before hitting Denny's or Applebee's, and the intact original parts of his body were impressively built up.

And the face: How could Rita not love that face, the ginger crew cut and facial scruff, the shit-eating grin, the watery blue eyes that were like her mother's and her uncle Terry's but full of delight and trouble instead of sourness and doom? The little cousin she'd proudly and proprietarily taken to the amusement park in summer at Salisbury Beach for the Tuesday night half-price-entry special, the cousin who made her feel so mature when she'd pull her own money out of her pocketbook to buy him ride tickets and fried dough, and the cousin who inflated her ego when, upon her attempts to explain some complex matter of politics or science, he would say, "You're wicked smaht, Rita. You're probably gonna go to Hahvahd, *ahn'cha?*"

But now, as they grinned at each other, he said, "Naw. *You* look great. You look even bettah than when I see you on the nightly news using your fancy policy talk."

Only Bobby could drop such bullshit on her, make her shriek with laughter. "Shut *up!*" she laughed. "I wanna push you but I can't anymore."

"Yeah, you can. Go ahead, push me. Right in the chest."

"No!"

"Go ahead. You think I'm not strong? I'm still a fuckin' barrel chest."

"No, Bobby, I am *not* shoving you!"

"Who's shoving who here?"

Rita turned. It was Jonah, slipping his hand around her waist. For a nanosecond, Rita was annoyed that Jonah had crashed their cousinly mini-reunion so quickly, before catching herself.

"Jonah, this is my cousin Bobby, who I told you about," she said. "And Bobby, this is my boyfriend, Jonah."

Jonah and Bobby shook hands. Bobby beamed. "Nice-ta-meech-ya."

"Likewise. Rita's told me a lot about you."

"Yeah, well," Bobby said, still grinning. "She probably told you what a little wiseass I was to her growing up and then how pissed at me she was when I told her I was signing up."

"I wasn't pissed at you," she corrected. "I was worried because I was already in Iraq and it was already becoming a nightmare, and then my mother tells me that you are *voluntarily* signing up to be a part of it. She turned to Jonah. "And *then* he e-mails me to tell me they're sending him to Ramadi when it's become the center of the insurgency."

"Cuz, I had to come over to find you, 'cause I missed you!"

Rita released a short, bitter laugh. "Well, I'd been sent away with my tail between my legs long before you finally got there."

"At least ya still got two legs."

"Whoa!" Jonah interjected. "I feel like I'm watching a Laurel and Hardy routine here."

Rita laughed and put an arm around him. "We've been putting on this show for many years, haven't we, cuz?"

"Well, look," said Jonah. "You're both here and alive and together today. That's the amazing thing."

Throughout the exchange, Bobby's grin never left his face. "Back with more fuckin' Arabs!" he crowed, gesturing around him. "I just can't get enough."

Rita cracked up with him. "You are the *worst!*" she said. She turned to Jonah. "He has no boundaries. *Zero.* He is the human embodiment of political incorrectness."

The three walked off the dance floor back toward the family table, Jonah slightly ahead. Lightly, Rita guided Bobby by the elbow. "Be serious and tell me how you are," she said.

But he turned to her with the same bullshit smile. "I'm fuckin' awesome!" he said. "How are *you*?"

"Stop it! Seriously. How's your head?"

"It's still sitting on my neck."

"*Stop it*. You still get together with the vets?"

"Three times a week."

"That's good. You still seeing—um—" Rita faltered, forgetting the name of Bobby's last girlfriend.

"Cheryl the amputee addict?"

Rita just rolled her eyes, exhausted already from trying to make Bobby cut the jokes. He'd privately nicknamed his last girlfriend that because he'd been the second amputee vet she'd dated in four years.

"Yes, that's who I mean," Rita said.

"Naw. That ended back in the winter."

"What happened?"

He shook his head, to suggest he was at a loss. "I just wasn't feeling that anymore."

"Oh. Okay. Well as long as you're doing okay."

"I told you I'm doin' fuckin' *awesome*."

"Okay! Good."

"How are *you* doin'?" Bobby pointed up ahead, to where Jonah was settling in at the family table. "What's goin' on here? You gonna get married?"

Rita snorted derisively. "No, I'm not going to get *married*. What would anyone ever get married for?"

"You been with him, what, a year now?"

"Nearly. He's a great guy."

"First a Palestinian, now a Jew. You just can't get away from the neighborhood."

"Please," she scoffed. "Jonah's never even been to Israel."

Bobby was uncharacteristically silent for a moment. "We gotta get him on the dance floor today and check out his moves," he then said.

Rita beamed. "You're right, we totally do!" She was glad the conversation had lightened. She turned to him. "I love that after all these years you still love coming to this thing. That makes me so happy."

"I love me some dabke," he said, inserting a giant guttural noise, as if hacking up phlegm, where the hard *k* went, and they both cracked up.

"Honorary Arab," she told him, as they rejoined the others at the table.

But no sooner had they sat than the synthesizer keyboardist, positioned with the drummers in the corner of the dance floor, directly beneath large Lebanese and American flags hung side by side, struck up notes to a brisk four-four beat. Nearly every adult under the large tent turned again toward the dance floor, eyes aglow with recognition and anticipation, hands brought together in rhythmic clapping. "Yalla!" called several of the older men. The musicians smiled broadly, having elicited from the crowd the response they clearly sought.

Rita and Ally turned toward one another, laughing. "The time has come!" Ally said.

"It always does!"

Jonah put a hand on Rita's arm. "What time?"

"This is the song to end all songs," Rita explained. "It's called 'Nassam Alayna Al Hawa.' It was sung by Fairouz, who is the ultimate diva of Lebanon and is worshipped by every Lebanese person on the planet, and it's all about missing the homeland, and whenever it's played all the old folks will start crying. Just look around you."

Sure enough, old ladies were dabbing tears from their eyes, clutching one another's arms as their heads bobbed to the beat.

And now the gentleman playing the synthesizer said into his microphone, "Ladies and gentlemen, a beloved classic of our mahrajan, Ramona Bistany and her daughter, Nicole."

From around a screen erected behind the musicians, out stepped Ramona Bistany—now likely in her early seventies and looking about half a foot shorter than Rita remembered her but every bit the diva still, nimbus of bottle-blond hair intact, face preternaturally smooth and plumped, in a peach-colored shirred chiffon dress and heeled sandals, smiling broadly and lightly clapping to the beat with the microphone in her hand, her long nails—painted peach to match her dress—carefully splayed. And alongside her was her daughter, Nicole, whom Rita remembered from church merely as a husky tomboy in button-down flannel shirts and Dickies. Now here she was alongside her mother, her own microphone in hand, her dark hair in a crew cut, in khakis with rolled cuffs and a polo shirt.

"Ahlan wa sahlan!" called Ramona, lacing her left arm around her daughter, who laced her right arm, in turn, around her mother's still tiny waist. "Welcome to the mahrajan!"

Rita, Ally, and Bobby all traded wide grins. "Looks like Nicole raided the boy's department at Filene's Basement," Bobby cracked.

"So I guess the whole tomboy thing wasn't a phase," Rita said to her sister. "Even having the world's most glamorous mother can't make you put on a dress if you don't want to."

Ramona Bistany then warbled out the first lines of the song, which, during the fifteen years of civil war in Lebanon, and even after, became the anthem of the Lebanese diaspora, sung everywhere by Lebanese who'd fled and nursed romantic memories of a halcyon prewar land. Then, holding Nicole's hand, she turned to her daughter expectantly, and Nicole sang the second line of the song in her not-bad tenor. Back and forth they went like this, all eyes on them, wet ones from the elders, everyone clapping to the beat.

Rita, smiling, shook her head. "So tribal," she remarked.

Ally shoved her gently. "You know you love it. Who's the only one here who learned Arabic?"

Jonah, perhaps feeling protective, put an arm around her. "Her Arabic blows my mind."

"It's so rusty," Rita allowed, "now that I don't use it every day."

"She's a very smart girl," chimed in Mary Jo. "Always has been."

Rita turned in surprised delight to her mother. "Did I just get a compliment from you, Ma? Do my ears deceive me?"

Her mother rolled her eyes. "Don't make me out to be some kinda Mommie Dearest," she snapped, making Rita and Ally collapse in laughter.

Ramona Bistany strode to the edge of the dance floor, began pulling people from their folding chairs. "Yalla!" she called into her microphone. "Hayaa linarquas! Time for dabke." Bit by bit, people rose, joined hands, made their way onto the dance floor. Wives tugged husbands, children tugged sittus and jiddes, until an ever-lengthening line began inching its way sideways, then curling to draw an arc past the musicians.

Charlie threw himself into Mary Jo's lap. "Come on, Nana, dance *dubee* with us, please, *pleeeeez*?"

"Look at those beseeching eyes, Ma," Rita gibed.

Mary Jo slowly stood. "How does your father manage to get out of this and not me?" she asked, of no one in particular. But she had an arm around her grandson as she said it.

Everyone cheered Mary Jo's acquiescence. "That's it, Ma!" Ally cried. "Keepin' it real at the mahrajan."

As a family, they threaded their way through the tables, joined hands, and attached themselves to the end of the line as it snaked its way around the dance floor. Ramona and Nicole Bistany sang together above the clamor. Rita had lived in Beirut long enough to know what the lyrics meant: "My heart is scared of growing up estranged. / And my home wouldn't recognize me. / Take me home, take me home."

Rita's right hand was enlaced in Jonah's, her left in Bobby's. To the right and then ever so slightly back to the left, everyone stepped, stepped, kicked, and stomped, repeating this sequence in endless cycles. Ramona and Nicole Bistany joined the end of the line as they continued to sing, linked by a silk handkerchief that each clutched in one hand.

Rita laughed, smiled first at Jonah, then at Bobby, who was keeping up with the steps flawlessly. She watched her mother between her nephew and niece, all traces of being put-upon lost, her face in a wide-open expression of pleasure.

Much later Rita wondered whether it was her instincts from Iraq, that adrenaline-induced hyper-attentiveness to one's surroundings so typical of veterans and others who've lived in a war zone, that made her notice, well before anyone else seemed to, the man walking toward the dancers at a strangely swift clip from the parking lot, bent slightly forward, in his hands a dark object that Rita at first could not decipher. Even as she continued to dance, her eyes remained fixed on him as he came closer toward them. Then she identified the object in his hand, and her heart was stabbed with terror.

PART ONE

THE OLD WORLD

CHAPTER ONE

THE COUGHLINS AND THE KHOURYS

(1912–)

In Lawton, the mills dominated everything. You could hardly believe that the city was part of the tranquil Merrimack Valley of northeastern Massachusetts, its lush, rolling green hills cleaved in two by a broad and gently winding river once lined with Pennacook Indians spearing fish, then with sparsely settled Yankee farmers of modest ambition. But by 1912, the year of the great strike that drew the world's attention, the mills along the riverbanks had grown so large and long that if you beheld the city from very high above you would have seen a swath of green violated by massive, miles-long blocks of brown brick spiked with dirty black towers and, in the instance of the Ayer Mill, a forbidding clock tower with a mansard roof that flared and then peaked like a medieval executioner's hood.

From the banks on either side of the river Lawton sprawled away over a claustrophobic seven square miles of further unloveliness: churches, synagogues, and municipal buildings constructed with a ponderously Victorian hand; dark brick, triple-decker tenements whose backsides, meeting close together, were a riot of rickety wood-slat porches, clothes-lines, and dirty alleys. At its borders, the anxious, needy city loosened back into green hills and the white-painted, black-shuttered homesteads of the surrounding colonial towns of Mendhem and West Mendhem, full of Protestant farmers with narrow eyes and jaws clenched tight against the winter cold.

But Lawton itself—erected hastily in the 1840s by Irish laborers to the scientific specifications of Boston Brahmin merchants looking to harness the power of the river to enrich their well-tailored pockets—was a dark city founded strictly for capitalist purposes, intent on squeezing as much horsepower out of its workers as out of its own river, which had been carved and dammed into roaring usefulness. Six days a week from shortly after dawn until dinnertime, the city's massive mills thrummed with the deafening clack-clack of thousands of looms and spinners, as dark-eyed boys and girls from the poorest quarters of Europe and the Mediterranean, in wool caps or with copious black hair piled up high on their heads, coughed and wheezed in vast rooms where the wispy remnants of lamb's wool floated in the air like tiny ghosts. Once, a man got caught in the looms and was thrown into the air and against the opposite wall, dying hours later in Lawton General Hospital, where nurses driven by a Christian sense of mission sweated uncomplainingly under severe white muslin dresses that covered every part of the body.

Fortunately for the Coughlins, not since the Civil War years had their kind had to break their backs stoning up the dam, laying miles of brick, or working the monster machines of the mill. They had been some of the first to arrive in the nascent city, in those still vernal American years of James Polk's presidency, poor and hungry and grateful for wages of any kind. But nearly seventy years on, by the eve of the Great War, the Irish of Lawton, once subservient to a Yankee middle class, now were that very middle class, part of a ruddy-faced network of mayors, judges, aldermen, police and fire chiefs, clerks and bookkeepers, emanating outward from Boston all the way to Providence in the south, Worcester in the west, and Bangor in the north. Alongside book-lined walls and player pianos, behind lace curtains, where women kept immaculate house or returned evenings from respectable jobs as teachers, nurses, seamstresses, and nannies, the Irish of Lawton peered out on the swarthy mobs flooding the streets with their placards and noisemakers in the frigid winter of

1912. Some of those Irish thought the strikers were ingrates who had a fine nerve to be choking up the city's lifeblood, others sympathized genteelly with the cause, but all of them felt well above those bands of Poles, French, Sicilians, Latvians, and Syrians who'd fixed the world's eyes on their Babel of unrest, goaded daily by headline-seeking carpet-bagger agitators from the Industrial Workers of the World.

Not long after the strike came the Great War, not long after which Frank and Annie Coughlin married. By the time the stock market crashed in 1929, they'd had Rosemary, Frank Jr., Terrence, Olivia, Tara, and baby Edward Coughlin, and they all lived in a fine, large Victorian with stained glass windows on the stair landing, in the Irish neighborhood on the south side of the river, just three blocks from Saint Patrick's Church, where the family occupied an entire pew in the seventh row on Sunday mornings. They were regarded as one of the finest, most attractive, and most upright families in their community; took part in many religious and civic groups; and spent most of August in a large rented house a block from the ocean at Salisbury Beach.

In 1942, Frank Jr., who'd been melancholy and shy his entire life, hanged himself in the family attic, where he was found by Olivia, who was seventeen at the time. This cast a pall over the entire family for the rest of their lives and considerably darkened their profile in the eyes of the community, some members of which speculated that Frank Jr. had killed himself to avoid service, after Pearl Harbor was attacked. But the truth was, nobody in the Coughlin family really knew why this shy and sweet oldest brother took his own life.

Terrence, who lost all of his boyish smirk after his brother's death and became a facsimile of his stoic father, trained as a branch manager at a regional bank and married Margaret Callahan, a woman whose unhappiness matched his own, an unfrivolous schoolteacher he met through his sisters, who had also become schoolteachers. Terrence and Meg married in 1945, as soon as Terrence (minus two fingers) got back from the war, and brought into the world Terrence Jr., Elizabeth, Mary Josephine, Anne, and Kevin, who died at six months. At this point Terrence Sr., whom everyone called Terry, watched his sisters and his younger brother, Eddie, pull away from him in fortune. Eddie, so bright, managed a scholarship to Holy Cross, then went on to Suffolk Law, while his sisters married executives on a fast track. They all moved to Mendhem and West Mendhem to raise families in gleaming new split-levels, far from the incoming Puerto Ricans they claimed had already begun to destroy Lawton, whose mill industry by the 1950s had mostly decamped to the South, where wages were cheaper and labor laws looser.

But Terrence and Meg stayed in the city, safely nestled with the Irish on the south side of the river, to bring up Terry Jr., Lizzie, Mary Jo, and Annie. His whole life, Terrence Sr. would mutter indignantly under his breath about the layers of superiors who dictated the terms of his work life. Naggingly, he knew that he should be exhibiting some gumption, some charisma, some *something* to advance into their ranks, but a foul, abiding misanthropy settled so deeply in his bones that it was all he could do to get through a workday with civility, let alone emanate the kind of crispness and cheer that tagged a man as promotable.

Still, he and Meg proved to be decent if not joyous parents and raised reasonably happy children. From an early age, Mary Jo became the family bookworm. Her classes with the nuns came easily to her, boringly even, leaving her to wonder whether she would ever be challenged. To her shock, Sister Frederick had once handed her back a book report with a B-plus on it, noting sharply, "If everyone here gives you an A or an A-plus every time, you'll think you're smarter than the sisters." For Mary Jo this B-plus stung, but she was also secretly pleased by what Sister Frederick had said.

Mary Jo worshipped her older brother, Terry Jr., a slim, handsome boy who was tall by the age of twelve and had the demeanor of an angel. He excelled in Thursday-afternoon catechism class at Saint Patrick's and could flawlessly recite Bible stories, beaming with pride as he did so. Terry was an altar boy and, on Sundays, aided Father Ken in the Mass with an air of grave self-importance.

One Thursday afternoon when she was nine, Mary Jo walked around to Saint Patrick's to pick up Terry after catechism and then go to the candy store together.

"Terry's in the sacristy helping Father Ken," Mary Jo was told by one of the other twelve-year-olds in front of the church.

Mary Jo thanked him and slipped inside the church, dipping her fingers into the font of holy water just inside the great doors, crossing herself with it. The church was vast, cool, empty, and silent, its vaulted ceiling floating high above her, votive candles winking coyly in their racks, the entire space permeated with the smell of old wood and incense—a deep, mysterious fragrance that Mary Jo found infinitely calming, the smell of Sunday mornings when she nestled shoulder to shoulder among her siblings and parents. It was strange to be alone in the cavernous church, with its stained glass images of a sad, handsome Christ going through the stations of the cross staring down at her, and she tiptoed down the main aisle, her head aligned with the tops of the pews, until she came to the altar, which she respectfully skirted until she entered a side door, after which she walked down a narrow, dark hallway, then turned a corner to find an open door. Inside, on the far side of the room, which appeared to be Father Ken's office, she spied Terry standing, his back to her, his pants and underpants down around his knees and hands limp at his sides, while Father Ken, also angled away from her, embraced Terry, his head buried in Terry's neck. Mary Jo heard Father Ken making a strange noise. Her brother was silent.

Instantly, she turned away, fled back down the hallway, then through the empty church itself, as softly as she could, until she emerged outside and sat, dazed, on the church's front steps. The other children had departed, and she was alone now, shaking, her mind spinning, trying to make sense of what she had just seen. She was nine years old and had no understanding of sex, but sensed on some gut level that what she'd seen was wrong, out of sync with the way the world should be. Yet, was there something she hadn't understood? Had Terry perhaps been hurt or sick, and was Father Ken examining him or helping him? She had to ask Terry when he came out, which he did, about seven minutes later, his brow knit tightly, his head down, his hands thrust into his pockets. Mary Jo noticed that a tuft of his shirt, in the back on the right, remained untucked from his trousers and also that one of his shoelaces was poorly tied.

"Come on," he muttered, barely pausing next to her before stalking off down the sidewalk, along which she hurried to regain his side. She wanted to ask him what had happened, but as he stared down at the sidewalk the look on his face—screwed up into itself and either angry or pregnant with tears; Mary Jo couldn't quite tell—rebuffed her. She reached for his hand, but he flicked hers away.

"What's wrong?" she asked him.

"Shut up," he snapped.

At the candy store, he reached into his back pocket and produced a dollar bill. "Go get what you want," he said, handing it to her.

She was slightly awed. "Where did you get that?" He usually had but a few nickels and dimes for her.

"Just go get what you want," he repeated, sharply. "We have to get home."

Mary Jo was so confused. She could not enjoy the novel experience of having so much money to spend on candy, even as she had Mr. Clooney fill a bag for her. When she came out, she offered him the open bag heavy with Chuckles, Zagnuts, and Red Hots, but he brushed it away.

"You better hide that at home," he told her, then stalked on ahead.

"Terry!" she called, running again to catch up with him. "What's wrong?"

He stopped. "I said shut up!" he yelled at her. "Just shut up!"

This time she knew better than to follow him. At one point, he rounded a corner, and she lost him, and all her life she would remember that corner—at which sat the Fitzpatricks' blue house, with the Virgin statue in the front yard in front of a blooming lilac bush—as the corner where the brother she had known disappeared from their lives. He would become sullen and, starting as early as seventeen, would drink heavily for the rest of his life, and until Father Ken was transferred to a parish in

Rhode Island nine years later, Mary Jo would glare at the priest, trying to damn him with her pale blue eyes, every time she saw him.

In early 1912, during the same icy winter when the strikes raged in Lawton, a sixteen-year-old boy named Girgis Khoury thrummed with excitement as he walked, his canvas bag slung over his back, up a steep, scrubby hill in his Syrian mountain village of Chartoun, home from a day of studies in the nearby city of Aley. From the top of the hill, beyond a vast expanse of limestone villages nestled on the slopes of mountains, he dimly spied the sprawling concentration of civilization that was Beirut, and beyond that the indistinct blue of the Mediterranean. Beyond even *that* was where his dreams lay. In his bag was the letter he'd carried with him faithfully since he'd received it before Christmas:

> *My dear brother Girgis* [the letter read in Arabic],
>
> *To begin, I relay my greatest love to Mama, Baba, Sittu, Elias, Salma, and baby Nour, and to all the aunties and the uncles and the cousins, and to all the church. I am very sad it will be my first Christmas not with the family, I will miss Mama's cookies, but Ammtee Joumana says she will make them for me.*
>
> *Brother, it is so cold here in December! True, it gets cold on Mount Lebanon in the winter, but it is nothing compared with Lawton. Ammo and Ammtee had to buy me a heavy coat of wool with a hat, scarf, mittens, boots, and I am still cold! It is good you are not arriving until the spring, which comes very late but is very beautiful here, very green, especially in the country outside Lawton. Summer last, we took the tramway all the way to the beach and we had to stay a night in a hotel, it is such a long ride. The water is so much colder than the Mediterranean! We went the weekend of the Fourth of July, which is when the Americans celebrate their freedom from the British, and there were fireworks all up and down the beach, with the American flag hanging everywhere. A beautiful sight. We will see it together soon.*

Ammo Boutros and Ammtee Joumana are ready for your arrival. They are ready to have you work in their grocery store with me, and there you will find that Ammo Boutros has for the most part everything you might have in Chartoun—olives, figs, bulgur, grape leaves, pita, kibbe, everything you are familiar with, so you won't be homesick for food. A lot of it comes from a supplier in Boston who ships it here from Beirut.

You will like it as it is mainly other jabali who shop at the store, from every mountain village you have heard of but never visited. Everyone is here, it is like being home, but without Moslems or Druze, and also the buildings look very different. Everyone is Christian except for some Jews like the butcher nearby. You will have to go to school and learn English as soon as you arrive. Arabic or schoolbook French won't do you much good here. Everyone is here, Girgis! English, French, Italian, German, Polish, so many jabali, which everyone here calls Syrian, not really caring whether we are from Damascus, Beirut, or the mountains. Latvians and Greeks, too! So many Irish, who have been here for many years and who run everything, the police etcetera. Almost everyone works in the mills, Girgis, which are so huge. Though I am proud to say that it seems as many jabali here have their own stores or businesses as work in the mills.

You will share a room with me behind the store, with Ammo and Ammtee and our baby cousin upstairs. Ammo will pay you four dollars a week and you will send half of that home as I do. Together, our remittances will help the family a great deal and I wager they will have double the goats and another cow in six months' time.

And also, I trust Baba received my last remittance?

There, Yousef dropped down a few lines, as though he were thinking.

Oh, brother! I must admit I miss lemon and fig groves and I miss stone homes with red tile roofs and I miss being able to see the sea from the top of the hill and I miss my family! My heart aches when I think of Mama, always looking so worried! After you kiss everyone for me, kiss Mama again and tell her in secret it was an extra one from me.

I await your arrival, Brother. Let's make a good sum and go home for good, build a big new house, and not worry about crops year after year. Let's live like the House of Khazen!

Once more I ask you to relay my love and prayers to all the family, dear brother. April will come soon and your eyes will pop from your head when you see the Statue of Liberty in the harbor. Then you'll know it's not long before we are reunited.

Yousef

Every time Girgis read the letter, and he did so nearly every day, he became so giddy with excitement he could hardly concentrate on the here and now. That was the case that evening at dinner, in the dining room of his family's stone house with its simple tile floor, crucifixes or pictures of Christ or the Virgin on every wall. Girgis was a sweet-faced, if not exactly good-looking, teenage boy, his black hair glossy atop his head, his dark, serious eyes set slightly too close above a nose that had only recently become prominent, giving him a comical, owlish look. The family ate a simple salad, a fattoush, tossed with lemon juice, olive oil, and bits of fried pita bread; then a yakhni, a stew of okra and lamb, that his mama and Sittu had made. The Khourys were not unaware of their fortune in being able to have meat at the table so frequently; such wasn't the case with poorer households, with whom Baba was known to occasionally share some of his lamb, so they might have such a stew occasionally or make kibbe.

Nour, his baby sister, barely touched her bowl.

"Girgis," said his mother, who he thought was the most beautiful and wondrous woman on the face of the earth, the very image of the Virgin Mother herself. "Go sit by your sister and help her eat. She always listens to you."

And so Girgis did just that, holding the spoon aloft before Nour's tiny pink mouth and singing a silly song, about the friendship between a bird and a lamb, until grim-faced Nour could hold out no longer and cracked a wide smile, laughing, at which point Girgis, delighted with his triumph, gently fed her.

Everyone laughed but Sittu, who threw her hands in the air. "What are we going to do when the second-born son is no longer here, too!" she cried, on the brink of tears, as she often was. "Look how well he takes care of his sister. Look how well he helps his Baba with the olive press. Elias is still too young to help!"

"Mama, stop," said Baba, holding up a hand. "We will be fine. Elias will be thirteen soon. There's more opportunity to be had in America, for the boys to help us out."

"Everyone's leaving for Amrika!" Sittu exclaimed, tears flashing to anger. She smacked her palm atop the table. "Half the village! There won't be any boys left for girls to marry."

"It's not forever, Sittu," Girgis pleaded. "It's to make money to bring back home."

"And not everyone is leaving," Mama said gently to Sittu, her mother-in-law, with whom she had labored for years to share a tenuous peace.

"But we're losing our best!" lamented Sittu.

Girgis privately conceded that Sittu was half-right. In the past decade, it did seem as if half the village had left—for Canada, the United States, Cuba, Mexico, or Brazil—chasing fortunes. Not just the men, but whole families, or half a family, leaving the other half to wait for remittances that went toward livestock, a new tile roof, a new grove of mulberry trees for harvesting silkworms. In the village church, Girgis knew of parents or children grieving over news that relatives had died of sickness aboard a ship crossing the sea.

But Girgis didn't fear that such a thing would happen to him on his crossing. He was young and healthy; his family—with their sizable groves of lemon, fig, and olive trees—had never wanted. They were hardly rich Orthodox Beirutis like the Sursocks who spent their summers high in the mountain resorts of Aley to escape the heat, but they were no peasants, either.

Weeks passed, and the snow began melting on the mountain peaks. Fruit blossoms sprang to life in the orchards, and wildflowers sprouted on the roadsides, riotous exclamations of blue and yellow. Girgis and his siblings wore new clothes to church on Palm Sunday, and then it was his final Easter in Chartoun—gorging on Sittu's mamoul, those pretty cookies with patterns on top and pistachio inside, so buttery and powdery all at once; coloring eggs and then cracking them against one another in the ritual contest; the procession through the streets with the large crucifix carried aloft by young men, Nour atop Girgis's proud shoulders. His mother had taken to holding him close and stroking his hair for long seconds at a time, saying, over and over again, "Ibni, ibni," *my son, my son,* or "Aini, aini," *my eye, my eye.* How could he leave Mama?

And yet . . . New York! He had seen pictures of the Flatiron Building, so slender and so tall, almost like a book standing upright, and girded in steel! Of course, he knew he would only be passing briefly through New York, but still. Girgis felt terribly important and manly walking through the streets of Chartoun, as villagers approached to tell him of their own families abroad and to give him random bits of advice they'd heard back, such as that American men should not greet one another with kisses or hold one another's hands while promenading.

And then, suddenly, it was an afternoon in early May, and his family was putting him and his trunk into the back of a motorcar in Aley bound for Beirut, everyone crying, crying, even Baba and Elias, his mother pressing her rosary into his hands.

"Take it! Take it!" she cried, through tears. "Think of me every time you pray on this."

"Mama, this is your favorite rosary."

"Take it!" Mama redoubled her tears. So Girgis thrust it deep into his trousers pocket and surrendered to his mother's embraces and sobs.

"Go, go," said Baba as the motorcar engine clamored to life. "Go, take care of your brother and make us proud and come back to us, Girgis, in not longer than two years."

"Yes, Baba," he said, twisting around to watch his family recede out of sight as they waved after him, to watch Aley fall away behind him as the motorcar drove out of town, leaving white dust in its wake—the church spires, the Druze in the street with their voluminous garments and strange tall hats, the outdoor markets, the walls of warm yellow limestone that would haunt his dreams.

The following week, glued to the deck of the ship, his head dizzy from several nights of seasickness and the foul smells of vomit and too many people living in close quarters, Girgis watched the New World emerge. Soon enough, everyone was calling *Brooklyn, Brooklyn!* and pointing to a landmass to the right lined with large, low brick buildings that were dark and forbidding, Girgis thought, so different from the warm glow of limestone. *Warehouses*, some passengers were saying in English. There was land on both sides of the ship now, Brooklyn to the right and, a countryman named Fouad told him, with the casual smugness of someone who had made the passage before, Staten Island to the left. Then, as their passageway opened, there was New Jersey.

"Right now," Fouad said, "we are sailing down the line between two different states, New York and New Jersey." Girgis nodded. The distinction didn't mean much to him. It was all America, unfolding before him in a mighty panorama of massive buildings, piers, freighters, and small craft, under a steel-gray April sky flecked with rain.

The Statue of Liberty appeared through the drizzle, a dim gray shape that was nonetheless so well known to everyone on the ship that its first sighting sparked a hysterical roar of shouts and tears from the decks, while hundreds of fingers pointed. Girgis watched, mesmerized, as the ship neared, then slowly passed before, the monument, whose features loomed ever clearer. Her face was sphinxlike, yielding nothing, hardly welcoming, he thought, while her sinewy, manly raised arm reminded him of his own mother's strong and hardworking arms, and those of Sittu and every other village woman he'd ever known. And oh, he wished his family could be alongside him now, in this thrilling moment!

"Can you believe you are really finally looking at her?" Fouad asked. "It's still exciting for me the second time."

"Ana bi helem," Girgis said, over and over again, shaking his head slowly. *I am in a dream.*

And indeed, the next twenty-four hours passed as though he were in a dream, and he would always remember them as such, in part because he had not slept a sound full night in nearly a week. There was the docking at Ellis Island and the endless lines, the interminable waiting amid the pungent, oniony odors of families who had not properly bathed in days, the thousands of people surrounded by mountains of their belongings, and the alien, flat bark of English from the mouths of police officers and customs officials, the eye exam with a buttonhook that had become the stuff of dread legend back home, with everyone claiming to know someone who knew someone who had trachoma and was sent back immediately to the old country. There was the interrogation by a white man alongside a Syrian interpreter who made a point of looking at Girgis with kind and encouraging eyes, and then Girgis was given some papers, and he had arrived, on the other side of the passage.

"Find me at the end of the process," Fouad had said to him earlier, and so now he did, and he and Fouad loaded their trunks onto a ferry headed across the harbor to the great island, Manhattan, whose phalanx of towers, seen from over the water, astonished Girgis.

"Look there," said Fouad, pointing at a spire that rose above the rest, with an almost mosque-like flare at its tip. "That is the Singer Building, forty-seven stories high, the tallest building in New York, one of the tallest in the whole world. They make all the buildings here now from steel, so they can go as high as you please." Now he pointed to another soaring building, clad all in limestone save a few stories at the top, where a steel skeleton still showed. "And there is the Municipal Building"—Fouad said this English word, *municipal*, slowly for Girgis, enunciating each syllable—"which will be for the government, when it's finished. And that," he said, pointing to a spire that looked like a cathedral, "is the Woolworth Building, the headquarters of a company with stores around the country."

Girgis and Fouad spent the night on blankets on the kitchen floor of yet more jabali cousins of cousins, who lived in a corner of lower Manhattan the white people called Little Syria, a neighborhood that, Girgis mused, could have been an old country mountain village transposed to a grid of streets walled with large buildings. The faces, names, food all looked the same, while Arabic lettering adorned the windows and the sweet smell of nargileh floated from cafés. But Girgis also noted that his people looked prosperous, men in well-tailored suits and women in carefully embroidered dresses and large picture hats. He thought for the first time that perhaps his family might be happier here than back home, especially if they could have all the people and pleasures of home around them, starting with nargileh and strong coffee.

And then, near noon, Fouad was seeing him and his trunk onto a New York, New Haven and Hartford Company railcar, which, because it was the cheapest line available and made many stops along the way, did not arrive in Boston's South Station until ten that night. As instructed in a letter from his brother, Girgis spent the night in the station, alternately reading his English phrase book and sleeping in fitful increments on a hard bench with one foot on his trunk. In the morning, bleary-eyed and utterly disoriented, showing a porter the slip of instructions in English his brother had sent him, he was directed to another train, marked Boston and Maine. No sooner was he seated than he passed out cold, his head on the window, and he woke to someone jostling his shoulder, crying, "Khayi! Girgis!"

He looked up. The train had stopped in a station marked "Lawton," and the jostler was Yousef, his eyes wide with joy. Girgis, his exhausted heart exploding with gratitude, wept, stood, and embraced his brother tightly, kissed him on one cheek, then the other, then back again. "Khayi! Habibi!" he cried through his tears.

"Brother, you made it, you made it!" Yousef was giddy, laughing, earning the amused smiles of the white passengers staying in the car on their way to Mendhem and Haverhill. "It is like a dream, isn't it?"

"It has all been like a dream, Yousef. I'm not sure I am really awake."

"You are really here, Girgis, you shall see."

*   *   *

Girgis was there, certainly, and in his first weeks his heart felt crushed by the ugliness of the place. Though it was spring, thankfully, and not the depth of winter—whose iciness, Yousef promised, would shock him—there were still no warm limestone homes, no sweeping views from atop mountains, no vast groves of dates and lemons. Here, it was all two- or three-story wood-frame tenements, dirty with trash, skeins of laundry hanging in the back; and commercial thoroughfares of dark brick that lacked the scale, grandeur, and electric energy of New York. Fouad had been correct, it was nothing special to speak of.

Save, perhaps, the sprawling, endless immensity of the dark, dirty mills, which seemed the only reason for the city's existence. Some mornings, helping unload deliveries in his uncle's store, he would watch the neighbors—a motley assemblage of folk from all over Europe and the Mediterranean muttering in every language from Italian to Greek to Arabic to Polish—trudge off to those mills with their lunch pails, and he would silently pray thanks for having been spared that miserable-looking fate. Working in his uncle's store, he almost could have been back home, as if all the foods of their lives, which they had once harvested or made themselves, were drawn into one storefront for the benefit of their jabali neighbors desperate for olives, dates, figs, za'atar, salty cheese. In the back kitchen, his aunt labored all day making pita bread and sweets like baklava, while up front he, his uncle, and his brother stocked shelves, swept, kept the books, and dealt with a rotating cast of visiting Syrian wholesalers, some of whom traveled in from Boston or Providence, Rhode Island, to take orders.

At six, after the mills closed, tired workers would trudge into the store for bread and whatever else they might be able to afford that night. Finally, he and Yousef would clean the shop and close it for the evening, heading upstairs to the apartment, where his aunt had prepared dinner, after which they drank coffee and smoked on the back porch while Yousef taught Girgis English. Then, in the room they shared, Girgis often had to shove Yousef in the night to disrupt his snoring, which could get so loud Girgis was certain it shook the house. On Sundays, their only day off, they went with the other jabali to the Maronite church, which had been built a decade before, and then, it being summer, they often walked the few miles to the nearby farm town of Methuen to picnic alongside a small river with jabali families who'd settled there. The rolling hills, orchards, and farm plots reminded Girgis of home a bit and provided a welcome one-day respite from Lawton's grimy grays and browns.

He desperately missed his family. "These wara'inab aren't like Mama's," he said, low, to Yousef, as they ate stuffed grape leaves while they picnicked. "They're too big, and they're not lemony enough. Mama's wara'inab are so small and pretty."

"Shh," said Yousef. "Auntie Jou will hear you."

"I miss everyone."

"I do, too," said Yousef. "But the money we're sending is helping them. And we'll go back in a year or two. Besides," he added, smiling, "don't you like Irish girls? Creamy skin, blue eyes, and yellow or red hair?"

"They're not as beautiful as Mama," said Girgis, his eyes watering.

Yousef laughed scornfully. "That's what Americans call a mama's boy!"

And so went their lives for the next two years, with Girgis becoming gradually more proficient in English, and the opening, in their neighborhood, of a small jabali men's social club where they often went after they closed the store, or after dinner, to smoke nargileh; drink coffee; play basra, an old Arab card game; and listen on a Victrola to records sent from New York or Beirut of traditional dabke music, those familiar sounds of oud and hand drum that would bring homesick tears to the men's eyes and sometimes compel them to get up and dance, arms across shoulders, feet stomping in unison.

Yousef had been right about one thing: the cold. Come his first winter in Lawton, that of 1912–13, Girgis was shocked and dismayed by the frigid, often wet and icy weather that set in, of a bone-chilling depth the likes of which he'd never known in Chartoun, where, even on winter nights, the temperature hardly ever went below freezing. He shivered every day and night until April, when he saw daffodils in the city's common and knew that the worst was over.

Toward the end of their second winter in Lawton, in the very early spring of 1914, Girgis and Yousef began talking about going back to Chartoun before the following winter. They'd sent back a considerable amount of money, and they figured they could always come back to Lawton when and if they needed to. Girgis longed to feel the Chartoun sun on his face, to eat olives straight from the tree, to smell lemon blossoms, and, most of all, to hold in his arms his grandparents, his siblings, and his beloved Baba and Mama.

But then in June, the archduke Franz Ferdinand was assassinated in Sarajevo, and soon Europe was at war. Yousef and Girgis decided to wait until the fighting ended to book their passage back. But it didn't end, it only worsened and spread, and by November, the Ottomans were in the war as well, their men beginning to comb Mount Lebanon for conscripts. To avoid conscription, everyone who could, their brother, Elias, wrote to them in a letter, was giving the Turks a payoff, which the Turks saw as an acceptable option from Christians in the empire. "Baba says it's best you stay in Amrica and send us money," he continued, "because nobody knows yet what will happen here and we need to save."

By early 1915, Elias wrote, there were increasing numbers of Ottoman soldiers patrolling through Aley, which the dreaded, fez-hatted, mustachioed Jamal Pasha, who commandeered Syria for the Ottomans, had seized as his headquarters. There were rumors that the Ottomans might start requisitioning livestock and crops from jabali for their own war uses. This echoed what Girgis and Yousef had read in the small weekly Arabic newspaper that had been started in Lawton. And then in late April, that newspaper, called *Al Balad* (The Homeland), delivered chilling news: A plague of locusts had descended on Mount Lebanon, darkening the skies like a massive cloud and eating everything in sight. Soon after, another letter from Elias arrived: the crops of all the families in the region had been denuded, and food stores were reduced to whatever they might have preserved in jars or cans. "We will survive,"

Elias wrote, "but there are foods that we will have to buy somehow, so Baba asks if you can please send more money."

Girgis and Yousef were not alone among the jabali of Lawton who began sending back home 25, even 50 percent more money now than previously.

"I am so worried," Girgis said to Yousef. "I wish we were there."

"What could we do there?" said Yousef, who now told non-Syrians to call him Joseph, or the very American Joey. "Thank God we are here and in a position to send them money."

In the ensuing year, news of home in *Al Balad* merely worsened: Jamal Pasha was employing more and more jabali as spies; people were pointing fingers at their longtime neighbors in return for political and economic favor from the Turks; and in the summer of 1915, Jamal Pasha hanged in a public square in Beirut several Syrians he accused of being traitors to the Ottomans. Perhaps worse, he had blockaded the entire Mediterranean coast to impede the Allies, and no food or other supplies could get through. With that and Jamal Pasha's troops seizing all available livestock and crops for their own use, people were starting to go hungry. At the Syrian café in Lawton, all the talk became of the situation back home, of relatives not heard from in weeks, of remittances sent with no confirmation of receipt.

"Dear brothers, things have gotten really bad here," read a letter they finally received from Elias late in 1915.

Baba says thank you for increasing the money you sent, but it took us three times as long to receive it, obviously with issues related to the blockade and the war. Thankfully we were able to buy some much-needed supplies. There is so much else I wish to tell you but I fear given circumstances related to mail into and out of the region I cannot.

"What do you think he means?" Girgis asked Yousef.

"I wonder if they are thinking of going to hide in Qadisha Valley," answered Yousef. They'd heard through the jabali grapevine that more and more families were fleeing to those remote parts northward in the mountains, to live in caves and farm surreptitiously until the war was over and the Ottomans were, it was hoped, defeated.

Months passed through 1916 with no word from Elias. It was becoming common now for jabali, when they wrote to relatives in America, to relay all the available news of an entire village, perhaps of a vilayet, or region, with the understanding that mail got through spottily, and then for jabali in the New World to relay such news received in their letters to everyone they knew. And so it was that an Aley man who was now a tailor in Haverhill, Massachusetts, wrote to them that fall—when it seemed all of New England was punch-drunk with another World Series win by those Red Sox and that Babe Ruth everyone was so gaga about.

"My countrymen," the letter began.

May God and his Holy Mother bless and protect you. I have some news from my cousin to share with you about Chartoun. He tells me the village has been hit hard by famine, with Jamal Pasha's men taking what little food was left there and no packages or remittances getting through. He was there recently and said that he nearly gasped to see how bony the children were, fighting for orange rinds, and how precious was a mere bag of flour or beans. He said he visited a once fairly prosperous farm with ample lemon and olive groves where the elders and one of the little ones had recently died and there was starvation and sickness among the survivors, but he did not know the family name. However, to me, it sounded like Beit Khoury . . .

The letter infuriated Yousef. "Why would he send this to us to make us sick with worry when he is not even sure who he is talking about?" He tore the letter into pieces. "What a stupid ass."

"But who else in Chartoun has *ample* groves?" insisted Girgis. "We have the biggest groves."

One night, the brothers were in the café, playing cards with some others, when Ammo Boutros, who usually liked to relax at home with his

Arabic religious books after closing the store, came in, gently put a hand on Yousef's shoulder, and signaled both brothers to come out of the café.

"They are all gone, all passed, except little Nour, who is with a family in the Qadisha Valley. A friend in Aley telegraphed me. Half of Chartoun is dead from starvation. I'm sorry, my nephews, your family is gone except for your little sister, may God protect them. You are my sons now."

Girgis's eyes grew wider and wider, then he howled and fell to his knees. "Alean lakallah!" *I curse you, God!* He brought his fists to his eyes and punched them again and again, as men poured out of the café and tried to tear his hands away from his face, to hold them behind his back. "Mama! Ya, mama!" he groaned, twisting away from the men's embrace.

"Ya, khayi, khalas," Yousef cried, throwing himself over his brother, bringing him down to the ground again, weeping with him. "They are with God now. We will survive, we will survive."

Somehow, over the next two years, they did, but it seemed that misery would never end. No sooner were they finally in touch with the family in the Qadisha Valley that had taken in Nour, who by then was six years old, than the flu plague, which was racing around the world, descended on Lawton, forcing the quarantine of the sick in a ghastly tent city and ultimately taking nearly two thousand lives. The shroud of death hanging over the city by the American Thanksgiving holiday, as another unbearable winter loomed, eclipsed the relief of the Armistice.

The brothers did not board a steamer until 1921, by which time the jabali region was not only its own state, called Lebanon, and distinct from Syria but under French supervision. Girgis was not as seasick on this trip, perhaps because he'd found his sea legs on the journey over. In Alexandria, on the stopover, he and Yousef smoked nargileh in cafés alongside the Corniche, the seaside promenade, which they generally agreed was not as beautiful as Beirut's.

And then the Pigeon Rocks were emerging on the horizon, the steamer's great horn was bellowing, and they were docking in Beirut, whose port Girgis, who was now twenty-five, had not seen for nine years, since the day his ship pulled out, when all his family had been intact. He thought of all this as he stood on deck, watching the city emerge, and he became full of feeling, his eyes watering.

Yousef put an arm around Girgis as the brothers gazed at the ever-closer port, and at one point Yousef merely looked at him and shook his head sadly.

"Nihna ashbah," he said. *We are ghosts.* "I feel like a ghost."

Early the next morning, they hired a friend of their cousin to take them by truck on the long, high journey up into the Qadisha Valley town of Bcharre. After the war ended, several families from around Aley had come out of hiding in the mountain caves or the monasteries and settled in Bcharre, and it was one of them, Beit Nader, who had taken in Nour in the final days of her father's, then her mother's, life. She'd been only three at the time, that horrible fall of 1916.

Umm Antoun came to the door, fabric draped over one arm, her hair cut just above the chin and her dress just over the knees, in the new style. She was young, with four children of her own, and her smooth olive skin and lovely dark eyes instantly reminded Girgis of his own mother. The memory stabbed him with grief.

She beamed to see them and kissed them each three times. "Let us thank the Holy Mother and her Son for getting you here safely," she said, waving them inside. "I want to tell you about Nour before you see her."

Girgis looked at her, alarmed. "Why?"

"She is not well. Not normal. She screamed and thrashed about for weeks and weeks after—" Umm Antoun paused. "After the events, and since then she has never been the same. She keeps to herself. She doesn't talk much. At best, she eats nushkrallah."

Girgis and Yousef looked at each other, then followed Umm Antoun out into the yard, where her children played. In the far corner, alone and apart, tracing lines with a stick in the dirt, was a little girl with her black hair pulled back in a single braid, wearing a simple gray dress and black shoes.

Yousef put a hand on her knee. "Ya Nour, ukhti hilweh, my beautiful little sister, do you know who we are? We are your brothers, Yousef and Girgis."

But Nour just shook her head and continued tracing with her stick, gently pushing Yousef's hand away. Yousef looked at Girgis, who tapped Nour's knee.

"Ukhti sagheere, little sister, you remember me, yes? Girgis? You remember sitting at the table with Sittu, Mama, and Baba and me and Elias and Salma?" As he recited the names, he felt overwhelmed and his eyes welled.

Nour slowly shook her head and continued tracing with her stick.

"And you remember the song I'd sing you when I fed you?" Girgis continued. "The song about the bird and the lamb? Al tayir wa al hami?"

She shook her head again.

Softly, Girgis sang:

If a bird can fly
Oh father, if a bird can fly
Then why does that sweet bird
Ride on the back of the lamb?
Why would a bird with wings
ride on the back of a lamb?

And as he sang, she looked up—he could see his mama's beautiful, kind eyes in her eyes!—and smiled indulgently, as though she were acknowledging his efforts. Whether she remembered the song or not, Nour put her little arms around his neck, where she then buried her face.

When Yousef, Girgis, and Nour returned to Lawton in the spring of 1921, the siblings rejoined the Sunday picnics. Nour, who shared a room with her brothers, did not—nor would she ever—lose a certain dazed, shell-shocked expression. She went to school during the day, urged by her older brothers to learn English as fast as possible, but advanced slowly in the language. Sometimes Girgis would come into the kitchen and find Nour standing in the middle of the room, hands at her sides, one messy braid down her back, staring into space.

But at the Sunday picnics, Nour at least seemed capable of playing dollies with another little girl her age, Marguerite Daou, the youngest of six children in a farm family from Bleibel. Marguerite was very loud and bossy for such a little girl, everyone noticed, no matter how much her parents, Abu and Umm Beshara, told her that such behavior was unbecoming. As Nour grew increasingly fond of Marguerite, her friend would come to visit more often at Uncle Boutros and Auntie Jou's house, until, by the time Marguerite was thirteen or fourteen, she finally began catching the attention of Girgis, who was both scandalized and mesmerized by her outspokenness. She even had the temerity to critique Auntie Jou's method of rolling out phyllo for baklava.

"That's not how my mother and aunts do that at all," Marguerite said sternly.

To this Auntie Jou merely smiled, shook her head, and said, "There's more than one way to do things, Margie."

But Marguerite actually stamped her little boot and said, forcefully, "That is *not* the way to roll out the dough!"

Auntie Jou came around the table and smacked Marguerite across the face. "Don't you *dare* talk to elders that way! You are a guest in this house, Marguerite Daou."

Marguerite stood there, her hand on her raw cheek, stunned and, for once in her life, silent.

Yet her forthrightness transfixed Girgis. As soon as she turned sixteen and left Lawton High School, knowing the essentials of reading, writing, and figures, if not very much more, Girgis asked her father if he could marry her. Abu Beshara, Marguerite's father, approved of the offer and called Marguerite into his parlor. Girgis sat there terrified, trying to smile at her as she glowered at him. He knew from listening to her conversations with Nour that she was in love with the movie star Ramon Novarro and that she never mentioned him, Girgis, whatsoever. And now here he was about to bid for her hand with her father's blessing.

"Girgis has asked to marry you, and I think he would make you a very good husband," said Abu Beshara. "He is a good man," her father continued, "a devout Maronite, from only three villages away from ours, with many cousins in common, and he will provide for you well. Of course, it is your choice, but we think this would be a good one."

But he had barely finished speaking before Marguerite snapped, pointedly in English, "May I leave now?"

Her father nodded, and she flew out of the room and up the stairs, her low heels clattering on the wood. Girgis, his face burning crimson, looked away from Abu Beshara.

"Give her some time," said Abu Beshara, unruffled. "She's lived nearly her whole life in America, and it's different here, so we can't make her do anything, but she has good sense."

After that, Marguerite did not come to his aunt and uncle's house but instructed Nour to come to hers, draining the kitchen of girlish chatter, which Girgis had always enjoyed overhearing when he came up from the store. Rather than settling down with Girgis, Marguerite got a job as a shopgirl in the ladies' section of Feinstein's Apparel in downtown Lawton. With her modest employee discount, she acquired clothes, such as a fox-trimmed winter coat and matching cloche hat, that made her the height of fashion by local standards. Girgis saw her seldom now, but when he did, they darted their eyes away from each other quickly.

Then one day Nour said to him, "Why don't you ask Margie to the picture show on Sunday after Mass?"

Girgis turned, startled. "You mean ask Abu Beshara?"

Nour came closer to him and said, in a low, conspiratorial voice, "You should ask Margie directly. That's what she wants."

This information surprised and intrigued Girgis. *Really?* "You won't say anything to anyone else, will you?" he asked his sister, and she shook her head solemnly.

The next day, he ventured into Feinstein's Apparel, where he found Marguerite putting dresses on hangers, her back to him. He called hello.

She turned, gasped slightly, then settled herself and betrayed the shadow of a smug smile. "Hello. Can I help you?"

So she was determined to play a game, Girgis thought. Why was he pursuing this troublesome girl? Reaching out for a hand in marriage was not supposed to be this convoluted. And yet—he thrilled a bit to the intrigue she was pulling him into.

"Would you like to see a picture after Mass Sunday?"

At that, she turned her back to him to return to her dresses. And she said, "I'll meet you in the alley behind the movie house at one."

There, on Sunday, is exactly where Girgis found her, in her fox-trimmed coat and cloche. Sitting in the back row of the movie house, they watched Harold Lloyd in *The Freshman*. Marguerite thought the picture was hilarious and laughed in a loud, unselfconscious way, as though she were at the pictures alone. Several times, Girgis discreetly turned his head to look at her and wondered why he'd fixated on her for so many years. He thought he wanted a typical wife who would obey him without exception, in the old-country tradition, but his desires were apparently more complicated than he'd assumed.

At the picture's end, Girgis proposed they go to the drugstore, to which Marguerite answered, with studied brightness, "Alrighty!" to show him that she was modern. At the drugstore counter, they had burgers and a drink called a milkshake, which was whipped up in a thing called a blender. It was unusual for them to eat American food, and they were somewhat self-conscious about it.

"I'm usually home helping Mama with Sunday dinner right now," Marguerite observed. "Scooping out peppers or squash." She spoke English better than he, unaccented, and she didn't bother slowing or simplifying her words to accommodate him, which meant, to his embarrassment, that he had to take a moment to process what she'd said before answering.

"What did you tell your father?" he asked her.

"I told him we were going to the picture show!" she exclaimed, surprised that he'd think otherwise. "Why should I lie? He's approved you. And he's adjusted to the new world. He's been here nearly twenty years now."

But Girgis was baffled. "Then why did we meet secretly?"

Her lips curled in a smile. "For the thrill," she said, simply, regarding him keenly.

Thus began their courtship. He often felt mentally exhausted after an evening with her, because she insisted they speak in English to help him improve. Walking her home one evening, he was surprised when she pulled him into the narrow alley between her house and the next. "Here," she said, pulling his arms around her. "Please kiss me good night."

Girgis nearly froze in shock. "What if your father finds out?"

"We are dating," she said sternly, using a word that Girgis had only recently learned, referring to something he'd only recently seen, in the pictures Marguerite insisted they see. Men and women doing things outside the woman's home, outside the company of her parents. *What was this wild country?* he marveled.

"It is acceptable," she added. She closed her eyes, tilted her head up to him, and puckered her lips.

Gingerly, he pushed his lips against hers. They were the first lips he'd ever touched with his own, and the moment he did so, a memory of his own mother's lips on his cheek stabbed his heart, and he released a little cry, which embarrassed him, but Marguerite must have taken it for passion because she drew his arms around her coat more tightly and pressed her lips more firmly onto his.

Finally, Marguerite withdrew, exploding with that raucous laugh when she looked at him. "You look like a clown!" she cried, pulling a handkerchief from her coat pocket. "Let me get the lipstick off you." So here was yet another moment when Girgis turned himself over to her, Marguerite wiping his lips industriously, as a mother would do.

Now he was baffled, his head spinning. "So you will marry me?" he asked.

"Ask me again in three months," she said, jumping slightly to peck him once more on the cheek before running inside.

Five months later, the two of them stood before the priest in the Maronite church as the bride's and groom's crowns were placed upon their heads, Marguerite's family on one side and Girgis's on the other. Then, afterward, there was feasting and dabke downstairs in the basement for hours, with more than 150 people, including relatives who had come from as far away as Waterville, Maine; and Danbury, Connecticut. Holding aloft her immense veil as she danced, Marguerite was an exultant bride, so at ease in greeting and chatting with guests that Girgis could hardly believe she had only just turned seventeen. Yet that night, in a hotel overlooking the ocean at Salisbury Beach, she was shy as they consummated their union—shyer than he was, in fact—and Girgis assumed that marriage would subdue her. He was wholly wrong.

Their first year together was pleasurable enough, with Marguerite keeping her job at the department store, from which she'd arrive home brimming with stories and gossip and new accessories. In such a mood, she seemed not to mind cooking for him the jabali dishes she'd been making her whole life alongside her mother, and she appeared amenable to accepting help from his Ammtee Joumana to learn how to make meals just how he liked them, such as his extra-lemony wara'inab or his fattoush with very crispy, almost burned bits of bread. After all, what wife would not want to please her husband this way?

But once she became pregnant in the summer of 1931, her mood changed. It was partly that the department store, where she'd loved being surrounded daily by new fashions, let her go, not only because she was pregnant but because the financial crash had hit Lawton hard. Marguerite took up working in the kitchen end of the family store, alongside Joumana and Nour, to bake bread and make the other meze they sold. Often she found herself spending an entire morning making sfeeha and fatayar, the little triangular pies of lamb or spinach, hundreds of them, or chopping fluffy mounds of parsley for tabooleh, until she thought she would scream. She became increasingly sharp-tongued with Girgis, sometimes outright derisive.

"I wish you knew what it was like to take orders all day from your aunt!" she would snap at him in the evening. "I put down the knife for five minutes to massage my fingers, and she's breathing down my neck! I wish I were still working for Mrs. Feinstein."

Girgis would shake his head mournfully. How could he have married a wife so unlike his mother? Surely, he thought, children would restore joy to Marguerite.

But that didn't quite happen either. Over the next five years, they would have two girls, Irene and Nancy. Such a fact might have dismayed Girgis, who had been raised to believe that a father had no major reason to rejoice until he had a boy, but during, and for several weeks after, each pregnancy, Marguerite plunged into such an angry, brooding state of near indifference, and perhaps even resentment, toward her new baby, that Girgis ended up feeling far more protective toward the little girls than a father otherwise might. He fell madly in love with his dark-haired, dark-eyed daughters—my two princesses, or amiriti, as he called them. For the rest of his life, when he looked at them, even as grown women, he would remember them as wriggling bundles in his arms while their mother curled away from them in another room.

"I'm not fit to be a mother," she would cry when Girgis asked her what was wrong. "There's something wrong with me."

A few months after her pregnancies, Marguerite would inexplicably feel better and suddenly enjoy spending time with her baby girls, showing them love and warmth. Girgis would relax slightly and allow himself one or two nights a week at the social club, catching up with Yousef, cousins, and friends over arak, nargileh, and games of basra.

The third time Marguerite became pregnant, Girgis braced himself for his wife's seemingly inevitable plunge into darkness. By now it was clear to him that her crippling moods did not wane until months after the child was born. At the same time, it seemed not a day went by that he was not asked by his brother, his aunt and uncle, his cousins, or various friends when he would have a son, someone to carry on the name of Beit Khoury. He supposed he wanted a son as well, even though his nightly ritual of holding a daughter in each arm before supper left his heart feeling more than full.

Yet strangely, as the weeks and months passed and Marguerite began to show, she didn't seem to slide into the same despondency as previously, which was a great relief to Girgis. They had a boy, whom they named George Jr., as Girgis now often went by George, and immediately called Georgie, as they'd always planned in the event that the wet, crying creature pulled from beneath the sheet had a tiny penis. Girgis's first reaction was relief. He and Marguerite had fulfilled their ancestral duty. He delighted in having a son, even though he could not hold back at least one tear, remembering that his mama was not there to exult in her first grandson.

But his happiness paled next to Marguerite's. When she showed the new baby to visiting family and friends, she would beam and say, "Yes, I have a *son* now, my *son*, my son, *ibni*, my perfect son," her lips grazing Georgie's tiny, fuzzy pate with infinite wonder and tenderness. Girgis watched this with some degree of fascination. In her best moods during the prior few years, Marguerite had been loving to her daughters in her own erratic fashion. She wasn't above snapping at them, her brows knit in anger and frustration, when they cried or failed to eat their food.

But now Marguerite lavished on her firstborn son an almost worshipful affection. The depression that had engulfed her after the girls' births seemed nowhere to be found. In all the years to come, as the area suffered through the Great Depression and the next world war, then savored the prosperity that followed, with its televisions and highways, Marguerite arrayed her life around Georgie. The slavish devotion she'd never quite been able to show her own husband came easily to her in regard to her son, whom she cherished as her most perfect accomplishment.

CHAPTER TWO

GEORGE AND MARY JO

(1960s–1970s)

By age twelve, Mary Jo, the third of five children, was the undisputed brain of the Coughlin family. She was a very plain and sensible-looking little girl, with watery blue eyes, a freckled snub nose, and wheat-colored hair cut into short bangs in the front and a pageboy in the back. She seemed to barely tolerate her Mary Queen of Peace school uniform, with its Peter Pan–collared white blouse and itchy wool plaid skirt. When she came home, she would change into overalls and an old flannel shirt and spend the afternoon holed up reading, reading, reading. As young as eight or nine, she had a direct, humorless, self-contained quality that earned her the nickname "Dreary Mary" from her older sister, Lizzie, who was very flirtatious. She had little interest in the new diversion of television, and when she wasn't reading, she was usually holding forth at the dinner table about what she had learned in her introductory biology class.

"We found some undigested field mouse inside a frog's stomach today when we were dissecting it," she announced one night at dinner when she was in seventh grade.

Everyone at the table groaned in disgust.

"That's not appropriate for the dinner table," her mother said.

"And what's the point of that?" her father added. "What good is that gonna do you?"

"A frog's organs are laid out in a very similar fashion to a human's," Mary Jo replied.

"Stop!" protested Lizzie "You are making me want to vomit."

Their mother clanked her fork loudly on her plate. "I have *had it up to here* with the language at this table."

Mary Jo rolled her eyes a bit and sighed. It was another grumpy night at family dinner. Terry, her brother, had not said a word, or even lifted his face up from his plate.

Mary Jo had a haughtiness toward most other people and accordingly was not very social. All through junior high school, and then in high school, in the very early 1960s, her best friend was a Lebanese girl, Christina Kattar, with very glossy, straight long black hair pulled back in symmetrical barrettes, who shared her unsmiling braininess. Mary Jo respected Christina, suspecting that Christina might be even a bit smarter than she herself was, and she was also fascinated by the odd foods that Christina's mother would pack for her lunch, such as, on one occasion, a lump of raw lamb chopped up with onions and slick with olive oil, which Christina unwrapped from its tinfoil and proceeded, in a businesslike and highly unselfconscious manner, to eat with tiny shreds of a flat, paper-like bread.

Christina would regularly tell Mary Jo about how she intended to be an obstetrician and deliver babies. Mary Jo would complain to Christina about how unchallenging she found the classes at Mary Queen of Peace. "I don't see why we have to memorize poems about trees," she would say. "What good is that?"

But Christina seemed unfazed by this. "College will be more rigorous," she'd say calmly. Christina made it very clear she wanted to go to Tufts for both undergraduate and medical school; she would talk of this not as though it were something she aspired to and hoped for, but simply as something she knew would happen.

College. The word had a wild, fantastic, unreal quality to Mary Jo. Terry had been the first in the family to go, a great source of pride, studying business at a Catholic college in Mendhem, the tidy green suburb to Lawton's immediate south where it seemed more and more families they knew were buying small homes, moving out of Lawton as it filled with Puerto Ricans just as the city's big textile mills were closing up and migrating south.

Could Mary Jo possibly go to college as well? Every year, a few of the brightest and richest girls from Mary Queen of Peace went to Regis or Emmanuel, women's Catholic colleges in Boston that were considered the height of prestige among her nun teachers. (Of course, Mary Jo dimly knew, there were other women's colleges, such as Bradford, Wheaton, and of course Radcliffe, but they were for rich Yankees who went to debutante balls or for extremely elite Catholics, like the Kennedys.) She was starting her junior year in high school, and she began wondering whether she could perhaps get a scholarship.

One evening after dinner she broached the idea to her parents. "Christina Kattar is planning to go to Tufts and I'm going to apply for a scholarship to Emmanuel," she said.

"Emmanuel?" her mother exclaimed. "You're gonna move to Boston and get killed by the Boston Strangler? No way. You can go to the nursing program at Lawton General or Teachers College in Lowell."

"But I want a real bachelor's degree, like Terry," she protested. She looked at her father, who appeared to be focused on his newspaper.

"Putting Terry through four years of a private school is already breaking your poor father's back," her mother said sharply. "And Terry needs it because he wants to break into management. You don't need it to become a teacher or a nurse or a secretary. You just need a year or two."

"Maybe I don't want to be a teacher or a nurse or a secretary," Mary Jo insisted.

Her mother, an elementary school teacher, folded her arms over her chest. "Oh, really?" she said. "That's beneath you?"

I want to be a doctor, Mary Jo desperately wanted to say. *A doctor like Christina.* But she was afraid her mother would cackle in her face, which would surely destroy her. "It's not that," she said, more quietly. She turned again to her father. "Are you going to say anything, Daddy?"

Not diverting his eyes from the page, her father said, "I think you should listen to your mother. Lowell was just fine for her."

After that dispiriting talk, something in Mary Jo snapped. Prior to it, she'd always taken pride in staying head-to-head with, or at least only slightly behind, Christina Kattar on various exams and rankings. But she suddenly stopped caring as much. She certainly didn't need top grades to get into teaching or nursing school. She slid, but not *that* far down the scale, merely into the top twentieth percentile of her class. Still, everyone noticed that girls who'd once never so much as come close to Mary Jo in science or math now occasionally scored higher than she did.

Mary Jo affected nonchalance about it all. Concurrent with her academic slide was the fact that, for the first time in her life, she was falling in with the cool girls—Maureen Lynch, Janet Abruzzo, Ava Desroches, and the others—and taking up their habits of teasing their hair, putting on makeup, rolling up their plaid skirts after school to reveal more leg at the diner, and mooning over Elvis and Ricky Nelson. (And, of course, smoking, which Mary Jo had previously found disgusting.) Mary Jo now had the approval of her peers, a full social life, and the attention of boys from Boys' Catholic, and a part of her wondered why she had sneered at these things and deprived herself of them all her life. She found them pleasurable, and these prizes came with considerably more ease than perfect scores on chemistry exams. Girls in her new crowd talked offhandedly about their post–high school plans, much of which involved their prospects of marrying a doctor, lawyer, or business owner. Maureen Lynch, for example, was already dating a freshman at Boston College.

The following fall, Mary Jo started at Lawton General Hospital's school of nursing, living in a bare-bones dormitory with seventy-five other girls from the Merrimack Valley, a dozen of them from her own high school. She continued to be popular, and she became the informal organizer of near-nightly rounds of Forty-fives, a local card game that involved gambling with nickels and dimes. She found most of her introductory classes, such as tenets of patient care, bed making, and principles of antisepsis and nutrition, stupefyingly simple, and she was privately aghast at the nearly religious fervor that the instructors—some of whom had been nurses at the hospital since the 1930s, before the introduction of antibiotics—brought to these classes.

She was desperate to get to anatomy, physiology, and biology—classes that were taught by the hospital's doctors, all male, who exhibited varying degrees of boredom while lecturing. The doctors were patronizing, Mary Jo thought, as though they expected the nurses to generally understand, for example, what the endocrine system was and what it did but no more than that.

Mary Jo raised her hand in the lecture hall. "Excuse me, Doctor," she asked. "What are the other conditions we would want to rule out before making a diagnosis of hyperthyroidism?" She'd read enough to know that this was a standard part of the diagnostic process.

The instructor, a dry Yankee sort from southern Maine, turned and stared at her blankly. "As the nurse, you wouldn't need to do the ruling out or make the diagnosis," he replied flatly. "You would note your observations in your chart and alert the physician." He stared at her a moment longer, then shrugged to suggest that he'd dispatched the query. Some of the other students Mary Jo was seated with looked her way, then tittered and whispered.

"Thank you, Doctor," Mary Jo said. But she was humiliated and burning with rage inside. She thought briefly of Christina Kattar, perhaps sitting in just such a physiology class at Tufts, being given a proper answer to the very same question because *she* was training to be a doctor. Her rage doubled, and she gripped her pen hard. During the break, Peg Consentino, one of her handful of nursing-school friends from Mary Queen of Peace, came up to her to bum a cigarette.

"If you make the doctors think you want their job, Mary dear," said Peg, "none of them will ask you to marry them."

Part of Mary Jo wanted to scream. She often felt that most of her classmates were here foremost, in fact, not to get a nursing diploma but to land a doctor. It was an ongoing game, a competition, fiercer than their nightly rounds of Forty-fives. Which doctor had the brightest future; which doctor had smiled alongside his *hello* to which nursing student in the corridor of which floor of the hospital; which doctor was the handsomest, came from the best family—and, ultimately, which nursing students, once they'd earned their caps, received proposals from which doctors a year or two down the line.

But Mary Jo only scowled at her friend, who she knew was being (partly) flippant. "Boo hoo, poor me," she said. "As though that's why I came here."

For their two-day musculoskeletal segment, they had a young orthopedic surgeon named Dr. George Khoury. It quickly shot through the school grapevine that he'd grown up in the Lebanese (or what some still called the Syrian) section of Lawton, excelled at Holy Cross, went to Tufts for medical school (*Tufts!* thought Mary Jo. *There it was again.*), and did his residency at Boston City Hospital before returning to his parents' home to be a surgeon at Lawton General. Dr. Khoury was five foot seven, not fat but not exactly slim either, and wore thick glasses on a prominent nose below his thick, dark head of hair and brows.

"Good morning, future nurses," he'd said on the first day, and Mary Jo had found his teaching demeanor serious but not humorless, as evinced when he'd refer to the entire musculoskeletal system as "the bones, the meat, and the hinges," which had made her smile quietly to herself.

Dr. Khoury did not merely lecture at them. He was constantly interrupting his exegeses to point to random students and lob a question their way, seemingly obsessed with having his lessons properly absorbed. "And a pathological fracture is—" He pointed to Annie McCarthy, the strawberry pixie cut in the fourth row. "What is a pathological fracture, Miss?"

Annie sat up. "Me?"

"No, Miss, your great-aunt Tillie. Yes, you." Many of the girls erupted in semi-scandalized and delighted laughter. "What is a pathological fracture?"

Annie blushed deeply. "It's—it's caused by a pathology."

"Brilliant," deadpanned Dr. Khoury. "Now, can you tell us what that means?"

Annie struggled before shaking her head in embarrassment.

"I've obviously been speaking Swahili," said Dr. Khoury. "Who can tell us?"

Mary Jo raised her hand, caught his attention. "It's a fracture caused by disease weakening the bone. Such as osteoporosis."

"Very good. Or what else?"

"Or cancer or a cyst."

"*Very* good. And how would we diagnose it?"

"Clinical observation or X-rays."

"And how would we treat?"

"It would depend on the nature of the fracture and the underlying condition or reason."

Dr. Khoury paused briefly, considered, then smiled slightly. "Very good. What is your name, future nurse?"

"Mary Jo Coughlin."

"Very good, Future Nurse Coughlin. And if we suspected the underlying condition was, for example, a multiple myeloma, how would we determine that?"

By now, all eyes in the class were on Mary Jo. There had hardly ever been a back-and-forth like this among instructor and nurse. And now the doctor was throwing in big technical words like *myeloma*! Mary Jo stared at the doctor, perplexed. Was he challenging her to fail? But regardless, she knew—she was fairly certain she knew—the answer.

"Clinical observation, radiation, lab tests," she said. "But eventually you'd have to do a biopsy."

"Exactly," said the doctor. He sounded matter-of-fact, Mary Jo noted, as though he weren't shocked that a nursing student should know such things. "And with the advancement of fluoroscopy-guided biopsy at the moment, we are expecting some wonderful breakthroughs in biopsy in the coming years."

Then the doctor continued with his lecture. Many sets of eyes were still on Mary Jo—she could feel them—but she did her best to hold a neutral expression. She felt very good.

Once the students were on the floors of the hospital, Mary Jo began crossing paths regularly with Dr. Khoury. She found his large nose and his shortness—he stood probably an inch shorter than she did—adorable, and she often overheard him muttering funny, flat remarks like, "He's a nutjob" or "This is just screwy." He also remembered her.

"Good morning, Future Nurse Coughlin," he addressed her one day.

She laughed sharply, a bit surprised by his recollection. "Good morning, Current Doctor Khoury," she quipped back, quick with a smile.

"What brings you to the floor today?"

"We're following Dr. Hall on rounds."

"That must be very lively," he said, and winked at her, which, to her dismay, made her snort sharply with laughter.

The exchange had been caught by Peg Consentino, making her way down the hallway with a bedpan. "Sweet nothings," Peg said to her demurely before sashaying on.

"Oh, for God's sake, Peg!" Mary Jo called back, but as she walked on, she smiled a bit herself.

Soon enough, Mary Jo and her classmates found themselves on rounds with Dr. Khoury. They gathered around the bed of an old woman from Mendhem named Dottie Doherty who'd fallen and broken her femur. As soon as Mrs. Doherty saw Dr. Khoury walk into the room, she put down her copy of *Ladies' Home Journal* and beamed as though her own son had appeared.

"Good morning, Dr. Khoury," said Mrs. Doherty cheerily.

"Good morning, Mrs. Doherty," said Dr. Khoury, ever so lightly tweaking the old woman's big toe, which poked inelegantly from the sheet. "May I introduce you to some bright future nurses of America who are following me on my rounds this morning?"

"Make a specimen of me, Doctor, it's all for science," said the old woman, turning on her side and pulling back the sheet, then her johnny, to expose her bony white thigh.

"Gather round, future nurses," said Dr. Khoury, and the young women did so. "Mrs. Doherty has sustained an oblique, displaced closed fracture of the femur shaft," he explained, drawing a small line on the woman's thigh with his index finger. "This is very common in older patients who've lost key bone mineral density with age."

"Wonderful," said Mrs. Doherty dryly, evoking titters from some of the students.

"In Mrs. Doherty's surgery in a few days, we will utilize intramedullary nailing to stabilize the fractured femur so it can heal. Can anyone tell me what intramedullary nailing is?"

Mary Jo knew, but she determined to stay quiet to give someone else a chance to answer. But there was silence. She found it hard to believe that, after two years of nursing school, no one knew the answer, but no one seemed willing to proffer it.

"Anyone at all?" said Dr. Khoury, his voice betraying annoyance.

It was silly, Mary Jo thought, to withhold further. "You'll insert a rod and pin it to the femur," she said.

Some of the other students looked her way, irked, shaking their heads. Mary Jo was the class know-it-all, it had been well established by now, which earned her varying degrees of respect and irritation. "If I know something, I don't see why I shouldn't say so," she'd once snapped back, when one of her classmates had remarked, in sarcastic singsong, "Oh, Mary Jo *always* has the answers."

But now, Dr. Khoury merely said, "Yes, exactly," and went on to detail the procedure. He then sent the students outside so he could have a private moment with Mrs. Doherty, and when he emerged in the hallway, ushering the nurses on to his next patient, he fell in step alongside Mary Jo.

"That should be a very simple, classic pin," he said to her matter-of-factly.

She nodded. She desperately wanted to talk to him about something, and hesitated only a moment. "Isn't it exciting," she said, "what they're doing in Boston with arthroscopy? What Charnley's doing with whole hip replacements in England?"

"Extremely exciting," he said. "That's the next decade in the field." Then he stopped walking and lightly took her elbow while the other students went on slightly ahead of them. His brow furrowed as his eyes searched hers. "Why aren't you studying to be a doctor?" he asked in a low voice.

Mary Jo felt her entire face flush red. She looked down. For a moment, she considered covering for herself, for pride's sake, saying, *I chose to be a nurse.* But something gave way, and she said, with some bitterness in her voice that surprised her, "This was my option."

He continued staring at her—not with pity, exactly, but with a frankness that made her, glancing up into his eyes only to glance away again, profoundly uncomfortable. "Why don't you come work with me after you get your cap in May?" he asked. "I'm setting up a private practice in Mendhem. Orthopedics is going to get very exciting in the next few years."

Mary Jo was taken aback. "I was thinking of going into pediatrics," she said, truthfully.

He smiled and said, "Plenty of kids break bones," which made her smile.

"Well, thank you, Doctor, that's a very generous offer, and I'll think about it."

"I hope you will. I would work with you in a partnership. I'm not of my parents' generation."

She did think about it, for several weeks. Seeing him in the hospital coffee shop a few weeks later, she approached him. "Good morning, Doctor," she said.

"Good morning, Miss Coughlin."

"May I ask you something, assuming your offer still stands?"

"It still stands. And of course you may ask me something."

Mary Jo cleared her throat. "If I came to work with you," she began, then stopped. "Well, for starters, of course I would fulfill my standard nursing duties."

Dr. Khoury nodded, signaling her to continue.

"But," and again she paused. "You would share all information and new developments and new studies and best practices with me, and you would be open to my opinion on cases?" Mary Jo was a bit surprised to find herself trembling slightly.

Again, he looked at her searchingly. "Miss Coughlin, I would *solicit* your opinion," he finally said. "You would likely be evaluating patients before I even saw them, and you would be briefing me. And I would hope that *you* were following all new information and developments in the literature and sharing them with *me*. I told you, I want to open this practice in partnership with an excellent nurse."

It was more of an answer than Mary Jo had been expecting, but it was the answer she had been hoping for. "And you'll be able to pay a full-time nurse in your first year starting up?"

"I've budgeted a ninety-dollar weekly salary for a nurse in the first year, with a raise hopefully after that."

Mary Jo nodded slowly. "I can accept your offer, then, Doctor."

He smiled. "I'm very happy to hear that."

"But I'm going to hold off telling anyone until after graduation. It would just be too awkward until then."

"I understand."

The morning of their capping ceremony, a perfect day in May 1964, Mary Jo told Peg Consentino that she would be going to work with Dr. Khoury in his new office in Mendhem, adding that Peg was the first to know.

"Everybody already knows that," said Peg.

"You're the first person I've told."

"The girls knew he was opening his own practice, so a few of them asked him about work, and he said he'd already hired a nurse, and we all just assumed it was you." Peg, smoking as usual, had a cool, factual air about her as she relayed this. "It wasn't that hard to figure out."

Mary Jo was briefly flummoxed. "Oh," was all she could manage.

"Congratulations, MJ. You made out well."

"What about you next year?"

"I'm up for a job at Crestview." It was a local nursing home.

"That's good."

Peg shrugged and stubbed out her cigarette. "It's a job. I suppose you and Khoury will be married in about six months. That's what we're all betting."

"Peggy! I am going to *work* with him."

Peg raised an eyebrow. "You mean *for* him."

"I mean *with* him," she said, sharpening her tone.

Again, Peg shrugged. "He's *awfully* short." She rose, put a hand on Mary Jo's shoulder. "Congrats, MJ. I'm happy for you. I'll see you at the ceremony."

Mary Jo sat there for a moment alone. She felt as though Peg had just suggested she'd sold herself into concubinage under the cover of a nursing job. *Dr. Khoury offered me a rare opportunity to be a doctor's associate and not a bedpan-changer*, she told herself. She was very loath to admit, even privately, that she felt warmly toward him. It just didn't feel professional.

But in her first few weeks on the job—in a newly built, sleekly low-slung doctors' park off a leafy country road in affluent, Yankee-filled Mendhem, which felt a world away from the crowded city blocks of triple-deckers where she'd grown up—she found she was simply too busy to think about her personal feelings toward him. He hadn't explicitly told her, but she might have assumed, that she wasn't just the office nurse, she was the office manager, and her job included the many non-nursing tasks of getting a brand-new office up and running: ordering furniture and wall art, medical equipment, and a slew of office supplies; plunging into the byzantine paper-flurried world of health insurance plans, not to mention working out payments for patients without insurance; and greeting and managing patients at the front desk before she ever saw them in the examining room. Dr. Khoury already had a strong reputation in the Merrimack Valley, and it wasn't long before the schedule was regularly filled. Mary Jo came into the office each morning at eight o'clock, set up the electric coffeemaker, and then found she didn't stop until an hour after the office closed at six. Dr. Khoury proved good on his word and consulted her regularly on cases. She felt she was doing meaningful work and had made a wise choice in coming to work for him.

And then one day Marguerite came in.

Mary Jo had heard a bit from Dr. Khoury about his mother, whom he seemed to talk of in both reverential and terrified terms. She had married Dr. Khoury's father in 1930, at the age of seventeen. Dr. Khoury's father had owned a grocery store in the Lebanese section of Lawton, but to hear Dr. Khoury tell it, it was his mother who ran the store, made it profitable, and reined in her softhearted husband when he wanted to give all the stock away on credit to near-starving neighbors during the Depression. *I gave you life and I can take it away from you* was Marguerite Khoury's preferred threat, in Arabic, to her two daughters when she was angry at them, according to Dr. Khoury—who added with a laugh that she'd never said as much to him because "I was the only boy, hence her Messiah." This little anecdote made Mary Jo feel for the doctor's sisters.

Already, Mrs. Khoury had called the office a few times. "Hello, may I speak to my son, the doctor?" she'd asked. And Dr. Khoury always took the call in his back office, Mary Jo noted, even when he was swamped and otherwise would not take calls.

The first time Marguerite came into the office, it was unannounced. It was late morning, the waiting room was busy, and Mary Jo had her hands full both signing people in up front and preparing them for the doctor's examination and consultation in the back. The phone cradled on her shoulder, she looked up to find, rising not much higher than the long front desk, a woman, about five foot one, with ebony hair carefully set into an updo and protected by a transparent plastic rain bonnet, wearing a London Fog raincoat. She had shrewd, dark eyes set deeply behind cat's-eye glasses and carried a large, covered pot with steam rising from its lip.

"I'm the doctor's mother," she said flatly. "I brought yakhni for lunch."

"Excuse me, what?" replied Mary Jo, before she could catch herself.

"*YUCH-nee*," repeated Mrs. Khoury loudly. "It's a Lebanese stew. I have the rice in the car but I couldn't carry both pots with just my two hands."

"Oh!" Mary Jo leaped up. "Well, of course, let me take that from you." She reached for the pot.

"Be very careful!" Mrs. Khoury barked. "It's still very hot."

"Of course, I will." Mary Jo hurried the pot into the back, delivering it directly to the doctor, who was poring over a chart, preparing to see a middle-aged fellow who sat in a johnny in the examining room.

The doctor looked up. He didn't seem surprised to see Mary Jo carrying a steaming pot into his office. "My mother brought a yakhni?" he asked. "She said she might do that today."

"Yes," said Mary Jo, setting the pot down atop a stack of medical journals on the doctor's credenza. "She's outside."

The two hurried back out to the front desk. Mrs. Khoury was gone.

"I think she went to get the rice, she said," Mary Jo noted.

Indeed, in a moment, Mrs. Khoury walked back in, carrying a smaller covered pot. Over her arm hung a shopping bag, which contained, Mary Jo saw as she relieved the woman of her burden, two bowls, a serving ladle, two soupspoons, some folded paper napkins, and an aluminum foil package that contained, she soon learned, half a dozen Lebanese shortbread cookies stuffed with dates and nuts (which Mary Jo would find quite delicious with her afternoon coffee).

"I brought you yakhni and mamoul for your lunch," Mrs. Khoury virtually yelled when she saw her son. Then she glanced at Mary Jo and said something in Arabic.

Dr. Khoury rolled his eyes, laughed lightly, and said, "Ma, go sit in my office and eat with us in a little bit when it quiets down."

"Don't be crazy!" she barked. By now she'd attracted the attention of the entire waiting room. "You're busy, I'm busy. We're all busy." Then she switched back into Arabic and glanced at Mary Jo again. Her hands now free, she reached up to her son, who obediently stooped a bit to receive her kiss and pat on the cheek. Then Mrs. Khoury marched out of the office.

About an hour later, the doctor and Mary Jo found a quiet moment in his office to partake of bowls of, over rice, yakhni, which was a hearty lamb stew that Mary Jo found absolutely delicious.

"What's this unusual taste?" she asked the doctor.

"That's coriander," he said. "We call it 'kahz-brah.'" His syllables came out harsh and emphatic. Mary Jo tried to say the word, and the doctor laughed and said, "Close."

Then her memory was jogged. "Your mother was speaking Lebanese to you?"

"Arabic."

"Oh, right." She was a tad embarrassed. "What did she say to you when she came in?"

The doctor actually blushed, then laughed. "She said she didn't think you were feeding me properly, that's why she brought in the stew."

Now Mary Jo laughed, sharply. "So it's my job to feed you, too? That's why she gave me the evil eye!"

"I'm sure she'll grow to love you once she gets to know you. She's very—how shall we say? A force of nature."

I'm going to have to get to know her? thought Mary Jo. But she didn't say as much.

But, as it turned out, George was right. Secure in her knowledge that Mary Jo wasn't feeding her son sufficiently, Mrs. Khoury started coming to the office regularly bringing lunch, driving all the way over from Lawton to Mendhem in her boat-size 1958 Buick. There were days when Mary Jo ignored the bit of leftover roast and potatoes her own mother had packed for her, in order to sample dishes brought by Mrs. Khoury.

"It's so nice of your mother to bring us lunch every day," she remarked to the doctor.

"Ever since my father died, she's bored," he said. "No store for her to manage anymore. She runs all the activities at her church, but that's not enough. So she just cooks all day and then delivers the food to her kids."

One afternoon, one of the lunch pots was delivered by a tall, slim young woman with supple olive skin and beautifully set black hair crowned by a gray, broad-brimmed wool hat set far back on her head. Her eyes were lined heavily with makeup, just above a very grand nose and red-painted lips, and she wore a gray wool cape coat, set off by a matching navy patent-leather bag hooked on her arm, and heels.

"I'm Georgie's oldest sister," she announced. "Irene."

Mary Jo had heard about Irene. She was engaged to an engineer at Wang Laboratories from a Greek family—a union Mrs. Khoury had deemed acceptable after the fiancé had agreed to convert from the Greek Orthodox to the Lebanese Maronite church. Irene was a buyer in the ladies' department at the Jordan Marsh store in the new low-rise mall two towns over. The doctor had said that his sister, five years his senior, was the best-dressed woman in Lawton, if not perhaps the entire Merrimack Valley.

This chic woman looked out of place holding a giant, scarred pot, thought Mary Jo. "Oh, hello," she said. "I'm Mary Jo."

Irene smiled with an odd knowingness. "Yes, I know who you are."

This took Mary Jo aback briefly. "Oh. Well." She paused. "Mrs. Khoury couldn't come today?"

"Father Joe needed her to go over the books with him. At our church." Mary Jo nodded.

"Anyway," Irene said, holding the pot slightly aloft as though to suggest she wanted Mary Jo to take it off her hands. "Here's Georgie's lunch. I've been a good sister like my mother told me to be, and now I have to get back to my job." She sang the words with a sarcastic ring.

"You left work to pick up lunch for George and bring it over here?" Mary Jo asked, standing to receive the pot.

Irene arched an eyebrow at Mary Jo, as though she were some kind of idiot. In a lower tone, she said, "Georgie is *the son*. He *always* comes first."

Dr. Khoury, in fact, emerged from his office in time to hear the remark. "You don't have to listen to her," he told his sister, relieving her of the pot. "Don't be a martyr."

Irene seemed slightly embarrassed to have been overheard. "I don't mind bringing you lunch, Georgie," she said. She stooped down to kiss her younger brother on the cheek, where she left a faint lipstick trace. Mary Jo noted how her manner had shifted from stiff and sarcastic to softly adoring.

Dr. Khoury put the pot on the desktop and lifted the lid. "What is it today?" he wondered. "Oh, chicken and chickpeas. Yummy." He glanced at Mary Jo. "You'll love this one."

Irene glanced at her in turn. "I hope there's enough for both of you," she said.

Mary Jo laughed sharply. "There's enough for the whole waiting room!" she noted.

The doctor laughed in assent, but Irene looked at her reprovingly. "*Someone* has to feed him," she said, before pulling gloves from her handbag and sailing out the door toward her Ford Mustang sports car, which was the same cherry red as her lipstick.

"Let me guess," said Mary Jo. "Your sisters think I should be feeding you, too."

The doctor laughed good-naturedly. "They're very protective."

"She's very chic."

"She's a fashion plate," the doctor said fondly, picking up the pot. "Come back and have some of this when you have a moment."

In retrospect, Mary Jo realized that she likely fell in love with the doctor while they were sharing his mother's lunches in his back office, those stolen fifteen or twenty minutes when she would keep one eye and ear on the waiting room while also listening to his funny tales about his mother, who—on family road trips years ago—would make her husband, George (the doctor's namesake), pull off busy highways when she spotted grapevine leaves lushly growing on the roadside.

Mostly, Mary Jo marveled at the doctor's warmth. The doctor smiled and laughed readily and was also kind and tender with patients, especially children, whom he hugged and offered lollipops to while saying things like "Ouch!" and "That must have *hurt. You poor kid!*" But he also wasn't above light, good-humored gossip and gentle jabs. He was, in fact, more animated than many of the tough-skinned women in her own Irish family—and certainly more animated than the men, whose flat gruffness dissolved only when they drank, and then sometimes in scary, off-putting ways. The doctor, on the other hand, hardly drank, but seemed instead to be a coffee addict. Mary Jo always found herself looking forward to seeing him in the morning and, uncomfortably for herself, a bit sad to say good-bye to him in the evenings.

At home, she talked a great deal about the doctor, his kind ways, and the strange but delicious meals and pastries his amusingly bossy mother would bring in.

"You sure seem to like your boss," her mother would note. "You better be careful, there, Mary Jo."

"What does that mean?" she would ask, offended. She would talk about the doctor so freely, so enthusiastically, that she initially wasn't aware she was betraying affection.

"Just remember who's the boss," her mother would say.

Then something happened that—she was loath to admit to anyone, even to herself—she found devastating. The doctor apparently began dating someone.

One spring evening toward six, a tiny, dark-haired young woman in an A-line dress and matching shoes and bag stepped shyly toward the front desk. By this point, enough of the doctor's family, extended family, and family friends had come to the office for Mary Jo to realize instantly that the young woman was Lebanese, Greek, Armenian, or some combination of the above: the dark, deep-set eyes, the strong nose, the olive skin.

"Hello," the young woman said. "I'm here for Dr. Khoury."

"He's not seeing any more patients today," Mary Jo said. "Would you like to make an appointment for—" She began scanning the appointment book. "Actually, he has nothing until next week. Would—"

"Oh no." The young woman laughed shyly. "I'm not here for an appointment. I'm—would you tell him Mona is here?"

Mary Jo could feel her bright office face fall as the woman's words sank in. Ever so briefly, she paused. Then, "Of course—just one second."

She found the doctor in his office, immersed in a pile of paperwork. "Mona is here to see you," she said flatly.

He looked up. "Oh my goodness, that's right." The doctor stood, stuffed the file and a few others into his briefcase, grabbed his overcoat. Mary Jo stepped back to let him pass through the door—at which point he smiled at her uncomfortably and said, "Good night"—then followed him out to the front, where he greeted the waiting woman with, "Well, hello there!"

The young woman looked down briefly, blushed. "Hello to you."

"So, shall we eat?" asked the doctor, buttoning his overcoat and hurrying to the door to hold it open for the woman.

"Yes!" she said. She turned politely back to Mary Jo. "Good night," she said.

"Good night, Mary Jo," the doctor echoed. "See you tomorrow."

"Good night," Mary Jo called back. But once they were gone, instead of collecting her own things and leaving for the night herself, Mary Jo just sat there in the empty office for several minutes, feeling slightly stunned. Of course, she told herself, trying to be rational, it wasn't surprising that the doctor would be dating. He was a highly eligible bachelor, a prominent young doctor, even if he was barely more than five feet tall. Certainly in his own ethnic community he was seen as a good catch. Then Mary Jo chastised herself for having allowed herself to feel, amid all those shared lunches in the doctor's office, full of jokes and gossip, that something was happening between them. How stupid and unprofessional she had been, even if it was just in her own head! She was embarrassed to feel tears of humiliation—and something else, bitter sadness—rise hotly in her eyes.

"Oh, get a grip," she said aloud, to herself, in the empty office, before gathering her things and locking up.

Over the next several weeks, Mona became a regular presence, visiting once or sometimes twice a week toward closing time. She was a polite, shy, plain girl, a social worker at Lowell General Hospital who still lived with her Lebanese parents in Haverhill. She would sit with a book or magazine in the waiting room, and Mary Jo would steal narrow-eyed glances at her while both women waited for the doctor to emerge from the back. Eventually, Mary Jo determined that it would seem rude or strange for her to go on ignoring Mona, so one night, when—as usual—only the two young women were left in the front, Mary Jo piped up from her desk.

"How do you like it over at Lowell?" She'd tried to make her tone bright, but she still thought she sounded harsh and confrontational.

"Oh!" exclaimed Mona, as though she were surprised and honored to be addressed. "I really like it very much. They're really doing some very progressive things there."

"Like what?" Again, Mary Jo had meant to sound friendly, but the query came out more of a bark.

"Well." Mona sat up straighter, holding her book primly in her lap. "There's a wonderful new program for geriatric social work. I've recently gotten involved with that."

"Good luck with that," Mary Jo said. "I've got some girlfriends from nursing school working in geriatric. It's a backbreaker."

Mona blinked, looking slightly chastised. "I enjoy it," she replied, nearly murmuring.

Mary Jo turned her back on Mona to put away files. "I guess that's what matters." She was sounding just like her mother, the shrugging voice that said, *If you want to be an idiot, go ahead and be my guest!* She was very angry at herself for foiling her own attempt at being cordial. But then in no time, the doctor came out, and he and Mona were off to dinner, leaving Mary Jo alone in the office, her lower lip trembling.

"Had a nice time with Mona last night?" she brashly said to the doctor the next morning.

He must have caught something in her voice, because he turned and briefly regarded her curiously. "We went to Kowloon," he said. Kowloon was a Polynesian restaurant on Route 1 in Saugus built to look like a temple, with a giant tiki sculpture over the door. "I have a strong suspicion that all that fried food is not authentic Oriental cuisine."

Mary Jo shrugged. "Never been, so I can't say." She turned away abruptly, back to her work, but she could feel the doctor's eyes on her briefly before he headed back to his office.

Irene stopped in around noon to deliver lunch: two Tupperware containers, one of green peppers stuffed with rice and lamb, another of fresh yogurt. She wore a pink sleeveless top with black pedal pushers and low heels, and didn't bother to take off her opaque, pink-framed cat's-eye sunglasses.

"Your mother's using Tupperware now?" Mary Jo asked. She was still feeling punchy. "How modern."

From coral lips, Irene allowed what Mary Jo thought might have been the trace of a smile, then set down the containers and, still not removing her glasses, studied her for an uncomfortable moment.

"May I be so bold as to suggest something?" she finally asked.

This startled Mary Jo. "What would that be?" she managed.

Irene sighed. "I know this may sound retrograde," she began, "but would you please just once bring in lunch for Georgie? Just so we know that you can cook?"

Mary Jo let out a short, sharp laugh, her mouth gaping. "*What?*"

"I know it sounds backward. But then I can tell my mother."

"I'm his *nurse*, I'm not his *cook*. Or his mother."

"I know." Irene finally removed her sunglasses and regarded Mary Jo with sympathy. "But—it might go a long way."

Mary Jo felt her face flash crimson. "Toward *what*?"

Irene jutted her chin toward the back office. "We all know the two of you laugh and chatter the day away back there. He's very fond of you."

Mary Jo's horror deepened. She made a sound of protest, but no words came out.

"And moreover," continued Irene, indifferent to Mary Jo's indignation, "Mona Farah is actually a distant cousin of ours. Which is just—" She paused, shivered slightly. "You would think we were still in the mountains."

This was far more information than Mary Jo could handle in the middle of a busy day. "I really have to get back to work," she said, flustered.

"Of course." Unfazed, Irene put her sunglasses back on, turned, and departed.

Mary Jo sat there a moment, slightly shell-shocked, the container of stuffed peppers releasing steamy aromas before her.

"What was Irene going on about?"

Mary Jo turned. It was the doctor. "Your mother's new Tupperware," she said, thinking fast.

"Oh yes, Ma feels very up-to-date now, even though she's convinced there's something sinister about putting food in plastic. What's this?" He pried off the lid of one container. "Ooh, stuffed peppers, good. This is one of my favorites."

"That's probably why she made it," Mary Jo ventured flatly.

"Come back and have some with me when things slow down." With that, the doctor disappeared.

Mary Jo nursed her outrage over Irene's suggestion for several days. Her pique wasn't so much over the idea that she should be responsible for feeding the doctor, which she thought was absurd and indeed *retrograde*; it was more that Irene suspected she was looking for an in to his heart and to the family. How presumptuous! What had she done to make Irene think that, except to chat and laugh intermittently with the doctor, as any two colleagues in close quarters all day would do?

Then came the Sunday dinner when she broke down and asked her mother to set aside some of the prime rib and scalloped potatoes for her to take to work the next day. Enough for two.

Her mother looked at her suspiciously. "I thought the doctor's mother sent in Syrian food every day," she said.

"It's Lebanese food."

"We called them Syrians when I was a kid."

"Lebanon was part of Syria then, that's why." Christina Kattar had explained this to her a long time ago. "And I just want to balance out all the lunches he's offered me."

"Fine," said her mother. "I'll set some aside."

"And some pie, too?"

Her mother shot her another look. "Fine."

In the morning before the office had opened, when the doctor arrived while she was making coffee, she said, with studied casualness, and without turning toward him, "You can tell your mother she doesn't need to send lunch today. I made prime rib last night and brought some in today."

She didn't dare turn to see the doctor's reaction, but she heard none. So she finally turned, to find the doctor staring at her, a small, amused—and, to her, infuriating—smile on his face. "That was thoughtful of you," he said.

"Well, I made too much," she said, her words coming out overemphatic to her own ears, "so it just made sense."

"Okay, then. I'll let my mother know." He retreated into his office.

"Of course you will," Mary Jo muttered under her breath, profoundly annoyed that she'd capitulated to this machination.

In a lull at around two thirty, the doctor stuck his head out. "Eat?" he called.

She put her hand-lettered "We Will Be Back Shortly" sign on the desk and retreated to his office, where the doctor was putting Mary Jo's leftovers onto plates. "This looks delicious," he remarked.

"There's pie, too," she noted.

They sat, he behind his desk, she by the corner of the desk, in the chair the patient usually took. As soon as she cut her first bite of the cold meat and potatoes, she was dismayed. "I should've made sandwiches," she said. "They would've been better cold."

He shook his head, his mouth full, then swallowed. "I think this is terrific. Thank you for bringing in lunch today."

"It must be a little dull to you compared with your mother's exotic foods."

"It's wonderful. Thank you."

"Well, you can thank my mother," Mary Jo found herself saying sourly, even as she wondered why she was sabotaging herself. "She made it. I'm not much of a cook, frankly. I can do eggs and burgers and a meat loaf and that's about it."

Once again, the doctor shook his head and laughed mildly. "That's better than me."

An awkward silence ensued while they chewed. "That last patient needs wrist surgery, I think," he mused.

"Molinari?" she asked. "I was thinking the same thing."

The doctor grunted an assent. Chewing the cold roast, Mary Jo felt that today's lunch felt different. It was better, frankly, eating the doctor's mother's dishes, delivered hot. They glanced at each other, which provoked from the doctor a small, closemouthed smile as he chewed.

Then, as though reading her mind, he finally said, "I hope you don't feel you have to bring lunch. My mother is more than happy to do it. I told you she centers her days on it now."

She said nothing, just shrugged and continued chewing.

He laughed lightly. "Regardless of the unsolicited comments you hear from Irene. I've told them you're a nurse, not a cook."

Now she simply put down her fork, sat back, and folded her arms, unable to mask her annoyance at him but not knowing what to say.

He laughed, mildly alarmed. "What is it?"

"You are not making this any easier on me!" she declared, her face hot.

Amusement drained from the doctor's face, which softened. He set his plate aside and offered an open hand across the desk. "Mary Jo," he said. "Do you want to take this?"

She felt a flush of tears, and she swallowed them back down. She set aside her plate and took his hand, which was warm and slightly moist. "I just don't know how to handle this, because I work for you," she said, her voice raspy.

He gazed at her as he put his other hand over hers, rubbing it. "I haven't known, either. But I'm sure we can figure it out—if you want it. Do you want it?"

She brushed away tears with the back of her hand. "I suppose I do!" she exclaimed. "For better or worse." She rose and walked around the desk and sat in his lap, where they began kissing. She'd long wanted to stroke his pate of black hair, and now she did. She'd never felt so wild, so lawless, in her life, as she realized that life required a few key moments when one's tough wall had to come down if certain major steps forward were going to be made. She felt exhilarated—and monumentally relieved. She now held that adorable, funny man in her arms. *Her* arms!

"You're such a sweet man," she told him, overcome by a flood of warmth. "I've wanted to tell you for so, so long."

"You are such a smart and capable person," the doctor said. "No nonsense. I feel like there's nothing we can't do together."

"Except cook!"

"I don't care! We'll figure that out."

"But wait," she said, still in his lap.

"But what?"

"Mona," she said quietly.

He inhaled and frowned apologetically. "Mona is a very sweet girl," he said.

"But that's who your mother wanted."

"That doesn't matter. But there is one important question."

"What?"

"Would you be okay letting my mother teach you how to roll grape leaves?"

Mary Jo burst out laughing. "That's the condition I can have you under?"

"Well, thankfully, you're already Catholic. And she knows you're a hard worker."

She shook her head, finding the caveat so absurd. "Sure, I guess I can learn how to roll a grape leaf if that's what it'll take to get your mother's blessing."

George looked genuinely relieved. "I was afraid to ask you."

She dabbed her eyes, having laughed so hard she'd cried a smidgen. "What am I getting myself into?"

Sixteen months later, the day after Peg Consentino got her wedding invitation, she called Mary Jo. "You did it," she said. "You got a doctor." Peg had already married a car dealership owner.

"I guess you'll never believe me if I tell you that wasn't my ultimate goal in life, will you?" Mary Jo asked.

"Oh no, I would," Peg said agreeably. "I know you're not that kind of person. You just don't know how lucky you are, that's all."

Mary Jo didn't know how to reply to this. She felt lucky because she was marrying a man she found kind, warmhearted, adorable, funny, and brilliant; whose work she could share; and who talked to her about work as a peer, seeking her counsel and relying on her support.

But marrying George also meant joining his sprawling, incestuous, bickering, tight-knit family—infinite layers of aunts, uncles, and cousins; intrigues, petty rivalries, and grudges that went back decades, some back to the tribe's earliest years in America. And it also meant a lifetime of managing her future mother-in-law, the indomitable Marguerite, who, even after learning of her son's engagement, still barely addressed Mary Jo save to tell her which meals Georgie would prefer when, and how he liked his underwear folded and his bed made.

"I don't give a damn about any of that!" George insisted to her later, in private. "These are just ideas she gets in her head."

"Well," said Mary Jo, half-amused, half-simmering, "she certainly doesn't need to tell a nurse how to make a bed. We wasted a full week on that in school."

Nonetheless, aiming to be a good sport, Mary Jo yielded to Mrs. Khoury's demand that she come over one Saturday afternoon, about three months before the wedding, to learn how to roll a proper grape leaf. This was essential, Mrs. Khoury reminded her (not for the first time), "because the time will come when I'm not here and George will have to rely on you for this." Mrs. Khoury said this darkly, as though she could hardly bring herself to envision such a dire circumstance.

Mary Jo went over to Mrs. Khoury's house with the best of attitudes.

"I thought you were coming at one," Mrs. Khoury, in a housecoat and scuffs, greeted her, kissing her dutifully. "It's nearly two."

"I had to take care of some insurance forms for my mother."

Mrs. Khoury ignored her and marched her into the kitchen, where wet, green grape leaves were stacked high on a plate, alongside a pot of raw-lamb-and-rice stuffing and two cutting boards, laid side by side. Mrs. Khoury washed her hands and instructed Mary Jo to do the same. She had the small TV on in the kitchen, tuned low to the news, with its inevitable, endless shots of fighting in Vietnam and of President Johnson.

"You sit there," instructed Mrs. Khoury. *Honestly*, thought Mary Jo. *Not even a how are you? Small talk?* She sat down and resigned herself to her tutorial.

But almost from the start, she could do nothing right according to Mrs. Khoury. "That's too much filling!" she'd bark, amid aggrieved sighs. Or: "Now that's not enough." Or: "You didn't snip off the stem right from the bottom." Or: "You fold from the bottom, then the sides, not the other way." Or: "You put the leaf in the pot with the rolled side down." Or: "You're not packing them tight enough in the pot! They won't cook right."

And then finally: "I don't think you're ever gonna get this. You're not trying hard enough."

Mary Jo finally lost it. "This is my *first time*," she said forcefully, turning to the little despot in the housecoat and scuffs. "And frankly, you should be *lucky* I'm here because I have other things to do today, like take care of my own mother. I'm here for *you*. George told me he doesn't even care if I make grape leaves because he can get them from you or his sisters. Or from Salaam's."

Mrs. Khoury looked horrified. "You're going to make your own husband buy grape leaves from a restaurant?"

"He doesn't care," Mary Jo insisted. (*Did* he care, perhaps? she asked herself. Just a little?) "I'm here today to make you happy. So we can get to know each other."

But Mrs. Khoury seemed impervious to this sentimentalism. "These are things you have to know," she insisted.

"No," Mary Jo said firmly. "Maybe these were things that *you* had to know. But George loves me for me. Not because I'm his cook. If I make grape leaves or anything else for him, it'll be because I want to. Not because I have to."

Mrs. Khoury now looked truly unraveled. "You won't hold on to him that way."

Mary Jo laughed. "Oh yes I will. And you," she added, toggling her index finger between herself and Mrs. Khoury, "won't win this fight. George told me so." *Jesus*, she thought, *I'm really bluffing now*. "So you'd better back down if we're gonna get along. I'm happy to learn recipes from you, but you'd better stop the bullying. Right now."

Mrs. Khoury stared her down, stunned, for several seconds. Then she rearranged her face into a hurt look. "I was just trying to show you something nice," she said.

Mary Jo managed to put a hand on the woman's chubby upper arm. "Then let's keep going."

She turned studiously back to her grape leaf, rolled it, then placed it, fold down, in the pot, nestled snugly between two others.

"That was very good," Mrs. Khoury said. "Like a Lebanese would do it."

Inwardly, Mary Jo smiled. She'd won the day's battle. "Thank you," she said.

Mary Jo agreed to be married in their Maronite church, which Mrs. Khoury had insisted upon. Her own mother had balked about that slightly but ultimately relented, since Maronites were Catholic, at least, even if in the Mass they spoke a strange language that they claimed Christ had spoken, and burned an incense with a suspicious scent that hinted at rituals from faraway lands. During the wedding ceremony, Mary Jo and George had to wear golden crowns which made Mary Jo feel positively ridiculous.

George's family outnumbered her own by about three to one at the wedding and the large, lavish reception afterward in the ornate banquet room at Salaam's, which Mrs. Khoury had insisted on and paid for herself. Mrs. Khoury wore her own mink stole, and Mary Jo's mother wore one borrowed from a rich old aunt. The reception was the first time, but not the last, when her own family would be pulled to the center of the room for the line dances that wound their way around tables and chairs, set to what her brother Terry called "snake-charmer music." With the exception of her mother, though, who sat out the dance sourly, the Coughlins actually enjoyed themselves—found the whole thing a bit wild, perhaps partly because they all got very drunk.

She gave birth in a year, to a girl, Allison, and three years later to another girl, Rita. Despite protestations from Mrs. Khoury and other family elders that they had to keep pushing on until they had a boy, Mary Jo and George determined that they were a modern family who could stop at two kids rather than the three, four, or more that had been common in their parents' generation. Mary Jo went on the pill to ensure as much; she was a medical professional, after all, not some antiquated Catholic who believed the church's edict that birth control was evil.

Over the years, Mary Jo would note to herself with relief that, overall, she loved being a mother. George was a more affectionate parent to their daughters than her own parents had ever been to her, which liberated her to be more affectionate than she might otherwise have felt was seemly. George smothered his daughters with hugs and kisses when he got home, calling them habibti and hayati, which he told her meant "my life" in Arabic. Both Mrs. Khoury and her own mother had suggested Mary Jo take time off from work, at least until both her girls were about ten, but she had said firmly, "No, George needs me at the office," and conscripted both grandmothers into daytime babysitting. Privately, she feared she would unravel if she were home alone all day with toddlers, cut off from the medical profession and the outside world. Thankfully, George backed her up.

They bought a large, new split-level with three bedrooms and a giant backyard in Mendhem, on the rural, affluent border with Boxford, just down the road from a horse farm. The 1970s commenced; it seemed Nixon and scandal were on the TV constantly. George advanced in his career, prospering, mastering ever more complex and specific surgeries. He had incredibly high expectations for his daughters, which came as a slight shock to Mary Jo; she'd been raised to think of children as people you fed, clothed, housed, took to church, and generally raised to be literate, industrious, moral, and polite—not necessarily as investments that you bred for success and achievement. But that's what George wanted for his girls, which meant a great deal of planning, putting them into all sorts of lessons and extracurriculars, buying them stacks of books in the summer, getting them into the area's best private schools.

When a high school friend informed her that Christina Kattar, after Tufts Medical School, had moved to the New York area and become a gynecological oncologist but also reportedly remained single and childless, Mary Jo had merely pursed her lips slightly and said, "Hmm. Well, that's not a surprise. She always was very ambitious and intelligent."

Some women might want that instead of what she had, she told herself after several days of thinking about Christina. And that was fine. But thankfully she was not one of those women, she assured herself, and she was very, very satisfied with how her life had panned out.

CHAPTER THREE

RITA AND BOBBY

(1980s)

By the time Ronald Reagan was elected president, the ebony-haired and inseparable Khoury sisters, Allison and Rita, had a total of eighteen cousins on both sides of their family, ranging from William and Caroline, who were in college and struck them as impossibly grown-up and sophisticated, to four-year-old Jimmy, their Auntie Annie's youngest child.

Of all the families on either side, the Khourys themselves were the richest. This marker, in the Merrimack Valley generally, was measured by whose father was a doctor, lawyer, or business owner; who had the biggest house in the richest town (that being Mendhem, with West Mendhem a feeble second); who had a beach house; who drove European cars; who went to private (or perhaps the better Catholic) schools rather than public ones; and who dressed most like the Kennedys, with popped collars and shoes without socks. The Khourys met all these criteria, living well above the status anxiety that bedeviled the households of George's sisters. Nancy and Irene were a bit too prone to bragging about their new cars, home additions, or vacations; they were extremely invested in their husbands' success, each fearing that hers might fall short in comparison with the other's.

This was not a worry among the Khourys. On an upward trajectory since youth, his career based on medical expertise rather than the vagaries of entrepreneurialism, George worked hard and took his success for granted, while Mary Jo chafed at it somewhat. She knew she'd married well, that her own kids enjoyed advantages she couldn't have imagined for herself, but something stoic and suspicious in her kept her from surrendering to new comforts. She was frugal with family finances, until George could finally urge her to relax, and when her girls were as young as fourteen, she insisted they have after-school or summer jobs, delivering papers or scooping ice cream, just as any other kids would have. She would not give them handouts just because she could. And she was proud that her daughters had character, that they went to their minimum-wage jobs uncomplainingly, that they balanced school and work capably, as she had in her less cosseted youth, when she hadn't had a choice.

The Khoury sisters were close to their cousins on both sides, partly because everyone spent large swaths of the summer at their beach house, a Dutch Colonial a block from the water in Rye, New Hampshire, a town filled with former robber barons' mansions sitting high on manicured hills overlooking the surf. The Khourys' house, which they'd bought in the late 1970s for less than one hundred thousand dollars, was not especially handsome, but it was large, with a finished basement where, some nights, half a dozen cousins would sleep on couches or in sleeping bags, everyone waking up in the morning to the smell of not only salt air but bacon and pancakes, which Dr. Khoury—who'd arrived late the night before after performing two back-to-back surgeries—whipped up while torturing his nephews and nieces with off-key renditions of Neil Diamond songs.

"Uncle George, *stop!*" they would plead. "You can't sing!"

Rita would roll her eyes. "That never stops him," she would say. Much as her own mother, Mary Jo, had been as a child, Rita was a serious, highly studious, and skeptical little girl with a head of dark, tight curls, never without a book. As early as age seven or eight, she had displayed curiosity about the president (Carter) and about current affairs (inflation, pollution, the Iran hostage crisis). This marked her as very odd for a child, especially a girl, but she was the undisputed pride of her father, Dr. Khoury, who would often say to her, "I expect excellence from you. Great things."

"Yes, Daddy," she would say, dutifully. Rita had one overarching goal in life, which was to make her father proud. This motivated her every single second of every day. When she was taking a test in school, she visualized the A-plus or the 100 percent that she would present to her father when he arrived home from surgery late in the evening. With every essay she wrote, every book she read and later discussed, she was performing mental cartwheels and backflips for her father.

"Every generation only wants to see their children do better than they did," he would tell her. "That is the point of families, what keeps them evolving."

"I know, Daddy," she would say.

On the beach, the cousins of the Khourys—loudly roughhousing while Michael Jackson or the *Grease* soundtrack came out of the transistor radio or the boom box, disco rhythms mixing stickily in the sun with the crash of waves just yards away—looked as though they came from two tribes. The grandchildren of Marguerite Khoury, who spent her days and nights up at the house cooking in her housecoat and scuffs and waiting for everyone to come in off the beach, were dark-haired, olive-skinned creatures, the progeny of Lebanese mothers and Greek or Sicilian fathers, while the grandchildren of Meg Coughlin—who often sat up in the kitchen with Marguerite, knitting and watching suspiciously while Marguerite concocted her strange Arabian dishes—were towheaded, pug-nosed, white-skinned, and freckled.

Of all her cousins, Rita was closest to Bobby, one of the sons of her dour uncle Terry. At eight years old, Bobby had a honey-colored bowl cut and a chipped front tooth from a bike accident. There were several dyads and even one or two triads among the cousins, but Rita and Bobby were the famous pair in the family, always having their own conversations—which, heard from a few paces away, seemed to consist mostly of Rita lecturing Bobby in a schoolmarm tone.

Someone might hear Rita tell him: "I read one or two books a week in the summer, and I think you should try to read at least one a month. And then give a report on it back to me." Or: "If they only have French or Spanish in your school, you should take Spanish because it's more practical."

Bobby submitted mutely to his older cousin's edicts. There was a driven-home consensus in the broad family that the Khourys were smarter than the Coughlins, and that Rita was the smartest Khoury of all, so Bobby felt grateful Rita had taken him under her tutelage. He worshipped her, and in turn she mothered him, and everyone in the family knew that Bobby was Rita's favorite, almost like a godchild. The first summer when she had money from a job, she took him to movies and to the amusement park and derived a tremendous feeling of maturity by paying for Bobby to go on the Himalaya, a ride that whipped around and around while a DJ played hits like "Heart of Glass" or "Centerfold," and Rita, abstaining from the ride, waved back at him from the pavement, occasionally reading the book she had brought with her.

When Rita was fifteen and Bobby was twelve, she started having strange pangs of affection and tenderness toward him that were different from what she'd felt before. As had all the cousins, they'd tickled and horseplayed, especially in the ocean, their entire lives, but Rita suddenly stopped liking what she felt when they did this, and she started making a point of keeping a physical distance from him and often averting her eyes from him in conversation.

"Are you mad at me?" Bobby asked her once. He wasn't feeling what she was feeling, and he didn't know where her abrupt chilliness was coming from.

"Why do you ask me that?" she said, her arms crossed.

"You're kind of ignoring me. Are you too cool for me now that you go to Banner?" That was the private school in West Mendhem she went to, as a day student, where Ally was a senior.

"Don't be stupid," she snapped. "I'm just cold."

"Let's go under the outside shower together!"

"No!" she snapped, horrified. "I need a real shower."

Bobby merely shrugged and said no more.

But it wasn't just these unsolicited rogue feelings that were putting distance between her and Bobby. She'd just finished her first year at Banner, where several presidents and vice presidents had gone, and she'd met kids from all over the country and the world. Many of them were from New York City, Chicago, or Los Angeles, and some were from as far away as London, Monte Carlo, Lagos, or Bombay, where their fathers were diplomats or owned companies.

A few such girls, extremely beautiful blond girls who'd grown up on Park Avenue, plus a Jordanian British girl named Yasmin, who was the most stunning and sophisticated person Rita had ever met, found Rita a charming local curiosity and took her under their wing, allowing her to accompany them on the bus for shopping trips to Boston, where she learned to prowl thrift stores and cultivate a look of mussed hair, minimal makeup, a single dangly earring, an oversize untucked shirt buttoned to the neck, and ripped-knee jeans, all underneath a vintage trench and pointy-toed black boots.

"You look like a witch!" Bobby said to her the first time he saw her in such a getup, which was Easter Sunday after Mass at Uncle Terry and Auntie Carol's house, a very modest Cape Cod in the suburban-feeling southwestern corner of Lawton, the one part of the old city that remained completely white and Irish and hence was deemed the last acceptable part for such folks to live in.

"This is vintage," Rita explained patiently. "It's from Cambridge."

"You're different now that you go to Banner," Bobby said. He never shied away from flatly assessing her to her face. This assessment would take on a smirkier, more joshing tone as they aged, but Rita still detected in it the blunt, matter-of-fact colors of their childhood, when she felt that Bobby, who loved her most, was also the person who could see right through her.

"You think you're better than us now, don'cha? With all those Banner snobs."

"No, I don't!" she protested. But the accusation bothered her precisely because she *had* been feeling she was drawing away from her family, which had been the center of her universe for her entire life up to that

point. She'd slowly been realizing there was no future for her in the Merrimack Valley and that she likely would be fleeing as soon as she could.

"You're going to go to Harvard," her father had said to her, with
quiet certainty, at the start of her freshman year, and thereafter everything she did for the next four years at Banner was in the service of that
edict. She could not let her father down. Ally had gone to Georgetown,
which had made her father very proud, but he'd often said when they
were young that he wanted at least one of his daughters to get into to
Harvard, which was the end point, the nirvana, of the Boston-area immigrant family's dream, and now it had come down to Rita.

She needed an area of focus, something to specialize and excel in, to
distinguish her. As early as her sophomore year in high school, she started
homing in on the Middle East. This was a great land, her father had told
the family since they were children, a cradle of civilization, of language,
science, poetry. Look at the Sumerians, the Babylonians, the Assyrians,
the Persians! And of course the Phoenicians, the ancient, great seafaring
people of early Lebanon, from whom the Khourys descended. There was
a saying, her father told them: "Egypt writes, Lebanon publishes, and Iraq
reads." This showed just how cultivated, how literate the region had been,
earlier in the twentieth century, when its people modeled themselves and
their behavior after their colonizers, England and France, when anyone
who possibly could left the region for a time to study in those countries.
And look at Lebanon now! Her father would nearly weep, looking up from
the TV news or the newspaper. Chaos, war, destruction, fighting . . . and
all for what? It was barbarism. And it was *their* fault.

Who were *they*? When the civil war broke out in Lebanon in the
late 1970s, when Rita was very young, she never quite knew who *they*
were when all the elders would start lamenting. *They*'re ruining a beautiful country! *They* ran us out of Lebanon once, and now they're doing it
again! *They*'re not civilized; they'd rather fight and live in mayhem than
compromise and have nice things. *They*'re so obsessed with the afterlife
that they don't want to enjoy this life.

By the time Rita reached high school, she understood who *they* were:
Muslims. Turks had been Muslims, and Turks had made life miserable for

Lebanese Christians like her family many decades ago, torturing them, hanging them, starving them, or—at best—forcing them to leave for better lands. And now *they* were ruining Lebanon again, taking over the country because the Jews had run them out of Israel, using beautiful and peaceful Lebanon as their battleground against Israel, making the Christians and the Muslims of Lebanon—who had long lived side by side in peace—take sides, tearing the country apart, turning a cosmopolitan city like Beirut into a war zone where you could hardly go out for groceries without risking getting caught in cross fire between crazy militias, neighbor against neighbor.

The only Muslim Rita knew was Yasmin. She was a raven-haired, olive-skinned version of the Park Avenue girls, draped in voluminous men's-style shirts, box-shouldered blazers, long skirts, and pointy boots, wearing her mussed hair high on her head. Like the Park Avenue girls, Yasmin smoked cigarettes and drank every chance she could and was in love with the British pop singer Paul Young. Once Rita asked her whether she was a practicing Muslim, at which she had merely opened her mouth, astonished, then said, in her London accent, "Do I *look* like I am?"

Rita was mortified. "I don't know," she answered. "That's why I'm asking."

Yasmin paused, as though she were considering. "I think religion is bullshit," she finally said. "Of course, I'll fake stuff for my grandmother when I see her. But, Rita—I've lived in London since I was five. I'm British."

As Rita researched, she also questioned whether the Christians of Lebanon were so innocent. She hadn't noticed the news a few years before, at the age of ten, when Christian armies went into Palestinian refugee camps in Lebanon and massacred everyone, with the tacit approval of the Israelis, who were occupying the country; but reading about it in Banner's library now, at fifteen, she found this horrifying and brought it up at dinner with her father, who seemed startled.

"How do you know about that?" he asked.

"I read old magazines in the library at school."

"They had to do that to rout out the terrorists from the PLO. They use the refugee camps to hide."

"The story I read said that the PLO had already left the country."

Her father just sighed, waved his hand. "That country is a mess now," he said. "It's impossible to tell who is doing what to who, or why they're doing it. It makes Sittu so sad to see it in the news. I'm glad my father isn't here to see it."

Her mother piped up, "What class are you reading that for?"

"It wasn't for a class," she said. "I just started reading up on Lebanon in the library and went back and read some articles from a few years ago."

Her mother shook her head slightly. "I'm surprised you have time to read things outside your classes."

"I was just taking a quick break," Rita said.

And her father added, "She loves her ancestry."

Her mother certainly didn't have to worry that Rita was slacking. Being surrounded by many of the smartest and most talented teenagers in the world had sparked something ruthless in her. She was determined to excel, to be the best, and as a day student, a townie, she had a lot to prove. She earned flawless marks and raves on her essays, and she threw herself into the school paper, with an eye toward foreign policy and world affairs, nabbing interviews with politicians and dignitaries when they visited the school, which many of them had attended. She took Spanish, and if the school had offered it she would have taken Arabic, the rudiments of which she badgered her grandmother into teaching her, even though Marguerite would usually protest, "You don't need to know Arabic! You're in America!"

In the fall of her senior year, she devoured, and then wrote a long analysis of, Thomas Friedman's new book *From Beirut to Jerusalem*. A few weeks later, she elated her parents, but especially her father, by getting early admission into Harvard.

She now had a plan for herself: She'd become an Arabist in college, a Middle East expert, and she'd nail down the language, then she'd become a correspondent in the region for a major newspaper or wire service, just as Friedman had. She fixed this plan in her head with no intention of letting anything or anyone stop her.

Yet also by her senior year, she'd realized that she'd changed. She'd stopped courting the friendship of the pretty, rich girls from New York once she realized that they didn't share her intellectual hunger, and she now found that her closest friends were, for the most part, nerdy, brainy boys with bad skin with whom she could discuss the Iran-Contra affair for hours in the dining hall over coffee.

One night, she said to her mother, "Even at a school like Banner, most girls just end up caring about which jocky boys like them and really have no career goals or interests of their own. It's kind of depressing."

Her mother laughed sharply. "You think things were actually supposed to change since I was your age, just because of women's lib or something? Honey, that's how girls are, and that's never gonna change. You're just different because your father and I raised you that way."

The lovely Sunday afternoon following her graduation from Banner in June 1989—at which she wore a white summer dress like all the other girls, while the boys wore navy jackets and rep ties—there was a party for her at the house in Mendhem, just as there had been for Ally upon her graduation, with all the aunties and uncles and cousins, Lebanese food on the big back porch, and the uncles manning a barbecue out in the yard. Her maternal and paternal grandmothers, Sittu Margie and Nana Meg, were seated side by side, as had become their custom, talking over each other about the merits of their own children.

Rita sat beside them with her Banner friend Ira Zucker, from New Jersey, with whom she'd awkwardly attended the prom. Bobby, who was finishing up his sophomore year at Boys' Catholic in Lawton, where he was on the basketball team, sauntered up to her, a wicked grin on his face.

"Well, cuz," he said. "You did it. You're getting the hell out of here, and you're ditching us all for the big H."

She grinned back at him and stood to hug and kiss him. All the cousins had hugged and kissed hello since they were little. But now, doing so with Bobby, whom she hadn't seen since Easter, made her flush with discomfort. Here he was, fifteen, taller than ever, with muscles, his voice deep, with shaggy red hair and watery blue eyes.

"If you torture me today," she said, "I'll come back in two years for your graduation party and seek my revenge."

"Naaah," he said, his face suddenly serious. "I'm not here to torture you. I'm proud of you."

She frowned. "I never know when you're being ironic."

He laughed and extended a hand to Ira. "I'm warning you now," he told him, "that if you think she'd be a good girlfriend, she's just gonna nag you to death like she did to me growing up."

Rita smacked Bobby across a biceps. "You're a jerk!"

Bobby cackled, while Ira sat there, mouth open, at a loss for words.

Two days later, she was in her first Arabic class in Cambridge, in a summer program she'd enrolled in to get a jump on the language ahead of college. A fat workbook lay open in front of her.

"Marhaba! Ahlan wa sahlan," boomed the teacher, a portly, round-cheeked Egyptian man named Tarek. "Welcome. Okay, guys, tonight we start learning what's called MSA. Modern Standard Arabic. Does anyone know what this is?"

Rita knew, but she'd trained herself not to shoot up her hand, as she'd realized over time that doing this constantly alienated her from other students. But when nobody else answered, finally, she raised her hand.

"It's formal Arabic," she said. "What they use on the news, formal documents, stuff like that."

"Na'am," said Tarek. "Yes, exactly, correct. And don't listen to people who tell you it's stupid to learn MSA first and that you should learn a regional dialect, like Egyptian or Levantine. MSA is the backbone of Arabic, and you cannot call yourself a scholar of Arabic unless you know it. Trust Tarek on this and listen to no one else. Now, page seven in your workbooks, we take on the alphabet."

Rita picked up her pen and sailed through her characters, from *alif* to *yaa*, scratching from right to left. Walking up and down the rows, Tarek stopped and took note.

"You've already learned it?" he asked.

"I did," she answered. And she had—the better to stake herself out beyond the rest of the class. Her road ahead was clear now, with a blood-orange sun, half-set under the horizon, shimmering at its end. The language, the culture, the region—she would take them all back, make them her own.

PART TWO

THE LOST WORLD

CHAPTER FOUR

NABIL AND ASMAA

(2002)

On his way home from his job at the grocery store in Adhamiya, crossing the Bridge of the Imams over the Tigris with the usual after-work pedestrian crowd, the mu'then's call to Friday night prayers filling his ears, Nabil saw the boys. He saw them every day at this time, in an overgrown patch of scrub just to the left of the crowded corniche in Kadhimiya. They were roughly fourteen or fifteen years old, a good eight or nine years younger than he, and they were always shouting, playing kurat al qadam, some of them wearing cheap knockoffs of the green jerseys of the Iraqi national football team, some of them in trainers, some in plastic sandals, some barefoot. They came into Nabil's sight simultaneously with the soaring golden domes and minarets of Al-Kadhimiya Mosque, and together in his mind and heart, for a moment he could hardly name, they mingled: God and football, God and football, wings that lifted him up and out of the dusty, sandy monochrome of Baghdad and into a more verdant land, somewhere by a vast sparkling sea, Beirut or Istanbul maybe, New York or even paradise.

He quickened his pace, coming off the bridge, and recognized one of the boys as his cousin, Omar, whom he had not seen since the family visits and meals of Eid al-Adha some weeks before, when Omar had been smugly showing off *Tomb Raider*, the video game a friend of his father's had brought back for him as an Eid gift from a business trip to Amman. So now Nabil came down off the bridge and ran toward the boys, feeling a bit foolish because he had just turned twenty-four and some of the boys were not much more than half his age.

But an excess of energy overran his self-consciousness. He'd been cooped up in the store all day, the sides of his fingers still lightly serrated from tearing open boxes of canned goods, and he wanted to goof around a bit. He called out to Omar, who called back:

"Nabil!" Then, to the other boys: "Ibn ammi!" *It's my cousin!* Then back to Nabil: "Come join us! My side needs one more."

So Nabil ran to the makeshift field, dropped his bag at its edge, and joined in the scrum, quickly greeting the boys, most of whom he knew from the neighborhood, with handshakes and double kisses. In a moment they were playing again, and Nabil looked up as the ball hurtled directly toward his head, so he positioned himself and thrust his head out like a ram, rebounding the ball toward the other team's side, whereupon Omar dribbled it forward and kicked it neatly into the space between two book bags that had been set down as goalposts.

"Ya Allah!" the cousins screamed, embracing each other.

"Played like Younis Mahmoud!" exulted Omar, who, like many young men in Iraq that year, was obsessed with the phenomenal new striker for Al Talaba. Then, he whispered devilishly in Nabil's ear, "Uday will never lock *you* in Al Radwaniyah, shave your head, and piss on you."

Nabil's jaw dropped in shock, and he lightly slapped Omar on the side of the head. "Shut up, cousin! You'll get us jailed! Killed!"

"Let him try," boasted Omar. "I'll tell him to go to hell like Ammo Baba does," he said. Ammo Baba was the football manager whom the whole country loved for standing up to Saddam Hussein's rotten son, who oversaw football in the country and jailed and beat players when they fell short.

But as the other boys approached, the cousins ceased their banter; Nabil was fairly certain that the father of one of them, Adel, worked for the Mukhabarat, the secret police, and as Nabil's own parents had told him and his siblings from an early age, one must never, ever speak of the Great Leader and the government publicly, except to sing their praises in school or at civic assemblies. Even to joke like that with cousins could be risky, that is, if one did not know exactly where one's cousin, or his father, stood.

One of the boys, Marwan, bounded over. "Nabil al-Jumaili, the high holy keeper of the grocery shelves, I salute you, oh man of rice sacks!" he cried, before pouncing on Nabil, laughing like a hyena.

Nabil twisted out from under him and reversed the friendly headlock. "You have no brain, you son of dogs," he laughed, twisting the knuckle of his index finger into the scalp under Marwan's glossy black hair. In middle-class Kadhimiya, Marwan was from one of the poorer families, the son of the owner of a tiny, failing photo-printing shop, and, like so many teenage boys during the past decade of international sanctions, imposed on Iraq to squeeze out Saddam, had dropped out of school to help support his family by collecting automotive scrap or electronic odds and ends around the city and selling them in the street on the fringes of Shorja market. When he wasn't doing that, he was smoking fake Marlboros, drinking fake Pepsis, playing soccer, watching soccer on TV, angling to get his hands on whatever bootleg video games he could, or getting yelled at by his mother and grandmother for not spending his spare time continuing his education independently with a book.

Hamdullah that's not my family, Nabil would think. His family was comfortable; his older brothers and he had all made it through the University of Baghdad, they with accounting degrees (and now, low-paying but stable jobs in a small company that contracted with the Ministry of Finance), and he with his marketing and communications degree. Of course, his own degree hadn't gotten him more than a forty-dollar-a-month job with a three-person advertising agency for the gold market that ran out of an Internet café in Mansour—a job which he'd lost in four months, as soon as the agency lost its major client.

Thus followed four excruciating, humiliating months of pounding the pavement, looking for a job, peddling his Baghdad U diploma and his excellent English skills, all to no avail. There were hardly any white-collar jobs, especially for those who weren't closely connected to the regime.

Nabil desperately wanted to obtain permission from the government to work in Amman, Istanbul, or Beirut. His brothers, who tried to pull their few strings for him, said he'd have better chances if he had letters of interest from abroad, and yet he barely had the money to rent a computer at the Internet café to research opportunities. They had dial-up access at home, but it was so weak and unreliable that his efforts to use it for anything serious usually drove him nearly to tears of frustration.

After four such dispiriting months, Nabil left the house one morning determined not to return until he had a job. That was how he'd ended up managing a distant cousin's tiny grocery store, for three dollars a week, which he promptly turned over to his father for the family's emergency fund, save for a bit he spent on kebabs, cigarettes, and Pepsi. The job's only upside was that it gave him ample time to read; between receiving deliveries of chickpeas and weighing old ladies' bags of onions, he would turn back to pages on which he meticulously underlined every bit of unfamiliar English idiom. Later, he would show all the marked passages to Asmaa.

What bit of vexing English the past many years, in fact, had he not shown to Asmaa? What blip of confusion, what keen observation, what attempt at wit had he ever not presented before Asmaa, awaiting her clarification, coveting her opinion, craving her laughter? Could his cousin, his mother's sister's daughter, really be but two years older than he, given the power she wielded over him? When she strode into the house, her height unimposing but her voice as loud and assured as a man's, her curls unwieldy, her eyes glinting with gossip and ideas, his dim world lit up, and he could envision a future, a beyond. She made that possible. Asmaa his cousin, Asmaa his lifeline.

And would she come to dinner tonight? He asked himself this nearly every evening during the mu'then's call to prayer, walking over the Bridge of the Imams back to his family's house in Kadhimiya, the mournful cries from the minaret briefly soothing his mind, which worried, like fingers over prayer beads, the same gnawing loop of thoughts: *How long will I work in a grocery store? How will I ever get out of here and find a real job? How will I get to the Gulf? To Canada?* But suddenly, now, there were Marwan's lean arms around his neck, the offensive—but also, it privately galled him to admit, pleasurable—smell of Marwan's armpit sweat in his nose, and he was scrambling out from underneath, calling Marwan a son of dogs. After all, his own name, Nabil, meant "noble," "honorable," and through his whole life he had felt burdened by the need to prove as much, even in lighthearted moments such as this.

"Me, son of dogs?" Marwan cried, laughing. "You, who crawled out of the pussy of a whore!"

The stupid insult made Nabil laugh and snort mucus from his nose. And soon Omar was upon them, jumping on Marwan. "Insult my cousin," he cried, "and I will make one thousand Bedouin dicks rain down on your sister's pussy!"

Now it was Marwan who squirmed out from underneath. "They would just all fall inside, it is so wide!" he yelled, howling at his own joke, then running away to rejoin the game. "Ma'a assalama, Nabil, and the same to you, Omar, ya tanta"—*you faggot*—he called back amiably.

"Good-bye, you kiki"—*big sissy*—Omar replied.

Nabil moved on, trudging past the massive Kadhimiya Mosque, with its sea of men kneeling down inside, cheek by jowl, their one thousand backsides facing up to heaven. He turned onto a side street of spacious villas—contemporary, boxy, two-story homes—hidden behind high walls. He turned again, then finally seized the latch on the gate into the garden of his own home. The tedious, accursed workday was done. He would have a quiet half hour in his room with tea, cigarette, and his book before dinner.

But in the garden he found Bibi, his grandmother, waiting for him in the swing chair under the date palm trees. She smiled, relieved, when she saw him; stood up from the chair, from which her tiny feet didn't reach the ground; and waddled toward him, her black abaya framing a face whose dark eyes and fat cheeks Nabil dearly loved. Since he was young, she'd reminded him of a plum with a black handkerchief pinned around it, revealing only one side. He had to bend down nearly at a right angle to kiss her, she was so short.

"Mama says we need to go buy bread," she commanded him, putting her arm through his.

If only he'd thought to pick up bread on the way home! "I can get the bread, Bibi," he said. He wanted to preserve his reading hour.

"You need me to help pick it out."

He laughed. "Bibi, you think I don't know how to pick out samoon?"

"It's a woman's job," she said matter-of-factly. And Nabil, in a second's turn, with only the faintest of sighs, acquiesced. Everyone did what Bibi said. His father was master of the house in name alone; everyone knew that Bibi, with her barking voice and her frequent kisses to reward everyone for granting her wishes, was the true ruler.

"All right, Bibi, yalla."

They turned out of the courtyard and into the street, where Bibi began to nod hello to a stream of neighbors and passersby, muttering, "Al salaam alaykum" to all. She moved slowly, and Nabil, who'd nearly sprinted home over the bridge, resigned himself to the crawl, thinking about where he had left off in his reading, *The Catcher in the Rye*, which he'd bought from Abu Mazen, a bookseller on Mutanabbi Street who slipped him English-language works. This was how he perpetually improved his English, along with watching American and British TV shows via satellite whenever he could on TV Shabab. At the place where he had left off, Holden Caulfield was in a cheap hotel room with a fake-blond prostitute who'd just hung her green dress on a hanger, then sat back down in a pink slip. Nabil had sneaked reading that section in quiet moments today at the grocery, and ever since, the image had been stuck in his head of those three colors: blond, green, and pink. The thrill and the challenge of reading in English—and he made a point of reading only in English—was the slang. For example, all just from this most recent chapter alone: "horsing around," "I damn near broke my knee," and "like fun you are." If Asmaa wasn't around, he had no one to ask what these things meant, and he had to try to work it out from the context. But then again, Asmaa had long ago told him to note when books were written, as the slang might be out of date, so a Brit or an American, were he ever to meet one, might laugh at him and find him quaint if he used such slang.

Then he realized he was thinking of a woman in a slip as he walked with his grandmother, and an intense rush of shame overcame him. To think of such things in this moment was haram, and he banished the thought, reentered the moment. They were rounding the corner onto a dusty, crowded market street, full of honking, dirty Volgas and Peugeots; Bedouin men with keffiyahs wrapped around their heads, sitting in white plastic chairs alongside their piles of vegetables; the usual unemployed young men in soccer shirts, flared-leg jeans, and plastic knockoff Adidas flip-flops, hanging around smoking and laughing and drinking Pepsis, politely stepping aside for Shiite bibiyat; and grandmas like his own, who came charging through in their flowing black abayas, bags laden with groceries. The amplified prayers of the imam rained down from the mosque, and the familiar smells of diesel exhaust and kebab laced the air.

"Who took you to jumu'ah prayers today, Bibi?" he asked his grandmother, who (he noted, out of the side of his right eye) had a grimly determined look on her face as she scanned the market stalls. At seventy-two, she'd lived through her own husband's fatal heart attack (1974), Saddam's deportation of her sister and her sister's family to Iran on the eve of the Iran-Iraq War (1979), the loss of one son in that war (1985), and then the disappearance of a beloved nephew (1992), likely into Saddam's vast prisons, or perhaps to his death, for some perceived slight to the regime. Bibi, like countless Iraqis, had no idea what had happened to her loved one and was too afraid of repercussions to investigate.

Nabil often wondered how she'd gone on without going crazy. It was in part, he knew, her faith: her belief in Allah, Muhammad, Fatima, and Ali; her conviction that injustice ultimately would be avenged in the heavenly scheme. That, and her staunch belief that someone had to do the cooking.

Bibi was his connection to an older, more pious world. Nabil's parents were part of that secular, educated generation of Iraqis of the

1960s and 1970s, who'd left the provinces and moved to Baghdad, who had gone to a university and entered professional life. They observed the high holy days of Islam, such as Eid al-Fitr and Eid al-Adha, perhaps prayed casually from time to time, but otherwise gave little thought to religion. Bibi had not been happy to learn that her daughter—Nabil's mother, Neda—was marrying a Sunni, and a Jumaili, no less, one of the most familiar Sunni surnames in all of Iraq. Bibi had cried and wailed and told Neda that her poor dead father was weeping in his grave.

But Neda, who listened to the Beatles and disco, read Erica Jong, wore miniskirts and platform heels, and thoroughly embodied the new Iraq, sweetly told her mama that she'd have to set aside her Shi'a tribal ideas, that they weren't in Najaf anymore, and that she was marrying for love. Because that was exactly what she felt for twenty-four-year-old Uthman al-Jumaili, a teacher as she was, a romantic man with a lush black head of hair and a thick mustache she was secretly thrilled to say that her own lips had brushed several times before their wedding night. And so, Neda's and Uthman's mothers—who, by the time Saddam came to power in 1979 were both widows and hence hopelessly reliant on their children—had to make their peace with the marriage. And that is how Nabil's bibis ended up sitting side by side—Bibi Fatima in her black abaya; Bibi Amal with her carefully set hair and pantsuit, enormous patent-leather purse on her lap—at the iftar meal, chatting and laughing a bit more with every passing year until, eventually, it was not unusual for the two ladies to go shopping together.

And now Bibi answered him. "Asmaa took me to prayers," she said, naming his cousin. "A very good girl who cares for her grandmother. She took her lunch hour to fetch me."

Bibi was playing a sly game with him, Nabil knew. "Am I not a very good boy for taking you to buy bread after my long, hard day at the grocery store?" he asked, constraining a smile that curled at his lips.

"You are the very best boy and my favorite of all my grandchildren," Bibi replied dutifully, squeezing his arm.

Nabil loved this little game with Bibi. "And you are the very best bibi," he said, kissing the top of her head.

"Hamdullilah," she replied firmly. *Praise be to God.*

"And how were prayers today, Bibi?"

"Very beautiful. But they don't keep the women's area as clean as the men's. I can tell. It's even gotten worse since Eid."

Such were the ways his grandmother registered her resentment over gender segregation at the mosque. Never would she come out and say she simply found it wrong. No, it was always indirect quibbles such as this.

"Why don't you speak to the imam?"

She snorted contemptuously. "I have better things to do, and so does he!"

"All right then, Bibi."

He then noticed she was dragging him past her favorite bread man, comical Abu Nader, whose round, flat, char-pocked loaves beckoned with their yeasty aroma, truly one of the most wonderful and comforting smells in the whole city, along with the aromas of kebab and of masgouf, roasting on Abu Nuwas Street at night, the succulent fish sliced wide open until it was just as flat and round as khubz, the bread, with which, of course, it went so well.

"Umm Ali!" called Abu Nader, in his amusingly high voice. "Why are you bypassing me? With my bread right out of the oven?" Abu Nader raised his palms to God in an exaggerated gesture of despair.

"Yes, why *are* you, Bibi?" Nabil echoed.

"I'm coming back to you!" Bibi called to Abu Nader. Then, to Nabil, "I want to look at one thing."

It all dawned on Nabil. "I know why you needed to come out yourself for khubz, Bibi," he said, laughing. "I think I know exactly where we are going."

"Don't tell Mama," Bibi said flatly, which only made Nabil laugh more.

In a moment, they were in the covered gold market, a sea of luminous, glinting yellow on placards of black velvet as far as the eye could see. Bibi marched past the vendors toward her favorite, Abu Nassar, a reedy, chain-smoking man whose nut-brown skin was so wrinkled Nabil was convinced he could see grains of sand in the crevices. Sidelong, Nabil watched Bibi as she approached, an animal look of lust concentrating in her eyes.

All the wrinkles in Abu Nassar's face pulled back as he saw her and grinned broadly, exchanging a knowing look with Nabil. "Umm Ali!" he cried. "Hamdullilah that you have returned to me! I have set aside the earrings for you."

"I told you that you didn't need to do that," Bibi barked.

"It was my pleasure and my honor," said Abu Nassar, in a tone of exaggerated fealty, winking at Nabil. From beneath the counter he withdrew gold earrings in the shape of teardrops, intricately wrought, each with a small turquoise stone at its center. He laid the earrings in his palm, which he tilted toward Bibi.

She gasped lightly, put a hand to her chest. "Ya allah, they are beautiful," she whispered reverently. Nabil glanced at her; her eyes were wide open, rapt.

"They truly are," echoed Abu Nassar, with a patience acquired over years of understanding that he could not force a sale, but merely stoke awe, letting the jewelry do its own work, even in the many drab hours and days when people like Bibi were away from the gold market, their weary minds seeking comfort and wonder back in those corridors of glinting yellow on black velvet. Eventually, Abu Nassar had learned, he would make a sale. Gold was not just a solid investment in a volatile country, it was also a little piece of paradise amid a life that was often its own dusty, tense, claustrophobic hell.

Bibi picked up the earrings, put them into her own palm. Her face had gone slack, her eyes soft. "Such beauties," she murmured.

Nabil loved seeing his grandmother rendered passive and nearly mute by gold; it was far from the first time. He'd been accompanying her to the gold market, always on the pretext of more mundane errands, such as bread or chickpeas, since he was young.

"Bibi," he began, playing the age-old game. "They won't show under your hijab. They'll hurt."

"They'd be for your mother. Maybe I'd wear them to a wedding."
Bibi rarely went to a wedding, of course. But it was where older Shi'a
women, segregated from the men, danced together, opulently dressed,
joyfully preening and competing in their rare, unveiled finery. Any
adornment Bibi saw in the markets, including jewelry that she could not
flaunt on a daily basis, became part of her wear-it-to-a-wedding fantasy.

Nabil wanted to tell Bibi that his mother, perhaps the most practical, no-frills woman in Baghdad, who favored slacks and sneakers most
days, had little use for jewelry besides her wedding ring. But he knew
that Bibi knew as much. The point wasn't who would wear the earrings;
it was the sheer joy it gave Bibi to look at them, to surrender all her
worries and her grief to their winking gleam.

"Besides, gold is a good investment," added Bibi, voicing a belief
common in Baghdad. "Better than dinars. Safer."

Abu Nassar nodded slowly. "This is true, this is true," he said. He
glanced at Nabil. "Your grandmother is a wise woman." Then he winked
slyly at Nabil, which Bibi missed, her eyes intently fixed on the earrings.

"What's the best price you could offer me?" she asked.

"You know how deeply I honor and respect you, Umm Ali," he
said, his hand to his heart. "I am willing to go lower than I would for
anyone else. With that, I could make the earrings available to you in
three payments of three hundred thousand dinars each."

Bibi let out a small shriek, her round face popping open in outrage.
"Three payments of three hundred thousand dinars?" she exclaimed.
"Habibi, we are living under sanctions! Nobody has that kind of money."

Nabil stood by, watching amusedly. He'd witnessed a variation on
this exchange several times in the past year.

"I know that, I know that!" insisted Abu Nassar, his fist pounding on
his heart now. "More people are selling gold than buying, just for basics like
car repairs and food and gas. But Umm Ali, I must make my living too!"

Bibi calmed down, somewhat chastised. "I realize that, allah yusall-
mak," she said, her eyes flickering longingly back to the earrings. "We
are all having hard times."

Now it was time for Nabil to play his role in the drama. "I am ashamed I do not have the money to buy you the earrings, Bibi," he said. "I dishonor you. I promise I will work and save for them."

Predictably, Bibi turned to him, slapped his arm. "Don't be a fool!" she snapped. Abu Nassar and Nabil glanced at each other, struggling to repress laughter. "There are more important things than gold."

"Yes, Bibi, but you deserve gold," said Nabil.

At this, Bibi grunted and turned away, not quite willing to dispute this fact. Slowly, reluctantly, she handed the earrings on their black velvet board back to Abu Nassar. "The time will come for these, inshallah. And may God bless you and your family until then, Abu Nassar."

"And the same to you, honorable Umm Ali."

Nabil and Abu Nassar shared a smile as they parted. Bibi put her arm through Nabil's as they walked away.

"We'll get the bread now, Bibi?"

She snorted again. "There's enough bread in the house. I bought it this morning."

Nabil roared. "Bibi! You told me Mama sent us out to buy bread."

"She knew there was enough bread. She just wanted me out of the house for a few minutes."

Still, Nabil insisted they bring back two warm loaves of Abu Nader's samoon, for which he parted with a thousand-dinar bill in his pocket. Since he was a boy, he'd found the walk home with warm samoon agonizing, so badly did he want to tear into the round, flat loaves and stuff large, fluffy pieces into his mouth. Warm samoon was love, pure and simple, like a good-night hug and kiss from Mama and Baba, or like sleeping on the roof on an unbearably hot night in summer and feeling a breeze caress his cheek and neck.

Bibi seemed to sense his thoughts. "The bread smells good, doesn't it?" she chuckled, as though she shared his rogue desire to plunder it.

"It always smells good, Bibi. It's one of the best smells in life."

She nudged him. "Tear us some off."

"Bibi!"

"I told you there's already bread at home!"

And so Nabil did, tearing off a piece for Bibi, then one for himself, and the two of them walked on beside each other, contentedly chewing, their mouths swaddled in warmth and softness.

But it was impossible to eat samoon without thinking of what went so well with it, as samoon was paradise not only in and of itself, but as a canvas upon which to put other pleasures. And so, said Bibi, once she finished chewing, "I made bamia tonight. With extra cumin."

"That's how I like it," said Nabil. Instantly, he imagined on his tongue not just the soft, dry warmth of the bread but the fragrant, hot silkiness of his grandmother's okra stew.

"That's why I made it that way. For you, my favorite."

"Shukran, Bibi."

"Allah yohofthak."

And Bibi smiled to herself. They'd had exactly this conversation perhaps a thousand times since Nabil was a little boy, and it always ended with Bibi's blessing, *May God keep you.*

And then Bibi gave her inevitable follow-up: "Please get married and make my heart happy. Why are you waiting? You are twenty-five."

Nabil was used to this inquiry from Bibi, though it still didn't fail to briefly trouble his stomach. "I'm only twenty-four, Bibi."

"Your brothers are married with children already!"

"Bibi," said Nabil, launching his standard response, "I don't want to pursue that until I am well employed." He'd said that to so many people, so many times, he half-wondered whether he'd deliberately foreshortened his ambition in order to maintain the excuse. Maybe a grocery store was, in some regards, the best place for him to be.

But Bibi just snorted lightly. "If everyone felt that way in Baghdad, nobody would get married."

"Ya, Bibi," he clucked, aiming to quiet her.

Arriving back at the house, they found Baydaa, Nabil's sister-in-law, pacing the garden, burping Mena, Nabil's eight-month-old niece, who cried lustily. Nabil noticed that Baydaa, a petite administrative assistant at a construction firm's office in Mansour, had a filmy silk floral scarf loosely covering her head and tied and tucked about her collar. It was only the second time he had ever seen her head covered, and when he had casually asked his brother Rafiq about it after the first time, Rafiq had said, laughing, "She feels nervous these days, and she says it makes her feel more secure, like she's got all her hair tucked in."

She wasn't the only middle-class, college-educated young woman Nabil knew around town who had begun doing this in the past several months. It depressed him, partly because it showed they were bowing to Saddam, who in recent years had been urging Iraqi women to cover their heads, reversing decades of secularism. And so Baydaa, like many women, said instead that she was doing so out of a vague, general sense of security and practicality. All the talk was of how likely the Americans were to invade. Since the towers had gone down in the United States, life seemed more unstable than ever, perhaps since the worst years of the stupid war with Iran in the 1980s. People were acting strangely, becoming more religious. His own mother lately had seemed to be stocking their small house with twice the usual quantity of canned goods and cooking oil, creating small towers of rations in odd corners of the kitchen.

Baydaa turned toward them and smiled wanly, rolling her eyes over Mena's wails. "I can't stop her, so I took her outside," she said, kissing and embracing Bibi and lightly embracing Nabil. "But that's not helping either!"

"Did you nurse her today?" Bibi barked.

Baydaa and Nabil both laughed at Bibi's bluntness, Baydaa blushing crimson. "Of course I nursed her, Bibi!" Baydaa exclaimed.

Bibi brushed past her into the house. "My children all instantly quieted down when I nursed them," she declared. Nabil, following her, turned back and shot his sister-in-law an amused, sympathetic look, which she returned.

Inside, the house was happy mayhem. Nabil's father; Nabil's brothers Rafiq and Ra'ad; Ra'ad's five-year-old twin son and daughter, Ahmed and Rana; and cousin Omar, who'd cleaned up a bit after his soccer game, were all huddled around the TV screen, drinking tea from small cups, cheering on Rafiq and Omar while they duked it out over Omar's cherished new *Tomb Raider* game. Rana, upon seeing her Ammo Nabil, jumped up and threw herself into his arms, whereupon he scooped her up and spun her around twice.

"You're finally here, Ammo," she said.

"I'm finally here."

"Come play the game with us."

"I will in a minute, habibti. I want to say hello to Mama."

But before he did, he stooped to kiss his father. "Marhaba, Baba," he murmured, noting that his father needed to trim his silver-flecked mustache. But his father, like everyone else clustered around the TV, was engrossed in the game, and merely pressed an affectionate hand on Nabil's forearm for a moment.

"How was your day, my son?" Baba asked absently.

"Just like all the others, Baba." Nabil turned toward the kitchen.

"Nabil, you dog, come play!" Omar called over the din of the video.

"In a minute."

In the kitchen, full of the comforting smells of lamb grilling and okra stewing, he found Bibi fussing over the bamia; Ra'ad's wife, Farah, at the small corner table chopping tomatoes and cucumbers for a salad; and his mother, Neda, reaching up to take down a stack of plates from a high cupboard. She was short, like Bibi, her mother, only five foot three, and perched precariously on a footstool, so Nabil rushed to her side, reaching up.

"Hand them to me, Mama."

Which she did, gratefully, stepping down and then reaching up to kiss Nabil on both cheeks. "Thank you, habibi, and thank you for taking Bibi for *more bread*." She rolled her eyes at Nabil.

"You can never have enough bread for a large dinner," Bibi called from the stove, her back to them, which earned amused glances among Nabil, his mother, and Farah.

His mother stopped and looked into his eyes a moment. How much he loved this woman, Nabil thought, his lifelong lodestar of decency, wisdom, and strength, someone who knew that there was a large world outside Iraq and had told him since he was young that he would see it someday, somehow. Yes, she'd traded her university miniskirts and platforms for the long-sleeved shirts, slacks, and sensible oxfords of a secondary-school math teacher. But she wouldn't cover her head, even when Bibi implored her, before they walked to Shorja market together, to throw on a light scarf like Baydaa's.

"Why should I wear a scarf, Mama?" Neda would ask lightly. "There's no sandstorm today. And Iraq is secular; we're not in Iran or the Gulf."

"I just think you would call less attention to yourself," Bibi would mutter. "This isn't Karada or Mansour, where you can pass as a Christian."

And Neda, his mother, would laugh with an edge of bitterness. "Pretty soon they'll be wearing a scarf too, just to keep the clerics off their back."

"I'd rather disappear under a scarf than have to put up with remarks from annoying men who think this is Iran and they're part of the religious police," said Farah, from the table.

It was she, in fact, who'd urged Baydaa to start covering herself. "Just do it to make going about your day easier," she'd urged her, as though she were telling her to bring along extra diapers for Mena. Farah, who was from a richer family than Baydaa's and also had beaten Baydaa to motherhood by several years, had no problem telling Baydaa what to do in all manner of things, and petite Baydaa, by far the most timid woman in this extended household, generally deferred to her. Often Nabil hoped she'd snap back at Farah, who (in Nabil's estimation) thought she was far smarter than she actually was, but Baydaa seldom did. Her own grandmother had died several years earlier and her mother just two years ago, unable to access a certain chemotherapy drug because of sanctions on the country, and Nabil saw how Baydaa clung to Bibi, Mama, and Farah. Except for two aunts whom she didn't like, they were the only older women left in her life and she seemed grateful even for their remonstrances.

And just at that moment, Baydaa came back into the kitchen, carrying Mena, who'd exhausted herself crying and now slept on her mother's shoulder.

"Hamdullilah, she fell asleep!" Bibi exclaimed. And Baydaa, looking exhausted herself, nodded gratefully and sat at the table. Nabil sat down next to her and took Mena from her arms, just as Farah retreated from the kitchen with a tablecloth and plates to begin setting the meal on the dining-room table.

"Tell those video addicts to start winding down their game and wash their hands to eat," Mama called back to her.

His baby niece in his arms, the women in his life surrounding him, Nabil truly relaxed for the first time that day. In the kitchen with Bibi, Mama, and his aunties or, now, sisters-in-law, where the aroma of fried onions mingled with the sharper notes of cumin, cardamom, and nutmeg, was where he'd always felt happiest, listening to their gossip and their clucking and their good-natured teasing. He could kick a ball around just fine with his uncles and boy cousins, but with them there was always a vague unease, a performing, a holding of one's breath, an exhalation that did not occur until he was listening to women debate how to stuff kibbe or who was the Shorja vendor with the best prices for zaytoon.

In the kitchen, since he'd been a boy, he secretly thrilled to the women's subtle power plays, their half-whispered fragments of long-ago family secrets, and even their muttered jabs at the Almighty Ruler himself. It was the kitchen, after all, where, in tiny increments as he grew up, he learned of the deportation to Iran of Bibi's sister, Rana (for whom his little niece was named), and her children; of the death in the Iran-Iraq war of Abbas, the uncle he remembered; and of the night when Saddam's secret police came and took away, for undisclosed reasons, Nizar, Bibi's oldest nephew, who was never seen again by any of the family and either was locked away in Abu Ghraib or had long ago decomposed in a mass grave.

These were the three central traumas of the family in the Saddam years, the kind of traumas that nearly every family in Iraq had undergone, except, perhaps, families that Saddam kept in the gilded prison of his innermost circle. Because everyone was afraid of speaking of these traumas directly, with the full force of grief and rage behind them, they were talked about elliptically, shamefully, fearfully, which is why it had taken Nabil, who as a boy had excelled at deduction, a few years, perhaps until he was thirteen or fourteen, to fully comprehend the family's threefold loss.

Finally, he gently handed the sleeping Mena back to Baydaa and rose to gather glasses and platters and bring food to the table, falling in line behind Farah. She turned back to him and whispered over the din of the video gamers, "I have a girl for you to meet. A sister of my former colleague at the bank. Very pretty and very intelligent and cultured, because I know you like girls with their own ideas."

All this hit Nabil so abruptly, as he stood there with the large bowl of salad, that he could only laugh. "Have you set the date for the engagement party already?"

Farah laughed with him. "Why don't you start with tea at her family's house?"

Nabil felt his stomach tighten. "I'm in no position to date someone. I work in a grocery store. I'm embarrassing."

Farah took the bowl from him and arranged space for it on the table amid the platters of grilled lamb and vegetables, the steaming pot of bamia. "You can't put off your whole life until you have the perfect job," she said. "You're lucky to even have a job. Anyone who has one is lucky."

His exasperation with his well-meaning but condescending sister-in-law rose inside him, but he strove to quell it. "Let me think about it" was the best he could come up with. "I'm very depressed these days."

"We're all depressed in this city. That's why you need company," she retorted briskly. "You must hate being the last unmarried son in this house."

Stymied, Nabil merely shrugged—as if to say, *Well, that's life!*—and headed back into the kitchen for the water pitcher. When he returned, Farah was hectoring everyone to move away from the TV screen and toward the dinner table. Nabil's father turned off the video and moved toward the CD player. *Fairouz, Live at Beiteddine*, Nabil predicted—correctly, it turned out. It was all his father ever played since he got the CD last year, the voice of the great, aging Lebanese singer ringing out through the house, the beloved voice of the Middle East. "La Inta Habibi," his father would sing along with her through the house, *You are not my love*, taking his wife in his arms to dance and singing it to her, which made Nabil's mother laugh and push him away, crying, "Don't sing to me that I am not your love! That's not very romantic!"

"Okay," his father would agree, "I will drop the *la* from the song as I sing it," and then he would do so, which would only make his mother laugh more. "You think he could just pick a love song without a negative in it," she would comment, before indulging him and swaying in his arms for a moment and then going back to her business.

So now, hearing the familiar recording, everyone groaned as the family assembled at the table. "Ammo Uthman, *noooo*, please play another CD!" implored Omar, dramatically putting his hands to his ears. "Not the same Fairouz!"

"Fairouz is all you ever need," said Nabil's father calmly, sitting down at the head of the table.

"Yes, fine, walidi," joked Farah, "but please, just another album!"

"Just a few songs on this one, then we'll switch. Indulge me please, children."

"We live to indulge you, Father," said Nabil dryly, to which his father replied, with equal dryness, "You honor me, my son."

Platters were passed, pleases and thank-yous were muttered, silent bismallahs were murmured. Ahmed and Rana squirmed on either side of their mother, Farah, complaining about their large portions, saying they only wanted rice, and Farah sternly rebuked them, saying they'd get no rice at all, and no mann al-sama for dessert—that sublimely gummy, sweet confection of cardamom, honey, and nuts— if they didn't have their share of lamb, salad, and okra. Omar blabbed on endlessly about all the new video games he wanted—it was all he lived for, video games, as though he'd chosen to remove himself from Baghdad entirely and live in a world of fantasy tunnels and supersonic sky raids. Baydaa tried, mostly unsuccessfully, to spoon-feed Mena tiny dabs of hummus. Nabil's brothers, Rafiq and Ra'ad, who labored in government offices, complained idly about oppressive supervisors.

Nabil, wrapping some lamb and salad in a ragged piece of bread, felt both swaddled in, and suffocated by, the presence of his extended family, as usual. There was a heaviness, a grimness and austerity to daily life in Baghdad under Saddam, but there was still always this Friday-night dinner, this bubble of safety and intimacy, this temporary respite from the gray. He imagined he would always feel this way, and he found something both comforting and dismaying, foreshortening, in the inevitability, the fatalism of it all. His mother caught his vaguely lost expression and puckered an air-kiss his way. He smiled and returned it.

In mid-bite, Bibi frowned and pointed. "What's that?" she asked. She stood and reached across the table to the heavy wooden frame that held the painting of the ninety-nine names of Allah, a decorative staple in many Baghdadi homes, this one a version that Bibi had brought from her own house in Najaf when she moved in with her daughter. Bibi ran a finger across the length of the frame. "This is covered in dust!" she exclaimed.

Nabil's mother shrugged and laughed weakly. "That's Zahra," she said, naming the girl who came in weekly from Saddam City, the Shiite slum, to clean. "I tell her to dust, and she never dusts. Or she'll just do tabletops and ignore everything else."

Bibi gasped, indignant. "You've got to withhold payment from her until she does everything you ask!"

"I'm not as strong-willed as you, Mama. I get caught up in the workweek and I forget about it."

"You should just let me clean then."

"You have enough with the cooking, Mama."

"You talk about me like I'm some frail old lady."

This made everyone laugh—including, a bit, Bibi, who was not above laughing at herself. Then the doorbell rang and Nabil, closest to the front room, sprang up to get it.

"It's Asmaa!" cried Rana, who adored her older cousin.

Finally, thought Nabil, as he approached the front door.

He caught her stubbing out her cigarette in the garden urn that served just that purpose. "You bad girl!" he cried.

She exhaled in relief to see that it was Nabil who'd answered the door. "My lamb," she said, calling him just what she'd called him since they were kids, then, reeking of smoke, kissing him on either cheek. "Work held me so late. A document came in just an hour ago."

Asmaa worked in Karada for a small office that the government contracted with to translate business documents into English for communication with Iraq's few trade partners—Austria, Russia, and China, mostly. She was good at her job and all but ran the office, even as she dreamed of working in the Gulf, or, better, in London or Paris, Australia or Canada or the United States, as an interpreter for diplomatic or cultural matters. Still, she had an unusually high-level job for a Baghdadi these days, especially a woman as young as twenty-six, and she carried herself with a certain brisk bearing that suggested she had no time for Baghdadi malaise. She would not cover her head or refrain from wearing light makeup, even if she wore long-sleeved blouses (with slacks) or dresses with long hems. She would not even carry a scarf in her bag, a tactic employed by many Baghdadi women so that they might quickly veil themselves if they felt they were going into hostile territory, such as one rife with self-appointed clerical police. Her father had been Nabil's Ammo Abbas, who'd died in 1985 while unwillingly serving Saddam in the pointless war against Iran, when Asmaa was nine. Asmaa still lived not far from Nabil's home with her mother, Mariam, who since her husband's death had been crippled with anxiety and seldom left the house.

Nabil had worshipped Asmaa from an early age. Asmaa had always seemed to know everything, to read more than anyone else, to know exactly what was going on in politics, in culture, in Europe or America. By the time she was fourteen, her command of English was superb, and it only improved from there. She was expert at connecting to proxy servers to circumvent Saddam's censorship on what little, weak Internet access the country had, and thus always had the latest news from CNN or the BBC. She'd followed the news of the attack on the towers in New York obsessively, trying to divine what the events portended. She was sharp-eyed and intense, a stream of world headlines at dinner conversations, which often led Bibi to snap at her, "Get your head out of the news and find a husband!"

Nabil would parrot this to make her laugh, and she'd reply, "Same to you! Go find your wife!"

"Come inside," Nabil said to her now. Nabil found Asmaa beautiful. He always had. He understood that she might not be considered beautiful by conventional standards. Her eyes were vaguely crossed and her nose was faintly bulbous, her hair a riot of dark curls that she seldom relaxed, instead merely pulling them back in a ponytail or a bun. But from an early age, she had represented something to Nabil: alertness, movement, energy, restlessness. She wanted more than Kadhimiya, or Baghdad overall, had to offer her, but instead of falling into the familiar Baghdadi torpor that existed in the space between one's dreams and one's reality, Asmaa proceeded as though each moment in time were a stepping-stone to a bigger future that surely would come her way. Nabil couldn't match her forward drive but he was happy to siphon some of it from her when in her presence.

She stepped inside and set her bag down. "I have to tell you about something exciting afterward," she said in a low voice. "When we have our cigarette on the garden swing."

It had become a ritual between them when Asmaa came to dinner, the moment the two of them would slip away and smoke and whisper, free from the family din and Bibi's abrasive interjections. So Nabil said merely, "Great," and followed her into the living room.

"Pardon my lateness, my dear family," announced Asmaa, making her way around the table with kisses, including extras for Rana and Ahmed, who screamed her name and flung their arms around her. "I got held at work."

Bibi sprang up and began ladling bamia onto Asmaa's waiting plate. "Eat this before it gets too cold," she commanded.

"Shukran, Bibi." Asmaa set to her plate; Nabil noted that she didn't take the silent moment to murmur a bismallah of thanks. *It's all such bullshit*, she'd said of religion, any religion, to Nabil several times, echoing a feeling common among young, middle-class educated Baghdadis.

Just a stupid excuse for us to kill each other and make women's lives miserable. Nabil agreed with her, though he did find himself muttering prayers here and there, feeling mostly as though they were little nods to Bibi, who was fiercely religious.

"Amma Asmaa!" cried Rana. "Will you take us to the zoo tomorrow?"

Asmaa clucked. "Ya, habibti. What did I tell you about the zoo? Our Great Leader closed it for renovations last month." Asmaa said *Our Great Leader* so dryly, Nabil thought, one could hardly detect the acid in her voice. "But," she continued, "I'll take you to Mansour for ice cream and shopping, how's that?"

Rana smiled, appeased. "Very good."

Ahmed held up his fork. "Can I come too?"

"Yes, habibi. But I just bought you trainers last month, so no new trainers until your birthday."

"A Spiderman coloring book?"

"Definitely that."

"And Ammo Nabil will come too?"

All eyes turned to Nabil. He'd planned to hole up in his room the entirety of the next day, his only day off, reading and drinking tea and smoking, but there was little he could deny his nephew and niece, whom he loved madly, the sight of whose faces filled him with joy.

"Of course Ammo Nabil is coming too," he said.

"Yallah!" Ahmed stabbed his fork in the air, earning a scolding bark from Farah, which silenced him. A moment later, Nabil caught his chastened nephew's eye and winked at him, which put a smile back on his face. It was always like this at Friday family dinner, Nabil thought. It would always be like this.

The eating and the chatter continued—and then the power went out, plunging them into darkness. A collective groan rose from the table.

"It was too good to be true," Nabil's mother said. "Too much to ask that we could get through one meal with the lights on." The country's power grid, like everything else in Iraq the past decade, had been deteriorating. Nobody expected to get a full twenty-four hours a day of power.

"Should I turn on the generator?" asked Ra'ad, half standing.

Nabil's mother sighed. "The power might come back soon, so let's just light some candles."

"Yes!" exulted Rana and Ahmed. "We love candles!"

So candles were brought to the table and lit, bathing everyone's face in flickering light. That was followed by the clearing of plates, then the bringing out of fruit, pastries—the commonplace baklava and the slightly more special mann al-sama, both bought from a nearby pastry shop—Turkish coffee, a little arak for the grown-ups, and a cigar for Baba.

Asmaa stood and nipped Nabil by his shirtsleeve and headed toward the front door. Outside, he joined her on the garden swing, and she extracted two cigarettes from her purse, first lighting his, then hers. Nabil exhaled gratefully, taking in the warmth of the night and the heady smell of the lemon blossoms. He and Asmaa had been sneaking off for these cigarette breaks since they were fourteen, and forever they would make him feel clandestine and alive and, with just two glowing cigarettes between them, as though he could be the closest to who he really was, who in fact was someone that he himself did not fully know.

He watched Asmaa as she drew slowly on her cigarette, then tilted back her head and unleashed a blue plume skyward, high beyond the garden walls.

"So, lamb," she finally said. "How are you?"

"The same as ever. Stuck, stuck, stuck. I'm reading *The Catcher in the Rye*."

"I didn't slip that to you years ago?"

"I don't think so. Abu Mazen sold it to me last week."

Asmaa sniffed a bit, exhaling. "He's become a little bit out of date."

This offended Nabil slightly. Abu Mazen had been their favorite Mutanabbi bookseller since they were teenagers. "He's our number one!" he protested.

"I know, I know. I love the old man. But I just found a little store in Karada that has newer books." From the same bag from which she'd extracted the cigarettes she pulled a copy of a book, *White Teeth* by Zadie Smith.

Nabil flipped through it. "What's this?" he asked absently.

"You mean you haven't heard of it?" Asmaa was always doing this, nearly gasping with disbelief at Nabil's cluelessness. It was part of Asmaa's general air of superiority, which Nabil had long ago accepted as the price he paid for the worlds she opened to him. "This is one of the biggest books of the past few years in the rest of the world. Absolutely huge."

So Nabil merely nodded as he thumbed the pages. *Early in the morning, late in the century, Cricklewood Broadway*, read the first line. "What's it about?" he asked Asmaa.

"Oh my goodness," she gushed, again tilting back her head and exhaling smoke. "I don't even know where to begin. It's *so* good, lamb. It's about London, and immigrants, and Muslims, and colonialism, and all these families overlapping. It's just absolutely—" She paused, inhaling, and Nabil thrilled to watch her search for the word. "It's *brimming with life*," she finally said in English, stressing the words carefully. "It makes me want to go to London so badly. Right now!"

Asmaa wanted to travel even more than Nabil did, which was saying a lot. Since she was twelve or thirteen, she enjoyed running down her list of cities she intended to visit or live in one day, which usually included, in perhaps slightly shifting order depending on Asmaa's obsessions of the moment and whatever she was reading, London, Paris, Bombay, Tokyo, New York, Beirut, Berlin, Mexico City, Bangkok, and Rio de Janeiro. She liked to casually drop names of neighborhoods and museums and even clubs and restaurants she'd heard of in these cities, as though she'd been there, and when she did, part of Nabil would inwardly scoff at Asmaa's pretentiousness while another part of him aimed to commit the places to his own memory, so that he might casually drop their names himself one day. Such was his relationship with Asmaa. Ultimately, she nourished him more than she irritated him.

So now he continued to flip through the book, trying to assess how hard its English would be for him. "You'll lend it to me when you're done?" he asked.

"Of course, lamb." There had never been a book that entranced Asmaa that she had not nearly ordered Nabil to read, and their post-dinner retreats to this very swing often involved discussing the books in question.

Quietly, they finished their cigarettes. On the other side of the garden wall, what sounded like a young man passed, singing that hit of a few years ago by the Lebanese superstar Elissa with Ragheb Alama.

"Hey, you're off-key!" Asmaa called. Nabil put his hand over his mouth in delighted shock, stifling his laughter.

On the other side of the wall, the humming stopped abruptly. "Inchabi"—*Shut up*—the young man called back sourly before walking on, which only made Asmaa and Nabil laugh harder, silently, their hands over their mouths, before falling back into silence.

"What did you have to tell me?" Nabil finally asked.

"Oh, yes. Well," and she dropped her voice so that no passersby on the other side of the garden wall could hear them. "I was talking to an Austrian client today who was just on business in Washington, D.C."

Nabil immediately scoffed. "Did he see the bombs they're going to drop on us?"

Asmaa laughed weakly. "Not that I know of. But he did tell me of all the work that is going to open up if America comes. The military, contractors, engineers, journalists. They're all going to need interpreters and translators. And the pay is incredible. There are interpreters in Afghanistan right now making the equivalent of one hundred thousand dinars a day."

Nabil regarded her skeptically. He found it hard to believe that any common translator could make that kind of money.

"Yes!" Asmaa hissed in a whisper. "So I gave him my work e-mail and asked him to pass it on. And if you keep up your English, you can get work, too."

Now Nabil looked alarmed. "You didn't pass on my name, did you?"

"No. I merely said that I also had a cousin with excellent English proficiency."

The entire exchange was making him anxious. "You weren't afraid about passing on your e-mail?"

Asmaa set her face hard and leaned in closer to him. "I want them to come," she said grimly. "Nothing is ever going to change here otherwise. I can't stand to stay here if nothing changes. Can you?"

"The damage they'll do!"

"Nabil, what damage hasn't already been done?" By now they were talking in sharp whispers. "This is a prison. I would sneak away and apply for refugee status if it weren't for my mother. Anything has to be better than this. Something has to change."

Nabil looked away, pained. There was a saying in Iraq, that if you so much as thought bad thoughts about Saddam, the Mukhabarat would knock on your door instantly to take you away to Abu Ghraib. To even privately ponder a change, an uprising, freedom, seemed foolishness, never mind to say something aloud. Baghdadis had their solaces: soccer, families, weddings, holidays, outings for masgouf, evenings alongside the Tigris, whatever TV and movies they could get their hands on (increasingly now, with more people hiding satellite dishes on their roofs). Some people, like Asmaa, had a job that gave them some window onto the outside world and a sense that they were making at least partial use of their university education. And then of course there were books, Nabil's great escape. For the most part, these things anesthetized the dark, constrained feeling that one was living behind walls, in a dictatorship, that one would never realize the full extent of one's gifts, ambitions, or desires.

But not entirely. That Asmaa dared speak her discontent aloud both unnerved and thrilled Nabil, because she was also speaking his own.

"Do you think they will take him out and leave everything else in place?" he whispered. His body trembled to say the words.

Asmaa, too, replied in a whisper. "The military hates him, and even his bureaucrats hate him." She mused. "They would have to take out his sons, too. And probably some of the people closest to him."

Nabil ran through the calculations in his head. Could it ever possibly be done—like a surgeon cutting out a tumor? Removing Wondrous

Uncle and a few layers surrounding him and leaving everything else intact? Weren't Americans capable of achieving anything, great or terrible? But then he shuddered.

"I am just so scared of another war," he whispered. His first memories were of being at war with Iran, of the suspicion of Persians the government had tried to foment. His own family had Persian roots on his mother's side. He remembered fathers and uncles coming back without a limb, or—in the case of his own Ammo Abbas—not coming back at all. No sooner had that stupid, pointless war ended, in 1988, than the country was at war with the United States over Kuwait. He vividly remembered being thirteen years old, terrified by the reverberations of the American so-called smart bombs annihilating government buildings in Baghdad; two of those bombs had hit the air-raid shelter in Amiriyah and killed hundreds of civilians. True, life the past decade had been lousy, with the sanctions, with everyone's income plunging, with typical daily amenities and even necessities like medications being so hard to get. But it had still been without war, which was saying something.

Yet Asmaa gave him what he thought was a rather hard look. Carefully, she stubbed out her cigarette in the elaborately carved stone receptacle used for that purpose, which Nabil regularly emptied of butts himself. Ali, the gardener from Saddam City, always "forgot" to do it.

"If they're going to come, they're going to come," she said simply, again in a whisper. "We have no say in the matter. At least it'll shake things up and something good might come from it for us. Our education is a total waste otherwise."

Nabil considered this for a long time. How could things get any worse? They were stuck, stuck. The whole world out there was talking about the Internet, and they were lucky if they could get a dial-up connection for a few minutes a day and had to do backflips to latch onto a proxy server so they could actually see what the rest of the world was discussing—whether their own country would actually be invaded or not! It was a horrible way to live.

"Will you e-mail my name, too?" he finally asked softly. "Do you need my CV?"

Asmaa smiled, triumphant. "Not yet," she said. "Let me just mention it, and we'll see if anything comes of it."

He nodded. "Khosh. Shukran."

Asmaa smiled. "Anything for you, oh most wondrous cousin."

For a few moments, they were silent, listening to the dim sounds of video game mayhem from inside the house. "Should we smoke another cigarette before going in?" Asmaa finally asked, already reaching down for her purse.

So they did, feeling decadent. "Is Zaid still flirting with you?" he asked. Zaid was Asmaa's office mate, a stocky bachelor from Amiriyah who gelled his hair daily into a spiky immobile sculpture and talked mostly about the care and maintenance of his 1998 Peugeot, which he felt set him off from the lot of poor Baghdadi bastards driving ugly, boxy Toyotas from the early 1980s.

Asmaa laughed. "He's a moron." She used the English word. "Spends the whole day telling me about this Russian beauty he chats with online every night over his proxy server, then asks me if I want a date."

Nabil laughed too. "A real class act." He'd been to the movies a few times with Asmaa and Zaid; she'd asked him to come to signal to Zaid that it was an outing among colleagues, not a date. Nabil was perversely fascinated by the incredible height and rigidity of Zaid's hairstyle.

"He's a chauvinist deep down," she added. "He can treat me like an equal as a coworker and a friend, but he'd stop if we were dating."

Nabil's lip curled in amusement. "Is that your way of saying you'd consider dating him?"

She let out a short, shocked laugh. "No! You know I'm waiting for Brad Pitt."

"Maybe he'll come along for the invasion."

"Aha! I can dream!"

Their laughter settled eventually into silence. It was the familiar awkward silence of their nonconversation about Nabil's own romantic yearnings. Nabil deeply dreaded this topic, even with Asmaa; it created the vague sick feeling in his stomach of being examined, considered.

His eyes flickered away from her gaze, upward into the sky, and she put a hand on his knee.

"Something will come up soon," she said. "A job. Your English is nearly perfect."

But Nabil suddenly found her insistent optimism irritating. "Nothing will come up!" he snapped. "This is it," he said, pointing up beyond the walls of the garden, as though to signify Baghdad.

Uncharacteristically, Asmaa was silent. Nabil could see chastisement in her eyes, as well as pity and love. During the summers of their childhood, they would hold hands in the pool, plunge down, stare at each other, their eyes burning with chlorine, cheeks puffed up like frogs', and compete to see who could stay down longer. Later, they would lie in the sun, shelling pistachios, while Asmaa told him rambling stories she'd read about adventuresome girls solving mysteries, and Nabil would listen, drowsy and warm, lying on his naked stomach with his feet in the air, or perhaps on his back with one hand blocking the sun and one knee latched over the other, content to make himself the vessel for Asmaa's vivid narrations.

"Wait until the Americans come," she finally said, infinitely quiet. "We'll get our break."

He shrugged and stubbed out his cigarette in the stone urn.

Back inside, the power had come back on and everyone had regrouped around the video game on the TV screen. Nabil and Asmaa stood there a moment, watching, as drowsiness set upon Nabil. He kissed Asmaa good night, wandered into the kitchen, and did the same to Mama, Bibi, and his sisters-in-law, all of whom were sitting, rapt, as Bibi read the fortunes foretold by the patterns of the grounds in the bottoms of their tiny coffee cups.

"Sit and have a coffee and have me read your cup," Bibi instructed him.

"No, Bibi." He knew where that would lead—to Bibi's envisioning of his future wife, of her beauty and kindness and fertility. "I'm exhausted, I'm going to bed. Good night to you all."

"Good night, habibi," said Mama.

He retreated to his room in the back of the house. Its walls were bare save for a giant poster of the footballer Younis Mahmoud, an action shot of him in midair, mid-kick, thigh muscles bulging. It was the only poster Rafiq had left when he moved out of their shared room into the tiny bungalow behind the house with Baydaa after his marriage. Nabil flopped down in bed and picked up *The Catcher in the Rye*, happy to be leaving Baghdad once again. He made the mental shift in his head: The air was not balmy and citrus-scented but frigidly cold, snow flurry cold, Christmastime in New York City cold, a sort of cold Nabil had never known. The skyline was not low and boxy, the color of sand, and spiked with minarets, but infinitely vertical, massive, jagged combs of skyscrapers with millions of nighttime twinkles, infinite flashes of yellow below as cabs crisscrossed the grid all night long, stopping and starting in front of restaurants and clubs. So very long ago, before Iraq meant nothing to America but Ali Baba and a magic carpet.

He found that Holden Caulfield, too, after having sent home the call girl, lay on his bed. *I felt like praying or something, when I was in bed, but I couldn't do it*, Nabil read. *I can't always pray when I feel like it. In the first place, I'm sort of an atheist. I like Jesus and all, but I don't care too much for most of the other stuff in the Bible.*

He sighed, laid the book down, and reached for cigarettes at his bedside. There was no God, he thought. That much was certain. He fell into his nightly ritual before bed, smoking and staring at the popped thigh muscles of Younis Mahmoud, at the scrunched look of fury on his handsome face. Nabil thought about his scuffle with Marwan that afternoon, of Marwan's smell. He rose and turned the lock on his door, then lay back down. He fixed on Younis Mahmoud's thighs and inhaled, his right hand slipping to the zipper of his jeans. Then, for the usual minute, he flew away high above the golden domes and spires of Kadhimiya.

CHAPTER FIVE

RITA AND SAMI, PART 1

(2002-3)

The bar called Barometre was not the typical Beirut bourgeois pleasure spot. Since the Lebanese civil war ended, in 1990, the city—whose coastal front looked toward Europe and mountainous backside spilled into the Middle East—had slowly crept out of chaos back toward its prewar habits of glamour and decadence, so that by the early 2000s, the city's affluent young people and their peers from Europe and the Gulf were partying nightly until dawn, on Rue Monnot in Achrafieh, the traditionally wealthy Christian neighborhood. There, in cavernous, dramatically lit clubs that shook with sound systems and flowed with champagne, big-haired women in tiny dresses and spike heels vamped for swaggering men with gelled hair and crisp white dress shirts, their BMWs and Mercedes parked outside. Many in this crowd had grown up in France or the United Kingdom or Canada, in wealthy families waiting for the crazy men in their homeland to exhaust themselves with their senseless bombing and shooting, and they'd come back to Lebanon in the 1990s to find their once prosperous neighborhoods reduced nearly to rubble, the sandstone and arch-windowed facades and Orientalist balconies of handsome old Ottoman-era apartment houses riddled with bullets.

But that didn't stop their ancestral entrepreneurial instincts from reemerging. So they opened restaurants and bars, clubs and boutiques, borrowing from the aesthetics and foods they'd grown accustomed to in London, Paris, Toronto, and New York, and then invited the Anglos they'd come of age with in those cities. Shouting in Arabic, English, and French, everyone would drink and smoke until four or five in the morning, then pile into taxis and go to BO18, a club in an outlying industrial neighborhood that had been built into a giant underground bunker on the site of a former Palestinian refugee camp where a massacre had taken place. Banquettes were in the shape of coffins, and at a certain point near sunrise, the roof would open halfway, and cocaine- and Ecstasy-fueled revelers would find themselves dancing under the dawn sky, looking at their own reflections in the mirror-lined underside of the unopened half.

Such was the energy of Beirut as it clambered back to life in the first years of the new millennium, war-scarred but pulsing with ambitious, narcotic, hedonistic energy. But with rare exceptions, the pounding late-night clubs were too much for Rita and her expat journalist friends, and most evenings after deadlines they found themselves eating meze and drinking arak or Almaza, the national beer, at Barometre. It was a tiny, purposely unglamorous hole-in-the-wall run by an unreconstructed Lebanese communist, hung with pictures of 1980s Lebanese Marxist fighters and Palestinian nationalist writers, favoring a soundtrack heavy on the pan-Arabic nostalgia of Fairouz, Abdel Wahab, and Umm Kulthum. It was not unusual for the entire room to stop grumbling about sectarian political jockeying in the nation's feckless parliament, or about the double indignity of Syrian occupation in the north and Israeli occupation in the south, to sing along when Ziad al-Rahbani's beloved "Ana Mosh Kafir," about the religious idiocy of the 1980s civil war, came on the stereo.

The first time this had happened, Rita had surprised herself by tearing up, feeling a profound sense of lineage and country.

"Look at you, chérie!" Salma had exclaimed in her extremely husky voice. "You are getting all chauvine for your homeland! I love, love, *love* it."

And Rita had laughed and brushed away her tears, feeling profoundly embarrassed. While at Harvard and in the years after, she had developed a certain characteristic hardness and did not like to betray vulnerability and feeling. They were girlish traits that would not serve her well in foreign correspondence, a field that was still overwhelmingly male and macho.

Barometre was in Hamra, the neighborhood in the part of the city that snubbed out into the Mediterranean, flaring upward in high cliffs upon which sat the handsome red-roofed buildings of the American University of Beirut. The area was the leftist intellectual heart of the city, the enclave that had been the center of nightlife and culture in the years before the war, and Rita loved that so much of it seemed frozen in the blocky mid-century design of the 1960s and early 1970s, and that from the tiny balcony of her studio she could see the old sign for the Cinema Al Hamra, each letter its own square panel.

By the late fall of 2002, she'd been working in Beirut as a correspondent for the Middle East bureau of the *American Standard* for eighteen months, and she'd fallen deeply in love with the hectic, traffic-jammed, car-honking, food- and drink-obsessed city. She loved the mild winters and the steamy summers that necessitated spending holiday afternoons lounging by the Mediterranean at Le Sporting, the beach club; or going up the coast to Batroun, to the more rustic beach shack Pierre and Friends. She loved walking the Corniche, looking out to the sea on one side and on the other up to the wall of hotels, some of them shelled to mere concrete carcasses, while threading her way among joggers in T-shirts and tiny shorts, as well as pious women covered head to toe in black.

She loved the winding, narrow streets themselves, the graceful old Ottoman buildings with their arched windows and delicate balconies, still standing despite having endured fifteen years of bullets and bombs. And, even when—despite four years of intense study at Harvard and two summers learning the language at the American University of Beirut— she heard Arabic she still couldn't fully understand, because she was still acclimating herself to some of the peculiarities of Levantine Arabic, she loved that the sound of the language always reminded her of her own grandmother, the redoubtable Marguerite Daou Khoury, who had died six years earlier. Everywhere she looked, she saw people who resembled her own father's family, with dark hair, faintly olive skin, and prominent noses—the noses often surgically altered among Beirut's rich women.

So, at Barometre that lovely late fall evening, after she'd filed her latest story on regional unease over and resentment at her own country's likely impending invasion of Iraq—a story she now seemed to file a version of every week—she settled at a table with Salma, who'd become her best friend in Beirut. They'd met a year earlier at one of the endless weekend parties where liberal, university-educated Beirutis—the kind who traveled continually into and out of the city—mingled with an ever-rotating crowd of post-collegiate Europeans, Australians, and Americans, who were flooding Beirut the way their counterparts ten years prior had flooded Prague and Berlin after the Soviet Union collapsed. It was the allure of a city with a glamorous past that had only just started wriggling itself out from under the detritus of war and deprivation. In Beirut, expats had found that everything from food, drink, and drugs to music, apartments, and hospitality was plentiful and cheap.

Rita had been at a Saturday-night party at somebody's cavernous, high-ceilinged, candlelit apartment in Clemenceau where the rent was a mere four hundred dollars a month, everyone drinking Almazas and passing around hashish and talking about the global repercussions of the attacks in New York, which had occurred only two months before. Serge Gainsbourg and Brigitte Bardot were on the stereo. At some point, Rita and Maher, the portly freelance photographer from Damascus she both worked and socialized with, wandered into the kitchen, where they found a strikingly tall, slim, tawny-skinned young woman, with spiky hair, deep red lipstick, kohl-rimmed eyes, and a vintage black leather jacket, regaling a small crowd in French, making ample use of her cigarette as a prop.

There was something performative and commanding about her, and Rita found herself compelled to listen, even though she hardly understood, having eschewed French in high school, finding it snooty and ornamental. Increasingly, in Beirut, even as her Levantine Arabic improved with every passing month, she wished she knew French. Working-class Beirutis, like shop owners or the drivers of unmetered service taxis, those unmarked cars you merely stuck your arm out for and entered to share space with three or four other passengers on a generally common route, were always happy to practice Arabic with her or speak to her in the little bit of inglizi they knew. ("Hello! How are you? New York Yankees! Michael Jackson!") But it seemed that bourgeois Beirutis always answered her Arabic in English—only to, after a moment, turn away from her and continue toggling between Arabic and French with their friends.

"What is she saying?" Rita asked Maher, who knew French.

Maher squinted, concentrating to listen. "She's telling a story about trying to buy a rug in Istanbul . . . ," he began, stopping to listen to more. Suddenly, everyone, including Maher, laughed. Rita felt left out. It was a common feeling for anyone living in a foreign country, a daily feeling. Being a journalist, she'd long ago lost her timidity about asking someone else to translate.

When he finally stopped laughing, he said, "The merchant thought she wanted to sell him her pussy."

"Aha!" Rita laughed.

She and Maher wormed their way into the woman's magic circle, which included a late-thirtysomething writer for *Libération* named Cyrile, whom Rita vaguely knew.

"Hello," said the woman musically.

Maher babbled something to her in French, and Rita caught her own name and the typical words *américaine* and *journaliste*. The woman turned to her, smiling, offering a hand.

"Hello," she said. "I'm Salma. I'm a journalist too, but I don't do important stuff like you and Maher. I do arts, design, food, culture."

Rita shrugged. "That's important."

"I mean they're all nice things if you're not living in some camp."

Cyrile put a hand on Salma's arm. "Chérie," he said, "those can be nice things even if you are living in some camp."

Salma brushed his hand away. "Then you go to Burj Al-Barajneh"— the sprawling Palestinian refugee camp near the airport—"tomorrow and bring them some pictures of Damien Hirst and champagne."

Everyone laughed, including Rita, impressed by Salma's quick tongue. The two women spent most of the rest of the night drinking, smoking, and talking. Rita almost instantly liked Salma, who reminded her of a sardonic, smarter version of her friend Yasmin from high school. Salma's family had left Beirut for Paris in 1976, the second year of the civil war, when Salma was still a baby. Salma's was a typical story: growing up and going to a lycée in France and then a university in the U.K., all the while hearing from weeping elders stories of the beauty and dolce vita of Lebanon before the war. Then of course, she heeded the postwar gravitational pull back to Beirut in the 1990s, like so many others, their dual or even triple citizenship intact.

Salma wrote stories here and there for the *Daily Star*, the English-language paper, and *L'Orient Jour*, the French-language paper, as well as a variety of French and British papers and magazines, about Beirut's slowly reemerging art, design, and fashion scenes. She complained constantly about the lack of money and how desperately she wanted a staff job in another city, but when she was not living in comfort in her parents' palatial mid-century-modern apartment in Achrafieh, complete with a Filipina who cooked and cleaned, she stayed at her family's apartments in Paris or Montreal while visiting siblings, cousins, and friends studying or working abroad. Wherever Salma was, her life was a whirlwind of visits to contemporary art museums, galleries, performance spaces, and boutiques, not to mention the restaurants and bars du jour. Notebook in one hand and digital camera in the other, she collected material wherever she went and always managed to find an outlet to sell it to, even if she spent half her time trying to get paid. She and Rita were perfectly matched; they did the same thing for a living, and hence were professionally bonded, but worked in spheres separate enough that competition never complicated the friendship.

"What are you doing tonight, chérie?" is how Salma would begin a typical phone call. "Come with me to a live installation in a garage near the Beirut River. It is a digital meditation on the loss of the war years."

"What does that mean?" Rita would reply. As far as she could tell, all contemporary art in Beirut was a meditation on the loss of the war years. The conflict had torn the country apart for fifteen years and was the only thing that any artist who had come of age at that time could focus on.

"Well, that's what it says on the e-mail!"

Rita laughed. "Sure, I'll go."

So that evening, they had gone to the installation, a somewhat grating sound-and-light show whose relation to the war years Rita could not discern, though she refrained from saying as much to Salma, who was engrossed. Later they'd ended up, as usual, at Barometre, which Salma vastly preferred to the flashy clubs frequented by many of her Achrafieh neighbors, and were sitting at a table with Cyrile and Lise, a Dutch photojournalist, when Rita noticed that, at a nearby table, a man in a group of people who conversed variously in Arabic and English seemed to keep staring at her as he drank and smoked. (Restaurants thick with cigarette smoke had been one of the dismaying aspects of life in Beirut, along with homicidal motorists, that Rita had had to make peace with, doing so in part by stealing puffs from Salma so as to feel at least part of the general smoky aura.)

The man was handsome, Rita conceded, Arab, wild haired and stubbled, with transfixing green eyes, an aquiline nose, and an indifferent, amused expression. A very ragged old T-shirt clung loosely to his lean frame, and one wrist bore several leather and hammered metal bracelets. Their eyes met; he smiled slyly at her as he exhaled smoke, and she found herself blushing and looking away.

She murmured to Salma, "Do you know that guy over there with the messy hair and the bracelets?"

Salma glanced his way. "I can't believe you haven't met Sami yet," she said. "The world's most glamorous Palestinian refugee."

"What? He lives in the camps?"

Salma laughed sharply. "Ha, hardly! He's from one of the richest Palestinian families, going back seventy, eighty years. He's lived everywhere *but* the camps. We went to school in Paris together for two years. I figured he'd come over to the table sooner or later to say hello, and I promise you that within sixty seconds of meeting him, you'll hear his

Palestinian diaspora story. It's his obsession, and it's his secret weapon with Western women."

Rita laughed, intrigued. "Really?"

Salma exhaled cigarette smoke. "Really. And look, here he comes now."

It was true. He was now at the table, his cigarette still burning, leaning down to give Salma three Beiruti kisses, exchanging with her French hellos and how are yous. "Assieds-toi, joins-toi à nous un instant," Salma said, and suddenly he was pulling an empty chair from a nearby table and pulling up close to Rita.

"Who's this?" he asked Salma, but smiling intensely at Rita.

"This is my friend Rita Khoury, from Boston, a writer here for the *American Standard*."

Sami shook her hand. "Khoury? A lubnani?"

"Half," Rita answered. "My mother is Irish."

"You speak Arabic?" he asked her in Arabic.

"I do my best," she answered accordingly.

"Ah! Very impressive!" Back to English.

"Thank you. What about you? Do you live here?"

"Just down the street on Abdel Aziz. I'm a grad student at AUB."

This caught Salma's attention. "You've started finally?" she asked, a teasing note in her voice.

Sami grinned. "Va te faire foutre, chérie," he said affectionately—Rita at least knew that much French; it meant *Go fuck yourself*—and Salma laughed in reply. "I'm starting in January. I had family things to sort out this fall."

"Ah, of course, of course," murmured Salma. "Family always comes first, yes?"

He grinned again, then turned back to Rita. "So," he began, at the same time summoning the server. "What do you think of your homeland? How long have you been here?" He turned quickly to the server to order a round of Almazas for the table.

Rita detected a note of challenge in his question. "Eighteen months. I love it!"

"Eighteen months. So you're obviously over the romance period and now you just put up with the same shit we all do on a daily basis, correct? The power failures, the shitty Internet, the crazy drivers, the corrupt politicians, the small fortune you spend on bottled water. All that?"

"Those are all the things that make you a real Beiruti, right?"

He smiled condescendingly. "You'll get sick of it soon enough. Come on, you grew up in the States, a functioning country. Same here. I grew up mainly in Paris after my family was pushed out of Palestine by the Zionists." (Rita felt Salma's triumphant knee nudge her own under the table.) "So I know how a real city runs. Salma, too."

"Paris has a stick up its ass," Salma interjected. "Nothing new has happened there since the 1980s."

"It's true," joined in Cyrile. "The whole city is an old museum."

Sami raised a finger. "But at least it didn't destroy itself for nonsense religious reasons."

"T'es con!" exclaimed Salma, exasperated. "You're just laying it on extra thick tonight because you have a new audience member." And she gestured at Rita. "If you preferred Paris so much, you'd be at Sciences Po right now studying for the civil service with all your friends."

Sami blew air upward from his lower lip. "There's no place in the French civil service for Arabs."

"Ah, khalas, enough please," Salma protested. She turned to Rita. "Like I said, he's laying it on extra thick. He must fancy you."

Sami smiled, raising his cigarette to his lips, as though he were semi-conceding his contrariness. "I'm just saying, let's be honest about the dysfunction."

Now it was Rita who'd had enough. "We just got out of a civil war!" she exclaimed.

"*We?*"

"Well," she began, slightly sheepish. "You know what I mean."

Several more rounds of Almaza ensued. Sufficiently drunk, Rita smoked freely with the others. The evening crept past midnight; the room filled, and the rowdiness increased. A new track came over the speaker.

"Oh, I love this song!" declared Salma, standing with her cigarette in one hand, grabbing Rita by the other. "Let's dance." She sang along with the song, a French dance hit from the 1980s: "Marcia, elle est maigre, belle en scène, belle comme à la ville." Half the room rose to dance, and when Rita at one point turned to face Sami, he laced one arm around her waist and held his opposite hand up against hers in a goofy attempt at a tango. Fairly wasted now, she obliged him for a moment.

She found him walking her home along Hamra Street at one thirty in the morning, both of them weaving slightly. Drunkenly, in her own head, she was torn between inviting him up and forcing herself to submit a friendly but responsible good night.

"You have to work tomorrow?" he asked.

"I work every day. This isn't a nine-to-five kind of job."

"But you were off the clock tonight?"

She laughed. "A drink after deadline is mandatory. To wind down."

Now it was his turn to laugh. "Are you wound down?" With immaculate casualness, he threw an arm over her shoulder.

She reluctantly allowed it to stay there. "I think I'll regret how much I wound down tomorrow."

"Ah," he clucked. "No regrets—ever!"

"Life isn't really like that."

He winked. "You have to work at that philosophy. I do."

They were standing now in front of her apartment building, its wall a scarred slab of mid-century marble framing glass doors. He pressed himself against her, then pressed his lips, with their ticklish sensation of surrounding stubble, to hers. He tasted like cigarettes and beer, which she found both off-putting and sexy. As they kissed, a shiny black Mercedes SUV passed, the Lebanese pop siren Haifa Wehbe blasting from its powerful speakers.

Sami paused in his kissing. "Ah, Haifa! A perfect soundtrack for us."

"This is my first act of PDA in Beirut," she confessed. It was true. Despite Beirut's bohemian vibe, public kissing was frowned upon in the city.

"We can take it upstairs then."

Now she pulled away, laughing. "You mean *I* can take it upstairs. Which is exactly what I should do now." And she did, but not before an added few seconds of locked lips.

"À suivre?" he'd said, just before she went in.

"What?"

"To be continued?"

She pulled a notebook and pen from her bag, scrawled her number, and handed it to him. "Call me," she instructed him, before letting herself inside. In the lift up to her studio, still tasting his beer and cigarettes on her lips, she wondered if he would.

He did, in fact. Three days later, while she was on deadline, which she shared with him.

"What's the story?"

"The latest Palestinian suicide bomber. What we call the daily blowup." The bombings had been going on just over the southern border nearly every day all year—two Israelis killed in front of a falafel stand, a dozen Israeli and Arab students killed on campus, eight Asian guest workers killed in the red-light district. And the Israelis seemed to respond to each atrocity by seizing more land in the territories, to which the Palestinians responded with more suicide bombings. On and on it went, in a dizzying and eventually numbing cycle.

"Ah." Sami paused. "Well, I'm sure your President Bush's road map to peace"—he said the words pointedly—"will settle all that. Even as he's so sweetly delivering American-style democracy to Iraq."

She chuckled. "No comment. I'm a journalist. I have no opinion."

"Do you have an opinion on getting together again?"

New e-mails were popping to life on her computer screen. "Can I formulate one after this deadline?"

"Suicide bombers will always come before me, I suppose."

"Yep. That's just how it goes. Sorry."

But once her work was done, she called him, agreeing to meet at Pacifico, a fashionable Mexican restaurant on Rue Monnot whose dim amber lights on plaster walls and slowly whirling ceiling fans gave it the air of Latin America in the 1950s. She found herself putting on makeup, a skirt, and boots with a moderate heel—niceties she usually had little time or patience for.

They sat at the bar, each with a margarita, a stone bowl of guacamole between them. She remarked to Sami, who himself had put on a jacket and suede slip-ons, that he seemed to know everyone on the staff.

He lit a cigarette, and, feeling bold, she followed suit. "Well," he said, "like you, I need to unwind at the end of a long day. So I have my favorite places. Beirut's come a long way the past few years."

"How'd you spend your day?"

He shook his head slightly. "Things to sort out. All sorts of family drama and paperwork."

"You're going to start graduate classes at AUB in January?"

He inhaled and exhaled first before he bothered to answer. "Very likely," he finally said. "Again, a lot depends on the family situation."

She nodded, reminding herself to modulate her journalist's impatience at not getting anywhere. "And your family—they're all in Paris?"

He nodded slowly, as though he were processing the question, or ruminating over it. Rita found she couldn't take her eyes off his slender hands, flecked with black hair, and found it hard to stop herself from reaching for one of them. She cut her eyes away.

"My parents are there still," he replied. "Though they've both been remarried for several years now. And I have a brother who's a banker in London and a sister who's a banker in Toronto."

She laughed mildly. "So you're the only non-banker in the family?"

"Well, my mother is an art history professor and my father is a surgeon."

She brightened. "Mine too! Orthopedics." She felt the usual stab of affection and longing for her father that followed thoughts or mentions of him. "What about yours?"

"Thoracic."

"Wow. Heavy stuff."

Again, Sami nodded. "He's a brilliant man."

She caught a note of rue in his voice. "You're not close?"

He stubbed out his cigarette, readdressed his margarita. "He's a lot to live up to." Then, with what to Rita felt like a studied new note of anger, he added, "No, actually, the problem is that my father is one of that generation of kids that were absolutely ruined by the displacement. And has made his kids pay the price."

Rita knit her brow. In some ways, she felt she was working: Here was someone telling her something charged and vague, and it was her job to extract the specifics: the who, what, where, when, and why. After a few years as a journalist, she found that this had become a reflex. In casual conversation, she had to remind herself not to ask follow-up questions, that she didn't need to know everyone's life story, that she wasn't always on a deadline.

But in this instance, she didn't stop. "When was your family displaced from Palestine? After the 1967 war?"

"Huh?" He seemed surprised. "Oh, no. By then, we'd been in Beirut for decades. We went to Paris in 1976 because of the Lebanese war. But my grandfather pulled the family out of Nablus, to Beirut, in '42, '43, I think. He saw the writing on the wall. He became one of the major shareholders in Middle East Airlines here in Beirut."

"Oh," Rita began now, somewhat confused. "So, I mean, you weren't technically displaced then."

He frowned at her, as though he were disappointed in her. "How much have you read about the nakba?"

She had actually read a fairly good deal about the nakba, the great, forced Palestinian exile from the homeland in 1948 amid Israel's forming, and she knew that many wealthy Palestinians, such as Sami's grandfather seemed to be, had left well in advance of the nakba. But she also sensed that, for Sami, the subject was touchy, as it often was. So she merely smirked and said, "I've read about the nakba, thank you."

"Lebanon sucks for Palestinians, you know," he persisted. "No citizenship, can't work."

"But of course your family has citizenship, right? Being here so long." He didn't reply, so she then dared to ask: "Your family's Christian, right?" She was nearly certain it was true, based on all he'd told her.

"Yes, we have citizenship, and yes, we're Christian." Their voices were rising. "But you know I'm not talking about us. I'm talking about the people in the camps!"

"I know you are! I was just *in* the camps, working. I cover the Middle East, so I'm not totally clueless about the plight of the Palestinians in Lebanon, thank you very much!"

By this point, her voice had spiked so high she cut through the din, earning a glance from the ponytailed bartender.

"Hey, come on, you two," he said, gesturing at their margarita glasses. "More drinking, less politics. The war is over."

Rita smiled at him apologetically, embarrassed at her loud American voice, and turned back to Sami.

"Let's rewind," she offered. "I mean, who am I . . ." She trailed off.

He smiled, also conciliatory, then briefly played with the second and third fingers of her right hand on the table, sending an expected shock wave through her. "Your family was very smart to get out of the region so long ago," he told her.

"Some did," she said. "Really just my grandfather and great-uncle and great-aunt. Almost everyone else died in the famine in the mountains around World War I. That really haunted my grandfather all his life."

"Well," he continued, "you're still lucky they were mountain peasants. The wealthy had no incentive to leave, so their kids and grandkids were the ones who had to leave in the 1970s, start over again in Europe or North America."

She shrugged. "I guess every few decades or hundred years or so, people have to leave their country."

He laughed sharply. "Just in some places. Fucked-up postcolonial places. Not everywhere."

Then he looked down into his drink. Their hands were only inches apart, and now she took his second and third fingers and stroked them between her index finger and thumb. He glanced up at her, and for the first time that evening, she thought she spied his vulnerability rather than his arrogance.

"You have really beautiful hands," she said.

He smiled slightly, amused. "So assertive, Miss Khoury."

Now she laughed. "You think so? I guess I'm just one of those assertive American girls."

"No peeping out from under the burkha for you."

And they both laughed, earning an approving and relieved glance from the bartender.

Later, drunk on seven margaritas between them, they hailed a service taxi. He began kissing her in the car, but she gently pushed him away, careful not to upset the driver, whose prayer beads swung from the rearview mirror. However, there was no avoiding Fadi, the burly night concierge at her apartment building, who watched her and Sami under heavy-lidded eyes as they crossed the lobby toward the elevator, then awkwardly waited for it.

"Bonsoir," she called to Fadi once it arrived. He nodded grimly in return.

Finally, they locked lips in the elevator, continuing once they were in her dark, sparsely furnished apartment, the living room dominated by a large framed poster of the 1966 Baalbek music festival, the dining-room table crowded with her laptop, printer, and various notebooks filled with her scrawl. While she turned on the kitchen lamp in order to retrieve and light a candle, he idly picked up a notebook.

"What's this? 'Risk of destabilizing region . . . ,'" he read with theatrical gravitas, "'escalating hostilities . . .'"

She snatched the notebook from him. "Get out of there!" she laughed, drunker than she realized. "That's highly classified!" She wrapped her arms around him. They stumbled to the couch and began unbuttoning each other's shirts. He was the first man she'd taken home in the eighteen months she'd been in Beirut. Amid the endless assignments and deadlines, the all-consuming vortex of Middle Eastern geopolitics, of which she intended to be the master storyteller, she hadn't realized how hungry for physical intimacy she was, and she felt she was nearly devouring his lean body as they kissed and groped.

He must have felt it too. "You're a wild woman!" he marveled.

She laughed heartily. "You really think?"

"I surrender to you, Rita Khoury!"

She reached for his belt buckle, laughed again. "Good boy."

Thus, their courtship began. Life became an almost unmanageable whirl for Rita in the late fall and early winter of 2002: long days and nights at the paper's bureau; short reporting trips with Maher to the West Bank, Jerusalem, the Gulf, or Amman; working with a team of staff and stringers in New York and Baghdad to cover the United Nations' weapons inspections under way in Iraq amid increasing threats of war.

But now she no longer took a service taxi home to an empty apartment. Instead, she always found Sami there, reading, smoking, drinking wine, her dinner at the ready, the leak in her bathroom faucet fixed, the prints she'd bought in Sidon finally framed and hung on the wall.

"Chérie, you have what every woman dreams of!" Salma exclaimed to her over a brief midday coffee. "You have a househusband!"

Rita grinned. "He says he's biding his time while he waits to hear from AUB about starting in January."

At this Salma smiled skeptically, before shrugging. "Of course! Enjoy him while he's free."

But Rita had detected something in Salma's face. "Wait," she said. "What? What was the smirk for?"

Salma leaned forward, put a hand briefly on Rita's. "Chérie," she began. "You have to know something. Sami has been getting ready to start his graduate work at AUB for three years now. It's, how do you say, a joke around town. 'Oh, have you heard Sami is about to start at AUB?' It's what he says to feel more respectable about himself. The truth is, he lives on his family's money and he . . ." Salma trailed off, shrugged. "You know, he enjoys himself. Long nights out drinking and dancing, talking politics and books, sleeping late, Paris or New York or skiing for a week here and there to break up the monotony of Beirut."

Salma shrugged again, lit a cigarette, as though to signal that she'd painted her picture. "I'm not saying it's wrong, per se, but you should know. That's his life."

Rita laughed defensively. "That sounds like your life, too!"

Salma gasped slightly, sat up. "That's very unfair," she said. "You know I'm always working on stories. Not everyone can go to Harvard and then bounce right into one of the best papers in the world."

Now it was Rita's turn to be stung. She pursed her lips, but hesitated before speaking. "I'm sorry," she finally said. "I didn't mean to say you don't work. I know you work. I see you."

"And it's not like the States here," Salma persisted. "Not everyone gets their own place right out of uni. People live with their parents until they get married, and sometimes even then. And they help out at home in different ways."

Rita was chastened. "I know." And she did. To know the Middle East was to understand this thick-as-thieves quality of extended families—tribes, really—this prioritizing of clan over one's individual ambitions or desires, even into the upper reaches of the bourgeoisie. It had been a mark of her own family once, something that had weakened in the passage of time between her father's generation and her own, somewhere in the interval between the 1950s and the twenty-first century.

"Anyway, darling," continued Salma, "I'm just saying, enjoy Sami but don't have any illusions about him. He'll probably go on being your househusband for as long as you want him to."

They laughed together, having lightened the air between them. "That may not be so bad!" Rita mused. "At least for now."

Later that day, she worked with the *Standard*'s Middle East team filing that night's story: U.N. inspectors had finally arrived in Iraq to search for weapons of mass destruction. Then she leaned back at her work desk for her weekly call to her mother.

"Can you call me back in ten minutes, honey?" Mary Jo answered. "I'm shopping for Thanksgiving and just got home with all the groceries. Eight bags."

"Sure." Rita hung up. Keenly, she felt a stab of desire to be back in Boston, to crunch leaves underfoot and feel a cold snap. In Beirut in mid-November it was still balmy enough most days to swim in the Mediterranean up the coast at Batroun. She also missed her mother's rough, salty affection.

"That's better," said her mother, ten minutes later. "I'm sitting down with a nice cup of tea now and can enjoy you. So tell me everything."

"All's well," Rita began. "Just the usual. Busy. Iraq, Iraq, Iraq. That's the main thing. Then the Israelis and the Palestinians. Beirut is stable, as usual. I hired a driver last weekend to visit Dad's family's old village up in the mountains, Chartoun." Not having mentioned Sami yet to her mother, she didn't add that he had accompanied her and done a good deal of the translating with the locals. "So pretty up there, and the people are so nice. They had me in for coffee, and we looked at old pictures together. It was nice but I think they still think I want to take away their land."

"Ah," her mother chuckled. "Dad and I will have to get there soon."

"That would be amazing." But that's all Rita said. For eighteen months, she'd been trying to get her family to come visit her, but they always claimed they were too busy, that they'd make the trip the following year. She sensed no great desire on her father's part to see the land he was from. He'd talked about doing so a great deal in the 1970s and 1980s, during the civil war, but seemed to have lost interest in the 1990s, when it actually became possible, and dropped the subject entirely after 9/11, contenting himself with dispatches from his daughter. Her father didn't like her being posted so far away and wanted the *Standard* to post her in its Washington bureau—a move that Rita told him was probably many years from happening. The people at the Washington bureau paid their dues elsewhere first, scattered around the globe.

"What about on your side of the world?" Rita asked her mother now.

"Well," she began. Rita could hear her pausing to sip tea. "Speaking of Iraq, guess who's joining the army?"

"I have no idea." She couldn't think of anyone she knew from high school or college who would do such a thing.

"Your cousin Bobby."

Rita paused briefly, stunned. "*What?*"

"He's joining the army. He signed up last week."

.   "I thought he was becoming an electrician!" Bobby had barely graduated from high school and, afterward, working at some kind of customer-service phone job out of a converted factory in Lawton, had started talking about going to a technical institute. But Rita had not followed him closely in the past decade. At Harvard and then afterward, when she was working her butt off as an intern and then a junior reporter at the *Standard* in New York, she'd drifted out of her childhood closeness with him. A gulf grew between them. Encounters at family holidays took on an awkward, rote quality, with him making the usual gibes about her being too fancy-pants for him with her Cambridge and then Manhattan life.

"Oh, shut up! You don't change," she'd respond lamely, feeling both shamed and irritated. "How about you, what's up with you?"

"Oh, you know, nothing special," he'd respond with forced cheer, in his martyr's voice. "Just tryna get by here in the Merrimack Valley on a high school degree. Workin' for the weekend and that kinda shit."

And she would smile uncomfortably. How could they have once been so close and now have so little to say to each other?

So now her mother said: "That was his plan, but then 9/11 happened, and you know how he's been since then."

It was true, Rita conceded. After 9/11, he'd started forwarding to her and everyone else he knew those stupid, patriotic, anti-Muslim stock e-mails: cartoons of Uncle Sam standing up to a wild-eyed, turbaned Taliban caricature; THESE COLORS DON'T RUN emblazoned beneath the American flag; that sort of thing. Or, worse, saccharine anecdotes about 9/11 cleanup crews finding crucifixes or images of Christ's face etched among the mangled ruins. The whole Irish side of her family had gone in this direction after the towers came down—a development of some embarrassment for Mary Jo who, when her own husband and kids mocked the knee-jerk patriotism of her siblings, would merely shake her head and say, "They're very traditional." Mary Jo had married up and out of the reflexive, defensive love of cops, country, and pope that marked families like the one she'd come from, whether they hailed from Lawton or Worcester or Southie or Revere. She still went to church on

weekends—alone, her own husband and family being too busy or indifferent to accompany her—but she was skeptical about what the priests
said, especially with the sprawling sexual-abuse scandal that had broken
in greater Boston the past year. "I have my own version of my faith,"
was how she would justify her church attendance when Rita would ask
her how she could still support the archdiocese after all she knew. "It's
personal. And believe me, I wasn't naïve all those years about the priests."

So now Rita said to her mother, considerably upset, "I can't believe
he's signing up now, of all times! If we weren't facing a war and he were
just going for the free education, fine. But now? He's gonna die!"

"Rita, don't say that! You don't know that."

"He's gonna get sent either to Afghanistan or to Iraq as soon as
we start that stupid war. And we *are* starting that war. I predict before
the end of the year."

"You really think so?" Her mother's tone softened. "I don't know
what to think from the news."

Rita lowered her voice, careful in case others might still be in the
bureau. "Everything you're seeing now with the weapons inspections
and the talks is just a charade," she said. "This administration wants to
go to war, and they're just going through the necessary paces."

Mary Jo was silent a moment on the other end. "God help us,"
she finally said.

"Exactly."

"Well." Mary Jo paused again. "Maybe you can talk to your cousin
when you come home for Christmas. You are coming home, right? It's
hard enough not having you here for Thanksgiving."

"I'm gonna try. So what's the latest with Ally? I haven't talked to
her in two weeks."

"She's goin' steady with that fellow Gary you met last time."

"Oh yeah?" Rita suppressed her disappointment. She'd found
Gary insufferably dull and even borderline offensive in his remarks, like
the one about Condoleezza Rice being "no Rembrandt," as though he
were anything more scintillating than an average white guy in Dock-
ers who worked in a tech pavilion on Route 128. Rita wanted more

for her sister, but she also had to admit that Ally didn't necessarily. Like her own father, Rita sometimes imposed her own standards of excellence on others.

So while her mother recounted a dull-sounding getting-to-know-you dinner with Gary's parents, she turned over in her head the idea of telling her mother about Sami. Doing so would mean admitting to herself that she was taking Sami slightly more seriously than his current role—which Salma dubbed HWB (houseboy with benefits)—might suggest. She was suddenly a bit surprised to hear herself ask, "So, Mom? How would you feel if I brought someone home for Christmas?"

Her mother stopped short. "What? Who? Your friend Selma?"

"Salma, Ma. Like Salma Hayek."

"Sorry, honey. You know I've struggled my whole life with those kinda names."

"No, Ma. Not Salma. She has her own family here. It's a guy."

Rita waited patiently through the inevitable pause. "A guy? Someone you're involved with?"

"Yes. The past few months. A great guy. He's a grad student at the American University of Beirut." (Rita allowed herself this half lie.) "His name's Sami. But spelled *S-A-M-I* here. Anyway—I don't know, I just thought I'd invite him home with me. If you're okay with that."

Another pause. "I guess you'd want him to stay in your old room with you?"

Rita was glad her mother couldn't see her blush. "Or maybe in Ally's old room since she has a full bed?"

"Well," her mother mused. "Lemme talk to your father about it." She paused. "Is he a Muslim?"

"What does that matter?" Rita snapped. "God, you sound like Bobby."

"I wasn't saying anything bad about it!" her mother protested. "I was just curious."

"Well, no, for your information, his family isn't Muslim, they're Orthodox Christian. Do you feel better now?"

"Oh, Rita, stop it," her mother snapped.

"They're Palestinian Christians who left Palestine for Lebanon a long time ago, before Israel officially formed, but he grew up mostly in Paris during the Lebanese war. And now he's back—like a lot of people."

"Oh!" her mother repeated, brighter still. Rita's mother loved Paris, an upscale affectation that Rita found amusing. Mary Jo had made her husband, who was indifferent to the idea of a vacation that didn't involve golf and the beach, take her there twice. Before each trip, she had assiduously practiced her beginning French with audiotapes.

"Ha. I knew the Paris thing would impress you."

"You know, you can be a very sharp-tongued little girl. You always have been. You get it from your Aunt Nancy."

This just made Rita laugh harder. Her mother disliked her Aunt Nancy, her father's forbidding second sister, after Irene. "I love you, Ma."

"Sometimes I wonder."

She brought Sami home. His own family was atheistic and indifferent to Christmas anyway, though his mother was disappointed he would not be in Paris at that time and made him promise to come in January or February.

"I don't really have the money right now for the ticket," he'd first said when Rita proposed the idea. "And it'll be expensive so close to the date."

"I'll buy your ticket." She'd asked herself if this was wrong, then decided it wasn't. She, after all, had invited him. And she felt it was worth it. She was always the single sister, the single cousin at holidays, "the career woman" too busy for a relationship, and she was tired of it. He was handsome and sophisticated, and she wanted to show him off. So she'd buy his ticket. But then she was extremely puzzled, but also touched, when he spent what had to be close to a thousand dollars on a case each of arak, Ksara wine, and olive oil to ship ahead to her family as gifts, not to mention dozens of tea towels made by artisan women in Byblos. She'd been on continuous deadline right up until seven hours before their flight and had had no time to do her own gift shopping.

"Ahlan wa sahlan!" her father greeted Sami at Boston's Logan Air-port, giving him three kisses, which she thought was adorable, her father trying to show his familiarity with the old country when he'd never set foot there. Sami greeted him in kind and also embraced her mother, when Mary Jo had merely held out a hand for a shake, which prompted from her a startled laugh and a vaguely reproving, "Oh my!" In the car, Rita shyly held Sami's hand in the back seat, as though to reassure him, while her mother ran down who would and would not be coming for Christmas dinner. They pulled off the highway into Mendhem, its white clapboard homes framed by black shutters, electric candles in the windows. A twenty-five-foot fir, encased in lights, stood on the town common, not far from the white spire of the Unitarian church.

"Such a pretty American town," noted Sami. "Like in a movie."

"You have to say it like a local and say it's *wicked chahming*," in-structed Rita.

"*Wicked chahming*."

Rita and her parents laughed. "You still sound like you're from the Far East," said Mary Jo jovially.

"Ma!" Rita rolled her eyes for Sami, who squeezed her hand.

Her family loved Sami. "He's so handsome!" Ally whispered to her the next day at dinner. "Hang on to him!"

Sami, Rita noted relievedly, had muted his tendency to play the smirking provocateur and seemed content to act the courteous, curious guest, dutifully asking her relatives all manner of questions about their lives and interests. He successfully feigned interest in Ally's exhaustive enumeration of the benefits of Pilates, her new obsession.

"What do you think of my family?" she asked later, when they'd slipped out of the house for a quick private walk (and, for Sami, a smoke) on the edge of the country road at the top of the driveway.

"They're lovely," he said. "They've come a long way from the mountains, haven't they?"

She laughed lightly. "They have no connection to that. They're New Englanders. Their life is work, family, the beach, and the Red Sox. And not even necessarily in that order."

"What do they think about your fascination with the old country?"

She stole a puff from his cigarette, then exhaled the smoke in a plume mixed with condensed breath into the cold evening air. "I think they wonder why I want to live in a war zone with bad Internet. And it doesn't matter how many times I tell them it's not a war zone anymore, because in pictures, it can still look pretty beat up, as beautiful as it is to me. Let's face it."

Sami gestured around at the winding country road, the large homes set far back from the street, the Volvos and Saabs nestled in expansive driveways, the Christmas lights twinkling from windows and wound around shrubbery. "Not a perfect picture like this."

She took another drag on his cigarette. "I'll get them there eventually, and they'll see how beautiful it is. My goal is to get my father up to the Qadisha Valley."

Sami smiled and put an arm around her. "So many goals!" he exclaimed.

On Christmas Day, extended family poured into their house—all the Lebanese aunties, uncles, and cousins, and about half the Irish ones, too. On such occasions, Rita was not a foreign correspondent on a career fast track; she was merely a woman, who, along with her mother, sister, and aunts, was expected to help expedite sixteen appetizers, then a vast dinner including both ham (Irish) and lamb (Lebanese), then about fourteen desserts, for a crowd that this year, at its peak, totaled forty-one. Meanwhile, her father relegated himself to the showier tasks of carving the meats and making sure everyone's wineglass was filled. Yearly, Rita and Ally rolled their eyes over this gendered division of labor, but, out of loyalty to their mother, they did not protest it.

All of this meant that Rita had to leave Sami to his own devices for much of the afternoon. So when she looked for him, having completed her share of clearing and washing in the kitchen and, wineglass in hand, finally ready to relax, she found him in a corner, chatting with Bobby, whom she'd wanted to talk to all day. She felt slightly unnerved to see her cousin talking to Sami.

Bobby grinned widely when he saw her coming. "They finally let you out of the kitchen?" he cracked. Then he turned to Sami. "My cuz gets a rude awakening when she comes home and finds out that women's lib never happened."

She smiled and shook her head at him. He would never change! Here he was, twenty-seven, and he was still that brat who'd been her little brother in the absence of a real one. "Well, it was great to see you in there with us, cuz, pitching in and doing your part for gender equality," she tossed back.

He cackled. "Hey, I was entertaining your boyfriend!"

Sami looked up, pleased. "Oh, you told him I was your boyfriend?"

"His words, not mine," Rita said, sitting down. But she made a point of putting an arm around Sami and pecking him lightly on the lips as she did so. And at that very moment she caught what she was nearly certain was a flash of rage in Bobby's eyes.

Or had she just imagined—feared—that?

"I heard some news about you," she ventured.

"Oh yeah?" There was the old Bobby grin. "What's that?"

"That you're joining the army."

"Joined," he corrected her. "I start BCT in South Carolina in six weeks. I'm in the gym every day getting jacked!" He flexed his biceps with clownish machismo.

She raised her eyebrows, felt her lips tighten. "Bobby," she pleaded. "Why now of all times? We're going to go into Iraq and you're gonna get sent there."

"Why now? Of *course* now. That's why I joined."

"But—" she sighed, stopped herself. He just looked at her, then he glanced meaningfully at Sami and then back at her.

But Sami had caught his glance. "Don't hold back because of me," he said. "I'm not in al-Qaeda, even if I look like I am."

All three of them laughed. "Half this fucking house looks like they could be," Bobby cracked.

"You are the worst!" Rita cried.

"No, but seriously," Bobby continued. "We can't let this shit continue over there. If it happened once, it'll happen again if we don't stop it."

Rita put down her wineglass. "Oh please. You cannot really believe that Iraq is a threat. You can't believe that bullshit."

"He's a fucking evil fucker! He tortures his own people."

"A lot of dictators do! That is not a reason to invade. If it were, we should be invading eight, nine countries right now."

Bobby just sat back and folded his arms over his chest. "They can't do what they did and just get away with it."

"I agree," Rita said, more calmly now. "That's why we're in Afghanistan. But doing what I do for a living, I feel pretty confident that Saddam had nothing to do with it. He's a two-bit tyrant from a poor country. Bobby, honestly."

Bobby looked from Rita to Sami, then back again. "What do you think?" he asked Sami.

Sami considered, sipped his wine. "I think if this is something you feel strongly about, you should go," he said.

Rita looked at Sami, mouth open. "You have got to be kidding me!"

But Sami just sat there and shrugged. Bobby thwacked him lightly on the arm. "Thank you!" Then to Rita: "Hey, maybe you'll get sent there too and we'll see each other. We can hang out with the camels."

Rita groaned. "This is not even funny," she said. Then, suddenly feeling too great a rush—of frustration with Bobby, of extreme irritation with Sami for egging him on—she abruptly stood, grabbed her wine, and walked out of the room. Back in the kitchen, she found Ally making coffee.

"What is it?" Ally asked, when she saw the look on her sister's face.

"I just can't believe Bobby is joining the military," she said, and then surprised herself by bursting into tears. "What an idiot!"

"Oh, sweetie!" Ally embraced her, then whispered in her ear: "I know. But that's Ma's side of the family, right? You're the one who always said they were Archie Bunkers."

"I know," Rita snuffled. "It's just," she added quietly, "he's my baby cousin, and I don't want him to die."

At that moment, her mother walked into the kitchen. "What the hell is this?" she asked, seeing her two daughters in a tearful embrace.

"Rita's upset because Bobby's joining the army and she thinks he's gonna die in Iraq," Ally explained flatly.

Mary Jo stood there for a moment, looking dumbfounded, then she tenderly stroked Rita's hair, tucked a tendril back behind her ear. "She pretends that she doesn't care about her family, living halfway around the world, but she really does. Deep down."

Rita and Ally looked at each other, then burst into laughter. "You always know just what to say, Ma," Rita observed.

Later that night, as they prepared for bed in Ally's girlhood bedroom, Rita said to Sami: "I can't believe you said that to Bobby."

"Said what?" Sami's bare back, dusted in black hair, was to her. Rita loved how it tapered to his lean waist.

"That you think he should join the military if it means that much to him. I was trying to talk him into quitting before he actually starts."

Now he turned to her. "I would not discourage any young American patriot from bringing democracy and more McDonald's and Starbucks to the Middle East," he said, seeming preternaturally calm. "We savages must be civilized."

"I knew it!" she cried, heedless that her parents in the room down the hall might hear them. "You were just fucking with him, about something so serious!"

"And he came away twice as confident, because he got a blessing from an actual Arab."

She paused, stymied. She agreed with Sami. If Bobby were anyone else, she'd hold him in contempt. But, of course, he was not.

"He's also going because the military will open up opportunities for him," she said. But she immediately heard how feeble she sounded.

"Such a great reason to invade another country that's done nothing wrong," said Sami.

She flopped on the bed, defeated. "I know. Forget I said that. The whole thing just makes me sad."

He stretched out alongside her, kissed her tenderly. "You just love your family, that's all."

She kissed him back. "You understand that, right?"

"They're wonderful."

"No, but I mean, you would feel the same way about your brother or sister or cousin, right?"

After a long interval, he said: "I don't believe in tribes. When we only put the tribe first, we don't think about the whole. Look at Lebanon. It'll never evolve as a government, because it's all just tribes."

"I know what you're saying." And Rita did. She witnessed firsthand in Beirut the daily horse-trading, the favor-swapping among cousins, and cousins of cousins, and how it reduced the country's parliament to little more than a joke. "But family is a hard thing to rise above."

This made him smile indulgently and pull her close. "Let's do it in your sister's bed," he whispered.

"If you're really quiet."

"I'm always quiet."

"Not true."

The last thing her father said to her before dropping them off at Logan was, "Tell your job to put you in D.C. Get out of there before it's too late. Stop making Mom and me worry."

"Daddy." She hugged and kissed him. "I still have a lot of time to put in. Nobody comes back to D.C. until they've put in major time overseas." She didn't tell him that there was no way in hell she would pass up the opportunity to report from a war zone; it was the mark of authenticity, the stepping-stone that made a journalist's career. "Beirut is secure. You'll come, right?"

He ignored her request. "What if you have to go to Iraq?"

"We don't know that yet." Though she all but did.

She and Sami flew to New York to ring in 2003 with friends, including Rima, Sami's investment banker cousin from Dubai, who lived in a new high-rise downtown and carried an Hermès bag that looked like it cost three thousand dollars. Rita saw friends from Harvard, some of whom were uniformly in awe of the fact that she was based in the Middle East, some of whom had already spent hours in the cold New York streets protesting the impending war and intended to do more of the same.

Over lunch, one such friend, Rishi, whom she'd worked with at the *Crimson*, the Harvard daily, and who now worked for an affordable-housing nonprofit in Brooklyn, kept giving her what she felt was a regretful, recriminating look. At one point, he actually looked at her, twisted his mouth, and shook his head slightly.

"What *is* it?" she finally asked.

He shook his head again. "You know that your paper is colluding in this war, right?"

It obviously wasn't the first time she'd heard this argument. "I don't agree with that," she said staunchly. "Every day over there, we are reporting out the facts as they emerge, and that includes the tremendous opposition of average Middle Easterners to U.S. invasion." That much was true. She'd spent many hours talking to people throughout the region about their horror at the prospect of troops coming in. But she still couldn't believe how much like boilerplate she sounded.

Rishi laughed sharply. "You are not pushing back on this crap intel about weapons that Bush keeps pushing! You're just putting it out there like a press release."

"Well, (a), I don't think that's entirely true, and (b), that's not me. That's the team in New York and Washington. We have a very different perspective from where we're sitting. Believe me. Palestinians I talk to think the whole thing is a Zionist plot. So there's obviously a multiplicity of perspectives."

"And what's yours?"

She smirked. "If I expressed it, I'd be fired. We're supposed to be blank slates."

Rishi smirked back, again shook his head slightly. "All right, then. So tell me about your love life instead."

She was glad he'd changed the subject. She proceeded to tell him about Sami.

Two nights later, she and Sami were back in Beirut, jet-lagged. Salma had them to dinner at her parents' sprawling, balconied Achrafieh apartment, all low-slung mid-century furniture and abstract art on the walls. Salma's parents, Nicolas and Hélène, were older versions of Salma, stylish people who had Jimi Hendrix and jazz on the stereo and seemed always to have a drink in one hand. At one point, they passed around a hashish joint, which Rita—startled by the thought of getting high with a friend's parents—declined but Sami accepted. At a certain point, everyone moved to the enormous dining-room table. Cherry, the family's tiny Filipina maid and cook, who lived in a small, windowless room in the back and wore a pasted-on smile that did little to offset wary eyes, served a dinner of fattoush, lamb, and roasted cauliflower.

"It took me three months to show her how to roast cauliflower so it's not too hard and not too burned," Hélène announced in a French-Arabic hybrid, in full voice, as Cherry spoke neither language, only Tagalog and English. "After our last cook left. And I am proud to say that she finally found the right balance." Hélène smiled approvingly at Cherry, who seemed to understand she was being spoken of and smiled back deferentially.

"But you would not believe some of the cauliflower we had to suffer through," Hélène added.

Rita wanted to ask Hélène why she didn't just roast the cauliflower herself, rather than put so much effort into teaching someone else, but of course she did not. She knew by now that one of the favorite pastimes of Beirut's rich ladies was training their cooks, barking at cowed Syrian, Sri Lankan, or Filipina women in sweat suits as they labored to master the intricacies of preparing a fluffy tabooleh, baking a perfectly crispy manouche, or stuffing a tiny, perfect, succulent grape leaf.

Salma raised a palm. "Mama, please. You are making us look so bourgeois in front of my friends."

Hélène laughed. "We actually live very modestly compared to some people we know."

Nicolas turned to Rita, knife in one hand and fork in the other. "It's true," he said. "By the standards of our neighborhood, we are very moyen."

"That means middle class," Sami murmured to Rita, nudging her under the table.

"What I really want to know," Salma enunciated in her friends' direction, as though eager to move on before her parents further incriminated themselves, "is how your American holiday went. Sami, did you successfully integrate yourself into the Khoury family?"

"He was a huge hit," Rita answered for him. "And for the most part, he behaved himself."

"I always behave!" Sami protested.

"Oh please," said Salma. "Spare us."

"But he really did, for the most part," insisted Rita. "Everyone thought he was very handsome and sweet and charming." She beamed at him as she said it.

Sami laughed lightly. "Even your patriotic cousin Bobby?"

"Oh, Bobby," echoed Rita. She wished Sami hadn't mentioned him. "Well . . ." she began weakly.

"Bobby is *very* excited about going to fight the terrorists in Iraq," said Sami.

Hélène perked up. "Is he really? But service isn't mandatory in America, is that right?"

"No, it's not," Rita said. "But he suddenly seems to have found a calling."

"He's going to be a freedom fighter for the Iraqi people," Sami added dryly.

An awkward silence settled over the table. Rita glanced quickly at Sami as though to reprove him, but he was concentrating on his plate, a vaguely smug look on his face.

"Well," Nicolas finally said, rather grandly. "The fact is this. If the Americans and whoever else they can get to go with them can do this right, they're probably doing the country a huge favor. The people are too scared of Saddam to rise up and get rid of him themselves. They're traumatized."

No one said anything. Rita supposed she could quote the dozens of military specialists and Arabists she'd either interviewed or read about, countless experts who knew the region well and said that Saddam was like the lid on Pandora's box, which the United States removed at its peril. But she did not. She felt awkward about challenging Nicolas in front of Salma.

She didn't have to, though. Hélène, instead, shook her head. "War is just stupid," she said. She'd stayed in Beirut, Rita remembered, through most of the civil war, somehow maintaining her well-tended life amid the bombs and checkpoints. "Stupid, stupid. It ruins everything nice."

She seemed upset now, and Nicolas reached across the table and took her jeweled hand.

In January, in journalistic circles in Beirut, all the talk over dinner or drinks was about the impending war, the logistics and intricacies of settling in Baghdad before the invasion occurred in order to cover it once it started. The largest outlets, like the *Standard*, were renting villas not far from Saddam's Republican Palace on the Tigris, pouring obscene sums into fleets of armed security men, fixers, drivers, and translators, not to mention insurance, the extortionate visa fees Saddam's government demanded of the foreign press, plus a great deal of general wheel-greasing along the way. Meanwhile, smaller outlets were setting up correspondents at the Brutalist, bunker-like Al-Rasheed Hotel, with its swimming pool and landscaped gardens, which suddenly seemed to be the only word on the lips of every reporter or human-rights worker Rita knew. She grew edgy.

"I want to get to Baghdad," she told her editor in D.C. by phone. "I need to cover this. How many correspondents do you have who actually speak Arabic?"

"Sit tight," her editor said. "We're working on it, but it's a huge puzzle to put together, who to put there, who to keep where they are. Every single staff member we send, we're talking like another hundred thousand dollars in various expenses. It's insane."

So she sat tight, covering from Beirut what by now seemed like the run-up to an inevitable invasion. But her anxiety mounted and she began smoking four, five cigarettes a day, cadging them from colleagues or from Sami. Too many colleagues whom she liked just fine but still privately considered rivals were leaving for Baghdad or had already left. Almost every night, postdeadline plans seemed to consist of good-bye drinks for people who'd received their war-zone training, flak jackets, helmets, and tickets for a flight to Amman, where they huddled with other journos and aid workers, awaiting the formation of an SUV convoy and a complement of steel-nerved drivers for the fifteen-hour trek over the border and across an endless, desolate expanse of desert to Baghdad. Tales were rife of drivers gunning their vehicles at breakneck speed to avoid being ambushed by thieves, Iraq's legendary Ali Babas, who would strip passengers of the tens of thousands of American dollars of survival cash they were bringing into Iraq, which did not take credit cards and where no one got anything without hefty bribes. Thieves would also pinch laptops, satellite phones, and every single other piece of equipment or gear one might be carrying that could command black-market interest.

But then it would be only a matter of days before Rita would hear through the grapevine that the members of the latest convoy were successfully installed in their villa, or in a suite of rooms at the Al-Rasheed, and her impatience flared. Her daily cigarette intake rose to eight, then twelve or thirteen.

"Aren't you worried about missing me?" Sami asked her late one night after he'd finally pried her away from her laptop and into bed.

She would indeed miss him, she knew. He had brought comfort and fun to the slim margins of her Beirut life that weren't occupied by work. It was hard for her to criticize him much for what seemed like an extremely slow (perhaps even fully stalled) uptake into graduate studies, because she benefited from his lack of a real professional life. He spent much of his time taking care of their apartment, improving it, greeting her arrival home with food and wine, organizing all sorts of administrative matters for her like the paying of bills, sweet-talking the concierge for favors or repairs, or securing drivers for weekend trips to the beach or the mountains. She'd never had someone in her life like that, at least not since her mother. Far in the back of her head, she wondered whether there was something fundamentally wrong with dating a man who seemed to have no ambition but to drink, smoke, read, argue about politics, and take care of her. Then she would tell herself to relax, that the reverse gender arrangement had existed for centuries and nobody had questioned it.

So she replied, enlacing herself with him: "Yes, I will really miss you if I go. But I have to cover this. This is the kind of thing that gets you made bureau chief eventually."

He shuddered in a parody of arousal. "So ambitious!"

Then, in early February, the day after Colin Powell went before the United Nations with his charts showing maps of Iraq's alleged weapons of mass destruction, holding up a vial of anthrax that he said symbolized far greater stores squirreled away by the rogue regime, Rita got the call she'd been waiting for.

"Can you be ready to go to Amman for war-zone training in a week?" her editor asked. "You'd spend about ten days there, then get in a convoy to Baghdad. You'll live and work out of the paper's villa in a team under Rick Garza, who's already there."

Her heart leaped. Ricardo Garza was her idol. He'd been covering Middle Eastern wars and conflicts for the *Standard* since the 1970s, spoke three Arabic dialects fluently, and was generally considered among the top five best-connected and brainiest foreign-affairs writers in the anglophone world. Rita had longed to be him in high school and college and had written three separate papers on books he had published.

"Thank you for coming through for me," she told her editor. "I promise I won't let you down."

Her editor laughed. "More than anything you have to promise to keep yourself alive. There is a huge discipline to taking care of yourself while reporting from a war zone. Rick will show you."

"I hear you."

"You'll get more details from us tomorrow."

She put down the phone and slipped away from her desk to the balcony with a cigarette. Blessedly, nobody was there at the moment, so she could light her cigarette and savor her triumph, staring out over the Brutalist and bombed-out rooftops of Beirut. *I just climbed another rung*, she thought. No foreign correspondents were A-rank until they'd served in a war.

Back at her desk, she called Salma first. "I'm going to Iraq," she nearly whispered, so that no one would hear. "Well, to Jordan first. In a week."

Salma drew in breath. "Oh my God." She paused. "Aren't you terrified?"

"I'm excited!" Rita whispered. "I've been hoping for this."

Salma was silent on the other end for several seconds. "It's scary," she finally said.

"We get so much training, and we're in a villa with a wall around it that has security twenty-four-seven."

"No. I meant the whole thing. The fact that it's happening."

Rita was taken aback. "Oh. I mean, yes." She felt embarrassed that she'd not quite known what Salma had meant.

Salma remained silent a few seconds longer. "Well! We'll have to have a good-bye party. At Barometre, obviously."

"That would be nice."

"I'll miss you!"

"I'll miss you! But I'll come back to Beirut."

"No, of course!"

Again, Salma went silent. Rita hadn't considered that the call might be so awkward. She'd merely felt charged up.

"Have you told the househusband yet?" Salma finally asked.

"No. Not even my family. I called you first."

"When are you going to tell him?"

"Tonight, I suppose. I guess now he'll have no excuse not to go to school."

"Chérie, please. I wouldn't count on it."

They both laughed. Rita realized with a sudden pang that she truly was going to miss Salma.

She waited, in fact, to tell Sami until later that evening, when she met him at Mayrig, a very rustic Armenian restaurant in a series of stone-walled rooms that had just opened in the Gemmayze district not far from the port. Sami had been wanting to go there, particularly to have a certain kind of kibbe stuffed with dried sour cherries and yogurt.

"So, habibi, I found out I'm going to Iraq today," she said bluntly, after they'd ordered wine.

He looked up from the menu. For a moment, she thought she saw a flash of deep hurt and betrayal in his eyes, of raw fear, before he seemed to rearrange his face, raise his eyebrows. "Really? Wow. Well, bravo. That's your dream."

She shrugged slightly, embarrassed. "It's a big deal."

"Are you going to be one of the lucky embedded reporters and get to experience it all just like an American soldier?" His tone was acid. Only a few days before, the U.S. military had said it would allow certain journalists to live and travel with certain units, fully trained and armored for a war zone. The announcement was controversial, many saying there was no way journalists could be neutral or get out the whole story if they were bonding 24-7 with American soldiers.

"No," she said. "We'll actually be in Baghdad before the war starts, probably. I'm going to Amman first for training."

"Jordan." He rolled his eyes. "Such a good little friend to the Americans."

She'd expected he'd not be happy to hear the news, but not quite this much. She said nothing.

"When do you leave?" he asked.

"In a week." She took his hand across the table.

He didn't pull it away. To her dismay, she saw tears well in his eyes before he ashamedly brushed them away.

"We made such a nice home together," he said.

"Sweetheart, I'll be back! This conflict can't last that long. Whether it's right or wrong to go in—"

"Well, it's wrong, for one thing!" he interjected.

"I agree," she said impulsively.

"You do?"

Then she shook her head and flicked her hand, as though to undo what she'd just said. She practiced what she thought of as "opinion discipline," in which she aimed to let a small downturn of her mouth signal feelings about matters she was not, as a reporter, supposed to express outright.

"Aside from that," she continued, "Iraq can't put up a fight. It can't go on that long."

"It'll be a fucking mess, and you'll be stuck covering it for years."

"Impossible," she said. "They would rotate us in and out, they wouldn't keep one person there for longer than a few months. And I don't want to stay! You know I love Beirut. I love our life together. I love Joujou." That was the little yellow kitten they'd just adopted from a friend. She was fond of stroking Joujou while it lay on Sami's tummy when they watched TV together before bed. Sometimes she forgot whether she was stroking Sami or the kitten.

Her words seemed to soothe him, before he sighed again. "What am I going to do with myself when you're gone?"

"You can start classes at AUB."

"It's too late. The term's already begun."

"Well." She paused. "You can go see your parents."

"Paris is disgusting in winter."

Now she was exasperated. "Sami," she said sternly. She was about to say *Be a grown-up*, but she caught herself. It was implicit in her tone, anyway. Then, of course, she softened, as she always did. Treating him like a little boy was just part of their dynamics, whether it was right or wrong. She squeezed his hand. "I'll be back."

He looked up, his large, green eyes veiled by his long lashes. "You promise?"

"I promise."

After she completed the emotionally arduous task of telling her family the news, after she packed, after she was sent off in a long alcoholic evening with colleagues and friends, she flew to Amman, from which she had reported before, where the *Standard* had a bureau slightly larger than the one in Beirut and she lived out of the Marriott, utterly anodyne except for its opulent lobby. Amman, prosperous and secure, full of Westerners and Middle Easterners who worked in banking or real estate or international aid and development, felt a bit like Beirut in places—if Beirut hadn't been beaten up in a civil war for fifteen years—without the romantic proximity to the sea.

She spent the first half of every day in sessions with a team of cheerful Jordanian and British former military officials, employees of a private international conflict-zone preparation corporation, who walked her and about a dozen other journalists bound for Iraq through the rudiments of strapping into a Kevlar helmet and flak jacket, donning a special jumpsuit and mask in the event of chemical attacks, how to behave if kidnapped or held hostage, and what to do if one suddenly found one's or another's limb hanging by a thread. Then, after several hours of such exercises, accompanied by a great deal of gallows humor, she'd walk to the *Standard*'s offices and jump into that day's multi-bureau, multi-time-zone coverage of the countdown to inevitable war, including the likelihood that the United States, England, and Spain would go ahead and lead an invasion without authorization from the United Nations and over the objections of France and other countries.

She was booked into an SUV convoy to Baghdad set to leave on Saturday, March 8, when Rick Garza, the bureau chief in Baghdad, called her. She still could not quite believe that she now communicated with one of her college idols as a daily matter of course. She'd told him as much and he'd laughed.

"You're gonna sit tight in Jordan for now, actually," he said now. "We're getting ominous hints from the Information Ministry flacks here that journos should get out before the invasion. They keep saying they can't promise us security. We keep asking them why, but they won't give us straight answers. We think they're trying to warn us about Saddam's guys trying to take us hostage, use us as human shields if troops try to take Baghdad. Already, most journos are packing up and leaving. It costs a fortune to hire a driver to Amman right now."

"No, you're kidding!" she cried, dismayed.

"I'm not. You'll have plenty of collegial company in Amman soon. I may leave soon, myself, at least for a while, and we can report together from there."

"But when can I finally get in?"

"Probably after the invasion, when we see how everything shakes out."

"You're kidding!" she said again. "I thought I was going to help cover it."

"I know." He sounded truly sorry for her. "It sucks. But it's always like this in a conflict zone, Rita. You have to play the safety thing by ear, day to day, based on what you know. You have to walk the line."

"I know," she said. She knew she should probably be relieved that she didn't have to go to Baghdad until the fighting was over and the country was under control. But that's not how she felt. She'd been psyching herself up for the journey for two weeks, and now she was crushed.

"Listen," Rick added. "At least when you get here, I have an amazing interpreter for you. We took him on about a week ago. His name's Nabil al-Jumaili. Sweet, sweet kid from Kadhimiya who went to Baghdad U, like all the smartest kids here, and he speaks amazing English. He reads in English constantly. We got him through his cousin, who's one of my interpreters. She's also amazing."

"That's great," Rita said. But she'd been only half listening. She was still sore about the delay.

He continued: "There's so many smart kids here dying for normal opportunities, to be part of the real world. It's like they've been living in an open-air prison all these years. That's a story you can definitely get started on when you get here."

CHAPTER SIX

NABIL AND RITA

(2003)

Nabil woke up tense, bolt upright, overalert, and unrested, as he had done nearly every morning since the night the bombings had started weeks ago. Those dull, concussive jolts rocked the ground under the house, even if they were miles away—which they generally were. Kadhimiya was a residential neighborhood, and most of the government buildings the U.S. planes targeted were closer to the center of the city. He heard a cock crowing two rooftops over and the twitter of birds outside his window, where sunshine poured in through the crosshatch pattern made by the electrical tape they'd put on all the windows of the house to prevent them from blowing out in the event of an explosion nearby.

Nabil sat up in bed, rubbed sleep from his eyes. It was another perfect early April morning in Baghdad, another day to witness the surreal spectacle: Massive concrete government edifices sporting gaping holes or half-collapsed into rubble or expelling wisps of black smoke; the charred carcasses of cars or tanks by the roadside; the American soldiers in endless convoys or manning checkpoints, where the faces of the white ones roasted pink in the sun under their camouflage Kevlar helmets, their eyes obscured by sunglasses and their cheeks bulging with

chewing tobacco. Baghdadi men in drab pants and soccer jerseys standing in long lines with empty blue plastic jugs as they waited for car oil,
younger men wheeling office chairs stacked with computers and desk
lamps through the streets as they picked clean the last bounty of the
looted ministry buildings, to the utter indifference of the U.S. soldiers.
The intermittent noise of bombs whizzing and then detonating, or the
rhythmic clack of machine-gun fire, either near or far. The countless
mangy dogs, cats, and sometimes donkeys that wandered through the
chaos, looking for food. All of which played out under a vast, flawless
blue spring sky and the best weather Iraq had to offer.

He was meeting her today for the first time: Miss Khoury. She'd
finally come in late last night from Amman. Mister Rick had said today
he'd start as her interpreter, with Ali, that young macho bodybuilder
from Al Sha'ab, as their driver.

He stared face-to-face with Younis Mahmoud, the football god,
who greeted him from the wall. It was the first face he saw every day,
just before he knelt for morning prayers, which he'd fallen into the habit
of saying again since just before the invasion. For that reason, he often
thought, with a private laugh, Younis Mahmoud might as well be God
to him. Then he dressed in his only fully clean shirt and pants, to make
a good impression; gelled his hair; and went into the kitchen to make
coffee, where he found Bibi at the table, making dolma, rolling grape
leaves around dollops of rice and lamb.

"Sabah el-kheir, Bibi," he mumbled.

"Sabah el-nour, habibi." She barely looked up from her work.

He watched her out of the corner of his eye while he brewed coffee
at the stove. She seldom left the house now unless she had to, too scared
of bombs and guns and thieves. He knew she missed her regular excur-
sions to the gold market, to marvel over some piece that she had no real
intention of buying, but that nonetheless gave her a fantasy to occupy
her mind and a feeling of having done something with her day. She was
mostly housebound and restless and depressed, like many women and
girls in Baghdad since the invasion, but at least now, with Saddam dead
or in hiding and his secret police dispersed, there was no fear in having a

satellite on the roof, and the TV options proliferated. Under virtual house arrest, the family spent days watching everything from Arabic-dubbed *Dallas* and *Melrose Place* to freewheeling Lebanese and Egyptian talk and entertainment shows to Al Jazeera, which Nabil found the greatest blessing. Before the invasion, one had to be so furtive to get any real news, any sense of what was really going on outside Baghdad as the coalition troops advanced, because the state TV network trumpeted only that Saddam's army was ready to annihilate the invaders. That certainly hadn't happened.

He poured coffee from the little metal pot into two cups for himself and Bibi, then sat next to her, tearing off a piece of bread on the table and spreading gaymar, soft white cheese, on it.

"You start with the new girl today, yes?" she asked him.

He grunted, his mouth full, and nodded his head.

"Al-Khoury. Arabiya?"

"Amrikiya-Lubnaniya."

Bibi raised her eyebrows. "Ya, na'am? Interesting."

"She's been in Beirut the past several months."

Bibi laughed. "I hope she likes Baghdad!"

Nabil laughed, too. If she'd gotten used to Lebanese beach resorts and nightclubs, all manner of beautiful people coming and going all the time, she was certainly in for a surprise. After a few minutes, he stood, kissed Bibi atop her head, and wished her a good day.

"And a safe day for you and all of us, God willing," she muttered, her fat fingers taking up the dolma again.

He found his father, nephew, and niece already in the living room, his father reading through a stack of the new newspapers that had proliferated since the invasion—a cacophony of unfettered opinion that had exploded since Saddam's fall. Ahmed and Rana were glued to *SpongeBob SquarePants*, laughing maniacally. The headmaster of their primary school had been shot dead en route to work two weeks ago by bandits who dragged his body out of his car and then drove off with the car, and the school had not reopened since. The primary school in Dora where his mother, Neda, taught was still functioning, even though about half the students were no-shows, their parents too scared to let them leave home.

So Nabil's father had been idling around the house, obsessively reading or watching the news; getting into minor tiffs with Bibi, his mother-
in-law; and trying to make himself useful by spending long afternoons in
traffic, pleading his way through American checkpoints in his best English,
to make runs for rations like soybean oil and flour or to visit friends or
relatives in the hospitals, their bodies burned or torn up by shrapnel, thanks
to their being in the wrong place at the wrong time after American fighter
jets acted on intel alleging that major weapons were stored there—intel
that was always bad but that nonetheless resulted in the destruction of a
neighborhood, leaving family members dead, mangled, or homeless, living
in crowded rooms with relatives or, worse, in tents alongside the rubble
heaps that had once been their homes. Iraq was free of Saddam, but it
was in a state of chaos, and nobody—least of all Nabil, who worked with
Americans and saw daily how efficient they could be when they really
wanted something done—could understand why the invaders had let it
happen. They'd had more than enough manpower to maintain electricity
and prevent looting, arson, and theft, but instead they'd mainly just stood
by and let all hell break loose.

Now his father rose. He'd lost weight from stress in the past several months, smoking far more than he should, and Nabil could again
see—ironically, he thought—traces of the handsome man his father,
Uthman al-Jumaili, had been back in the 1980s, the first decade of Saddam, when the family would pack picnics and head to Pig's Island in the
Tigris to rent paddleboats.

"I'll drive you to work," his father said.

"No, Baba. I'll catch the minivan."

"Khalas," his father snapped. "I'm driving you, and that's it. Why
do you want me to sit here picturing you in a minivan that gets caught
in a gunfight? At least this way if they fire on us, we go together."

Nabil smiled. "What a nice thought, Baba."

Ahmed looked up from the cartoon. "Ammo, have you seen a gunfight
yet?" Rarely allowed to leave the house or garden, even called down off
the roof at dusk, Ahmed was obsessed with whatever was going on out in
the streets of Baghdad, hyper-attuned to the noises of war in the distance.

Nabil scratched his head. "No, hamdullilah, but you can hear them everywhere."

In the old 1987 Toyota, Nabil's father played Iraqi news radio as they cruised down Fourteenth Ramadan Street, the commercial strip, toward Mansour, where the *Standard*'s armed villa was. The radio presenter was talking about how an American leader, this Paul Bremer, was planning to come soon to Iraq to oversee the transition of power from the Americans to the Iraqis.

Nabil laughed. "Baul Bremer," he repeated. "She can't pronounce the *p*." There was no *p* in the Arabic alphabet, and it was a source of hard-earned scorn among advanced English-speakers like him and Asmaa that most Arabs said things like "Bebsi" instead of Pepsi. Nabil was less likely to admit how he, himself, a few years before, had struggled to make the strange sound, as it felt the same against his lips as a *b*. Asmaa had drilled him for a week straight until she was satisfied that he could finally make the distinction.

Nabil's father just shook his head. "The transition," he repeated sardonically. "That's going well."

"They're going to be here forever."

"At least you and Asmaa will have work."

They both laughed.

They slowed along with the traffic, nearly coming to a standstill, which always made Nabil nervous. He glanced to the left and right, noticing other drivers doing the same. On the side of the broad, two-way boulevard that was Fourteenth Ramadan, he saw four men carrying furniture out of a storefront and into a white van. *Were they thieves?* he wondered. Then, as his father's car crawled forward, he saw, unmistakably, a pair of feet in beat-up loafers sticking out of the back of the van.

He jerked his head back to look straight ahead. "There's a dead body in that van," he said quietly to his father.

"Where?"

"Don't look. But in that white van those guys were loading."

His father was silent a moment. "Maybe it was just a guy sleeping."

"Not from the way the feet were positioned."

His father said nothing and turned onto Mansour Street, until the massive, unfinished Rahman Mosque loomed into view. It was one of Saddam's many monstrosities-in-progress, a sprawling concrete edifice in which large domes semi-encased smaller domes, like a hideous assemblage of Russian dolls or a villainous palace from the Star Wars series. Yet Nabil had to admit it exerted a strange fascination over him, as did many of Saddam's enormous monuments around Baghdad, all of them marked by gigantic renderings of swords and missiles, or of Saddam's own head soaring ten, twelve meters high. Nabil wondered what would happen to these markers of Saddam's obscene ego now that the man was either dead or, more likely, cowering in hiding somewhere.

His father pulled onto a palm-lined side street and stopped in front of the high-walled villa. A foreign ambassador who'd decamped for Europe as early as the previous December had sublet it to the *Standard* at an astronomical sum. Prior to the invasion, the *Standard*, like all foreign outlets in Baghdad, had had to shell out endless thousands of dollars in baksheesh to all sorts of Baath Party functionaries just to be in the country; to have drivers, translators, and the requisite government "minders" along on every story; to constantly renew visas. All that had deteriorated a few weeks ago when the Americans had finally taken over Baghdad and the tattered remains of the active Baath bureaucracy collapsed for good. The tables were suddenly turned, and now formerly officious Information Ministry hacks were all but begging foreign journalists to keep them on as freelance helpers.

"Good luck with your new lady boss," his father said, kissing him good-bye. "I'll pray for you until you come home tonight."

Nabil shook his head. "Ya, Baba," he merely said. "Let me know you got home safe." Then he stepped out of the car. Mohsen, one of the villa's three Kalashnikov-armed guards, greeted him through the gate, which he unlocked, letting Nabil into the well-tended garden, a sanctuary with lemon and date palm trees and not one but two of the requisite swinging love seats of the middle-class Baghdadi garden.

"She's waiting for you," Mohsen said. "Not so sexy, though."

Nabil merely shook his head and smiled as he passed.

Inside, "the bureau," as they'd renamed the villa, was buzzing as usual, its mix of about a dozen American, European, and Iraqi staffers propping their Thuraya satellite phones against their shoulders while they clicked and clacked at computers or scribbled into notebooks. Al Jazeera, BBC, and CNN played soundlessly on three different screens mounted on the wall, and Umm Nasim, the tiny black-eyed, black-veiled widow, a friend of Mohsen's grandmother, who now lived in a small room in the villa and cooked and cleaned, moved around the large room with a cart, serving tea, coffee, and bread and cheese—the morning routine.

"Where's Asmaa?" Nabil asked Umm Nasim as she handed him a small cup of her satisfyingly bitter coffee.

"She's out with Mister Rick at a press conference."

He nodded in acknowledgment as he sipped. "How did you sleep, Umm Nasim?"

She shook her head dolefully. "Not well. I could hear bombs all night, rat-tat-tat." She made the sound of gunfire. "Inshallah my son visits me today."

"Inshallah."

She trudged on with her cart.

A young woman in a white collared shirt like a man's, jeans, and Nikes, her dark curly hair pulled back in a sloppy bun, approached him, her arm outstretched, smiling. "You're Nabil?" she asked in Arabic. "I'm Rita. I've heard very much about you."

He shook her hand. Her Arabic sounded good, he noted, her American accent noticeable but not egregious. Still, he replied in English—that was his job, after all. "Thank you," he said. "I've heard much about you, too."

"How was the drive here today from Kadhimiya?" She now spoke English as well, and focused on him very intensely as she talked, her eyes boring straight into his. She clutched her Thuraya tightly, he noticed, as though she expected it to ring at any moment.

"Not very bad," he said. Then he lowered his voice. "But I swear to you I saw a dead body in the back of a van. On Fourteenth Ramadan Street. I saw the feet."

Her eyes widened, and her brow furrowed. "You sure it wasn't just someone lying down?"

"My father said that. And I said, no, not from the position of the feet."

"Hmph." She sighed lightly. "Well, I wouldn't be surprised. How has your family been?"

"We do not go out except for Asmaa and me, and my mother, to and from work. But despite that, we are okay."

"Hamdullilah."

He smiled slightly. "Hamdullilah," he repeated. It was unusual to have a Westerner around who was at ease with Arabic. Most of them relied on interpreters, who could tell a Westerner anything they wanted—and, often, did.

They were both silent a moment. She did not avert her gaze, whose intent he could not exactly discern: Sympathetic? Still sizing him up? Finally, he averted his own, to her Thuraya.

"It works well?"

"Hmm?" Then she saw him glance at the phone in her hand. "Oh. Yes. Well, it depends on where I am."

"Of course. Mine too."

She nodded toward the back. "Do you want to come to my desk and go over stuff? Do you need a minute to settle in? Rick and Asmaa are at a marines press conference."

"Umm Nasim told me."

"Oh, okay. They should be back in a bit, assuming no issues come up on the way back."

He nodded. "I follow you." Then he corrected himself: "I will follow you."

She'd set up a desk in the corner with her laptop, notebooks, the usual mess of cords running all over the desk and along the floor to the outlets. The entire front room of the villa was a chaos of cords, and one had to walk carefully so as not to trip on them and bring down three desks' worth of computers. He spied two pictures in frames on her desk. One was of what he assumed to be her very large family on a beach in America. He picked her out of the picture, in a bathing suit. The other was of her and a young man, a good-looking, ponytailed Arab man, arm in arm, with the sea and giant outcroppings in the background that he knew from pictures he'd seen were Beirut's Pigeon Rocks.

She dragged a chair for him from nearby and set it by her desk. He sat in it and faced her, his small coffee cup still in his hand. She took a swig from a large plastic bottle of water, then smiled at him again—not unkindly, he thought. He smiled back.

"Is this your first time interpreting?" she asked.

He nodded. "Asmaa encouraged me to do it."

She smiled broadly. "Your cousin is a force of nature. Rick says she's one of the best interpreters he's ever worked with, and he's been doing this a long time."

He grinned, proud of his cousin. "She's always been like that."

"She's talked Rick out of some bad pinches, a few angry crowds."

Bad pinches. He'd never heard that before, but he more or less understood it from the context. He made a note of the phrase and nodded. "She is very persuasive." He glanced up at the TV screens. Al Jazeera was showing crowds of men in Sadr City furiously shouting down the American occupation. CNN was showing a clip of Justin Timberlake dancing at a concert.

"Do you like interpreting?" she asked.

"I like it very much. I am happy now I can utilize my education. But I wish only the country is more safe. It is a very scary time."

She frowned and sighed. "It is a very scary time. We're all a bit shocked at how badly the post-invasion has been handled."

Nabil exhaled in relief. So at least she privately agreed that her country had screwed things up royally.

"But," she continued, "we still have to get the best stories we can. And so, on that note, are you ready to hit the street with me, the fruit markets? New York wants a story on what life after the invasion is like for Baghdad women."

Nabil couldn't suppress a slight, derisive snort. "To hear that they are all so free now? Iraq wasn't Saudi Arabia. Or Iran. No women had to cover themselves if they didn't want to."

She smiled and nodded her head. "I know. Listen, we push back a lot on their ideas from New York. But sometimes we have to give them some version of what they want."

Push back, Nabil noted. There was another one he hadn't heard before. He was going to learn a lot of new terms from this Rita. So he merely nodded.

"Of course, it is as you wish."

"But please," she insisted. "I want your thoughts and your insights. I need them. Don't hold back with me."

He smiled. "I will not."

And she smiled back. "Good. Will you tell Ali to get the car?"

Ali was the main driver for the villa, a full-lipped eighteen-year-old from Al Sha'ab, in Adhamiya. He spent most of his spare time on his family's roof working out with a set of weights and was prone to wearing too-tight T-shirts to show off the results; Nabil found him not only woefully uneducated but visually distracting. But he went into the kitchen, where Ali was reading a comic book and smoking, the biceps of the arm holding the cigarette flexed upward.

"Miss Rita wants us to go to Fourteenth Ramadan to talk to women shopping," Nabil announced, all business.

Ali exhaled. "Fourteenth Ramadan? It's so close. You can walk."

"You know it's too dangerous to walk!" Nabil snapped. "It's time to do your job." He turned on his heel and exited, feeling important.

Miss Rita had covered herself—in a full, hideous black polyester abaya that covered her from her head to her knees, reducing her face to a small oval. Nabil broke out in laughter.

"What?" Rita protested. "Umm Nasim gave it to me."

"I told you, this is not Saudi Arabia." He had prepared for this. "Take that off and come with me."

He led her back toward the kitchen, where the air was still acrid from Ali's freshly extinguished cigarette. "I'm sure Asmaa would do this for you if she were here." He took from his own bag an old pashmina scarf of his mother's and a pin, stood facing Rita, who had doffed her abaya and held it, balled up, in one hand. He relished the chance to fold a hijab. Since he was a child, he had been entranced by hijabs—their pleats, their clever folds and tucks, their soft lines. He would beg Asmaa to let him practice on her, and she would indulge him, all the while joking that he should go to work for the religious police in Iran.

"Look," he began. "You just need a simple square scarf like this. You fold it into a triangle and then you put the big part over your head. I may do it for you?"

Rita smiled and shrugged. "Of course. Thank you for showing me."

He did as much. "Then you pin it under your neck. Open your mouth in a big O while I do it so you have room when it is finished." She did so. "Then you take the ends and wrap them around your neck and tie them in the back. Now you see?" He guided her to her reflection in the glass door of the stove. "Very simple." He took a moment to tuck away one stray tendril of curls that marred the oval of her face. "There. You don't have to look like an old auntie from Saddam City."

She laughed. "I just don't want to draw attention to myself on the street."

Coming back into the main front room, they found that Rick and Asmaa had returned. Asmaa spied Nabil and Rita together.

"Ah, so you've met!" she cried. She'd met Rita already, late the night before upon her arrival.

"Yes, we have," said Rita, "and he just showed me how to tie a hijab properly."

Asmaa laughed frankly. "I told you you didn't have to wear that polyester tent. You look like a normal Baghdadi girl who covers now." Asmaa, in fact, was unpinning and unwinding her own head scarf. She'd now taken to wearing it out to work with Rick so as not to invite questions or rebukes from the various tribal sheiks or Shiite clerics they often interviewed, but she usually tore it off the second she was back in the villa, indifferent to Umm Nasim's muttering and head shaking.

"And," Asmaa added, "he is an excellent hijab wrapper because he's been practicing on me since we were little. He wanted to wrap me up like a Saudi woman just because it was fun for him."

Rick and Rita laughed, and Nabil could feel himself blush crimson. "I will reveal something about *you* later," he threatened.

"Ah!" Asmaa cried. "But I have no secrets!"

There were moments like this, amid the collegiality of the villa, when Nabil conceded to himself that he'd never been happier, never felt more useful, more needed, more free. He would look over at Asmaa, conferring with Rick, and marvel that she'd managed to find them both work that not only felt challenging and important but paid generously by the standards of sanction-era Iraq, so much so that they could stockpile American currency for their families against what had suddenly become an uncertain future. Sometimes, after stories were filed to New York, and they'd all partaken of Umm Nasim's cooking for dinner, Rick would break out a bottle of scotch or some other whiskey and nearly the entire bureau would have a small glass, while smoking, as Rick and Ted, a Brit, would relate stories from their days covering Serbia or Chechnya. Either that or they all would talk freely about Iraq's fall, whom they'd spoken to that day, and what they thought would happen. Or sometimes they would just discuss dumb things like *X-Men*, a bootleg DVD of which Mohsen and Ali were obsessed with, to the point that Rick and Ted had nicknamed them Cyclops and Wolverine.

It was a strange feeling, Nabil would think, this warmth and gratification while Baghdad burned and chaos reigned in the streets. Nabil could feel his whole body stiffen, particularly the back of his neck, which had been giving him trouble, every time they exited the villa gates— particularly when it was time to go home and make his way back to Kadhimiya at night, sometimes after the U.S.-imposed curfew of ten p.m., in which case he was always afraid that American troops would shoot at him before he had a chance to show them his ID card from the *Standard*.

But inside the villa, it was always safe, always certain. It felt, especially when Asmaa was there, a bit like being home with one's family.

Shortly, he and Miss Rita ("Don't call me that," she had already told him. "Just Rita.") were in Ali's 1982 Toyota Corona, making the brief drive back to Fourteenth Ramadan Street, where people shopped under the watchful gaze of U.S. troops in one of their now ubiquitous Humvees, a gunner sitting on high in the turret. Nabil watched Rita as she stared out the window, drawing her notebook and pen out of her bag.

"And so this begins," she said, seemingly more to herself than him. "I thought I'd never get here."

He found it a strange remark, the idea that someone would have been so anxious to leave Beirut to come to a war zone, when he'd have preferred just the opposite, but he made no comment.

Alighting from the car in front of a large fruit market, where women both with and without hijabs were picking through produce and haggling with vendors, she turned to him. "Are you okay if I ask questions in Arabic and you pick up on any mistakes? I have to start transitioning from Levantine to Iraqi."

"Of course." He hadn't expected her to try to speak Arabic. Now he'd really get a sense of how good she was.

No sooner had he answered than she all but beelined up to a middle-aged woman in a full black abaya whose hands were full of lemons. "Min fadlak, ya sitt," she began, then, with phrasing he knew from Lebanese television to be Levantine, she explained that she was from the *American Standard*, a large newspaper, and could she ask a few questions.

"Actually, here," he interrupted her in English, "we would not say 'ya sitt' to address an older woman, we would say 'ya hejia.'"

"For something that small, you can tell me later," she said flatly. "Only interrupt if you think I'm not getting my point across."

Getting my point across. Well, that was another new one for him as well. He made a private note. Moreover, he didn't think his point had been a small one. But, well, Miss Rita was the boss.

"Of course. I'm sorry," he said.

The middle-aged woman smiled indulgently at the exchange. "Of course you may ask me," she answered. "We are free to speak our minds now. And your Arabic is very good."

Rita smiled. "Shukran, ya hejia." She turned to Nabil. "Did I say it right?"

He nodded. "Very good."

The woman, too, smiled approvingly. Then she shook her head slowly. "What can we say about the invasion? We knew it was going to happen. We knew Saddam couldn't really hold back the Americans. So now, everything is uncertain—"

Nabil gently interrupted to translate everything up to that point.

"I got that," Rita muttered, scribbling furiously in her notebook. Nabil paused briefly.

"You don't want me to translate?"

"Huh?" She looked up. "No, no, of course I do. I just wanted you to know that I am following, for the most part."

"Okay. Go on, ya hejia."

The woman took in breath. "So now, everything is uncertain. Very scary. We have friends who were hurt in one of the bombings, who've been in the hospital with wounds—" The woman made cutting gestures on one arm with the other.

"Shrapnel wounds," said Nabil.

Rita nodded, still scribbling furiously while occasionally looking up at the woman with an intense, concerned expression. "I got that," she said.

There she goes again, Nabil thought. What did she need a translator for, if she was so proficient?

"And it is very upsetting," the woman continued. "We've had hardly any electricity. It only comes on for a few minutes at a time. We can't understand," and her voice rose as she spoke, "why if the Americans have all these soldiers here, they can't do a better job keeping control. Why did they let common thieves steal everything out of the government buildings? Don't we still need those buildings to run the country?"

She was talking faster and faster, becoming agitated. Rita laid a gentle hand on her arm to entreat her to stop for a moment.

"Can you translate that for me?" she asked him.

Oh, he thought, triumphant. So now she wants me to translate. But he did, while she continued to write it all down in a chicken scratch that fascinated him. How could she read it later? No sooner would she come to the bottom of one page then she would flip it over and start writing down the side of the opposite page. She bit her lip while she scribbled, he noted.

"And how is it for you in Iraq now," she asked in Arabic, once she'd stopped writing, "as a woman?"

The matron furrowed her brow and turned to Nabil. "What did she say? Am I a woman?"

"She asked, what is Iraq like for you now, from a woman's perspective?"

The matron laughed a short, high laugh. "From a woman's perspective? I'm fine as a woman. I want my electricity back and to be able to not worry when I go out and shop and for us to have a normal life again." The woman gestured at the Humvee stationed across the street. "I'm not sure if they are making us more safe or making it worse because we don't want them here. Why aren't they doing their jobs and stopping the thieves? Why did they come here? Just for the oil?"

He translated all this for Miss Rita. "Are you happy that Saddam is gone?" she asked the woman.

This much she seemed to understand fully. She laughed again. "What good does it do if the city is falling apart? At least Saddam was a strong man who knew how to keep the peace in the streets and to make the country work."

Nabil translated this for Rita. He had profoundly mixed feelings about her words. Certainly he would not be in his current job, working so freely without Baath Party minders (who, before the invasion, had demanded hefty cuts of his salary), if the coalition hadn't forced out Saddam. And yet—well, the woman was right.

"I got most of that," Rita answered him, scribbling. Why did she constantly have to let him know what she understood? This would become a tiresome dynamic between them. She raised her head to the woman. "But," she began in Arabic, "Saddam very bad man, yes? He killed many people, yes?" Rita gestured at the woman's black abaya. "Many Shi'a."

Nabil was surprised to see the woman's enraged affect collapse and her eyes quickly glaze over with tears. The woman stared at Miss Rita helplessly, while Rita held her gaze, brow furrowed.

"Let me tell you something about Saddam!"

It was the fruit vendor, a brown-skinned man in his sixties in a dingy dishdasha, with about four of his front teeth missing. "Saddam is a very bad man," he shouted in Arabic. Briefly, Nabil had to marvel at how readily Baghdadis would shout such things aloud now, when only a few weeks ago, preinvasion, they wouldn't have dared whisper such heresies about Great Leader without abject fear of instant disappearance into Abu Ghraib or an even more remote prison.

"*Very* bad man," the fruit vendor continued. "We hate Saddam. But we hate Americans more. Saddam is still an Iraqi. We don't want them here!" He gestured at the U.S. Army Humvee across Fourteenth Ramadan Street, where four soldiers in camos and flak jackets, all holding M16s, chewed their tobacco like cows chewing cud, unsmilingly surveying passersby from behind their opaque wraparound sunglasses. "So they scared off Saddam, hamdullilah. Now get out!"

"But," Miss Rita began in Arabic, "maybe American soldiers have to stay until Iraq has a new democratic government?"

"Democracy isn't good for Iraq!" the vendor cried angrily. "Too American. We need one strong leader."

Rita scribbled this down, then said to the woman and the fruit vendor, "Thank you for talking to me. I wish safety for you and your families."

At this, the woman and the fruit man dropped their scowls. The woman broke into a smile (also partly toothless, Nabil noted), raised her palm to Rita's face, kissed her on either cheek, and said, "Allah yus-allmak," as did the vendor, who quickly filled a small plastic bag with fruit and handed it to her.

"I cannot without paying you," Rita protested, fishing dinars from her bag, which earned protests from the vendor, which in turn compelled Rita to offer fewer dinars, which the vendor finally accepted. She seemed well versed, Nabil thought, in the regional tradition of elaborately rebuffing the offering of gifts until one finally accepted or struck some sort of compromise.

The two of them bade a final "ma'a assalama" to buyer and seller and moved on. "Not a bad start," she remarked.

"They were really yelling at you."

"I wanted them to. I play devil's advocate and ask questions that will provoke them until they give me a stronger quote about what they're really feeling."

He nodded, intrigued. Now here was another term, *devil's advocate*, he'd never heard before, though he understood its meaning from her context. And it had never occurred to him to deliberately goad someone into saying what you needed him to say. He could learn a lot from this Rita.

She was already marching straight toward two more women, both unveiled and with dyed blond hair, likely in their forties, browsing in a gold shop. Nabil hurried after her. By the time he caught up, she'd already introduced herself, explained that she was from a large American paper, and in turn she introduced Nabil.

The two women looked at each other tentatively before one, the slightly taller, spoke. They were sisters, she said, and it was their ritual to spend one afternoon a week shopping and browsing in Mansour together, grabbing a kebab at Al Saha nearby, perhaps having a pistachio ice cream. This was their first time back out together since shortly before the U.S. invasion, and they were relieved to see that everything appeared more or less normal, even though they were tired of not knowing from day to day what exactly was going to happen in the city, or the country.

More scribbling and judicious head nodding from Miss Rita. "I see that you are both uncovered," she finally said. "May I ask why?"

The sisters—one had a far better color job than the other, Nabil could not help noticing—looked at each other again. The one with the better color job shrugged. "Well," she began, "we are Christian, so we don't cover, obviously, but there are Muslim women too in Baghdad who don't cover. It is not required here."

"Even though Saddam did start to encourage it the past few years," added the other.

Her sister nodded. "That is true. That is true." She emitted a short, derisive laugh. "To make Iraq appear pious for the other Arab countries!"

Nabil laughed a bit with the ladies. Miss Rita looked up at him needfully, and he translated. She chuckled, to signal that she appreciated the sarcasm, while she scribbled. "Are you worried to be Christian in Iraq now?" she asked.

Nabil smoothed out some of her wording before the women nodded, absorbing the question. "That has never been an issue here," the one with the worse dye job said. "We visit our friends in Adhamiya, Kadhimiya, and they visit us in Karada. We go to each other's weddings. We have a Shiite family next door and a Sunni family across the street. We all live together happily, peacefully. My friend next door comes to church with me and prays before the Virgin sometimes."

Her sister nodded thoughtfully. "That's true. Or she'll ask you to bring a prayer to the Virgin."

"But now," continued the first sister, "we don't know what will happen. We can talk freely and we don't need to hide our satellite dish and can watch any news we want, which is wonderful, but even just coming out to shop makes us very anxious when it used to be a pleasure. Our husbands didn't want us to come out today."

"Yours especially," noted the other sister.

Rita lightly touched the woman's arm and asked Nabil to translate up to that point, which he did.

"But we insisted," continued the sister after he'd finished, "because you have to have some normalcy and pleasure in life. But already our neighbors had their car stolen right out from under them. They were driving back from Najaf and bandits with qinaa over their faces stopped them with guns on the road, told them to get out of the car, and drove away with it!" The woman's voice was rising now. "Can you believe that? Such a thing would have been unthinkable even just six weeks ago. They had to walk three kilometers until they found a petrol station that could call for a ride for them."

Nabil translated while Rita scribbled. She then asked: "And how is life for you both now as women since the invasion? Has it changed?" Nabil quickly interpreted her words.

The sisters seemed puzzled by the question. "As women?" one repeated.

The other considered, rocking her head back and forth slightly. "I suppose we don't feel as safe. Just as we said. Very fearful. Not sleeping as well."

"Do you feel more free?"

"We feel less free, because of the lack of safety."

"You have to understand," said the other. "We are both educated women, we both work, and as you can see, we dress like normal modern women in America or anywhere else."

"Are you more afraid now because you are Christian?"

Nabil nearly gasped. He could not believe how blunt this Rita was! But then again, he thought, he'd better get used to it, and prepare to sometimes soften her questions, because this, after all, was her job.

The sisters glanced at each other. One opened her mouth, then stopped.

"Speak," commanded the other sister. "We're free to speak our minds now."

She nodded, conceding as much. "The religious sentiment has always been locked down here by Saddam," she said. "The divisions. He wouldn't stand for it, even though of course he favored the Sunni for all the best jobs and benefits. Now—" she paused, then spoke in a lower voice. "I do worry about the imams and what they will say about us. I do worry."

The other sister briefly squeezed her hand. "So you can see why we want order in the streets again!" she said sharply. "So tell your government to bring some order!"

Nabil translated, and Rita said, "I wish I had the control of that issue." She nodded toward the gold vendor's shelves of jewelry gleaming on black velvet frames. "Are you thinking of buying gold today?"

"Buying?" laughed the better color job. "No, we are thinking of selling." She pulled up a sleeve to reveal a gold bracelet with small stone inlays, then discreetly pulled down her shirt collar to reveal a chain. "'We are talking about collecting as much money as possible if we have to leave Iraq soon."

"So if you want to write about how we feel as women, we are angry that we have to sell our gold!" laughed her sister.

"And we are very angry about the bombings in Al Sha'ab and Al Shula," added the other, with force in her voice.

Nabil dutifully translated. The woman was referring to the bombs that had fallen in two different residential neighborhoods in late March, leaving gaping craters in the road; turning entire homes into rubble; and, what was most gruesome, killing or injuring dozens of civilians, including children, whose bodies were charred until they were nearly unrecognizable, or blown apart, sending limbs and extremities flying through the air, to land in horrible, random places. A head might be found lying on its side atop a burning car or a torso sitting in the entryway of a destroyed car repair garage, slammed up against an oily, naked chassis.

Nabil, who had rushed over with Rick, Asmaa, and Claude, the paper's French photographer, had never seen such horror. He'd had to fight back vomit as he numbly translated for Rick and Claude the wails all around him of family members, especially mothers and grandmothers, screaming up to the sky, "Why? Why?" It had been ghastly. Up until that point, it seemed as though America's bombs had, as was promised, been precise, that they were hitting only government buildings, which had been evacuated long ago in anticipation of attack. After they came back to the villa, to help Rick and Claude file the story, he and Asmaa had sat briefly in the immaculate garden, smoking but not talking, stunned by what they'd seen, heard, and smelled. (He had never before known the sickly sweet, densely meaty odor of burning human flesh.) Eventually, Asmaa had simply said "Oh my God," again and again, and begun crying.

Miss Rita had not yet been in Iraq during the bombings. "But they are not sure the bombs were American, correct?" she asked now. "One was small, it might have been Iraqi."

The sisters looked at each other. "We would not have bombs dropping in Baghdad at all if the Americans weren't here," one said. "We didn't live like this before. We had our safety, and most people knew that if they just did not say bad things about Saddam, you could go about your life in peace."

"Freedom without safety is not really being free," said the other.

When Nabil translated this for Rita, she muttered to him, "That's a really good quote," as she scrawled it down.

The afternoon proceeded like this. Rita had a nice touch, Nabil had to concede, different from Rick's style, which was more impassive. Rita joked with people when joking was appropriate, made wry remarks that he translated back to them, and didn't hesitate to show sympathy when it was called for. But, like Rick, she was also indefatigable, barely wrapping up one conversation before starting another, constantly glancing around her as she scribbled to see what else was going on or whom else she could talk to.

Nabil felt his hunger grow. Finally, after two o'clock, he began to feel light-headed. "Can we stop for lunch?" he asked.

She looked at him, startled. "Are you hungry?"

"Aren't you?"

"I never get hungry when I'm reporting. It sneaks up on me later."

He had to assert himself. "I can't think well when I get hungry."

She considered this for a moment. "Okay," she finally said. "Let's eat something fast."

"A shawarma?"

"Sure."

"Follow me. We are near Al Saha. Very famous restaurant."

"I've heard of it."

They were a mere block from Al Saha, which sat on the ground floor of a massive concrete building on a corner of Fourteenth Ramadan. The interior was vast, crowded, with a great deal of black marble and brass fittings and Al Jazeera running on TV sets mounted high on the walls, the type underneath the correspondent reading, WHERE IS SADDAM HUSSEIN? Nabil led Rita to the queue at the counter.

She pointed to a large, garish photograph of fried chicken that read beneath, in English, "Kentucky." "Ha," she said. "I love that. Black-market KFC."

He wasn't quite sure what she meant, so he merely said, "Very popular here." Then, after a moment, he added: "I can't believe it, you're not interviewing anybody."

"It's not easy, believe me. I'm trying to give you a proper lunch break."

"Thank you, boss."

They both laughed.

At the counter, he ordered them each shawarma, a salad, and a Pepsi, and she pulled dinars from her bag, asking for a receipt so she might be reimbursed back at the villa. Food in hand, they found two unoccupied black stools at a counter in the back of the restaurant and sat.

She clacked her Pepsi against his. "Sahtein," she said.

He smiled. "That's Lebanese. We don't say that here before eating. We say bela'afya."

She repeated the phrase.

"Correct. Very good. There's a lot of small differences, aren't there?"

She nodded while she chewed. "Do you know how I started Arabic?" she said after she'd swallowed. "With Modern Standard. A lot of good that did me. I had to completely relearn once I got to Beirut, and now I guess I have to completely relearn again."

"Well, do not worry," he told her. "I will take you through it."

She smiled. "How'd your English get so good?"

This irked him slightly. "Anyone educated here learns English in school."

"I know!" she exclaimed. "But, I mean, yours is really good. You know a lot of idioms."

"I read a lot in English." Then, though it somewhat galled him to admit it, he added, "Asmaa really pushed me. From when we were very young."

"Aha!"

"Every book she read she gave me to read when she was done." He chewed a bit and smiled. "I was her project."

She washed down her bite with Pepsi. "I had a cousin like that," she said. "Well, I still have him, I should say. I was very bossy with him. And now he's in the army."

"He misses taking orders."

"Ha!" She laughed. "Maybe that's it. I made a monster."

"Is he in Iraq?"

"He's in the reserves in the U.S."

She seemed to become a bit morose after that, picking at her salad. Nabil stayed silent. Finally, she asked him, glancing at and nodding toward the TV, "So, what do you think is going to happen here?"

"Ah!" he smiled. "You're back to the reporter."

"Occupational hazard."

He frowned in confusion.

"It's a term," she said. "It means something you can't avoid, because it's part of your job."

"Ah, okay. Gotcha." He was proud of that colloquialism, *gotcha*. "Well, to answer your question." He paused. "I am very, very, very afraid. You see what is going on. There is no order in the streets, no electricity, no water. My family is trapped in the house, scared to go out. It is no life. I am scared for my mother every day when she goes to teach. Why would the Americans let this happen? Why are they just standing around and watching people steal and make crimes?"

She shook her head. "I don't know. The troops say they were trained to fight, not to be police and keep the peace. I think they either didn't realize—"

They were knocked off their stools to the floor by a stunning jolt. To Nabil, it felt as though the planet itself had just been sideswiped by a passing asteroid. There was a brief, strange moment of silence in the restaurant, about five or ten seconds, before a great clamor of wails and lamentations rose up, particularly from the front, near the street. Nabil sat on the floor, his food all over his shirt, dazed for several seconds, before he looked over to find Rita in the same state, covered in food, her hand to her head.

"Are you okay?" he managed to ask.

"Holy fucking God," she said slowly, then repeated it. "What happened? What happened?"

Nabil had gotten to his knees and looked around. "Look," he said.

Slowly, Rita got to her knees as well, hand still to her head. The wide glass front windows, which the restaurant had not thought or chosen to cover with plywood or at least reinforce with tape, had exploded inward. Dozens of people were covered in blood and food, screaming, crying out to God, staggering about, surrounded by shards of glass amid the tables and chairs, most of which had fallen over from the blast. There was pandemonium in the street beyond, an overwhelming cacophony of car alarms.

For several seconds, perhaps nearly a minute, the two of them just knelt, staring at the scene in mute shock, rubbing their foreheads. Al Saha staff members were rushing forward from the kitchen with towels, rags, and buckets of water to tend to the wounded up front. Oddly, Al Jazeera continued to run on the TVs, a report about a school in the West Bank. Nabil looked to his left to find that a portly man of his father's age, with the thick, dyed-black mustache worn by nearly every middle-aged male Baghdadi, had also been knocked from his stool and was sitting on his backside, rubbing his eyes, amid the remains of his own fried-chicken lunch.

Nabil crawled toward him. "Inta zein, Ammo?" he asked, putting an arm on the shoulder of the man, who nodded a slow yes.

"I think so," he said. He stared at Nabil, his eyes filling with tears. "My son, what is happening to this country?"

Nabil said nothing, then, "Can I—" He was going to help the man up.

But Rita called, "Nabil!"

He turned. She was standing, bag in hand, wiping food from her face and shirt with her napkin. "Come on," she called sternly. "We have to go find out what happened."

"But," and he gestured toward the wounded in the front, "we have to help them."

"No! They are being helped. We have to work. Come on."

She strode toward the exit, threading her way through diners who were only just gingerly picking themselves up off the floor. Nabil turned one last time to the portly mustachioed man, who said, "Go, go. I am fine. Thank you, my son. May God be with you."

Then he hurried after Rita. The people up front, many of them howling and crying—and mostly grown men, Nabil noted relievedly, no women or children that he could see—were being tended to by the restaurant staff and other patrons who had not been as badly hit. He saw a great deal of wincing and howling as people plucked glass shards from their bodies and made compresses from towels or napkins. There was a great deal of blood, spattered on clothing, tables, and the floor, but, Nabil noted with relief, everyone seemed to be intact. He saw no stray body parts, no great gushing dark pools of blood that signified imminent death.

Rita was already in the street, which was paved with shattered glass from all the storefronts, every one of which had had its windows blown out. A large dressmaker's sign, featuring a photograph of a stiffly smiling, typically over-coiffed and made-up Baghdadi bride, lay smack in the middle of the street. Rita had waded right into a crowd of young men, some of them with Kalashnikovs slung over their shoulders, who were screaming and cursing as they stared at the blown-out front facade of the well-loved Al Saha. Some of its large potted palms had been thrown into the street by the blast.

"Death to America! Death to Bush!" the young men had already begun chanting.

"What happened? What happened?" Rita was asking them in Arabic. Nabil, still feeling dazed and disoriented, approached her, ready to, as she put it, "work."

"Very big bomb! *Very* big," several of the young men cried in English. "This way."

They followed the crowd down a side alley that led into a network of smaller, residential streets where modest, walled villas—not the more lavish homes of other parts of Mansour—stood in rows. Everywhere, Nabil saw blasted-out windows and residents standing around, or pacing, dazed, some of them cursing openly. But it was when they rounded the corner that he truly moaned in astonishment and horror.

A huge gash lay in the middle of the road, perhaps twelve meters deep by twenty-five meters long by eight meters wide. It was filled with rubble, in which Nabil could make out the details of household interiors—a rust-colored couch, a sentimental watercolor picture of old Babylon still in its frame, a cream-colored electric kettle. On all sides of the crater, what had been homes were now heaps of rubble. The neighborhood had been completely flattened, pulverized to half detritus, half dust. People stood at the edge of the crater, staring into it, either dumb and dazed, trying to comprehend what had just happened, or wailing. A middle-aged, unveiled woman in Western clothes, a white blouse, jeans, and sneakers, knelt on the ground, sobbing, pounding her fists into her forehead, yelling "Oh my God, oh my God," over and over again.

And then Nabil looked down and saw what he hadn't yet seen as he'd surveyed the full vista: a hand, a woman's hand, he surmised from the gold ring still on the fourth finger, lying in the dust just a meter from him, its thumb and index finger bent back, which gave the strange impression that it was reaching out for something. A bundle of meat and a bone protruded from its back end, which had been crudely, not cleanly, hacked off. Nabil just stared at it, shocked and mesmerized.

"Look," he finally said to Rita, who stood a few paces from him, taking pictures with a digital camera and scrawling into her notebook. He pointed at the hand.

She looked at it, grimaced, then looked at him. "I've seen that before," she said. "In Tel Aviv. Is that the first hand you've seen?"

He nodded. She shook her head. "I hate to say this, but nothing is as bad as the first one." To this, he said nothing. "Come on," she added. "Let's talk to people."

She walked toward the kneeling, wailing woman in jeans, knelt down beside her. "Ya khala," she began, continuing in Arabic: "Can you tell us what happened?"

The woman began speaking through chokes and sobs. "My son, my son, I lost my son. He was working in the courtyard. I left him just for twenty minutes to buy food. I can't even find him, he is buried under the house." She gestured behind her. There was no house to speak of, just a small mountain of wreckage, in which Nabil could make out, as in the crater, household details: a floral printed shirt, a sneaker, a TV remote control, a toilet seat.

Nabil translated, and Rita scribbled. "May I ask your name, ya khala?"

"Umm Yusef," she replied numbly.

"And was your son Yusef?"

"Yes," the woman replied, amid a fresh wave of tears. "He was fifteen years old. I was keeping him home from school because I was afraid to send him out." She looked up at them, with what seemed an angry revelation. "Why were they bombing here? This is a neighborhood, there are no government buildings here, no weapons. I thought I was keeping him safe by keeping him at home. Now, how will I live without my son? I don't want to live. I wish God had taken me too. This will be no life."

The woman folded into herself with gasping sobs. Rita put a hand on her back and rubbed it. "Ya khala, I am so sorry. Where will you go?"

"I have a sister in Dora."

Rita looked up at Nabil. "We can take you to Dora," she said. Nabil repeated the phrase to the woman, to make sure she heard it well. "We have a driver nearby. We won't leave without you."

The woman didn't reply, just kept sobbing. "I don't want to live. I don't want to live. God take me now too, so I can be with my son."

"I am so sorry, ya khala," Rita said again. But as she spoke, Nabil noticed, she was already surveying the landscape again. Silently, she nodded at him to move on.

He was loath to leave the woman alone. It was an odd and alienating feeling, he thought, to be "working" amid such chaos, to know one's primary job was merely to observe and pull information and feelings from people rather than to join rescue efforts. Groups of men, dusty and some spattered with blood, were trying to pull back large chunks of wall wherever they could, to see whether anyone lay beneath, still half-alive. Other men were walking around with garbage bags and gloves, retrieving chunks of flesh or body parts.

Three teenage boys, their soccer jerseys covered in dust, came running up to them. "Did you hear what this was?" they shouted to Nabil. "The Americans thought Saddam was at Al Saha, they had a bad tip. They were trying to hit Al Saha, but they missed, the dogs."

"They were trying to hit Al Saha?" Nabil repeated, shocked. He and Rita had barely escaped with their lives, he thought. They and nearly a hundred other people in the restaurant.

"What, what?" Rita demanded. "What about Al Saha?"

Nabil translated back for her.

"How do they know it was an American bomb?" she asked.

He translated this for the boys. "Look at the size of the crater!" they shouted, gesturing back at it. "Saddam doesn't have bombs that size!"

"Do they live in the neighborhood? Do they know anyone who died in the bombing?" Rita asked.

No sooner had Nabil translated than the boys exploded with pointing and explanation. Nabil had to ask them to slow down, take a breath. "There was the Malouf family," said one of the boys, the smallest of the three. In the front pocket of his jeans, Nabil now noticed, was a pistol. "The grandmother and the father and the little son, Kassem, all died. Kassem already had lost a leg from an infection that they had to amputate last year. He was eleven years old."

"And over there," pointed the second boy, "was Abu Kassem's brother, Abu Nazar, and he died and his daughter, Leila, died too."

"We think so far about eight or maybe nine people have died," said the third. "We can't find Umm Fouad, the grandmother from that house." He pointed to another heap on the opposite side of the deep gash in the road.

As she scribbled, Rita asked, in Arabic, "How do you feel about the invasion?" A moment before he could echo the question, Nabil realized she had formed it flawlessly, so he was quiet. Her Arabic seemed to sharpen in a crisis, he noted.

"Death to Bush!" cried one boy.

"They said their bombs would be so precise, would only kill Saddam and his friends," said another. He gestured sweepingly. "Why are they doing this? What did these people do? They were our friends, our neighbors."

Nabil glanced several meters behind them. Alongside the crater, a middle-aged man in drab office attire, a white shirt and black slacks, crouched and wept, his head in his hands, while a man half his age held him. The neighborhood was so much like his own, he thought. He could easily picture the same scene on his street. His family had packed their bags and fled Baghdad a week before the first bombings to stay with his mother's cousins in Najaf, but they were back now. What if the Americans got "intel" about Saddam's associates or weapons caches in Kadhimiya? Would they be next?

He caught Rita's eye as it strayed. "It's Ali," she said.

Sure enough, Ali was hurrying toward them, a cigarette in one hand, his forehead beaded in sweat.

"I heard the bomb," he announced. He stared in awe at the crater, surveyed the Mansouris picking through the wreckage like zombies or weeping. "They said on Fourteenth Ramadan that they thought Saddam was at Al Saha."

"We know," Rita said. "We were at Al Saha when it happened."

Ali flicked away his cigarette and scowled. "This is *precision*? These are devils."

"We have a lady here we need to drive to her family in Dora."

They walked back toward where Umm Yusef had been, to find she was no longer there. "I don't know where she went," Rita said, scanning the scene.

But something had caught Nabil's eye as he stared into the crater, something he'd spied jammed between two large pieces of wall. He'd thought at first it was an object of some sort, but as he looked at it, he realized it was a human figure, small and charred, positioned as someone might lie when sleeping on the side, arms and legs splayed away from the trunk. He squinted and discerned that the figure had a full left leg but a stump on the right. The several men who had been searching for human remains had missed it thus far. Nabil just stared at it for several seconds, perversely engrossed in his examination, his stomach churning, before he finally pointed at it.

"Look," he said. "It's a body. I think that's the little boy they mentioned. Kassem. You can see he was missing one leg."

The three of them drew closer to the edge of the crater.

"Yes," Ali eventually said. "That's a body. That was a little boy."

Nabil watched Rita as she stared wordlessly at the body. Her mouth opened as though she were going to form words, but then it closed again, and she continued to stare at the form, her face unreadable. She, too, seemed mesmerized. Slowly, she stepped forward until she stood at the very edge of the crater. Then, not taking her eyes off the body, she pulled her digital camera from her bag, raised it to her right eye, and snapped. She then moved a few paces to the right and snapped again. She put the camera back into her bag and pulled her notebook and pen from the back pocket of her jeans.

Nabil watched her as she wrote, looking up every other second to regard the body again, "in the crater . . . wedged in rubble . . . body little boy . . . amputated . . . burned head to toe."

"How old would you say he was?" she asked, not taking her eyes off the body.

"I would say eight or nine," he answered.

"8, 9 y.o.," she scribbled. She then continued to stare at the body. She shook her head slowly. Then she turned to him.

"I can't believe they didn't send Claude out with us today," she said.

Claude, the photographer.

"I asked if I could have Claude last night," she added.

Nabil said nothing. It hadn't been what he thought she was thinking.

She looked away, scanned the scene. Her eye caught the middle-aged man in office attire, still weeping and rocking under the arm of the other man. She sighed heavily. "Let's go talk to that poor guy," she said. "Then I'd better get back and file."

She walked and he and Ali followed. Then she stopped and turned back to them. "And you know something else?" she added. "What do you want to bet the paper doesn't run that picture I just took? I bet they wouldn't run it even if Claude had taken it."

She walked on, and Nabil followed. *Here we go*, he thought, as they surrounded the weeping man. *Time to work again.*

An hour later, back at the villa, Nabil and Ali, joined by Umm Nasim, who brought them small glasses of sweet tea, stood smoking, watching the three TV screens, as Al Jazeera and the BBC broadcast the very images from the bomb site that they had just seen—the keening survivors, the enormous crater, the men picking through the rubble for body parts—while on CNN a correspondent related the incident without showing tape. Miss Rita was at her makeshift desk, working the phones and e-mail, trying to get American military officials to confirm or deny that coalition forces had dropped the bomb and to tell her why. She'd pulled off her head scarf the moment they entered the villa's garden, and now it lay in a small heap beside her laptop.

Ali exhaled smoke, shaking his head. "Dogs," he muttered. "They won't even show what they did."

"I know," Nabil muttered back. He felt the same stomach sickness he'd felt after hearing about the bombings in Al Sha'ab and Al Shula, only worse this time. One imprecise bombing on the Americans' part he could perhaps forgive. But now there were at least three he knew of! Dozens and dozens of people who'd had nothing to do with Saddam's evil had died; dozens more had been left without relatives, homes, or possessions.

And as for Rick, Miss Rita, and Claude: He knew it was their job to get out the story, but to see how mechanically they went about it, with no time for tears or outrage—he found that slightly appalling. He'd noted how, in the weeks before Baghdad fell, Rick had laughed with other correspondents after the press conferences at the Information Ministry when Muhammad Saeed al-Sahhaf, Saddam's press minister, whom the foreigners called "Baghdad Bob," had continually declared that Saddam's army was slaughtering American soldiers at the gates of the city and proclaimed that Baghdad would never fall to the Americans. Of course, it had been laughable—everyone knew that the Iraqi army stood no chance against the American-led troops—but it was the scorn with which they laughed that privately infuriated him.

They had no idea what it felt like to have a Godzilla-like foreign power about to take over their country. Uncomfortably, he found himself having strange feelings of loyalty to Saddam, of wounded pride for him, as he nursed a fantasy that somehow the Republican Guard would push back the coalition. Saddam was an Iraqi, after all. A monster, but *their* monster, not a marauding foreign monster. And today, not for the first time but certainly the most sharply yet, he felt dirty for helping the Americans, just because they paid well and it made him feel more important than working in a grocery store.

"Look at her," Ali muttered, flicking his gaze toward Miss Rita. "She showed no emotion. Even looking at that boy's body. She likes us to think that she is an Arab. No, she's not. An Arab would show emotion."

"She's doing her job," Nabil muttered back. But, of course, he'd had exactly the same thoughts.

"Nabil!" It was Miss Rita calling him, so he walked to her desk. "Can you take the other sat phone and call some professors and get some reaction?" She asked him to do this often, call around to a group of political-science professors, most from the University of Baghdad, all of whom spoke English anyway, to get analysis for her stories. "I won't just use American analysis," she said, and he knew she felt she was being very virtuous for aiming to include the Iraqi point of view in her stories.

"Of course." So he did just that, managed to get hold of one or two professors, who were still, remarkably, showing up for their classes. The professors said exactly what he thought they'd say, which was that if America was trying to win the hearts and minds of Iraqis in order to get them to support a new, supposedly democratic government, its bombing campaign was having the opposite effect.

"I figured that's what you'd get," Rita said when he delivered the quotes to her.

Near six o'clock, Rick and Asmaa returned. They'd been doing a story at Abu Ghraib, west of the city, which the coalition was using for prisoners of war, which mainly meant Iraqi soldiers who hadn't been smart enough to desert and go home. None of them had been very enthusiastic about fighting for Saddam's losing cause—as much as they might've said they were before the invasion, out of fear of the slim chance that Saddam would remain in power. But Rick and Asmaa had heard about the Mansour bombing, and Rick immediately joined Rita in working on the story.

"Nasty day," Rick pronounced loudly, to the room in general, on his way to Rita's desk.

Asmaa grabbed Nabil's arm and led him back toward the kitchen. "I need a cigarette and a tea," she said.

He followed her into the kitchen, where she fished cigarettes out of her bag, handed him one, then lit both his and hers. She refilled the electric kettle from their stockpile of bottled water, and flipped its switch. Unlike the rest of the city, the villa never lost electrical power, because the newspaper had paid the equivalent of twenty-five thousand American dollars to install a backup generator.

Asmaa leaned against the counter and exhaled, looking at him bitterly. "This is at least *three* times now their bombs have killed dozens of innocent people. Rick wants to go to Al Kindi tonight to look at victims."

Al Kindi was the nearby hospital that, since the invasion, had been flooded with the hemorrhaging and the burned, among them small children. The smocks of its overtaxed doctors and nurses, not to mention its very floors, were often smeared in blood.

Tears welled up in Asmaa's eyes. "I don't know if I can do it. It was bad enough seeing men being held like dogs at Abu Ghraib today just because they were part of the Iraqi Army. They are not the enemy!"

It was disconcerting for Nabil to see Asmaa about to cry, something she rarely did. "Tell Rick you don't feel well," he said. "I'll go with him."

But she shook her head. "No. Thank you, but no. This is my job, and we are being paid well for it. This is part of the job."

"Maybe I can come with you."

"You can ask al arabiya," she scoffed. She meant Miss Rita. Among Nabil and the other Iraqis in the villa, Asmaa called her "the Arabic woman," satirically, because Rita loved to remind them, in various ways, that she was half-Arab.

Nabil laughed lightly. He had noted Asmaa's chilliness around Miss Rita, and he imagined Rita had, too.

Ali wandered into the kitchen and requested a cigarette from Asmaa, who obliged him. For several seconds, the three of them said nothing, just glanced at one another and sighed.

"I will not be able to get out of my head what I saw today when I try to sleep tonight," Ali finally said. "That little body with one leg all crouched up in the dirt."

"The boy, Kassem?" Nabil asked.

Ali nodded and exhaled, in his trademark sideways plume, which vaguely mesmerized Nabil.

"I have images like that stuck in my head from Al Sha'ab," Asmaa said. "The worst one is a woman's head that looked as if it had rolled right up to the wheel of a car and then stopped."

"As if it didn't want to get run over," Ali added.

Just then, Miss Rita came into the thick cloud of smoke that hung in the kitchen.

"It's true," she announced flatly. "It was an American missile. They had some intel that Saddam was at the restaurant." She saw Asmaa's pack of cigarettes on the counter. "May I?" she asked.

Asmaa shrugged. "Of course."

She lit a cigarette. The four of them stood there, awkwardly, nobody saying anything.

Finally, Ali murmured, "It had to be an American bomb. Saddam had nothing that big."

Rita nodded. "I know. We still had to confirm."

Asmaa shrugged again. "That's our job," she said airily, with a barbed accent on *job*, which earned a quick glance from Rita, who then turned to Nabil.

"I guess our deadline on the wonderful new status of women in Iraq is off the table until tomorrow," she said.

Off the table. There was a new one, too, he thought. But he grimaced to acknowledge her sarcasm. "Sometimes a big bomb changes the plans," he said.

Now Rick joined them as well. Nabil regarded him afresh for a moment. Rick was a handsome, broad-shouldered, light-brown-skinned, silver-haired man in his early fifties, who (he had told Asmaa, who had told Nabil) had grown up very poor in a city in Texas called El Paso, very close to Mexico, where his parents were from. But Rick had shown a capacity for writing from an early age and had become the first person in his family to go to college—he went to the University of Texas in Austin—and after that had been one of the fastest-rising reporters at a big paper in Houston, winning many awards, until the *Standard* had plucked him, at the age of thirty-one, and put him in Central America, because of his bilingual capacities, back in the 1980s. That was the beginning of how he had become one of the most respected war correspondents in America.

"And all because I loved to read as a kid," Rick had remarked to Asmaa, who related this back to Nabil, with the underlying message that in America, if you were talented and liked to read, no dream was too big, no matter how poor you were or where you came from.

So now Rick entered their wreath of cigarette smoke (he'd made himself quit two years ago) to fix himself a tea. "So much for precision, huh?" he asked. "So much for great intel."

Nobody said anything. They were five in the small kitchen now, somewhat cramped.

Nabil watched Rick regard Asmaa, whose chin trembled slightly. Then Rick turned to Nabil. "Can you relieve your cousin tonight?" he asked.

Relieve? What did he mean? He stared back at Rick, looking, he feared, like an idiot.

"Can you go to Al Kindi tonight with Rick instead of Asmaa?" Rita asked.

"To give her a break after the prison," Rick added.

"Oh no!" Asmaa insisted. "I'm going! I'm fine."

"You need a break."

"No, I'm fine! This is my job."

Rick shrugged; all were silent briefly. "Can we all go?" Rita finally ventured. "With Claude?"

Everyone turned to Rick, who shrugged. "Sure. Let's get through this together."

They extinguished their cigarettes and left the kitchen together. Nabil found Claude, the Frenchman, who was tall and reedy, with (Nabil thought) extremely large ears, hunched over images he was uploading to Washington.

"Rick wants you to come with us to the hospital to take pictures of the victims from the bombing," he announced.

Claude looked up, his right hand on his computer mouse. "Have you done this before?" he asked. "Visited a hospital after a bombing?"

Nabil shook his head. Asmaa had gone the last two times.

"Did you have dinner?"

Again Nabil shook his head.

"That's good." Claude stood and stuffed his camera into his shoulder bag. "Because you would lose it anyway. Oh," he added, "prepare for the survivors to scream at you. They'll want to know why it happened, and they'll think we have the answers."

Nabil must have paled, because Claude looked at him again and softened, then briefly caressed his shoulder with his large hand, sending a shock wave of sensation down Nabil's body. "I'm sorry," Claude said. "Your country does not deserve this."

Nabil had no words for that, so he merely turned the palms of his hands heavenward, as Bibi did when she prayed, as though to say, *What can we do about that?* Claude's hand on his shoulder, he noted briefly, had left the imprint of a caress, a salve, that, to his chagrin, quickly faded.

They convened with Rick, Rita, and Asmaa in the garden. Ali came around with the car, and they all stuffed themselves in, the women sharing the passenger seat in the front. Nabil's stomach churned. They were out now beyond the walls of the villa, the sun was setting in Baghdad, a city he no longer knew, and anything could happen.

CHAPTER SEVEN

RITA AND SAMI, PART 2

(SPRING 2004)

She'd had too much to drink—again. She'd been drinking too much. They would all file work until ten thirty p.m., Baghdad time, just thirty minutes before the citywide curfew began. Then Nabil, Asmaa, and the other Iraqi staffers would be hustled by the villa's six new Kalashnikov-armed guards into two of the villa's four new armored cars to be taken home for the night on a wild, high-speed, herky-jerky slalom through the city, every night a different way home to throw off potential kidnappers or insurgents. Rita, Rick, Claude, and the other Westerners in the villa would wait for their sat-phone calls, to know they made it home safely, then Umm Nasim would say "Hamdullilah," tidy the kitchen, and go to bed in her own tiny room in the back. It was mid-May 2004, slightly more than a year after the Americans took Baghdad.

And then someone would pull a bottle of Maker's Mark or Johnnie Walker out of a desk, put on a Bruce Springsteen or Bob Marley CD, and the shots would go around and around in a haze of cigarette smoke. Often, they were joined by Ali, who was now living in the villa, sleeping on a couch in the side room with his sneakers on the floor beside him, because it was safer to bring the $250,000 armored car back behind the villa's newly erected blast walls (in addition to the original walls), on a street where the *Standard* had paid for a checkpoint at either end, than it was for him to sleep at home with his family in Al Sha'ab with such an expensive vehicle outside.

They all knew that going to bed fuzzy-drunk and waking up slightly hungover only five or six hours later, often to slight or major reverberations of the house as bombs detonated perhaps a hundred meters away, was not wise. It dulled their senses, slowed their reflexes, and only further soured their mood for the next day's work, which, whenever it took them outside their villa turned armed fortress, had become an exercise in getting what they needed to make a story and then scurrying back to the villa without being kidnapped or killed.

Just two days prior, Rick, Ali, and Asmaa had been driving back from Karbala, Ali flooring it as usual on the highway at 150 kilometers an hour, when a white van that had first appeared as a dot far behind them on the flat road grew ever closer. Rick had lain down in the back seat, so as not to be seen, when the van suddenly gunned past them, and two men, whose heads were wrapped entirely in keffiyahs except for eye slits, began shooting wildly at them with Kalashnikovs aimed out its windows.

Asmaa had screamed, and Ali slammed the brake, which had the intended effect of letting the van plow on ahead of them.

"What's happening?" Rick had called from the back seat.

"They shoot at us, but now they leave," Ali had replied, breathing hard.

For several seconds, Ali and Asmaa had sat rigid, terrified, wondering whether the van would screech to a halt on the empty, endless expanse of highway, and whether the men would jump out, point the guns, force them to stop, and take them hostage. It was happening all over Iraq now to foreign journalists, contractors, even aid workers, and to the Iraqis who drove them, translated for them—even cooked and laundered for them. The insurgents didn't distinguish between foreigners who were in Iraq to enforce the occupation and those, like themselves, who were there to report it, or to care for the sick or wounded or hungry, or to rebuild infrastructure. Any Westerner, especially an American, and any Iraqi working for a Westerner, was a target for murder—or at the very least a hefty ransom fee.

In a video they had all watched just two nights ago, riveted yet full of dread, Nick Berg, a young American repair contractor, seemed too calm to know he was about have his head hacked off with a long knife, but that's exactly what had happened. A collective cry of shock and horror rose up among them as they watched the video, Rita putting her hands to her face and pacing away from the screen, saying, "Oh my God!" over and over again, until she finally found the courage to turn and see one of the men parading around the room with Berg's severed head, blood dripping from the neck.

That evening on the highway back from Karbala, the white van hadn't stopped but had sped onward, until it was merely a dot on the horizon again. Asmaa had still sat bolt upright in the passenger seat, shaking, her hand gripping the door handle. It was Ali who told Rick that he could sit up again.

"What the fuck was that?" Rick had asked.

"They look like mujahideen, but they just fucking with us," Ali had said. "Shooting for fun to show who's the big man on the road."

Rick had snorted. "Yes, that was so much fun."

Asmaa had cried briefly. "This is just becoming too much," she'd said. "Too much. Just when you think it cannot get worse, it does."

Rick, he later told Rita, had wanted to put a reassuring hand into hers from the back seat, but he had restrained himself. Instead, "Take a few days off, Asmaa," he had said. "Spend time with your family."

But Asmaa had shaken her head. "The less time we spend with our own families, the safer they are," she'd said. Rick reported that back to Rita and Claude, and the three of them were stricken with guilt for endangering the lives not just of the Iraqis they worked alongside and loved but of their families as well. They discussed asking Nabil and Asmaa to simply come and live at the villa. Rick said he'd have to bring it up with the paper first, because to invite them would likely cost tens of thousands of dollars more in life insurance, when the *Standard* had only just agreed to cover Ali.

So these were the things they talked about late at night over their drinks and cigarettes—their unexpressed celebration of making it alive through another day in Baghdad—while guards surrounded the villa and patrolled the roof. They talked about the burned-to-a-crisp corpses of the American contractors that insurgents had strung up on the bridge in Fallujah, how they had swung there in such odd, gruesome poses, like charred ballet dancers, and about whether the Americans had crossed the final line with the photos of humiliation from Abu Ghraib, American soldiers giving the thumbs-up alongside naked, hooded Iraqi prisoners forced to stand like Christ on the cross, or to crawl on all fours like dogs. Ali told them that they should hope that if they were ever kidnapped, they would be kidnapped by the Shi'a-led Mahdi Army, and not by Sunnis, because everyone knew that Sunnis were vicious and would decapitate you or burn you to death, while Shi'a, with some rare exceptions involving power tools drilled into the leg, would merely keep you for a few days, or weeks, to score political points, until somewhat traditional negotiations occurred to obtain your release.

And everyone agreed with Ali. But that was also because everyone knew that the Shi'a, long degraded by Saddam, were ascendant and hence not filled with the murderous, mortified rage of the Sunnis.

That particular night, Rita knew in her gut it was not a good idea to accept the glass of Maker's Mark from Claude, that it would have been a better idea to take her cue from Umm Nasim and go to bed. This gut feeling, in fact, had been growing, as she realized that a year in the inferno of Iraq—with only three short breaks, two to Beirut and one to Boston for the holidays—was grinding her down. Finely, like the sand that blew constantly through the air here and covered one's clothes and face in a powdery film.

This day in particular had simply been too miserable. It had started at five in the morning with a mighty explosion, perhaps a car bomb a kilometer away, that had jolted the villa and awakened her with a scream. She could not get back to sleep after that, amid the wail of ambulance sirens, so she dressed and went downstairs, marveling that the blast had seemingly not awakened the others. She started the coffee in the kitchen and sat down in the dark, empty front room to check her e-mail.

Amid the usual queue of work messages, one popped out, from Bobby, titled "I'm comingggggggg!"

"My dearest beautiful favorite cuz," it began,

I got some major news to share with you. In August we're gonna be deployed to Camp Blue Diamond in Rammady (spelling?) to take some pressure off the Marines. You probably heard they are getting creamed there. I was thinking that maybe you could come down from Bagdad and do a story there and we could hang out! My Ma's scared that I'm going but I haven't been training up for a year for nothing and now we're all ready to finally put all this hard training to some use and its about time. It definately looks like we need more boots on the ground over there if we're gonna wrap this thing up and show that we're there to help build up the democracy and not just be like the occupiers forever right? I read all your articles online and I show them to my buddies here and say hey that's my cousin! I liked the article where you talked to the religious guys that definitely took some kahonies. It's so fucking weird (oh sorry your okay if I swear right) we are both gonna be in Iraq at the same time, I hope we can hang out! Okay anyway cuz I better go some other guys here wanna use the computer and I can't hog it all for myself as much as I wanna talk to you more. Definately write back to me even though I know you are crazy busy with your reporting and let me know if you think you can come to Rammady to write a story about us. Take care of yourself over there everybody in the family is woried about you and just remember that even though I give you a hard time I worry about you too and BE CAREFUL!

Love your wise mouth little cuz,
Bobby

Rita's stomach churned as she read. Ramadi was a nightmare. Twelve marines had been killed there only a few weeks ago in an effort to take the city back from Sunni insurgents. This had been exactly her worry, that Bobby would be deployed right into the heart of the Sunni Triangle instead of some relatively uneventful part of the country in the north or south.

Fucking Bobby! It still infuriated her that he thought of the whole idea of coming to Iraq as an adventure because he was bored with the prospect of staying home and being a car mechanic. She considered how sick with worry her Auntie Carol must be at the moment. The sad thing was, she would have no comforting words for Carol, were they to talk. Bobby was going into just about the worst part of Iraq to which one could be deployed.

"Dearest cuz," she wrote back, as she sipped the sour, watery coffee they relied on. What on earth was she going to say to him?

> *I'm sure you're not surprised to hear that I am not exactly happy that you are being deployed, as exciting as it may sound to you. I'm sure you know that it has gotten so dangerous over here in the past year. It is nowhere near what it was like last spring. We used to be able to walk around Baghdad fairly freely in our first months here, and now every time we leave the compound it's a major security production and we're scared for our lives until we get back. It's fucking hell, actually.*

She hadn't expected that burst of anger on her part, but she decided to leave it. Bobby might as well know what he was getting himself into. What she really wanted to tell him was what a botched joke of a war he was risking his life for. But she curbed herself.

> *Try to find out exactly what date you guys will actually be installed at Blue Diamond and I'll make some inquiries and see if I can come visit you and maybe even do a story about it. But I have to be*

honest, the highways out of Baghdad are a nightmare now. Some of my colleagues got shot at coming back from Karbala last week, and that's not even as dangerous as the Sunni Triangle. So . . . I can't promise but I'll look into it. And I don't blame Auntie Carol for being worried that you're leaving soon. I just hope they have enough body armor for you guys by the time you get here.

This was something else she'd been reporting on, that the military had actually not provided enough protective vests for soldiers, who had been asking family and friends at home to send them commercial versions. It infuriated her. Even on the simplest levels, they were fucking everything up.

But then she erased that line. It wasn't fair of her to keep scaring him when his deployment was now a done deal.

I hope you understand that I'm just worried about you. I suppose I admire that you want to serve your country.

Then she deleted that line. She simply couldn't subscribe to that bullshit.

Please give my love to Uncle Terry and Auntie Carol and everyone and tell them I missed them on Easter.

Briefly, she wondered whether she would even make it back alive for another Easter. She'd spent this particular Easter trapped in the villa, as usual, doing her best to piece together bits of information about a mass Mahdi Army ambush of a U.S. military convoy out at the airport. Nabil, sweetly, had given her a small chocolate bunny, and they had joked that it was only a matter of time until the bunny was kidnapped or decapitated.

Love, your MUCH OLDER AND WISER COUSIN, Rita (Meter Maid)

Concluding the e-mail, she hit "send."

She wasn't through her next e-mail, about a Coalition Provisional Authority press conference at noon in the Green Zone, when she heard noises in the kitchen. There she found Claude, barefoot, in a T-shirt and pajama bottoms, his hair mussed and sleep still in his eyes, fixing coffee.

"Sabah el-kheir," he muttered, and she returned the greeting. At some point, the non-Iraqi staff in the villa had taken to speaking small daily pleasantries—good morning, hello, good-bye, please, and thank you, alongside a few choice curses—in Arabic.

"Did the bomb wake you?" she asked.

Claude shook his head. "There was a bomb?"

Slowly, Rita shook hers as well. "Jesus. Maybe I dreamed it. Maybe a bomb in my dreams woke me up. I don't even know anymore."

Claude put sugar in his black coffee. "The first thing I thought today when I woke up was that it is the birthday of Céline. But it is still too early to call her."

Céline was his girlfriend in Paris, an advertising exec. Rita smiled. "What would you do if you were there with her today?"

"Ahhhh," he purred, warming to the thought. "We would take a day from work, walk in Buttes-Chaumont, or next to the Canal de l'Ourcq, sit at a café and drink beers in the afternoon, watch people pass, watch the old men play pétanque."

She closed her eyes and shook her head slightly, savoring. "And all in open space," she added. "Walking as slow as you wanted to."

"Yes."

She reached for a drag of his cigarette. Recently, she'd been breaking a self-imposed rule that she would not smoke until evening. "There's a press conference at the Green Zone today at eleven," she told him. "That'll be today's life-threatening journey."

Two hours later, the three TV screens were on, Rick and Ali had emerged from their rooms, Nabil and Asmaa had arrived, and the morning ritual of prioritizing and delegating coverage had begun. Everyone gathered around the big table with coffee and tea as Umm Nasim, swathed in black save the baleful oval of her old face, spread out breakfast arranged from supplies Ali had brought: the flat bread, the soft white gaymar cheese, a large pan of scrambled eggs, a plate of sliced tomatoes.

"Rita, I wanna put you on Bremer at the Green Zone," Rick said, his mouth half full of bread and cheese. "Ali can take you over."

"Because someone has to get the real story on what's going on in Iraq," she cracked. Asmaa chuckled along with her, which heartened her, because she'd often felt that Asmaa resented her, although she'd seemed to be warming lately. Save Umm Nasim, they were the only two women in the bureau, and Rita wanted them to get along.

Rick wiped his mouth. "Hey, listen, it's important. The CPA is under the gun to hand over power to the Iraqis by the end of June, and Bremer's the head on the beast. I'm curious if there's cracks in his optimism, with more and more photos coming out of Abu Ghraib. And what's more," Rick added, "you get to spend a few hours in the Bubble!"

The Bubble was what they all called the Green Zone, that surreal, hyper-defended city within a city dominated by American fast food, fat contractors from Texas and Omaha, lithe men and women jogging to the gym or to the pool in shorts and tank tops, and row after row of residential trailers, like some strange, low-budget retirement community in the California desert.

Ali rubbed his hands together. "Fried chicken for lunch."

Rita smiled. "Definitely fried chicken for lunch." Everyone knew that Ali loved fried chicken and fake Pepsi. It was his favorite meal, one they'd grabbed often at Al Saha before it'd become too dangerous for Iraqis and Westerners to be seen eating together there—or anywhere, really.

Rick determined that he and Asmaa would go to Adhamiya to talk to civil servants—cops and teachers and engineers—who were now un-employed and angry because the rising Shi'a power base had barred tens of thousands of Sunni from holding jobs in the new era in retaliation for their having belonged to Saddam's Baath Party. Nabil and Claude would join a convoy of journalists at Abu Ghraib, invited by the CPA and the U.S. military, to be shown how they were turning the place around after the scandal.

Thus everyone began the arduous process of putting on flak jackets, and Rita and Asmaa added full-cover abayas on top of them. They'd long since stopped wearing a simple head scarf along with a blouse and jeans; in the newly dangerous Baghdad, it was better to simply appear as a pillar of flowing black fabric.

Rita suited up alongside Nabil. "I'm sorry we won't be together today," she said. It was true. Most days they worked as a pair, calling themselves the Danger Twins. They'd developed their English-Arabic interviewing volley, which had caused prickliness in their first week together, into a well-oiled system in which each now had an instinct for when to keep silent and let the other speak. He improved her Iraqi Arabic and she, in turn, improved his English, each of them explaining idioms in passing. When he smiled, as he still sometimes did, and his eyes crinkled, he reminded her vaguely of Sami, and she softened inside for a rare, brief moment. She worried each night until he called her sat phone to say he'd made it home safely.

"I know," he replied. "No Danger Twins."

"Nope. How is your family?"

"Everyone is okay, except everyone is trapped in the house and making everyone angry. But the neighbor's son is gone. Nuri. He is fourteen. The mother is at our house, crying."

"What happened to him?"

"We think he is kidnapped. That family has some money. They are waiting to hear a request from the kidnappers, God willing. So that is why my nephew and niece are not allowed to leave the house and why everyone is driving everyone crazy."

"Jesus. Can we talk to them?"

"No, please don't." He looked genuinely afraid. "If Americans and journalists get involved, it might make it worse. For my family, too."

"Even if we don't use names?"

"Please, Rita."

She pursed her lips, chastened. "Okay. It's just hard to hear this stuff is going on."

He shrugged. "It is."

In the armored car, she lay down in the back seat as usual, out of view, while Ali floored it through Mansour, their chase car—full of armed men poised to jump out and shoot should their own car be ambushed—just behind them. Having to hide like this in the car, unable to gauge the mood in the streets, frustrated her no end. Instead she had to stare up at the tops of concrete buildings, the occasional minaret, and that implacable blue Baghdad sky. It was odd, she often thought, that Baghdad in spring could have such serenely perfect weather while the city itself was imploding. It had become common to see a thick plume of black smoke, from a car or a roadside bomb, rising grimly in relief against that flawless azure sky.

Eventually, from her low perch, she saw that they'd begun moving through a landscape of hideous concrete blast walls and concertina wire, which meant they were driving through the successive phases of security that led to the heart of the Green Zone. When Ali stopped the car, she knew they'd queued for the first of many security checkpoints, so she sat up and withdrew from her bag both her and Ali's press-clearance cards.

"Oh my God." She saw that there were at least twenty vehicles ahead of them before the checkpoint. "A mortar is gonna hit us before we make it up there."

Ali lit a cigarette. "Inshallah, no. But maybe." The Green Zone was always getting mortared, mostly with ineffectual rockets flying over the blast walls and landing in open space, although there had been exceptions—notably, the rockets that last year had hit one side of the Al-Rasheed, the ugly concrete hotel tower within the Green Zone that housed journalists and bureaucrats. The stairwells had been slick with blood from injured guests making their way downstairs.

She sat back in the car and sighed, irritated and tense. "Jesus Christ," she muttered. She was muttering this a lot, she realized. She wasn't handling the grind well. Rick had told her she needed to take up some kind of relaxation program—yoga or meditation. Rick said that he meditated for ten minutes when he woke up, which she found hard to believe, but perhaps it explained why he seemed to be able to keep his cool, day in and day out, after decades of covering war zones.

She asked Ali for a drag on his cigarette. He laughed and handed it back to her.

"How's your family?" she asked. She was becoming obsessed with the Iraqi staffers' families.

Ali exhaled. "Oh! I didn't tell you. They are leaving."

"They're leaving?"

"They're going to Damascus. My mother has cousins there. They hate it here now. They want to leave before the Shi'a take power because Adhamiya will not be a good place for Shi'a families then."

She knew what he meant. Ali's family was among the Shi'a minority in Adhamiya. Saddam had always tamped down those Sunni-Shi'a tensions, even if everyone knew that the country was run by Sunnis, and mixed neighborhoods had been peaceful, but now all that was breaking down.

"Are you going with them?" She dreaded asking. She was incredibly fond of him, sometimes preferring him, with his shrugging, who-gives-a-fuck-about-anything demeanor, to Nabil, who could be serious and finicky. He was also a fast and fearless driver.

"I can't. I have to stay here and make this good money to send to them. So I will put a Sunni friend in our house to guard it, and I will continue to sleep on the couch at the newspaper. So we are like a new family now."

She laughed ruefully. "I guess we are." She exhaled and shook her head. "We have completely destroyed this city."

"It will get better."

"Do you honestly think so?"

"At least Saddam is gone. That is a step."

She opened her mouth to protest but thought better of it. She was happy for Ali that he could still feel optimistic, even as his own family prepared to evacuate.

Finally, at the checkpoint, Gurkhas, those hired Nepalese soldiers, patted them down, then inspected their car before letting them through. They drove through another five hundred meters of blast walls before they came to a second checkpoint, where more security men, this time South African, doubled down on the prior routine, finally directing them to a nearby parking lot that was manned by more South Africans, one of whom body- and car-searched them one more time.

After that, they were on their feet in the surreal world of the Green Zone, crossing paths with the many young American CPA staffers—boys in khakis, button-downs, and crew cuts; girls with no-nonsense ponytails, skirts, and low heels—all of them chattering into their sat phones as though they were hurrying from one congressional building to another on Capitol Hill back in D.C., where most of them were from.

They showed ID, and were patted down, one more time at the gates to the palace, this time by American soldiers. After that, they hurried down the pathway, past the towering, well-tended palm trees, toward the palace itself. Whether one thought of the present project as a power handover, an endless occupation, or both, its peculiar ecology revealed itself now: the military men and women in camos; the civilian CPA bureaucrats who were inclined now to imitate their revered leader, Paul Bremer, by wearing combat boots with their shirts and ties; the tribal leaders in flowing robes, keffiyahs on their heads held in place by double circles of black cord; the everyday Iraqis who cooked and cleaned and hauled supplies to and fro, who might spend an entire day installing and repairing air-conditioning units so that every interior in the Green Zone would be properly chilled once Iraq's scalding summer set in.

Everyone was crisscrossing, barking into sat phones, calling out hellos. And then of course there were the journalists, from all over the world, the print hacks and the TV crews, hurrying into the palace alongside Rita and Ali to make the press conference in time. Rita saw the tall blond bombshell from Slovenian TV clacking across the pavilion in her impossibly high heels and tight cerulean dress, her crew behind her.

And then, pumping his short legs toward them from between two palm trees, came Ezra, from public radio back home, her own age. He was one of her closest friends here outside the villa. The prior year, before it became too dangerous to go to and from the villa at night for anything but the most important reasons, they'd spent evenings in the bar at the Al-Rasheed, gossiping about colleagues and mulling over plans, which they'd never executed, to take a four-day break together to Dubai to drink and lie by a pool without fear of being hit by mortar fire.

"How's life in the villa?" he called, falling into hurried step with them.

"What do you think, Ali?" Rita asked, in a sarcastic singsong. "How's life in our little villa?"

"Very fun!" Ali chortled. "Party all the time."

Rita laughed sharply. "It's like *The Real World: Baghdad*. We even have a hot tub."

They queued up for their final security check—bag searches and pat-downs—administered by American soldiers, before entering the Republican Palace. Rita hated that the pat-down for her and Ezra was cursory, while Ali's pat-down was thorough, as though he were being frisked for a homemade bomb taped to the inside of his thigh. Americans in the Green Zone viewed every non-VIP Iraqi who worked or entered there as a potential threat. Any one of them, went the American logic, could be ferrying details, maps back to the insurgents outside, to help them plan a mortar attack or a breach. The reality, she knew, was that such Iraqis were risking their lives daily for decent salaries they couldn't possibly obtain in the city at large. Each morning, they were forced to be sitting ducks as they waited in long, segregated security lines just to get inside.

And then they were inside the palace, whose colossal, cold opulence—endless vaulted expanses of marble and gold inlay, punctuated by elaborate mosaics along the walls and in the floors—never ceased to awe and offend Rita. It was one of the few times, in fact, when she wondered whether there hadn't been justice in taking out Saddam, when she thought about the obscene sums the man had spent on these hideously ornate palaces and monuments to himself throughout the country, dozens of them, while he let his own people suffer and scrape by under sanctions.

By the same token, the Americans could not have more thoroughly turned the gaudy edifice into an engine of Yankee bureaucracy. A voice on a loudspeaker regularly barked announcements (one said that the pool would be closed for cleaning in the afternoon). Fat marble columns served as bulletin boards for all manner of directives, including flyers announcing a yoga class, a Bible-study group, and a special "urban cowboy" country-and-western theme for the Friday night disco party at Al-Rasheed.

"You're alone," Rita remarked to Ezra as they began filing into the press conference room, greeting colleagues along the way. "Where's your interpreter?"

"He quit. He got too scared."

"That's happening a lot."

They took seats. Rita couldn't help noticing how few American journos were in the room now, compared with a couple of months before. Many outlets had pulled out after Al-Rasheed had been hit late last year, which left her feeling proud that the *Standard* had kept its staff in Baghdad at great financial and logistical expense. But she also worried that their newfound rarity as American reporters increased the value on their heads.

Half a dozen American and Iraqi functionaries of the transition filed in through a side door and took their places behind the lectern. The room quieted.

"I have to admit," Rita whispered to Ezra, "I always get a little excited to see Bremer's hair."

"He does have great hair," he whispered in reply.

Yet it wasn't Bremer who walked out to the lectern but a member of his so-called Governance Team, a bald, square-jawed suit named Collins, who'd left a job in public affairs for a major military supplier to do the same work for the CPA.

"Good morning and subbul kier," Collins began, his gesture at bilingualism rendered in flat Midwesternese. "Ambassador Bremer can't

be here today. He went north to Erbil this morning to say a final farewell
to tribal leadership there and won't be back until tonight." Then, reading
from a paper: "I've been asked to brief you on a rebooted effort between
the CPA, the Iraqi Governing Council, and tribal and religious leaders
throughout the country to stabilize key regions and communities in
advance of CPA withdrawal from Iraq next month. Ambassador Bremer
prepared this briefing before he left early this morning."

Ezra leaned over to her. "No hair today."

"I guess not. And I love that in his final weeks in Iraq, he's visiting
the friendly Kurds while the rest of the country is in hell."

What followed was more or less what she expected. The unrest in
Fallujah and Najaf was unfortunate and unforeseen, Collins read dully
from his prepared statement, but it had sparked an opportunity for
renewed negotiations among key parties that were crucial toward stabi-
lizing autonomous Iraqi leadership in preparing for the CPA's planned
exit in six weeks. The unrest actually had an upside, Collins continued,
because it made clear sectarian and logistical tensions, which would be
addressed in Iraq's forthcoming, autonomously penned constitution.

"Thank you," concluded Collins.

The room erupted in shouted queries. Collins had pivoted to leave
the lectern, but, sighing, acknowledged the frenzy in the room, the flash
of cameras, and pivoted back into place, balefully considering whom to
call on first. Dutifully, Rita stood, raised her hand high, called out Collins's name. Others were asking what she wanted to ask, so she scribbled
his answers into her notebook.

Did the CPA have any idea how much of the insurgency in Fallujah
was made up of former soldiers of the Iraqi Army, which Bremer had
immediately disbanded upon arriving in Iraq? No, said Collins, they
had no idea, but intel indicated that much of the resistance in Fallujah
was driven by foreign fighters with ties to al-Qaeda. Average Iraqis
didn't want this.

Collins called on someone from French TV, who said, "But that
isn't what we are hearing on the streets. We are hearing that as long
as American troops are still in Iraq, as long as their convoys are on the

street, as long as they keep raiding homes in the middle of the night and scaring women and children, there are going to be IED bombings, there are going to be snipers."

Again, Collins stated dully, that was the work of foreign fighters.

On and on it went like this. Rita leaned toward Ali. "I don't know why we even bothered to come today," she whispered.

"For the fried chicken," he whispered back.

To her surprise, Collins pointed at her joylessly and called her name.

"Thank you, Mr. Collins," she began, her adrenaline surging. "So, we are hearing more and more reports of ordinary Iraqis being kidnapped right from their homes or yards, being pulled out of cars while sitting in traffic, and it appears that some of this is sectarian or political, but a lot of it appears to be a new way of making money, of extracting as much ransom from families as one can."

Collins opened his mouth to cut her off, but she pushed on: "People are talking about having to scramble to sell their cars, their jewelry, their valuables, to part with their life savings to get their family members returned to them, if they're lucky enough to. And they're saying that when they take the cases to the Iraqi police, the police merely shrug and tell them to take it to the Americans, to the CPA. Can you tell us what the CPA is doing to make the Iraqi police more equipped to handle these crimes?"

Collins stared at her and sighed. "That's a very multipart question."

The flatness of his voice elicited some laughter in the room. Rita smiled. "I know," she said.

"I think Ambassador Bremer will have more on this to share with you in a few days," Collins continued. "I would merely state that, as many of you know, we have begun the process of transferring training of the new Iraqi police from private contractors to the military itself, which we are confident will result in a far more equipped Iraqi police force. But it's also important to remember that ultimately Iraqis have to take charge of their own systems of governance and order. All the technical support in the world from CPA or elsewhere is for naught unless Iraqis can unite."

"But from Sunnis there is incredible distrust of some of the new units—" Rita began, but Collins had already turned from her and pointed elsewhere.

"At least you pushed it," Ezra whispered to her.

Collins wished the room good day and exited through the side door, followed by his coterie. The room rose, everyone gathering up bags and cameras and recorders, emanating a general muttering of confoundedness and dissatisfaction. Rita caught the eye of Meg Warren, from the biggest paper on the West Coast, and smiled sourly. Rita had come to Iraq somewhat in awe of Meg, a tiny blonde in her early forties who had first covered conflict abroad a decade ago in Bosnia.

Now Meg came over to Rita, Ezra, and Ali. "I'm disgusted by that waste of time we just sat through," she said.

Ezra laughed. "I know. Oh, did you know that *all* the resistance to the new Iraq is coming from outside jihadis? Every Iraqi is actually very cooperative. Right, Ali?"

"Right." Ali went along with the joke. "Especially in Fallujah. Very friendly there."

Everyone laughed ruefully.

"Oh," Meg added, turning to Ali. "If any of you know a good driver, will you let me know? Ours just quit. He said it's not worth the risk."

Rita's eyes narrowed slightly. "So you're still leaving the Bubble?"

Meg affected a macho swagger. "Hell, yeah. This is what we do."

"True," Rita conceded. But Meg's response irked her as well. Had they all gotten soft in the villa without knowing it? What kind of stories was Meg developing outside the Green Zone that she herself had missed while she holed up in the villa, relying on merely e-mail and phone? She realized she was tensely digging her toe into her shoe.

When she refocused, she found Ali's eyes on her. "Lunch?" he asked.

"Yes! Absolutely! Fried chicken!" She turned to Ezra and Meg. "You wanna join us?"

Both declined, saying they had to get back to work. This irked her as well. What could they be working on that they couldn't take forty-five minutes for lunch? Suddenly, she felt very insecure about the work she had been putting out. Had they perhaps been noticing that her byline had been carrying dull news, dutiful summaries of press conferences?

She and Ali, weaving their way through journalists and bureaucrats, made their way out of the conference room and across the central rotunda into the dining hall, which reminded Rita of the sprawling cafeterias in the basements of the congressional buildings in D.C. A large photo of the Twin Towers dominated one long wall, as always, but now it was festooned with red-white-and-blue bunting.

"Oh, look," she sneered to Ali. "They dressed it up."

He laughed. "To remind people why they are here while they eat."

At this point, they diverged, as they always did, he to the hot-food bar, she to the salad bar. In line, she idly listened to two fortysomething American women with light Southern accents, each of them wearing a polo shirt, slacks, and low heels, discuss home renovations they planned to undertake when they got back to the States.

"When do you two ship out?" she broke in, aiming to sound genial.

They turned. "I'm leaving Sunday," said the blonder of the two, smiling beatifically.

"How are you feeling about it?"

She raised her eyes heavenward and shook her head. "I am counting the seconds. I just want my own bed so bad. And my dogs."

"And I'm going back with Bremer's contingent," said the other.

"Ah!" Rita said. "One of the diehards!" It came out sounding sharper and more sardonic than she'd intended.

The woman rolled her eyes. "Please. Those are my orders. I'd be going back Sunday with this one"—she arced her thumb sideways toward her friend—"if I could. I got here four days after the attack on the Al-Rasheed, and I am so ready to leave."

Rita nodded. "Oh wow. Since last fall, then?"

"Yes. I'm exhausted."

Finally, Rita introduced herself, mentioning she was from the *Standard*. "How are you two feeling about things as the CPA gets ready to leave?"

Instantly, the women's smiles melted away and their faces tightened. "You're from the *Standard*?" the blonder of the two asked, hardness in her voice now.

Rita nodded. "Believe it or not, we're not at the hotel. They isolate us in an armed compound in Mansour." She was trying to be chatty, self-deprecating.

"We know about your villa," the other woman said, coldly.

"And we're not authorized to talk to you," said the blonder one. Then they both turned their backs on her.

Rita just stood there, an uncomfortable half smile on her own face. She was used to this treatment from CPA staffers. They were almost entirely Republicans, and they hated the *Standard*. Ordinarily, she would not have even tried to get middling staffers to talk to her. But after seeing Meg and Ezra, she was especially impatient for new material.

Then the blonder of the two turned back to her. "But I will tell you something off the record," she said. "We have worked *incredibly hard* here, night and day, and we have done good work, and that will become evident eventually."

The second woman turned and said, more softly, "You have no idea how hard everyone has worked here. It's not all fun out by the pool like the stories say. We've tried to rebuild a country in just a few months under incredible stress and really scary conditions."

"I never doubted that!" Rita insisted. "Would you just talk to me a bit on the record about what it feels like to be leaving and what you want to do when you get back?" Optimistically, she reached into her bag for her notebook.

The blonder one looked slightly anguished, as though her instincts were at war. "You'll twist whatever we say and make us look like awful people. Your paper always does."

"It's like you're trying to make up for being so rah-rah at the start," said the other.

Rita wanted to concede her that point. Her editor in D.C. had been pushing them especially hard since late last year to "dig in," as he put it, regarding the occupation's failings.

Instead, she merely said: "It's definitely not our intention to make you look like awful people. Obviously, you're all doing your best with a highly flawed premise."

Instantly, she regretted her choice of words. "Well, there you go!" the blonder one said. "You just admitted it. You think it's wrong in the first place that we're even here. So how can you see any of the good?"

"That's not what I meant!" People in line ahead of them turned, curious, brows furrowed. Her tone had been escalating. "I meant that anyone would agree that the execution left a lot to be desired."

Again, the two women glanced at each other. The blonder one sighed, as though she were exasperated.

"Anyway," said the second one, "the fact remains that we're not authorized to talk on the record to press. So, off the record, *again*, I would merely say that we did the best we could with the situation we were dealt, and now we're going home. And I wish the people of Iraq the very best. I really do. The ball's in their court now."

The blonder one looked at her friend, then at Rita, then nodded in assent.

"And please stay safe as long as you're here," said the second. Then they both again turned their backs to her, stiff and silent, as though they were waiting to be away from her to talk.

Rita wanted the ground to swallow her up. She'd been rebuffed or even yelled at countless times in her twelve years of reporting and, like most journos, prided herself on her thick skin, but in this instance she felt strangely shamed, as though the women had seen right to the heart of her cynical, undermining, unpatriotic intentions. They also reminded her of the kind of bland, field-hockey-playing blond girls she'd gone to prep school with, girls whose friendship she'd initially tried to cultivate before she accepted that she was happier talking about the Marshall Plan with awkward boys from New Jersey or Michigan.

They were at the front of the line now, but she walked away, strode across the room, infuriated to find she was fighting back tears. She joined Ali in the hot-food line, smiled stiffly at him.

"No salad?"

"I changed my mind."

They were served fried chicken, macaroni and cheese, and stewed greens by Pakistani workers wearing smocks and paper hats; then they took their trays and sat opposite one another at the end of a long table. Instantly, Rita regretted that she'd abandoned the salad line. The sight of the processed, industrial food, shipped in from the United States via Kuwait, merely redoubled a queasiness she'd felt since breakfast, but she resigned herself to the meal and began pulling orangey fried skin off her chicken. Meanwhile, Ali was devouring his with both hands, gulping Coke simultaneously. She studied him as he ate.

Finally, he looked up. "What?" he asked, his mouth full. "Am I eating it the wrong way?"

"What? No. I'm just so angry."

He pointed to himself. "At me?"

"No, of course not. You're the best. At—" she paused. "At the situation." Her eyes swept over the room. "This is deeply fucked up."

He laughed, shook his head. "I don't think about it. I have no control over it. I'm lucky I have a job."

That softened her a bit. Who was she to fulminate, while his family was getting ready to leave the country? She smiled wanly at him. "We're lucky we have you."

"You see? Then everybody's lucky!"

She uttered a short, sharp laugh. "Right."

Five minutes later, Ali's sat phone rang. He answered it. Seconds later, he cried in dismay, "La, la!"—*No, no!*—then continued to listen. Rita's brows met, as she followed him. Someone had been killed, and now he was asking follow-up questions. Where was the body now? How was the mother? When was the funeral? He listened and nodded for several more seconds, at one point looking up at Rita and saying into the phone, "Of course, of course, I'll tell her." Then, "Ma'a as-salama," and Ali hung up.

"What is it?"

"You know Nuri, the boy of Nabil's family's neighbors?"

"Who was kidnapped?"

"They found him dead. His body got dumped at the end of their street."

"Oh no!" Her hands rose to her mouth. "Oh no! I thought they just wanted money."

Ali shook his head scornfully. "Nabil didn't tell you everything. The boy's father, that family, they did too many bad things for Saddam. He was—you know—he was a'ameel. Informer."

"You think it was Shi'a who took the boy?"

Ali shrugged. "Maybe not even Shi'a. Anybody with—you know, hiqid. I don't know the English word."

"What does it mean?"

"You know, when you did something bad to me a long time ago and I want to give you equal bad, I carry hiqid against you."

"Oh, you mean a grudge."

Ali cocked an eye. "That's the word in English."

She nodded.

"Okay. So anybody with this grudge word. Maybe a Baathist who lost a job because of the father."

"Why didn't Nabil tell me all this?"

"He didn't want you writing about it. That's why he called, to say he left the villa to go home and help the family prepare for the funeral, because they are crazy right now, crying and screaming. And to say please please please, Miss Rita, no stories. It will just make things worse."

"But these are the very things we need to be reporting on. To show the disaster here."

"Well," Ali said, folding his arms defiantly, "I am only telling you what Nabil told me. The family wants no journalists there, or they are afraid they will get more mashakil on their house. They want to have the funeral as quietly as possible and then go to Jordan."

She sighed, put a hand to her forehead. "Jesus Christ," she muttered. "I may as well go home."

"And you can leave anytime you want." Ali said it sharply, with sudden indignation in his eyes, which took her aback.

"I know. I'm sorry. I'm just—this is all so frustrating."

This time, he did not reply, merely shrugged and looked at her as if to say, *Well, so what?*

When they finished eating, there was the winding path out of the palace and the bag inspection and pat-down before they reached the parking lot. By now the sun was beating down mercilessly, and the temperature had surpassed thirty-five degrees Celsius; Rita dreaded putting on the polyester abaya again, but she did so. In the car, she slunk down in the back seat but refused to lie on the floor. Ali did not protest; he was indulging her, tired of scolding, she supposed.

Leaving the Green Zone was much easier and faster than entering it, and sooner than she expected, they were on the traffic-choked Qadisaya Expressway back to Mansour, a cacophony of bleats and beeps emanating from small, squarish, beat-up cars from the early 1980s. Back off the highway, they crawled through Beirut Square, lined with shops and shoppers, including some unveiled women. It had been several days since she had seen life, crowds, outside either the villa or the Green Zone, and she thrilled to the sight.

"Things don't look that bad," she remarked. "Seems pretty normal."

Ali grunted in reply.

They were driving slowly by a small, shabby chaikhana, a tea cart, where about half a dozen older men, some in dishdashas, some in shirts and slacks, drank tea and smoked nargileh.

"Let's pull over here and talk to these men and get a feel on the street," she instructed him, grabbing her bag.

Ali twisted around. "What? No. It's too dangerous. I just want to get you back. There's nowhere to park."

But she was already out of the car, twisting her abaya into place around her shoulders. "Take a minute to find a place and come meet me," she called back to Ali, not waiting for his reply.

As she approached the men, whose attention she had caught as she approached, she put her hand to her heart in the customary greeting. "Excuse me, gentlemen," she began in her Iraqi Arabic, which had improved much in a year. She named herself and the *Standard* and requested that the men allow her to ask some questions about how they were feeling about the current state of security and politics.

They eyed her, then one another, warily, none of them saying a word. They each had the same thick, dyed-black mustache—nearly every middle-aged man in Iraq did—and heavily creased forehead. One of the men shook his head in a sad manner and seemed to weakly wave her away.

"Have you had personal incidents of violence or crime in your family or your neighborhood?" she persisted. "I will not use your family name if you prefer."

Some of the men knit their brows and craned their heads forward as though they were trying to understand her. She wondered if her accent was completely unintelligible to them. Finally, one of the dishdasha men, the portliest, with the bushiest mustache, stepped forward and offered her a small glass of tea, which she accepted.

"Ahlan, ya anisa," he began, gently and slowly, as though to be understood. "This is my café. You are welcome to a tea, but please, only briefly. We are very afraid to talk to Americans."

"Of course, ya ammo, I understand. I will not stay long." To free her hands, she drank her tea in a single, ungainly gulp, which drew an amused smile from one of the men, then reached into her bag for her notebook and pen. But when he saw them, the café owner raised a hand in polite protest.

"Please, ya anisa, no notebook to show you are a sahafiya. Too dangerous."

She dropped them back into her bag. "Mafi moushkala. May I ask your name?"

The man glanced worriedly at his friends. "Abu Hussein," he finally said. Rita thought it was likely a falsehood.

"Thank you. And may I ask, it goes well, the business?"

He laughed. "I have no business left. These men come because they are my friends, cousins. They come just for the company."

"We cannot stay in the house all day," said one of the other men. "We have to get away from our wives for a few hours."

The men laughed, and Rita smiled. Her pulse quickened. At last!
She was reporting again.

"If a bomb goes off, God wills it," said another, the slightest of the
bunch, who lacked the third and fourth fingers of his right hand. "There
is nothing we can do."

At that point, Ali came up beside her, huffing, sweat on his forehead.
He flashed her a scowl to let her know he wasn't happy.

"This is my colleague, Ali," she said. "But if you please, gentlemen,
what do you think of the situation? Will Iraq be ready to govern itself
when the Americans leave at the end of June?"

They stared at her, uncomprehending, until Ali rephrased for her.
Then the men broke into laughter again.

"Saddam was a devil, ya anisa, but we were better off with him,"
said the slightest. "We are too—there are too many religions, too many
families, for us to have a democracy. We need a strong hand."

"But," broke in the so-called Abu Hussein. "The Americans must
go as soon as possible. The situation cannot improve at all until they
do. We are a proud people, and we do not like to be occupied like the
Palestinians."

All the men nodded gravely in assent, and Rita nodded with them.
"And what do you want," she continued, "from the new Iraqi government? Who should—"

But as she spoke, Abu Hussein put his hands to his heart. "And
now, ya anisa, you should leave. It is too dangerous for you to be on the
streets, and it is too dangerous for us to be talking to you. It is clear,"
and he gestured around her face, "that you are not Iraqi."

She pretended to simply not understand him. "How do you feel
that the Iraqi Army was disbanded?"

"Ya anisa, please go, and let God guide you home."

Rita held the man's stare for a moment. His large eyes, rimmed
black with exhaustion, were kind, yet pleading. She was utterly frustrated.
A year ago, he would have sat her down, served her tea and pastries,
shared openly with her. Now she could barely get two thoughts out of
him or his friends. Her very presence was anathema.

So she sighed. "Of course, ya ammo. I thank you and your friends very much for your time, and I wish safety for you and your families."

All the men smiled and muttered, "Ma'a assalama," which she and Ali returned before walking away. She was dispirited, but she couldn't blame Baghdadis for it. She was generally in awe of how kind, how resilient, they remained amid the hell they'd been through.

Impulsively, she turned back. "I am very sorry for the problems in your lives since the invasion," she told the men. "Very, very sorry."

They nodded and shrugged. "Thank you, ya anisa," said Abu Hussein. Then he added something she didn't catch. She turned to Ali.

"He said that you did not cause it," he said. Then he motioned for her to follow him.

They weren't twenty paces on when they heard the bone-rattling sound of a Kalashnikov from around the corner of a large concrete building, that visceral *tat tat tat tat tat*. She turned her head in that direction.

"Do not ask me to drive you toward the sound of the guns," Ali snapped at her. "I won't do it."

"Fine, whatever. I've given up."

In the car, she lay down on the back floor. She figured she'd given Ali enough grief for the day. Once again, feeling utterly defeated, she watched concrete rooftops fly by until she recognized the blast walls erected on their own street, the heavily armed funnel they had created to get into the villa.

Inside, they found no one but Umm Nasim, chopping onions in the kitchen while listening to Iraqi news radio. Rita was embarrassed to be the first one back. Rick and Claude were probably out getting real stories. She asked Umm Nasim to make coffee.

"Did you hear about the boy?" Umm Nasim asked in turn. "Nuri?"

"I did."

"His father was bad. But it was against God to kill him."

Rita said nothing. It drove her crazy that she could not write about the incident.

In the front room, she found that Ali had passed out on the couch, one of his arms hanging comically toward the floor. She sat before her laptop, opened her notebook, and started tapping out her dull story, leading with the men in the chaikhana and the fact that Baghdad had become so dangerous that Iraqis did not even want to be seen talking to foreigners.

That was how the hours slipped away into the realm of Maker's Mark. First, Claude came back, without Nabil; then, about an hour later, Rick returned, without Asmaa, who'd walked home over the bridge from Adhamiya to Kadhimiya, declining a ride because she said she wanted to clear her head after a long day talking to out-of-work Baathists.

"They're the educated middle class in this country, the people who would actually know how to run it, and they're leaving in droves," Rick told Rita. "Everyone was talking about Damascus and Amman."

"Well, at least they talked to you," Rita said bitterly. "I think today might have been my all-time low since I've been here."

"Everyone's coming up against that. Nabil and Asmaa are going to try to start smuggling folks into the villa here to talk to us. They don't want us coming and going at their homes."

She shook her head slowly. "Did you hear back from D.C. about covering Nabil and Asmaa to come live here?"

Rick pursed his lips. "I don't think they're gonna cover it. They said our costs are already through the roof."

"But that is such bullshit!" She threw down a pen as she said it. "They can pay to put fucking blast walls up and down the whole block, and they can't pay to help us protect our two biggest assets and their families? They're already paying to cover Umm Nasim."

Rick rose. Rita's eyes fells on his very large hands, the backs flecked with black hair. She found him attractive, and it irritated her that, on top of everything else, she'd had to carefully tamp down any such indications. She'd been sleeping alone for over a year now, and although most nights she yearned to be curled up in Sami's arms in Beirut with Joujou, the little yellow kitten, asleep on the bed with them, there were also nights when she pictured Rick lying alone in bed in the next room and allowed herself the fantasy of joining him. Not for sex, just to feel a man's arms around her as she fell asleep. Yet she was certain he saw her merely as a junior colleague, someone to be schooled. What's more, he had a girlfriend fifteen years his junior named Talia, a freelance photojournalist based in D.C., whom he talked about constantly.

Now he headed toward the kitchen. "The tough thing about covering war," he called back to her, "is that you don't always get the story you want, because you have to worry about staying alive, too."

"Where are you going?" she called after him.

She got his answer when he returned with a bottle of Maker's Mark and three small glass teacups. He poured them each a glass, and a glass for Claude, who'd been busy across the room running through photos. "Here," he said, pushing her glass toward her. "So Umm Nasim thinks it's tea."

Rita laughed sharply. "I think she's onto this trick already."

"But it shows we're trying to be respectful."

They wrote as they drank, something Rita had never done before, merging their reporting into one story to file, then were called to the table by Umm Nasim for the chicken she had roasted, which was sitting atop a platter of rice, alongside a salad and several small dishes of meze. It was the five of them tonight: Rita, Rick, Claude, Ali, and Umm Nasim, who beamed quietly as she watched her food go round and round. It was the only time she looked even remotely happy.

"Thank you, Umm Nasim, for this beautiful meal," Rick said in Arabic. It was one of the things he had taught himself to say flawlessly, and, in what had become a bit of a house joke, he said it before every meal, and Umm Nasim always replied, waving him away, "Do not thank me, it's my job, and I'll do it as long as God allows me to."

By the time they finished eating, they had edits back from D.C., which they addressed. Before they'd even finished, Ali had started watching *Friends* on the TV, dubbed into Lebanese Arabic, the episode where Rachel has a baby. Rick passed around more glass teacups of Maker's Mark. Occasionally, they heard the boots of the guards on the roof.

It was unusual for them to be doing this. Usually, after dinner, they continued working until twelve, sometimes one, as it was the middle of the afternoon in D.C. But this evening, everyone gave in, even Umm Nasim, who drank real tea and pretended not to know that everyone else wasn't. Rick had hidden the Maker's Mark below the sink in the kitchen, to which they would occasionally retreat for a refill. They smoked as they watched, Ali or even Rita translating throughout for Rick and Claude. It was a two-part episode, it turned out.

In a few hours, they were all in bed, the house dark and quiet. Head on her pillow, Rita realized she was drunk—drunker than she'd ever gotten during the evening "tea" sessions. She yearned deeply for Sami.

She rose from her bed, in just her tank top and boxer shorts, and walked out of her bedroom. She paused by Rick's closed door, put her ear to it, wondering if she could hear him breathing or snoring. She raised her hand to knock but restrained herself at the very last second. Even drunk, she knew there'd be no way to take back such an action.

She wandered into the front room, dim and quiet but for the low hum of the computers and the generator out back. Cords and cables snaked along the floor amid chairs and tables littered with empty plastic water bottles, notebooks, workbags, useless reports, and briefings they'd been handed at Green Zone pressers. She stood there, observing this odd, ugly room that had been the center of their lives, their only sanctuary, for so many months.

Weaving slightly, catching tabletops for balance, she sat before her laptop, clicked to bring it out of darkness. There she saw, sent only seven minutes before, an e-mail from Sami, whom she hadn't spoken to in over a week. "Unbearable yearning" was the subject line.

"The worst night so far," it began.

> *I can't sleep I miss you so badly. Life here has been drained of joy, of meaning. So much is happening here, so many new businesses and buildings and parties and bars, so many new people coming through, and I can't enjoy any of it. I wake up in this empty apartment, looking for you along with Joujou, the only other one who feels the same ache I do, and I go to bed hugging a pillow pretending it's you.*

Rita gasped a bit as she read this. She had just been doing the same thing! Smashing her mouth into her pillow and muttering, "Sami."

I've fallen into a rut. I can't seem to move forward with school or anything. I don't even want to go see my parents to get out of the heat here. I just stay in the apartment with Joujou and the climatisation, hoping the electricity doesn't blow (it's actually been pretty good lately), and read and look at your things and miss you.

By this point, Rita was crying. She hit "reply" and wrote, her fingers flying from habit, even if too much bourbon blurred her vision of the type on the screen:

Habibi, I feel exactly the same way tonight. I lay in bed thinking about you and Joujou and desperately wanting to be there. I was telling Claude this morning that I'd give anything just to be able to walk to dinner with you down to the Corniche, actually eat good food and drink good wine, then walk home without fear of getting kidnapped or my head blown off by a sniper. I miss a simple ritual like that so much!

I think it's very likely I'll be sent back to Beirut after the CPA leaves in a few weeks. The situation here has become an absolute disaster—an absolute, absolute unmitigated failure, a travesty, a nightmare, just like you predicted, and I guess I knew deep down in my gut your prediction was true. I certainly am not one to ascribe noble motivations to the Bush administration but even I can't believe the extent to which we fucked this up. We have created a nightmare here that may take years to fix, if it ever gets fixed. Poor Iraqis—they are living in terror. Just today we heard about a 14-year-old boy who was kidnapped then killed because apparently his father was a Baathist snitch for Saddam. I mean—people are being killed left and right. The Iraqi police aren't equipped. And the occupation just keeps making it worse with their crazy, paranoid raids that scare the shit out of oblivious families in the middle of the night. They drag the whole family out into the street in their nightclothes, humiliating the women and terrifying the kids, and then arrest the men in the house just because they find a Kalashnikov. Everyone here has a

Kalashnikov, it's like a household appliance! They're trying to protect themselves and everything they own from kidnappers and thieves!

She stood up, wove her way to the kitchen, found the Maker's Mark under the kitchen sink where Rick had stashed it before they went to bed, poured herself what she deemed to be a very modest glass, and then went back to her laptop.

"I can't even do my job here anymore," she continued.

We're either stuck in the villa trying to get whoever we can on the phone, no eye contact or no context while we talk, or we're in the fucking Green Zone, a fucking bubble full of ill-equipped idiots and George Bush neocon disciples, going to useless press conferences where Bremer's people tell me that even though roadside bombs are going off every four minutes we should believe them when they say we are making incredible progress and Iraq will be in great shape when CPA pulls out in six weeks. Fucking right. Not. Everyone knows they're pulling out early to make it look like the mission here's been accomplished in time for election season. And forget reporting on the streets. Ali doesn't want to drive me anywhere but to and from the Green Zone. The hardest thing of all, today, I made us stop on the way back to talk to some old men in a café. And the owner was so sweet, like most Iraqis are, but he was basically like, please go, it's dangerous for us to talk to you. A year ago it wasn't like that. Americans fucking coming in thinking they're the holy saviors and then their presence becomes the single biggest reason for the bombings. We're so toxic.

She stopped typing, sipped. She thought she heard Umm Nasim moaning back in her room, but she wasn't sure. Maybe it was just the low tones of the generator.

"I dread another summer here," she continued. She paused again, sighed.

If I get sent home soon, can we please spend two weeks on the beach in Tyre and eat good food and drink good wine and think about nothing? I can't stand another night of dried, stringy lamb and rice. They'll have to give me some time off after this stint. Just the thought of that makes every muscle in my body relax.

"And until then . . ." She paused again.

Until then I'm going to try to do what I can here, even if I can barely go out. I don't want to leave feeling like I threw in the towel.

I miss you more than I can say. Please know that and understand that times when I didn't call or write back right away, we were just overwhelmed. I can't wait to be back in your arms and for you to be feeding me fatteh in bed. I know that sounds dirty but I miss your warm, delicious fatteh so much!

B7ebak, habibi, aini, hayati!

Rita

She sipped again and hit "send," wove her way into the kitchen to rinse out her glass, then went into her bedroom and collapsed on the bed in her clothes.

CHAPTER EIGHT

EXILE, PART 1

Almost exactly one week later, boiling with rage and humiliation, Rita was sitting on a South African jetliner flying from Baghdad to Amman, avoiding the glances of her fellow passengers, the homeward-bound private contractors and CPA hacks and a few other journalists, none of whom she was close to, thankfully. Flights into and out of Baghdad were notorious for their corkscrew takeoffs and landings—gut-churning spiraling ascents and descents that dispensed altogether with straight angles in a bid to avoid rocket-propelled grenades fired from the ground. Rita had heard many a tale of passengers losing the contents of their stomach in the process, clutching vomit bags with white knuckles, crying in shaken relief as the plane either touched ground or finally straightened up at a safe altitude.

And here was the takeoff. She gripped the arms of her seat. She'd lived through the corkscrew before, on her brief breaks out of the country. It was wild, even perversely enjoyable if you knew what to expect; it felt a bit like being hauled up the first steep ascent of a roller coaster with no subsequent plunge, your back and head smashed down deeply into your seat as the plane thundered straight up into the atmosphere before righting itself. Then everyone on the flight settled back, relaxed. The worst was over. They'd all escaped hell without insurgents having shot a fireball into the plane's underbelly, and this meant that in ninety minutes they would each be in the utterly secure, anodyne confines of Jordan, having a burger and a beer before subsequent flights took them back to D.C. or Atlanta or Dallas or wherever they were going.

Sitting by the window, Rita looked down as the whole sorry, bitter, brown and tan expanse of Baghdad unfurled before her. She felt no relief, only frustration and fury. She'd left a job, a story, a whole population unfinished. She'd hung in there with Rick and Claude and their fucking hardworking Iraqi colleagues who'd risked everything. They'd been a family, a crew, muddling through day after day under life-threatening conditions, and now the *Standard* was doing this to her? *I cannot believe this is happening*, she thought. Tears rose in her eyes, but she gulped and pushed them back. She would die before she let anyone on this flight see her cry.

Part of her anger was directed at herself. If she'd only had not quite so much Maker's Mark that night, even just not had that final glass alone in the dark before the laptop, she might not have hit "send," and all of this could have been avoided. Pathetic, garden-variety drunkenness, of the sort displayed by the Irish side of her family, had set her downfall in motion. She cringed, massaged her forehead.

That following day had not begun well, obviously. She woke in her clothes, hungover and headachy, horrified to realize it was eleven o'clock. Cracking open her bedroom door, she heard the hum and chatter of work going on down the hall in the front room. Deeply embarrassed, she hurried to the bathroom for a shower, then put on jeans and a T-shirt and entered the front room sheepishly, calling out a sour good morning. Everyone was there; everyone turned to look at her, grinning.

"Well, good morning, Sunshine," Rick said, and everyone laughed. And had Asmaa just laughed hardest?

"I'm so sorry," she groaned. "I'll just get some coffee and be right there."

"Happens to the best of us in a war zone," Rick called back.

Umm Nasim was in the kitchen, at the sink. She glanced sideways at Rita. "Habibti, are you sick today?" she asked.

Rita glanced back at her, ashamed, as she fixed coffee. Certainly the old woman could put two and two together. "I just didn't sleep well," Rita answered.

"I'll make you a good lunch today."

The thought of food made Rita sick, but she managed to murmur a thank-you.

"What's the latest?" she asked in the front room, standing over Rick, Asmaa, and Nabil, who were running down a list of people they wanted to try to bring to the villa to interview. Rita glanced at the list and recognized the names of some of the cabinet leaders on the Iraqi Governing Council, as well as that of a woman who had already received death threats for announcing her intention to run for office when elections took place after the CPA vacated.

"We're doing palace politics today on who's up for the prime minister slot," Rick said. "Trying to get some folks in today to talk about Ayad Allawi."

Rita nodded. "Bremer's darling."

Asmaa looked up. "Who has not been in Iraq for decades until now." She added, "That's the kind America loves."

"True," Rita murmured. Asmaa, who probably had lost fifteen pounds during the past year and had chronic dark circles under her eyes, had reached a point of open disgust with American policy in Iraq. She'd once leavened her critique with a sharp wit, but by now the exuberance was gone, leaving nothing but bitter remarks and a haunted look. Rita couldn't blame her. The mere commute to and from the villa each day was exhausting and nerve-racking for her and Nabil. It was risky, stressful work that they were somewhat imprisoned by, with no other options and an urgent need to squirrel away money so that their families might flee Baghdad if they had to. Although she went out of her way to be nice to Asmaa, it was clear nonetheless that Rita favored Nabil, her daily side-by-side, with a devotion bordering on motherliness.

She sat down before her e-mails, which included a reply from Sami. It read:

My sweet one,

You have to publish this. This is the real story of Iraq that nobody is hearing. Please let the world know. You have a responsibility.

A million kisses to you today for safety and love. I miss you so much I ache.

S.

His "You have a responsibility" irritated her slightly. He'd grown up with French newspapers and didn't fully understand, or believe in, the concept of unbiased, nonpartisan reporting, as much as she'd tried to explain it to him. He'd say that nothing was purely unbiased, so why even bother trying?

So she wrote back:

Sweetness, that's not the real story, that's my drunken rant to you in the middle of the night! Which of course earned me a nasty hangover today and a late start. So many kisses to you too and talk to you soon. B7ebak.

Then she began plowing through her other e-mails, making calls. Her hangover dulled as the hours crept forward. Asmaa gave word that a security detail was bringing by for a lunchtime interview a member of the Iraqi Governing Council, one of the Shiites on the body, which set Umm Nasim to fretting that she had nothing special to serve him beyond the daily lamb, rice, and salad, but then the IGC member sent a deputy instead, a dour young man who merely parroted the CPA-IGC line that everything was proceeding apace for a smooth transition of power from the Americans to the Iraqis come the end of June.

"But so many Iraqis," began Rita, "are disappointed to see the IGC filled with exiles. Can you really get the trust of the country with so few members who actually went through the Saddam era?"

Nabil translated, and the deputy smiled, as though indulging a child's grievances, addressing only Nabil and Asmaa as he replied.

"He says that the members of the IGC have the full love and support of the Iraqi people, but they are afraid to say so publicly for fear of revenge from the insurgents," Nabil said, with a dutiful flatness that almost made Rita crack a smile.

She set to writing up the interview once the deputy had left. It was past four o'clock when she noticed she had an e-mail from Claude, who was sitting across the room, his back to her.

"You better look at this," read the subject line.

She opened the e-mail. Inside was a link from Fertile Crescent Follies, a blog purportedly written by a twentysomething Baghdadi woman that, every few days, and in bitterly scathing language, gave an unvarnished, Iraqi-civilian's-eye view of the dysfunction and violence playing out in the country. Launched shortly after the invasion, the blog, which everyone just called FCF, had developed a mass worldwide following and was read obsessively by every foreigner in Iraq.

Speculation as to the true identity of its author had become a bit of a parlor game in the Green Zone, at Al-Rasheed, and in the *Standard*'s own villa. Some people remarked that the tone seemed just a tad too robotically anti-occupation, too lacking in certain quirky and mundane daily details, for it to be written by a genuine twentysomething Baghdadi Everywoman. Others—including Asmaa—were convinced it was written by a stealth dissenter in the CPA or somewhere else in the occupation universe—a private contractor, perhaps, whose guilt at profiting from the chaos had pushed him or her to publish this anonymous takedown.

Rita, for her part, had sometimes wondered if the author was Asmaa, whose biting humor reminded her of the blog's.

She clicked open the link. Instantly, she gasped to see a photo of herself alongside the type. She recognized the photo immediately. Sami had snapped it of her—making a silly face as she held a piece of bread with a blob of lebneh on the tip—at a portside café during a day trip to Byblos they'd made in the fall of 2002. Her stomach began churning. The headline read:

"DISASTER . . . FAILURE . . . TRAVESTY . . . NIGHTMARE . . . WE
FUCKED UP . . . ILL-EQUIPPED IDIOTS . . . WE'RE SO TOXIC": AN
IRAQ WAR REPORTER FROM THE *STANDARD* FINALLY LOSES IT

A cold dread crept slowly over her entire body, worse than any fear
or dread she'd experienced thus far in Iraq. Two thoughts immediately
pervaded her. The first was that she could not believe that her own
boyfriend had betrayed her. The second was that, drunk and careless,
she had brought this on herself. And it was the second that galled her
even more than the first. She glanced around the room, terrified. Everyone was working, head down, except Claude, who shot her a pitying,
doomsday look. She quickly looked away. Then at the subhead:

*In one e-mail to her boyfriend in Beirut, she writes everything she
has been holding back in her "balanced" articles from Baghdad.
And it's as bad as you thought.*

Now she was hating the blogger as well as Sami and herself.

*We were forwarded an e-mail this morning from Sami Haddad, a
Palestinian graduate student at the American University of Beirut
who is the boyfriend of Rita Khoury, an American reporter for the
Standard who has been based here in Baghdad the past year (living out of the Standard's infamous villa in Mansour, which looks
like a mini-Green Zone). Sami wrote to us: "I know I am probably
ending my relationship by sending you this—*

You got that right, Rita thought bitterly.

*but this was simply too important. I know that Rita will feel the
same way one day. This is her real report of what's going on in Iraq,
very different from the 'balanced' and 'neutral' reports she says she
has to publish. I simply cannot stand to hear this and to know she*

is keeping this from the world at large. I even told her so. So, I will
pay the consequences of my actions in the interest of a bigger truth."

Then the blogger continued:

It's nice to finally hear an American on the ground here admit
what a disaster her country has made out of ours! We are just sorry
that she thinks the food is so horrible compared with her beloved
Lebanon. It's hard to make world-class cuisine when your homes
are being raided and your loved ones don't make it home from the
market with the vegetables because they died in a car bomb. But we
certainly hope Miss Rita is back on the beach in Tyre soon, sipping
wine and eating her delicious fatteh. Sounds like she might need to
find another man to make it for her though.

She felt her face burn red. Claude anxiously glanced her way
once again. She then skimmed, in their entirety, the very words she'd
pounded out last night in a bourbon haze. True enough, the part she
regretted most was having slurred Iraqi food. She could not have come
across more like a spoiled American—or, for that matter, Beiruti—if
she'd tried.

The account of the White House and the CPA, however, was brutal. Already, she was ticking off the likely chain of consequences. She
looked up, stared straight ahead for several seconds, then stood up and
walked over to the table where Rick and Asmaa were working. She
pulled up a seat.

"I need to interrupt you," she said quietly. "You need to read the
latest post on FCF."

They both looked up. "Can it wait?" Rick asked.

"No. You're going to be hearing about it very soon."

She sat there stoically while Rick and Asmaa read. She examined
Asmaa's face for any indication that she might not be surprised. But all
she saw in Asmaa's eyes was a slowly widening shock as she read.

"Oh shit," Rick muttered, his eyes tracking back and forth.

Finally, Asmaa looked up, made eye contact with her. Rita wasn't sure what she saw there. Awe? Respect, perhaps?

"I'm sorry you hate our food so much," Asmaa said, before getting up and walking into the kitchen.

"I didn't say that!" Rita called back. Now Nabil raised his head at a nearby table, alert to some sort of conflict.

Rita propped her head on one hand on Rick's table. "Jesus Christ."

It was Rick's turn to meet her gaze. "Jesus Christ is right." Then, lowering his voice, "Was that the whiskey talking?"

She felt her face burn crimson again, simply closed her eyes, and shook her head.

"Why didn't you just go to bed?"

"I don't know!" She felt tears rising and swallowed them back. "I decided to look at my e-mail late last night, and there was an e-mail from Sami saying he missed our life, and I just let loose."

Rick folded his arms over his chest. "You sure did."

"Just tell me what to do. Please. I'm totally paralyzed right now."

"You need to send the link to D.C. and alert them."

"I'll do it now. Rick, I'm so sorry."

He looked at her, shrugged. "I am too. I know where you're coming from, but you know this is probably uncontainable. You're shot as an objective observer."

She closed her eyes again to hold back tears. Mortification seized her every muscle.

Back at her desk, there already was an e-mail from her editor in D.C., complete with the link to the blog post, which had already been forwarded by staffers twice before arriving at him.

"Call me ASAP," was all it said. It was time-stamped 7:02 a.m. Likely it was the first thing he'd seen upon waking.

Take your punishment, she thought, picking up her sat phone. *Get it over with.*

"It's me," she said, when her editor picked up. "Rita."

"You did write it?" His voice sounded raspy, as though he were uttering the day's first words.

"Yep."

"It's not a hoax."

"Nope."

She heard a pause and a sigh. "This is not good for us, Rita. Not not not not good." On the final *not*, she heard the first eruption of anger. Institutional anger. She'd done the unthinkable. She'd shamed the *American Standard*, exposed the human flaws and passions in its impersonal, impassive editorial machine.

"I know."

"E-mails and calls are already flooding in."

"I know. On my end, too, I see now." Sure enough, they were. "Thank you!" read many of the subject lines. "Truth at last!" And also: "Shame on you—traitor." And: "So you hate Iraqi food? Poor baby. You can leave that hellhole whenever you want."

"What would compel you to do this?" her editor asked.

"It was an e-mail to my boyfriend."

"Yes, but you know the rule about divulging work information and work feelings in any sort of e-mail whatsoever. You never know who'll turn on you at some point."

She was silent. If she told him she'd been drinking, she'd doubly seal her fate. He'd likely find out eventually anyway. So, for now, she just said, pushing back hot tears yet again, "I'm sorry. I guess I've been here a while and I just cracked."

There was a pause that she interpreted as sympathetic. "That's why I kept a private journal during Bosnia," he finally said.

She said nothing to that.

"Listen," he continued. "Keep working for the moment. No byline for the next forty-eight to seventy-two. Obviously we have to have an internal discussion." He paused. "Maybe this will play itself out quickly."

"I doubt it."

"I do, too." A silence. "Listen. Take care of yourselves over there, okay?"

"Yep," she answered lifelessly.

She hung up, glanced at e-mail, saw Sami's name. "I'm sorry," read the subject line.

She clicked it open. "I thought about it a great deal before I did what I did," was all that the rest of it said.

She hit "reply," wrote, "Go fuck yourself," then hit "send."

In the ensuing hours of her professional purgatory, she watched through the portal of her laptop screen as her leaked meltdown became an international news item and bloggers' field day, with sentiment seeming to divide fairly evenly between the idea that she was an outspoken hero (to critics of the war and of American foreign policy in general), a traitor (Republican partisans), and a spoiled brat (Iraqis outside the country with strong feelings about their national cuisine). A total of three websites ran posts with recipes for fatteh—"the creamily satisfying Levant-region breakfast bowl of warm chickpeas, yogurt, toasted pita crumbles and pine nuts that Rita Khoury, an Iraq war reporter for the *Standard*, seems to equate with good sex," as one put it.

Calls and e-mails came in asking her for comment, but the *Standard* had instructed her to keep mum, while her editor in D.C. issued a statement attributing her e-mail to the intense stress faced by reporters in Iraq.

When news came in later that day that a car bomb had killed Ezzedine Salim, the erudite Shiite scholar who had been serving as chief of the Iraqi Governing Council, Rita's dismay was mingled with relief that some of the media attention shifted away from her—and that the fresh disaster gave her work with which to occupy herself. The saddest aspect of the assassination was that everyone had expected it would happen at some point. She huddled with Nabil and her sat phone to try to reach others on the council and within the CPA for comment.

On one call, Nabil announced that he was speaking alongside Rita Khoury from the *Standard*. A moment passed before he smiled awkwardly and answered, "Yes, yes, she is still."

Once they'd concluded the interview, she asked him, "What did he say to you at the beginning of the call when you mentioned my name?"

Nabil looked down, awkwardly. "He asked if you were still in your job after the e-mail."

She shook her head, amazed. "Wow. The head of the IGC gets assassinated, and they still have time to talk about my stupid e-mail."

"Well, you have to understand something."

"What?"

"Not one American here has come out and said what you said so strongly—including journalists. And people can believe it because you are from the *Standard*."

"But I didn't write it for publication!"

Nabil raised an eyebrow at her. "Are you sure you didn't? There is not much you forgot to say in it. It felt to me that you wanted people to read it."

She paused. She wasn't always very good at understanding her own intentions—she'd learned that much about herself.

"I was drunk when I wrote it," she half-whispered to him.

Nabil pursed his lips, seeming to consider this. "It was still very well written," he finally said.

"I guess I have that to be thankful for."

"But can I ask you something?"

"What?"

"You really hate Iraqi food?"

She dropped her head into her palm again. "That one line is going to haunt me more than everything else I wrote."

"But you think Umm Nasim's food is bad?"

"No, I don't. It's good."

He looked skeptical. "You think it's good?"

She laughed slightly. "I mean, I think it's perfectly fine. We're so lucky to have her. I hope to God she doesn't find out about that line. I just meant that I missed Beirut, certain restaurants, certain dishes."

He was looking at her intently now. "Rita," he began. "Can I tell you something?"

"Of course."

"I wish it were two years ago, before the occupation, and I could take you to my family's favorite place for masgouf on the river. Or I wish I could invite you to our house and you could have my grandmother's bamia. It is so good, Rita. It is really like tasting heaven. I think you would think differently about our food then."

He'd never seemed so deadly serious to her. It was more than she could take. She felt her face contort and began weeping, trying to do so silently. She grabbed Nabil's hand briefly, then hurried to her room, where she smashed her face into her pillow and wept uncontrollably.

It was the first time in Iraq she'd ever wept. The wailing survivors in the streets after the American bomb near Al Saha, sleepwalking through the wreckage; the tense faces of the hundreds of Baghdadis she'd interviewed in market stalls and cafés; the nerve-strafing car rides to get from here to there, day in and day out, Ali a necessary madman at the wheel; the constant ambient rat-tat-tat of Kalashnikovs; the doctors and nurses at the threadbare hospitals after car bombings, walking the halls like ghosts, their smocks and hands covered in blood; the victims dying on gurneys, their limbs gone or their skin shredded by fire or shrapnel; keening mothers and grandmothers in their black shrouds—she'd not cried through any of it.

And Nabil just wanted to turn the clock back two years so he could invite her for his grandmother's okra stew. For some reason, that had been the remark that had put her over the edge.

By dinnertime, it was clear that the Western blogosphere wasn't through with her—was, in fact, doubling down. She wasn't surprised at ten o'clock when she got an e-mail from her editor in D.C. saying, merely, "Call me."

Here we go, she thought. So she called.

"We're gonna call you back to Beirut, Rita," he said immediately. "If you stay in Baghdad, your byline is going to have a slant to it now. We can't put that genie back in the bottle."

She snorted aloud. "So Orientalist of you."

Her editor laughed grudgingly. "You've done great work in Iraq under more and more difficult circumstances, Rita. For the better part of a year, which is no small feat. We were probably going to rotate you out after the CPA withdrawal anyway to give you a break."

"No, you weren't," she snapped. "You know that'll be the most important time of all to be here, to see what really happens."

"We'll rotate someone in. Come on, this whole thing happened because you were burned out."

"Who are you going to rotate in?" She could feel blood pounding angrily in her temples.

"We're not sure yet. Maybe Marna Gelman in Jerusalem."

"Marna Gelman? She speaks *Hebrew*."

"She's very steady, Rita."

This stung her into humiliated silence. *Steady*, as in, not like her, not a hothead who popped off at the keyboard after too much to drink. Again, her stomach churned at the thought of telling her father she'd been kicked out of Iraq, as much as he'd not wanted her to go in the first place.

"Go back to Beirut and see your friends and take a breath and edit and assign and keep your byline out of the paper for a while."

She thought of Marna Gelman getting to know Nabil, becoming friends with him, becoming his new Danger Twin. It felt like more than she could bear.

"You know this is unfair," she said. "The world knows my unvarnished take on this place now. You should let me keep reporting here from that baseline, and let readers judge my fairness."

"You know it doesn't work that way here, Rita. Maybe some other outlet that's not as scrutinized but not here. You broke your vows. You're not a blank slate anymore."

"I'm in a unique position now for my stories to get more attention for the *Standard* than they have before," she persisted. "Rick can be the impartial voice of the paper, and I can be more freewheeling."

After a silence, her editor said, "That's not going to happen right now. I think you should gratefully go back to the Beirut office and lie low for a while."

Gratefully. She understood exactly what that meant. She was lucky they weren't firing her outright.

"Lisa will e-mail you tomorrow about a flight, okay?"

Now it was her turn to be silent. She knew what her mother would say right now. A very pointed *Go to hell.*

"Yep," she croaked. Then she hung up and just sat there, staring straight ahead. Behind her, on the other side of the room, Rick, Claude, and Ali were watching *Seinfeld* on satellite—Nabil and Asmaa had gone home—but, she had noticed, they weren't laughing. They weren't drinking tonight, either. She knew they'd taken note of her phone conversation, likely knew what it was about. She could not bring herself to turn around, face them, give them the news.

Then she felt a hand on her shoulder. She looked up. It was Rick. He sat on the edge of her table, crossed his arms.

"What's the word?" he asked.

"They're sending me back to Beirut." As soon as she said it, her voice broke and tears rose in her eyes, but she quickly squeezed them back. This room, this villa, this makeshift family, the knife-edged trips out of here and just as tensely back again, were almost all she had known for a year. She could not believe she was being banished.

"I lobbied so hard for you to stay, you know," Rick said. "I told them you were an indispensable part of the team here."

"So you knew this was going to happen?"

"D.C. called me earlier."

"I didn't hear you on that call."

"It was when you went to lie down for a while."

"Oh."

They were both silent briefly. Behind Rick, she saw Claude lower the TV volume, then lumber over her way, with Ali in tow.

"Rick," she began. "I'm so sorry I let you down." She swallowed back tears again. "I was so honored to work with you."

"Listen," he said. "You told the truth about a horrible situation. There's no shame in that. You just told it to the wrong person."

"It was so ill-considered. I'll kick myself for the rest of my life."

"No, you won't. I promise you won't."

By now, Claude and Ali were standing alongside Rick. "They're sending me back to Beirut," she told them flatly. "In a few days."

"That is fucking bullshit!" Ali exclaimed. "You just told the truth!"

"It is a thing of American journalists," Claude said. "They are supposed to be like robots."

"Does this mean they are going to fire Nabil?" Ali asked.

"They're gonna send in a replacement for me." She glanced at Rick. "Maybe Marna Gelman."

His eyebrows arched upward. "Are you serious?"

"That's what D.C. said."

"She speaks *Hebrew*."

"That's what I said."

The next few days were the worst. There was nothing else for her to do but help out with the reporting as best she could, all the while knowing she'd get no byline, and she'd not even be around to witness the very thing they were reporting on, life in Iraq after the CPA withdrawal. Worse, the generator blew out, and they were without air-conditioning for a full day and night in Baghdad's 125-degree summer heat, so they resorted to guzzling bottled water and mopping up sweat with endless towels, as it was too dangerous to venture respite on the roof. Their hands were so sweaty they could barely type or scrawl notes; anything other than lying flat on one's back, perfectly still, was excruciating, and even that was miserable because one's sweat quickly soaked the sheets and mattress. Rita had no idea how Umm Nasim, whose fleshy face glistened with sweat, continued to wear her polyester abaya, or cook while drinking hot tea, without passing out.

The morning after the call from D.C., when Nabil and Asmaa arrived, Rita began to inform them of her imminent departure.

As soon as she started to speak, they glanced at each other—Rita had long marveled at how they had exactly the same sharply bridged nose and Cupid's-bow lips—before Asmaa said, "We know already."

"How?"

They shared another glance, sheepishly. "Ali called us," said Nabil. "Well, he called Asmaa, and then she called me."

"Oh." Of course the Iraqis told one another everything, instantly. This was part of their livelihood, their survival. Iraqis working for foreigners were hustlers; they had to be. Interpreters, fixers, drivers, cooks, and maids secured new bosses for themselves as soon as they got news that a current one was leaving, even if it was weeks or months in advance.

"So I guess you know, Nabil," she continued, "your job is safe because they're going to swap me out with someone."

"Yes, we know," he answered gravely.

"Marna Gelman from Jerusalem," said Asmaa.

"You even know that?" Rita had to laugh. "Jeez. Well, yes, probably Marna Gelman, Nabil, who is a real pro and also who won't give you any guff about tolerating her Arabic because she doesn't speak a word of it."

The three of them were silent then, uncomfortable. "But I am still here another two days," Rita added.

Once again, the cousins exchanged a look. Still in a low voice, Asmaa said, "We don't really understand why they are sending you away just for telling the truth. There wasn't one lie in what you wrote."

"They don't want the whole picture?" Nabil asked. "You think they are still working with Bush?"

Rita closed her eyes and shook her head. "I broke protocol. We're not supposed to put our own feelings in writing. I wasn't careful."

"But you didn't write it for everyone to read," Asmaa said. "You were betrayed."

The remark might have upset her more if she hadn't thought she heard just the faintest note of schadenfreude in Asmaa's voice. Or perhaps she was just imagining it? She really didn't know anymore. She was exhausted and the dried sweat on her body felt like a rubbery second skin.

"Shit happens!" she answered, with mock cheer, and then stalked into the kitchen, where she sat, arms folded, at the small table.

In a moment, Nabil entered and sat across from her. "That was a very typical remark of Asmaa to make. She is like a sled hammer."

Rita smiled in spite of herself. "You mean a *sledge*hammer."

"A what?"

"A *sledge*hammer. I know the word you're referring to. It means a huge, heavy hammer. But the word is *sledge*hammer, not *sled* hammer. I don't even know why, but it is."

Nabil nodded, mouthing the word. "Okay. Good to know." They were never offended by each other's corrections of their English or Arabic. They wanted it that way; they'd worked that out several months ago—at this point, perhaps a hundred stories, dozens of trips, ago.

As though reading her mind, he asked, "Who will help me with words now?"

She shrugged. "Marna Gelman?"

They laughed. She looked at him, shook her head, moved to put her hand on his across the table, thought better of it, then did it anyway. "You have been my number one everything the past year," she said, her voice hoarsening. "You are so smart, Nabil. You and Asmaa both. You deserve a good life."

He bowed his head, his eyes welling up. "This was my first real job. Ever. Not for Asmaa, but for me. She got it for me."

"I know. And I will—" She paused. "Look at me."

He looked up, embarrassedly blinking away tears.

"I will do anything for you I ever can. I promise. You just have to ask. And you know how to reach me."

He held her stare for several seconds, then looked down again. "Thank you. I don't know what will happen here."

"Nabil."

"Yes?"

"Are you gay?" She said it almost inaudibly, under her breath.

He did not look up, but she saw his body freeze, saw him suddenly catch and hold his breath.

"I'm asking you," she continued in a whisper, "because that could help you leave. It could help your case."

He held his frozen pose for several more seconds. Then he slowly, resolutely, shook his head. "No, I am not. I know what that means, and I am not. I don't know why you ask me that. I am very offensive."

She scrutinized him, then slid her hand from his. "Okay," she said. "I'm sorry I asked. Truly. Pardon me."

But she was still leaning toward him, and hence did not notice immediately when Asmaa stepped in, an empty water bottle in her hand.

"Oh," said Asmaa, startled, stopping. "Am I interrupting something?"

Nabil was still looking down, his cheeks flushing crimson, and it was clear to Rita that Asmaa knew she'd stumbled on an intimacy.

"I was just thanking him," Rita said crisply, brushing away notes of conspiracy. "I wanted to thank you, too, Asmaa. I couldn't have made it through the past year without you both."

Asmaa seemed to be sizing her up. Rita held her stare. She allowed herself to see someone she'd half-willed herself not to fully see those many months. It was a woman not much younger than herself, who even looked somewhat like herself, educated at Iraq's equivalent of Harvard, smart, ambitious, hardworking—and trapped in a country whose future was currently a vision of hell.

"I'm very grateful for all the work you've put in," she concluded.

Asmaa's eyes on her hardened. She likely figured she had nothing to lose at this point, thought Rita, who prepared to absorb some sort of rebuke.

But then Asmaa's face seemed to soften. "Well, what I would like to say to you is something I spent a great deal of time pondering last night."

Rita nodded, as though to say, *Go on.*

"It wasn't fair what I said yesterday," Asmaa continued. "Everyone has the right to love and to miss the food of her own homeland, and that is not necessarily to malign the food of another culture. So for that I must apologize."

"You don't have to apologize," Rita said quickly.

"No!" Asmaa interjected. "Please just hear my apology, and then you choose to accept it or not. I'm sure if I ever will go on a long trip

to France or America or Mexico, or wherever I might go, I will reach a
point where I miss the food of my own country, just as you or anyone
would miss."

Then Asmaa just stood there, having said her piece.

"I accept your apology," Rita said.

"Thank you." Asmaa turned away to the refrigerator, retrieved a
new bottle of water. Rita stole a glance at Nabil, who was still looking
down into his lap, distracted, frowning.

Finally, the jet she'd connected to in Amman touched down in Beirut.
She'd fallen asleep briefly before the descent and now felt somewhat
dazed. Such a violent transition in one day, waking up for the last time
in the villa, the final work of packing, the bleary-eyed early-morning
good-byes to Rick, Claude, Ali, and Umm Nasim, who pressed prayer
beads into her hand and kissed her four times on alternating cheeks, the
slipping into the opaque-windowed armored SUV they'd hired to speed
her to Baghdad Airport, the crawling traffic getting out of Baghdad, then
the turn onto the dreaded Airport Road, site extraordinaire of some of
the most spectacular car bombings.

The driver, Mahmoud, an extremely fat middle-aged uncle or
cousin of Ali's—she'd not quite discerned which—accelerated, and she
gazed, to their left, at the shabby Shi'a district of Amil, where they'd
not spent much time. The ubiquitous knot of barefoot or flip-flop-clad
little boys, some of them shirtless, kicked around a soccer ball on a flat
brown patch of land just off the highway.

She felt not relief that she was leaving the cursed city, but extreme
anger with herself that her misstep had thwarted her need to stay here
and witness, chronicle, how it would all play out. She'd talked about this
with other reporters: you became addicted to the baking dung-colored
hell, attached to the stoic fatalism of Iraqis, compelled to share their
fate and muddle through and see what would happen. Only now she
realized she'd grown to love the ugly, dusty, doomed capital.

*   *   *

From the airport in Beirut, she took a taxi directly to Salma's parents' apartment in Achrafieh. She'd e-mailed Sami telling him to remove himself and everything that might remind her of him from her apartment before she returned, and he'd written back merely a meek, "Of course, chérie," but, still, the thought of going directly to the apartment was too painful.

In the taxi, she rolled down the window and inhaled moist, sea-salty air, a blessed change from scorchingly dry Baghdad. It was late May, and the weather in Lebanon was balmy and perfect. As they came into the city center, she looked up at a giant billboard for a French tanning lotion featuring a twenty-foot-long bikini-clad beauty with a body not found in nature and the requisite mane of blond hair, and she smiled, slightly happy to be back, for the first time that day.

Salma enfolded Rita in a hug—her parents were at their mountain house, where it was cooler, and she had the sprawling apartment to herself—and took her out onto the terrace, proffering watermelon, jibneh, gin and tonics, and cigarettes.

"I know it's selfish to say, but I'm so glad you're back," Salma said, cooling her forehead with the damp surface of her glass. "I can't run around anymore with these stupid girls. I want to move to Brooklyn."

"Don't move just yet. Please help me segue back into Beirut life. I am so tense, I can't relax. It doesn't feel right to be just lounging here on an open roof."

"Ya haram, you have some PTSD. My mother has it from the war years here. She hears even a little bang, and she has a nervous breakdown. I have all the Ativan you need."

Rita laughed. Salma's answer for nearly everything was a pill. "Thank you. It's so good to be with you again. I missed you so much."

"I missed you too, chérie. I just wish—" Salma then shook her head, as though to dismiss her thought as pointless, and continued dabbing her forehead with her glass.

"Wish what?"

"No, forget it."

"No, tell me."

Salma sighed. "I just wish I had warned you off Sami more strongly. But you were having fun and I didn't want to spoil it."

Now it was Rita's turn to sigh and shrug. "How could you have known he'd do something like what he did?"

"It's exactly the kind of thing he'd do," Salma replied sharply. "He's a lost soul, a poor little rich boy. He has no life, no future, so he spoils it for others because he's jealous. He was jealous of you."

Rita considered this, then shook her head slowly. "I dug my own grave. Partly because of this right here." She pointed at her glass, and they both cracked up laughing.

"Well," announced Salma, "there's more of that for you tonight, because I am going to be selfish again and drag you to a poolside party at Sporting that I have to go to because an Italian editor is in town. I can't bear that bourgeois crowd alone."

"*You're* bourgeois!"

"But I'm different."

Rita shook her head slowly. "I can't believe you are dragging me to a party my first night out of a war zone."

Salma cackled. "You're back in Beirut, baby! Parties and war, it's all the same to us. Come on, you can wear something of mine."

The next day, Saturday, Rita dragged Salma to Hamra, for moral support upon entering her apartment, which had last been the site of happy co-habitation. In the lobby, they caught up briefly with Fadi, the concierge, who had been taking care of Joujou, the cat.

"That is disgusting, what he did with your e-mail," said Fadi.

"He told you?"

"No. It was on Al Jazeera. I jumped up and said to my mother, 'She lives in the building!'"

"You're famous, chérie," Salma commented dryly.

The apartment was much as she remembered it. Spotless, thanks to Fadi's mother. A first look around revealed no traces of Sami, until some emerged: A bright red plastic pasta strainer he'd obviously bought after she'd gone to Iraq. A pack of American Spirits in the top drawer of the desk. A forgotten pair of black Calvin Klein briefs in the bureau. But there was no Joujou. Rita looked everywhere, enlisting Salma as well—under the bed and the couch, in the crevices of the closet, behind the dresser. She became increasingly agitated.

"I told him to leave Joujou for me," she told Salma. "I paid for him and his food."

Salma joined her in the bedroom. "SMS him."

So she did: *Where is Joujou?*

To her surprise, he texted back immediately: *Who took care of Joujou for a year while you were away?* Then: *Please leave me something.*

"I can't believe him!" Rita exclaimed, enraged, showing Salma the text. "He stole Joujou! He must have slipped in when Fadi wasn't looking."

"Oh, sweetie. Let him have the cat."

"That was my cat!" She was shaking, on the brink of tears.

Salma took her hand. "We'll get you a new one that's all yours."

When she entered the bureau Monday morning, braced to stoically accept whatever anonymous tasks awaited her as she served her tenure without a byline, and feeling surreally as though Iraq had never happened, she was shocked to find her editor from D.C. there, sitting at what once had been her desk, scrolling through his e-mails.

"Charles!" she exclaimed. "You're in Beirut!" Out of the corners of her eyes, she sensed the other bureau staffers watching her. She'd gritted her teeth on the way in and greeted some of them casually, as though she'd never been away.

"It's my big surprise treat for the office," he said. "I flew in Friday."

"That's the day I got back in, too."

"How is it to be out of the ninth circle of hell?"

"It feels very unnatural to be able to just walk the streets. I'm very on edge."

He nodded. "To be expected. Think of the transition your brain's going through."

"I know," she said dutifully.

An awkward silence ensued. He looked at her . . . what was the word? Ruefully?

"What brings you here?" she finally asked.

He jerked his head toward an empty office, then rose. She followed. He gently closed the door behind them, sat behind the desk, gestured for her to sit in the facing chair.

"I came over for a general check-in," he began, leaning forward, his hands folded on the desktop. "But I also came to give you some hard news face-to-face."

She felt the floor drop out of her stomach, her face blanch. "What?" she croaked.

"There have been many, many meetings while you were flying back from Baghdad. And the folks at the tippity top have concluded that you've become just too much of a story in and of yourself to play a role in any sort of foreign reporting that's not going to distract the critics and the *Standard* haters and keep them all over us, saying our Iraq coverage is biased."

Her whole body went hot with rage, which she determined to contain. "You've already stripped me of my byline for the indefinite future." She tried to keep her voice even. "Isn't that enough?"

"Have you read the blogs the past twenty-four to forty-eight?"

"No," she said coldly. "I tried to give myself a break from the whole thing at least for the weekend. And then I came in here today resolved to take my lumps and be a good editor behind the scenes and a team player. And even to reach out to fucking Marna Gelman for a chat."

"I know. But the chatter hasn't stopped. Fox is having a field day. How can we keep you on in any capacity at this point? I mean, that's the drumbeat."

She gave an ugly laugh. "You guys are such fucking cowards. Why didn't you stick up for me when this happened? I was doing good work over there—*in hell*, as you put it."

Charles closed his eyes and shook his head.

"But I know why," she continued. "You were too complaisant with the administration in the beginning, and you got called out on it by the entire world, and now you're using me as an example to show you've reversed course. I'm your scapegoat."

Charles simply opened his eyes and regarded her helplessly with upraised palms.

She released another sharp laugh. "You're too afraid even to admit it."

Charles picked up a pen on the desk and rotated it in his hands, saying nothing.

"So what happens now?"

He signed. "What happens now is, you are suspended pending review. I assume you'll be bringing the union into it."

She said nothing. Certainly she would not show him her hand.

"We will cover your flight back to the States. And we'll also give you a five-hundred-dollar flat sum to put toward any logistics this brings up. Maybe you want to stay in Beirut for a while."

She leveled a hard stare at him, and he continually glanced away, then back again. "After all the good work I've done for you," she merely said. "One of the youngest foreign correspondents you've ever had. Arab American, too."

He rubbed his right temple. "The *Standard*'s a tough place, Rita. You're not the first something like this has happened to."

"So utterly disposable if we make one false move."

"You're going into review. It's not necessarily over yet."

She rose. "I assume I work out all the logistics with Lisa."

Charles nodded.

"I hope you have a *great* time in Beirut," she said, finally injecting acid into her voice. Then she picked up her bag, turned, set her face in a mask, opened the office door, and walked through the bureau, neither speaking to nor making eye contact with anyone, until she'd passed through the glass doors and stood at the elevator, her heart pounding, desperately hoping that nobody would rush out to catch her before its doors parted. Nobody did.

Outside, her heart still racing, she simply walked, in a daze, the length of Hamra Street toward the water until she crossed the highway and found herself in front of the shabby seaside amusement park with the Ferris wheel, at the summit of which she'd made out with Sami in their first weeks together, all of nighttime Beirut and the Mediterranean arrayed dizzyingly below them. Adjacent to the park was an equally shabby café, populated at the moment with nothing but dozens of the ugly white plastic chairs she'd once joked to Sami she was certain were spawning through the Middle East, so nearly ubiquitous were they.

She took a seat, ordered an Almaza, fished a cigarette out of her bag, lit it, and stared out at the glittering sea, where hundreds of gulls swooped and cawed in a late-morning frenzy. Mortification—what Arabs called a'ar—began creeping in around her rage. She'd made it to a foreign bureau of essentially the best paper in the world before she was thirty—only to be sent home. All she could think about was what she was going to tell her father.

CHAPTER NINE

EXILE, PART 2

(2005)

Nabil always woke with a small moan of panic. And he did so now, his eyes adjusting to the alien setting, the interior of the minivan, which smelled sourly of sweat, including his own, despite its weak air-conditioning, and to his morning view from the window, which was half blue sky, half brown sand, with no other features whatsoever as far as the eye could see.

The petrified old man who'd been sitting next to him for the duration of the trip had nudged him awake. "Look," the old man said now, pointing up ahead out the driver's window, his eyes welling up frankly with gratitude. "We're are here. At al-Tanf. At the border. We survived the trip."

Nabil craned his neck forward. Sure enough, past a long line of vehicles queued in front of them, Nabil saw the border patrol, a massive concrete portal emblazoned with the Syrian flag, a large portrait of President Bashar al-Assad, and a sign reading, in Arabic and English, "Welcome to the Syrian Arabic Republic." He felt in his pocket for his Iraqi passport, fearful it might have fallen out or been plucked from him while he slept, patting it superstitiously.

It had probably been the first time he'd really slept in the past forty-eight hours, and yet he could not believe he actually had, so anxious had he been upon boarding the minivan at one a.m. on a side street near the mosque in Kadhimiya, helping others fit their single bags of clothes and possessions into the overhead compartments, then stowing his own. As the vehicle sped west out of Baghdad in the dead of night, he gripped the seat, sitting bolt upright, as tense as everyone else. Surely they would not make it to the border alive or without being kidnapped; there were simply too many tales of refugee minivans, especially those believed to contain mostly Shi'a, being ambushed by al-Qaeda or other insurgents, hitting roadside bombs, getting shot up with Kalashnikovs from both sides, or being attacked by thugs who knew that such getaway vehicles were rich with their passengers' life savings in dinars or gold. Often, the vans didn't make it past the dreaded Sunni Triangle just a few hours west of the city; if they did, there were still hours to go through remote desert with no angels to intervene if militias or thieves lay in wait.

And yet they'd arrived at the portal of another nation, one that had not descended into chaos and terror, with dozens or hundreds of deaths daily from east to west. He could not believe that in a few hours, after the border bureaucrats processed them in on a temporary visa, he would be safe in Damascus, reunited with his family, that he would scoop his nephew Ahmed and niece Rana up into his arms and hear their gorgeous cries of "Ammo, Ammo!"

He also could not believe he would never see Asmaa again. Every time he thought of the last moment he had beheld her, he fought back a fresh wave of both nausea and something darker, less familiar, and more frightening. Perhaps, he wondered, it was the beginning of madness.

His life, all their lives at the villa, had become very dark and small and fearful after Rita left. That was not because of her departure, though he missed her, but more because it had coincided with a nationwide explosion of violence and chaos that made the prior two years look tame. Now that the CPA had disbanded, American military, foreign journalists and contractors, and—most disconcertingly—everyday Iraqis were bombed, assassinated, or kidnapped at such a rate that at the villa, they spent much of their time merely trying to figure out which atrocities to cover, there were so many to choose from.

The paper had not sent Marna Gelman from Jerusalem in after all. She'd resisted, saying that life in Israel was occupational hazard enough. Instead, it had dispatched a thirty-three-year-old reporter from the American Midwest bureau, an Iranian American named Rostam Shirazi who was born in Cleveland, Ohio, spoke only English and Spanish, had never been in the Middle East before, and joked often that he'd gotten the assignment only because the *Standard* calculated he'd be less of a death risk since he wasn't white.

"But we can tell you look Persian," Nabil had told him.

"Really?" asked Rostam, who talked, Nabil secretly thought, in the same charmingly dopey cadence as Joey on *Friends*.

"It's true," said Asmaa. "Persians are thought of as especially beautiful by Iraqis."

Nabil managed not to roll his eyes. He could hear the flirtation in Asmaa's voice.

"Really?" asked Rostam again. "Well, I guess I'm in the right place!"

But the truth was that it really didn't matter much anymore what color anyone in the villa was, because hardly anyone left the villa. Meanwhile, few in the world outside could be persuaded to visit them; Iraqis weren't stupid enough to be seen coming to or going from a compound that many believed to be not the offices of a major American newspaper but a front for the CIA. Consequently, life in the villa had become a kind of soft prison where everyone spent as much time chatting, eating, watching TV, or playing Ping-Pong (a table for which Ali had imported, to everyone's delight) as they did working. Nabil noticed that body-conscious Ali was getting flabby.

And yet, every night after dinner, there was still the stomach-churning moment when Asmaa put on her abaya, and it was time for Ali to drive her and Nabil back to Kadhimiya in the armored car. The crazy corkscrew game began: Ali took a different, winding route each evening, making sudden 180-degree turns followed by heart-racing accelerations, all to throw off anyone who might have been following them. Then Ali dropped them in a different spot in the neighborhood each night to stump efforts to determine where they lived. Then came the tense walk to Nabil's home, the sidelong glances up and down the street as he and Asmaa undid the three locks on the garden wall, slipped inside, relocked the gates, and hurried across the ten meters of garden stones into the house.

And then the two of them were alone in the house, Asmaa pulling off the hated abaya, the two of them sitting on the couch, their hearts racing, praising God they'd made it home alive yet another night.

"How much longer can we do this?" Asmaa would whisper. The days when the two of them would sit out in the garden on the swinging sofa, smoking and laughing under the stars, seemed another, ancient life, a lifetime ago.

"I don't know," Nabil would answer. But they also knew they had little choice. Their entire family—Bibi, Nabil's parents and brothers and their wives and kids, and also Asmaa's mother, Mariam—had fled to Damascus late last November, a complicated and expensive exodus they had mostly planned before Ramadan and then executed four days after Eid. Only Nabil and Asmaa would stay behind; the family were taking considerable savings with them to Syria, but with all of them in a large apartment in Muhajirin that cost six hundred dollars a month while they tried to find work and put the children into school, they would run through those savings quickly. Nabil and Asmaa simply made too much money—an absurd amount of money by the standards of a devastated Iraq, and money their family would rely on—to leave.

And so Asmaa paid a local teenage boy named Akram to live in and guard her mother's house and she moved into Nabil's family's much larger house, where they hired another local teenage boy, Omar, to sit watch in the garden nights while they fitfully slept. Nabil stashed under his bed a pistol Ali had procured for him, while Asmaa slept in the adjacent bedroom, which had been his parents'. In the morning, over coffee in the kitchen, they would listen to news radio while waiting for the sat-phone call from Ali, saying that he was rounding the bend and that they should prepare to swiftly exit the house, triple-lock the garden gate, and slip into the car. Along with the reverse procedure late at night, it was the most nerve-racking part of their day.

One morning, no call had come from Ali, well past eight thirty a.m., his usual time. Asmaa, irritable in her abaya, spun her coffee cup round and round on the table.

"What is his problem today?" she muttered.

"Maybe a new checkpoint," said Nabil. "Or traffic." A strange fact of life in post-invasion, post-sanctions Baghdad was that it had been flooded with shiny, often enormous new cars from all over the world, luxury sedans and hulking SUVs, bought in a greedy frenzy by anyone with the means, and now the streets were choked with three times the traffic that had existed in Saddam's era—which, of course, made travel slower and more dangerous.

Asmaa let another seven minutes pass before she called the villa.

"Rostam, it's Asmaa. Has Ali left yet?" She listened briefly, then said to Nabil, "He left over an hour ago." She paused, then said, into the phone, "No. No, I should. I will. Okay. See you soon, hopefully."

She clicked off the call, then dialed another number. "Rostam says to call Ali and see what's going on."

While the call went through, Nabil idly studied his cousin's face, reduced to a colorless oval within her abaya. Despite himself, he began giggling.

"What are you laughing at?"

"I'm sorry." He couldn't stop himself. "Just you in your abaya. The times have made you a pious, humble woman. Bibi would be so proud."

Asmaa rolled her eyes. "Hamdullilah!" she emoted in a squeaky voice, raising her free palm upward, imitating Bibi, which set Nabil off on a new round of giggles.

"Hello, Ali? It's Asmaa. Where are you?"

Nabil then watched as Asmaa's face froze in shock and fear. After several seconds, she clicked off the call and put down the phone, her hand shaking.

"What?" Nabil asked.

"God help us," Asmaa whispered, putting an elbow on the table and holding her face in the palm of her hand. "God help us."

"What is it?"

"That wasn't Ali who answered."

"Why are you whispering?"

She drew closer to him and pushed the phone away as though, even inactive, it had ears.

"That wasn't Ali. I don't know who it was. But he said they had Ali and they were coming for me and you next, because we were infidels and spies for the Americans."

Now it was Nabil's face that blanched. "Who was it?"

"I have no idea. He just sounded like a thug. I don't think his accent was Iraqi."

Nabil suddenly felt more ill at ease in the house than he'd ever felt before. Were thugs just outside, in wait? "Maybe it was a lie just to scare us from going to work."

Asmaa gripped her coffee cup again. "Where is Ali, then?"

Nabil was stumped. "Do you think the night boy in the garden snitched on us?"

"Omar? He's fourteen years old. We've known his family for years."

"Yes, but they're Sunni."

"Nabil!" Asmaa looked genuinely dismayed. "Your father is Sunni!"

He shook his head, ashamed. He would not have thought in those terms only three years ago. "I know. But everyone's reporting people now if there's something to get out of it."

They were both silent a moment. "Should we go in the garden and see if he's still there?" Asmaa finally asked.

"I'm scared to," he admitted.

Several mute seconds passed, nearly a full minute, before Asmaa's phone rang again. The two of them sat there, staring at the phone as though it were a coiled serpent.

"Do you think they captured your number somehow?" Nabil asked.

But Asmaa boldly picked it up. "Allo?" she said, the standard Iraqi phone greeting, in a voice she willed into calmness.

Instantly, her face relaxed. "It's Rick," she whispered to him.

But then Nabil watched her eyes widen in horror as she listened, then brim over with tears as her head fell into her palm again. "Oh no," she moaned into the phone. "Oh God, no."

Nabil grabbed her arm. "What? What is it?"

She handed him the phone before throwing her head into her arms on the tabletop, sobbing.

"Rick, it's Nabil."

"Nabil, I have really bad news." Rick's voice was burry, thick. "Ali's body was just thrown in the street right outside the checkpoint. By a car that screamed up and then screamed away. The guards dragged him inside. He was shot in the head."

Nabil felt the room rock, as though the floor had fallen in. It had finally happened to them. So many Iraqis were disappearing or being found dead, yet thus far he and Asmaa had known only a few of them, vaguely, partly because, in the fortified villa, they were cut off from the network of Iraqi interpreters, stringers, and drivers that revolved around the Palestine and Rasheed hotels. Now they'd tasted it. The villa was a family, and they'd suffered their first loss. Worse, it meant that insurgents—or jihadists or Baathists or thugs, or whoever they were—were closing in on the paper.

"Nabil?"

"I'm here. I'm just shocked."

"I know. We all are. We're trying to work on getting in touch with Ali's family so they can claim the body."

"Of course," Nabil said dully.

"But listen. We have to work on getting you and Asmaa over here ASAP. I feel very, very uncomfortable with the two of you alone in that house in Kadhimiya with these assholes connecting the dots."

"Asmaa called Ali's phone, and some guy picked up and said they'd gotten him and they were coming for us because we worked for American spies."

Rick was silent for a moment. "Well," he finally said. "That's exactly how we thought it might go. So listen, both of you pack a bag with your essentials and your papers and sit tight while we arrange an armored car to come for you. Mohsen said he'll come and he'll call you from outside, and you have to rush right out into the car."

"Tell Mohsen not to come, please!"

"He says his friends will only bring an armored car if he goes with them."

"It could be a trap."

"I know. But we have to hope it's not, because we have to get you here. You and Asmaa should've just come here in the first place when your families left."

Nabil was silent. He knew Rick was right. They'd had that opportunity—the *Standard* had finally promised to insure them, at an exorbitant sum—but they'd declined it, convinced they'd be safe in their own home with each other, a pistol, and some teenage guards.

"So, stand by for the call," Rick continued. "Hopefully within the hour."

All this Nabil relayed to Asmaa as she continued to cry quietly, her head in her arms, as he rubbed the back of her abaya.

"I'm scared to leave the house," she said, muffled. "We should wait until night."

"But I'm scared to wait. Come on, you have to put a bag together."

Finally she rose, wiping her wet, splotchy face. "I did this to us," she said. "I've been thinking about it. I should never have pulled us into journalism. We'd be ordinary Iraqis now otherwise, minding our own business."

"Khallas," he said, clearing the breakfast things. "You had no idea it would go this way. And they probably would get us for something else at this point. So let's just focus on packing a bag and getting out of here." He was surprised to find himself becoming, in the dire moment, the stronger of the two, the planner. It was an odd sensation to have around Asmaa.

Stuffing the essential pants, shirts, underwear, toiletries into a duffel bag was the easy part. But what of papers? His Iraqi passport, of course. And his University of Baghdad diploma. Thankfully, his parents had taken most of their essential papers, their remaining jewelry and valuables, and a few albums of photos and other keepsakes to Damascus. He pulled a wad of American bills totaling five hundred dollars from deep inside a fist-size tear in the lining of his mattress, stuffed that into his pocket. He began roaming the rooms of the house, wondering whether he would ever see them again. In his room, he took down the poster of Younis Mahmoud, carrying it back into the living room. There he took from the wall the framed ninety-nine names of Allah, placed it on the table, took the yellowed painting out of the frame, and rolled it tightly with the Younis Mahmoud poster. Then he wondered how he could keep the roll from crumpling, lacking a poster tube. Then he simply decided it did not matter if the pictures crumpled; the point was to take something from the house should he never set foot in it again, so he slid the roll into the side of his duffel.

He remembered the pistol. He went back to his bedroom to get it, took out the bullets, and stared at it. Rick said journalists weren't supposed to carry guns, no matter how dangerous the setting. It compromised their status as journalists. But Nabil decided he didn't care, that it was very likely he might soon not be a journalist, but merely another Baghdadi trying to get through the day without dying, so he stuffed the pistol deep into the mass of his clothes, in the center of the duffel.

He sat on the couch, staring at the blank TV, waiting for Asmaa and for the call, obsessively running over in his mind whether there was anything he was forgetting. Eventually, Asmaa, still in her abaya, emerged with a lumpy bag and sat down next to him on the couch.

"Did you shut off all the lights?" she asked.

"I checked all the switches. The electricity's never on, anyway."

The house felt unbearably silent. Paranoid, Nabil thought he heard scuffling in the garden, but was too scared to peer between the heavy draperies to check.

"What if they can't get a car here?" Asmaa asked.

"It's just one trip from A to B and back, out of all the trips that happen every day," he said. "Ninety-nine percent of the time people make it to where they're going." But, of course, he'd been having the same thought. Several more unbearably silent seconds passed, filled not even by the hum of the overhead fan, which was still.

"Should we watch the news while we wait?" he asked.

"There's no power."

"Oh, that's right."

"Besides," Asmaa added. "I'd be afraid we'd miss the phone call."

"The phone is right here in my lap."

To that she said nothing. But eventually, still staring straight ahead, she put her hand in his.

"You have always been more like a brother to me, habibi," she said. "Really, my only sibling."

He had to resist the urge to give her hand back. "Why are you acting like you're in an Egyptian melodrama?"

"Sometimes we have to say these things."

"But why now?"

"Why not now?"

"You have a fatalistic tone that is making me very tense."

Now Asmaa in turn seem perturbed. "Well?" she asked.

"Well, what?"

"Don't you want to say something to me?"

"I can't believe you're making me do this now."

But she turned and stared at him resolutely.

"Yes," he finally said. "You are like a sister to me. Of course you know that."

She leaned in and kissed him on both cheeks, a satisfied smile on her face.

Finally, he put her hand back in her own lap. "Okay, then, fine. But let's have enough of this talk and just get to the villa."

Moments later, her sat phone rang. "Allo?" she answered. "Okay. Okay. Shukran." She clicked off the call. "It's Mohsen. He said they're pulling up in three minutes in an armored blue Chrysler Concorde, and we should slip into the back seat and get down."

Nabil rose, pulling Asmaa up with him, then throwing both of their bags over his shoulders. "Let me go into the garden and look through the gate for the car while you wait at the house door."

"I can carry my own bag."

"No," he said firmly. "So you can run right across the garden quickly. And don't bother locking the door. I'm sure squatters are going to take over the house anyway."

His heart pounded as he opened the front door, then strode, in a fashion he hoped was both unsuspicious and manly, across the garden, his peripheral vision absorbing the elements of his childhood, of family, of happiness: his mother's lemon trees, now dead and dry, and the floral-print swing chair, and the gash in the ground where his brother had bored a deep hole for groundwater. Through the slit in the metal gate, he watched down the length of the street until he saw it, a 1990s-era powder-blue Chrysler, plowing its way forward. Nabil undid the gate's three bolts, his hand resting there, until the car pulled up alongside the gate and the passenger-side window lowered just enough for him to see Mohsen and hear him say, "Hurry, get in."

He turned back and motioned for Asmaa to follow.

She closed the door behind her and hastened five or six steps before he heard the shot tear through the air and saw her fall instantly to the garden stones. He dropped the bags and ran to her, falling to his knees, lifting her up by the shoulders, and screaming her name.

"Get in the car, Nabil!" Mohsen screamed. "Leave her!"

But he merely called her name over and over again, trying to command her back to life. The shot, he discerned in his hysteria, must have been through her neck, because in that area, blood spread across the polyester of her abaya, crimson on black. Soon, it was all over Nabil's hands.

"Goddamn you, Nabil!" Mohsen shouted, running out of the car, pushing open the unlocked garden gate, grabbing up the bags, and throwing them into the back seat of the car. "Goddamn you, making me get out of the car. They're going to shoot again! Leave her!"

"I can't," he screamed back, sobbing, her body now fallen over his right shoulder. "Go without me. I want them to shoot me. I want this to be over."

Mohsen pried Asmaa's body away from Nabil and began dragging it to the car. "Get in the car, Nabil. Don't make us all die, please." As soon as he said that, another shot was fired, ricocheting off the near wall of the garden. It had to be some kind of a warning shot, Nabil understood amid his hysteria. Whoever or exactly wherever the sniper was—Nabil sensed he was on the other side of the far wall, in the neighbor's garden—he could easily take out both Nabil and Mohsen if he wanted to. They were like two fish in a fishbowl. But, still, Nabil sobbed, crumpled in a pile.

"Shoot me, please," he yelled, in the direction of the shot. "Please have mercy and end this hell."

No shot came. Instead, he felt Mohsen picking him up roughly under his arms and dragging him, his heels scraping the ground, across the garden. At some point, he yielded and made himself walk, before Mohsen stuffed him into the back seat next to Asmaa's body and the duffel bags, slammed the door, got back in the passenger seat, and slammed that door.

"Go, go, go!" Mohsen commanded the driver, who sped off down the street.

"Should we go to the morgue?" Nabil heard the driver ask.

"Too obvious," Mohsen replied. "Go back to where you picked me up, and we'll figure out what to do with her body together with Ali's."

Nabil didn't know who the driver was. He hadn't looked. He heard a final shot land somewhere several yards behind the car, in the dust of the street. He threw himself over Asmaa's body and sobbed into the wet polyester.

Everything after that ensued in a blur: Rick and Claude prying him off Asmaa's body, hustling him into the villa; Umm Nasim sponging blood off his arms, all the while crying and saying, "Allah yesaadna," God help us, over and over again.

"What about Asmaa?" he called out. "Don't take her to the morgue. We'll never see her body again."

Rick and Claude gently eased him down onto the sofa, Rick's arm still around him, handed him water. "Drink this, Nabil. Mohsen is taking care of Ali and Asmaa right now. Just breathe slowly, okay?"

Nabil willed himself to slow his breathing.

Then his sat phone rang. The three of them stared at it a moment.

"You don't have to answer it right now," Claude said.

But Nabil took the call. "Allo?"

"This is Nabil al-Jumaili?" asked a voice in what sounded to Nabil like a Tikriti accent.

Nabil said nothing. He glanced at Rick and Claude, who were watching him intently.

"We killed your sister because she was a whore for the Americans," the voice continued. "You are probably wondering why we let you live."

Again, Nabil, the hair on his arms standing on end, said nothing.

"Confirm something for us, and we will let you live. Confirm that the old lady Taqqya al-Daraji is living in the Americans' house in Mansour where you work."

Nabil suppressed a gasp. Taqqya al-Daraji was the real name of Umm Nasim. How had these men gotten the name of a widow who never left the house? He said nothing.

"You will die if you don't answer."

Nabil clicked off the call and related the conversation to Rick and Claude.

Rick's fingers flew to his forehead. "Jesus Chr—" He stopped himself. "How did they get her name?"

The three of them glanced toward the kitchen, into which the old lady had disappeared with the bloody rags she had used to clean Nabil's arms.

"We cannot say anything to her," Claude said quietly. "She is very safe here. They will never get in." Claude looked at Nabil. "You are both safe here now."

But safe was the last thing Nabil felt. "No," he said, slowly shaking his head. "I want to get out of here. I want to get out of Iraq. I want to get to my family before it's too late."

He felt Rick's grip tighten on his shoulder. "Nabil, listen. You can't leave. This is the safest place you can be."

"No!" His voice rose. "I'll take the risk getting out like everyone else. You can't keep me here." He felt a rage rising, something he had deeply suppressed. His good work for Rick and Claude had led to this moment. Rick and Claude, who could fly back to their safe countries if they really needed to, leaving the Iraqis here in this hell. Nabil felt a cold resolve settle in around him. "I am taking care of Ali and Asmaa, and I am leaving tonight, and you can't stop me. I am not your slave."

He knew his words stung Rick and Claude, who merely stared at each other.

"Okay," Claude finally said, slapping his hands on his knees. "You make your own choices, Nabil. And of course we will help you."

Nabil then glanced at Rick, who was looking downward, his own hands clamped on his knees. He then removed one hand and placed it over Nabil's knee, squeezing. "Of course we will," he said quietly.

Then came the hours and hours on the sat phones, while the bodies of Ali and Asmaa baked in the sun under a tarp in the armed villa's garden. His objectives focused Nabil and allowed him to keep his hysteria at bay; he'd interviewed so many Iraqis in recent months about these situations, he knew what to do, as though he'd been anticipating this moment. He knew the calls to make within the network of religious volunteers from Najaf who courageously drove between there and Baghdad to claim the bodies of Shiites and bury them in a collective grave in that Shiite holy city, which was not ideal but still comforted Nabil, because it was the home city of his and Asmaa's grandmother as well as Ali's. He felt he was doing the best he could under the circumstances.

By three o'clock, those volunteers had come and taken away the bodies, and Nabil's last glimpse of the cousin who had been his sister was of her blue sneaker as her corpse was lifted into the battered minivan, which was nearly the same shade of blue.

"And they will be washed and prayed over properly, you promise?" Nabil asked the driver, an old man whose eyes were vacant with fatigue.

"Absolutely, my son. By a pious woman in Kadhimiya who does this night and day before we bring the bodies to Najaf."

"Thank you." Nabil handed five hundred American dollars to the man, whose eyes widened.

"My son, this is too much."

"It is for the work you are doing."

The old man took his hand and kissed both his cheeks before departing. Nabil stood in the courtyard and watched as the minivan pulled away. "They are taking her away," he said, turning to Mohsen, who stood beside him.

Mohsen put a hand on his shoulder. "She and Ali will be with God soon. Come inside, it's not safe to stay in the garden. Let's get back to your calls."

In an hour, it was all arranged. Once again, Mohsen's expert skills of procurement, his seemingly endless network of uncles, cousins, and friends, had borne fruit.

"I will drive you to Kadhimiya tonight," he told Nabil, "and at midnight you will meet a white minivan on the side street south of the mosque. In front of the sat-phone shop that's between the religious bookstore and the kebab house. You know the one?"

"Yes."

"You will have three hundred dollars in cash to give the driver, Abu Shahad, who is my uncle's former business partner and a very brave man, former military, who has done this trip many times. He also has a gun under the seat. And you must show him your passport."

"Okay."

"And you must make sure you go to the toilet before boarding, because he will drive like a maniac and not stop until you get to al-Tanf, which is about six hours."

"Okay."

"Then another few hours to Damascus, but at least by then you are safe."

His bags were already packed. He also had Asmaa's bag. He spent the next hour opening its contents on the bed in what had been Rita's, then Ali's room. In addition to clothes—the jerseys and jeans Asmaa wore under her abaya, the bras and panties that filled him with strange feelings of trespass to touch—Asmaa had also packed her passport, her Baghdad U diploma, paperwork related to her mother's house, and her two favorite books, *Middlemarch* and *The Prophet*. This inclusion surprised Nabil not one bit. Briefly, he flipped through the pages of the Gibran. His eyes caught the words, "Verily you are suspended like scales between your sorrow and your joy." Asmaa had often quoted that line.

Inside *Middlemarch* was a manila envelope holding photos: a wedding picture of his aunt and uncle, another of Bibi and their grandfather, a family photo during Ramadan of (Nabil was fairly certain) 1986 or 1987, a school picture from when Asmaa was eight or nine, in pigtails, the hint of a know-it-all smirk on her face, and a Polaroid of Nabil and Asmaa at the pool at the athletic club the family had once belonged to, the scene of their childhood intrigues, their warm bodies rubbing against each other on towels as they shelled pistachios, licked ice cream, and drank lemonade. "Nabil and Asmaa, Nabil and Asmaa, tizin be fed libas," Bibi would always say. *Two little butts in the same pair of pants!* That expression had always made them howl with laughter.

And at that moment, looking at the picture, he began howling. The horror, the terror of the past two hours, the bottomlessness of the realization that he would never have another conversation with her, that he would never again look into the face that was a mirror of his own, broke over him, forcing out his sobs, until he crawled on the bed into a fetal position, smashing his head into the pillow, clutching the photo, wishing he could cry out his insides. Claude and Rick came into the room and rubbed his back, saying his name over and over again, for a stretch of time he could not mark, until finally, his wails subsiding, he sat up, wiped his face, and told both men, "I have to continue."

They helped him. He packed into his own bag everything of Asmaa's that was not clothes, save a red-checked button-down shirt she wore so often that he associated it with her, but not before holding the shirt up to his nose and inhaling, wondering if he could smell Asmaa in it. What had Asmaa smelled like? He'd never considered the matter before, but now it seemed of utmost importance.

After the three of them carried his bag into the workroom and set it down, Rick and Claude pressed a wad of bills into his hand.

"It's a thousand dollars," Rick said.

"The paper let you give me that much money?"

"It's from Claude and me. We'll get reimbursed, don't worry."

"I can't take that much money from you."

"Nabil, please. Just stuff it away. Maybe ask Umm Nasim to sew it into the lining of your pants or something."

"Thank you, guys."

Rick swallowed him in what felt like an awkwardly protracted hug, followed by Claude. "We are indebted to you, Nabil," Rick said. "You know how to reach us, and you know we'd do anything for you, so don't hesitate to contact us. Let us know as soon as you can that you made it to Syria."

"I will."

Uneasy hours still yawned in front of them. He sat, numb, on the couch. Rick made a few calls and then, rather than pounding away on his keyboard in his usual fashion, drifted from his desk and sat wordlessly by him on the couch, at intervals rubbing his back.

At length, feeling like a zombie, Nabil wandered into the kitchen and found Umm Nasim at the table, chopping parsley finely. She looked up at him with her small black eyes and shook her head.

"I am saying many prayers for you, ibni," she muttered. "I am very worried about you."

"I know. Thank you."

"There is so much danger out there. There are Sunni bandits everywhere."

"I know, but we have a good driver. Thank you for taking such good care of us here, Umm Nasim. And will you stay?"

She let out a rare, sharp laugh. "What choice do I have? I can't even leave this house. Inshallah, this craziness will end, and my sons will come back from Bahrain."

"Yes, inshallah." Umm Nasim's sons had both found construction work in Manama six months before, which had scandalized the villa somewhat. What sons would leave their widowed mother in a war zone, a virtual prisoner in a walled American compound? But Umm Nasim had insisted they were doing it for the future, that they were saving to buy a home in Damascus, where they would all soon be reunited.

At dinner, Nabil barely ate, his stomach in knots. He feared eating too heavily, anyway, knowing that for hours in the van there'd be no stopping for personal relief. After the meal, everyone sat uneasily in front of the TV, where *Seinfeld* ran, the volume muted. Rick and Claude were drinking whiskey—as was Mohsen, which worried Nabil a bit, since Mohsen was his driver, but perhaps Mohsen was just building up some liquid courage.

"We may as well pack up and go home too," Rick said, out of the blue, as though he'd been brooding on the thought all day. "We're all alone now."

"You'll find new interpreters," Nabil assured him.

Rick just shook his head and scowled.

At eleven-thirty, Mohsen stood up. "Let's do this," he said—a piece of slang he'd picked up from Rick. A final round of good-byes ensued, Umm Nasim crying. Nabil picked up his duffel and took a last look around the room that had been his second home for two years: the folding tables, the unsightly riot of cords and cables that snaked over the floors and along the walls, the corner with the couches and the TV. It had been his first real job. He had no idea what he would do for work in Damascus or even if he'd find work.

He stepped out into the courtyard, tense, with Mohsen. They'd agreed not to tell the guards that he was leaving, but he thought they probably had deduced as much from the day's prior events. For all he knew, one of them was the snitch, profiting from his betrayals. And, of course, the guards' lives were at risk, too—they were all working for Americans.

But their discretion was likely sabotaged by Umm Nasim, who hurried into the courtyard with a pot of water in both hands. She splashed the contents over the rear end of the car, in the Iraqi going-away tradition. "Allah wayak," she cried. Good luck! "May God travel with you!" Then she surprised Nabil by kissing him for the first time, four times on both cheeks.

"God bless you, Umm Nasim. May we live through this."

Mohsen then opened the trunk. "Get in with your bag," he said.

Nabil gaped at him. "You're joking, right?"

"It's safer that you are not seen at all."

Nabil looked hard at Mohsen. If he acceded to him, he'd have no idea where Mohsen was driving. He suffered his first flash of paranoia about Mohsen. Could he trust him? But this was Mohsen, he thought, who had put his own life at risk day after day, who spent the least amount of time in the safety of the villa. Mohsen, who had enlisted countless friends and cousins in procuring everything they'd needed to make work and life run smoothly for them—which was exactly why Mohsen was so vulnerable to bribes and threats.

Nabil scowled slightly and climbed inside the trunk, which smelled of petrol. "Just get me to the mosque."

"We'll get there. Just be quiet." Then Mohsen closed the trunk, plunging Nabil into darkness and the overwhelming odor of petrol.

He heard the engine turn over and visualized the route: the crawl as Mohsen edged out of the villa's own walled perimeter, the various slow turns. Nabil waited for what would feel like the turn onto the long north-south artery of Fourteenth Ramadan Street, but it never came. Mohsen kept twisting and turning. What was going on?

At one point, he heard rough Iraqi voices. The car came to a stop. More voices, including Mohsen's, though he couldn't make out what was being said. His stomach and sphincter seized with terror. Any second, he thought, he would hear gunshots and then silence where Mohsen's voice had been. And then the trunk would fly open, and men whose faces were wrapped in black scarves would look down on him, laugh, tell him he was going for a different sort of ride, or—more mercifully, he thought—shoot him dead on sight as they had shot Mohsen. *Fine*, he thought. *Just let it happen. Just let it be quick.*

But it didn't happen. The voices subsided, the car moved on, and Nabil relaxed incrementally. He never felt the straight line of Fourteenth Ramadan. Mohsen must be twisting and turning all the way to the mosque.

Finally, the car stopped, the engine quieted. In seconds, Mohsen was lifting the hood of the trunk. Nabil instantly recognized the familiar side street south of the mosque, the red neon sign that blared BEST KEBAB.

Mohsen helped him out of the trunk and then pulled out his duffel. "We made it."

Nabil found himself shaking all over, a delayed reaction. "I thought we were going to die when you stopped."

Mohsen laughed. "So did I, my friend. But I think they were just some young thugs who'd taken over that block. I offered them a hundred dollars and they let me pass."

"A hundred dollars? That's ridiculous. Where did you get that?"

"Rick gave it to me and said to offer it to anyone who stopped me on the way here."

They kissed four times. "I will miss you like a brother," Mohsen said.

"Mohsen, leave. Come with me tonight. You are such a target now."

But Mohsen shrugged, lighting a cigarette. "I have too much family here, and they need the money too badly. And Nabil—I really don't care. Let them shoot me."

"What if they do worse? What if it's torture?"

"I have a gun to shoot myself in the head before it gets to that point."

"Ya, Mohsen." They both laughed.

"Look." Mohsen pointed across the southern pavilion of the mosque. "There is your van and Abu Shahad standing outside." They both waved to a middle-aged man with a dyed black mustache and a potbelly. "Tell him not to fuck this up."

"I won't put it quite like that."

They kissed again.

"Come to Damascus," Nabil said. "We'll start our own paper."

Mohsen smiled and shrugged. "Maybe."

"Thank you for everything. You kept us safe."

He picked up his bag and walked toward the van.

Hours later, after the unbearable tension of speeding west through the Sunni Triangle, and then into the no-man's-land of the desert, after he had jolted awake at the border at al-Tanf, after they had been processed and crossed the border—all of them exhausted but wearing slack smiles of relief that they'd made it without road bombs or ambushes, finally able to smoke, relieve themselves, unpack a snack—they were back in the minivan, soaring across the Syrian desert toward Damascus as the sun rose behind them. The old man next to him patted his arm and smiled.

"Hamdullilah," the old man said, then repeated it.

"Hamdullilah," Nabil echoed him.

Suddenly, his entire body was so loose with relief that it ached all over. Only then did he realize that he'd held every muscle tense for the past two days. His jaw ached worst of all. He wanted to weep tears of shock and grief, but he was simply too tired, his arms shaking with fatigue. He pulled a keffiyah down over his head to block out the light and almost instantly, save a few violent spasms, fell back into a deep sleep, during which he dreamed that he was on the garden swing chair, talking with Asmaa, but she was nowhere to be seen beside him on the floral cushion.

"Where are you?" he asked her, exasperated.

"I'm right here beside you." She was laughing, delighted by his bafflement.

"No, you're not."

"I'm right here under the chair."

He looked. "No, you're not."

"I'm above you, cousin!"

He looked up. "No, you're not. But I can hear you. Asmaa, stop this right now! Where are you?"

"I'm just on the other side of the garden wall, lamb!"

"Stop teasing me! Where are you?" Nabil craned all around, alarmed, Asmaa's laughter now echoing in the top of the newly lush, overgrown lemon tree, its quivering yellow fruit and green leaves almost neon in their brightness. But her face and body were nowhere to be found. They were liquefied into the cool blue Baghdad night of his dream—vital, mesmerizing lodestones that he would never grasp or behold again.

PART THREE

THE NEW WORLD

CHAPTER TEN

A FRESH START

(2007)

"You're putting on a *lot* of makeup," Rita said, frowning into the mirror. It wasn't by any means her first time prepping for TV. She knew the makeup artists had to lay it on thick, almost like plaster, so she didn't appear sallow under the harsh lights, but this time around it seemed excessive.

"I know it seems that way," said the makeup artist, an upbeat Asian woman roughly her own age, somewhere just south or north of forty. "But we just got new lights in the guest studio and they are *so harsh*. I promise, you won't look made up."

"That's all I ask. It's not really my style."

"No worries. I totally understand."

A few minutes later, she was seated in the guest room, a fake nighttime panorama of D.C. behind her to signify her location, a tiny microphone clipped to the collar of her blouse, a tiny digital bud in her ear. In her head, she ran over the language she wanted to use, making sure it was forceful and unsubtle and, above all, concise, able to be transmitted in increments of a few seconds each, before she was inevitably interrupted by the host, who'd ask the opposing guest to rebut her. And tonight, she'd been briefed, it was Senator Obama's foreign policy staffer, a ginger-headed wonk named Amos Osgood, whom she remembered from Harvard, where he had been two classes above her. Obama loved his Harvard wonks; everyone knew that much.

She heard a click in her ear. "Rita, this is Kelsey, the producer. Can you hear me okay?"

"Yep."

"We're going live in ninety seconds, just a heads-up."

"Okay."

"Great."

She felt the familiar prick of resentment: *She* should be on the other side of the interview, *she* should be the one asking the tough questions. She still got to do that in her new life, to an extent. But ultimately she was supposed to declare, to opine, to frame, to explain—not to inquire, not to maintain a posture of either curiosity or skepticism. And since curiosity and skepticism had been her natural postures since she was a child, it was sometimes hard to assume the posture of expertise, of certainty. Even tonight, for example: Was she really certain of what she was going to say?

Then, of course, she'd remember that she should be grateful for having landed on her feet, given her journalistic disgrace. She was by now making twice the salary she'd made at the *Standard*. Her opinion was sought on a daily basis concerning topics she felt passionately about. But she'd admit only to herself (and occasionally, over wine, to her sister, Ally, or to Salma) that every time someone called her for quotes—a former colleague or, worse, a female journalist as young as she'd been when she'd started at the *Standard*—every time she heard furious typing on the other end of the line as she spoke, she felt an inconsolable pang of loss, inferiority. She desperately missed being a journalist.

The screen in front of her came to life, and she heard the network's familiar whooshing audio logo. In her ear again: "Okay, guys, we're live in five, four, three, two, go."

There was Jack McCourt on the screen.

"And we're back!"

Rita always marveled at the sonorous and mannered voices of TV anchors.

"Today in Washington," Jack barreled on, "commanding general of coalition forces in Iraq David Petraeus appeared before a skeptical Congress for more than *six hours*, warning against a quick pullout from the somewhat more stable but still deeply troubled country. Petraeus called the situation there, and I quote, complex, difficult, and sometimes downright frustrating, end quote, and said that getting U.S. troops out of there would be, quote, neither quick nor easy. Meanwhile, our latest poll, no different from any other poll: Americans want troops *out* of the country ASAP, saying enough is enough. So, tonight, my guests: Amos Osgood, foreign affairs staffer for U.S. senator and presidential candidate Barack Obama; and Rita Khoury, formerly Iraq correspondent for the *American Standard*, currently senior analyst for the Foreign Affairs Foundation. Thank you both for being here."

"Thank you," Rita said, concurrently with Amos.

"Rita, let's start with you. You've come out already in the *Washington Post* saying you agree with the general, a quick pullout would be a *bad idea*."

"Absolutely, Jack, very bad idea," Rita cut in.

"Tell us why."

"The surge was a smart move; it's helped, but the country is still so unstable. You know, the Bush White House wants us to believe that casualties are down because of the surge, but they're not. They're at an all-time high if you factor in not just coalition but Iraqi deaths, as we seldom do. My own cousin, who is serving there, just lost his leg to a roadside bomb right outside Ramadi."

Jack interrupted: "So why wouldn't we want to get the hell out of there ASAP?"

"We can't do that to Iraq. Iraqis don't like that we're there, but they know that at this point they still need us. We made this mess; we have to clean it up. We'll go right back to pre-surge-level chaos if we pull out fast. And we'll leave a vacuum where al-Qaeda and similar terrorists groups who've already gotten a foothold can really explode."

McCourt talked her words right back to her: "We made this mess; we have to clean it up. Amos Osgood, what say you?"

"We've been cleaning it up since the top of the year with the surge, Jack."

Amos, Rita thought, still sounded exactly like the supremely self-assured alpha who'd monopolized the foreign-policy class she'd taken with him in college. And now here he was, hitching his wagon to Obama, hoping to make it to the White House.

"Finally," Amos continued, "Bush and the military did what had to be done, and vast swaths of Iraq, including Baghdad, are now secured, vastly safer than they were a year ago. But we can't commit to being there forever. Iraqis need to hear we'll be out by 2010 to accept this one last chapter of American presence."

"Out by 2010," McCourt echoed. "Rita, that seems reasonable, right?"

She suppressed a slight smirk. Since she'd started doing TV, some colleagues had told her that when she disagreed or felt she was being baited, she had a tendency to smirk slightly before speaking, which would come across as smug.

"It seems reasonable, yes," she began. "But it's still an artificial cap that, respectfully, Senator Obama is putting out there because he's running for president, and Americans are demanding a pullout."

"That's unfair," Amos interjected.

But she pushed on: "I think, yes, we should move as fast as possible to help Iraq secure itself and get out, but the truth is, if we don't have total assurance by mid-2010 or any moment, frankly, that that's the case, it's a grave mistake for us to leave. We are just leaving a giant hole in the region and basically turning Iraq over to Iran."

"We've put a tremendous and really dangerous strain on our troops," Amos cut in again. "We have soldiers serving a second or third tour in this surge despite evidence of extreme fatigue, psychological trauma. That's unacceptable."

"Amos, you're absolutely right." No way she was letting him win on this point. "You should talk to my cousin. You should also talk to Iraqis who've lost multiple relatives—or their own limbs. A lot of them weren't even able to leave the house to buy groceries the past four years, until the surge tamped things down this summer."

"But at what point do we tell Iraqis," McCourt interrupted, "'Okay, guys, time to put your own house in order?' Why can't they get on the same page politically?"

This time Rita couldn't suppress her smirk. "You know, Jack, the thing is, going into Iraq, we didn't want to face the complexity of the situation. These resentments between Shi'a and Sunni run back over a thousand years, and then they were exacerbated and exploited by Saddam for two whole decades before we came in. And then you add to that the interests of the Kurds and the Turkmen, plus Iran breathing down their necks. This country has never known democracy or true civil society before. You don't just fix that overnight. Saddam was like a lid on the tensions, and we went in there and pulled off the lid. We made this mess."

"Rita Khoury, formerly of the *American Standard*, still not mincing words."

She laughed uncomfortably. She hadn't seen that coming.

"Amos Osgood, foreign affairs guy for Senator Obama, land this plane for us. What can we expect after Petraeus's big report?"

"I think we can expect support for what he's asking, Jack, especially from Senator Obama. Petraeus is a tremendous commander. But when he's president, the senator will keep his promise to the American people and to Iraqis that the American presence in Iraq will draw down definitely. This can't go on forever."

"Rita Khoury in D.C., Amos Osgood in Chicago, thank you both. Smart thoughts on both sides."

She and Amos both gave their thank-yous. She held her thin smile.

"Okay, Rita, you're off the air," the producer said into her earbud. She dropped her smile, relaxed her shoulders. "Did I do okay?"

"You were great." Suddenly the producer was in the room with her, unclipping her mic.

"I kind of feel like I came off as Debbie Downer ruining a campaign ad for Obama."

"Not at all. Thanks for being with us again tonight."

In the elevator exiting the studio, she checked her BlackBerry. *Well done,* read a text from Jonah. *Still not mincing words!*

This made her laugh out loud. Via text, she repeated her Debbie Downer line to him.

No way, he texted back. *You came off like your brand. Uncomfortable truths nobody wants to hear.*

Again, she laughed. *Really, I have a brand? Can you meet me at Busboys in 20 minutes and tell me more about it over much needed glass of Malbec?*

For a nominal fee, he texted back.

How much?

Come meet my parents in Westchester this weekend.

This took her aback. They'd been dating about three months, since they'd met at a friend's party in a beautifully refurbished town house on Capitol Hill, a neighborhood where no Beltway yuppie would've dared live just fifteen years ago. She had found herself constantly making eye contact with a good-looking, dark-haired guy, perhaps a few years younger than her, amid a conversation of a half dozen people on the usual party talk of early 2007: Hillary versus Obama versus John Edwards. Eventually, she had wandered to the kitchen for a wine refill, at which point she turned around to find him there, ostensibly for the same reason.

"Oh, hey!"

"Oh, hey!"

"I'm Jonah."

"I'm Rita."

"I know."

"Oh, you do?"

"You're kind of famous in wonk circles."

"Oh God!" She blushed. "That's like saying someone's kind of beautiful in, like, I don't know, aardvark circles."

He laughed appreciatively. "Or, umm . . ."

Now she laughed. "Come on! I know you can pull this off." Already she knew that the next day she'd tell Salma that it had been his eyes—his large, dark, kind eyes that reminded her of Sami's—that had done her in.

"Rather smart in carrot circles."

She laughed again, pouring wine for both of them. "How do you know that carrots are dumb?"

He shrugged. "They don't have much to say."

"Maybe they're just thoughtful. You were very quiet in the conversation just now."

"Oh, thanks." He sipped. "Now you're calling me a carrot."

She was having a good time, and she felt cheeky. "A cute carrot."

He raised his eyebrows in gratitude. "Why, really? Thank you. You're a hot tomato yourself."

"We've got a salad going."

"And just so you know," he added, "I'm riding hard for Barack."

She rolled her eyes slightly. "Of course you are. All the boys are."

"You're a Hill girl?"

She paused, sipped. "I'm not a fan of her war vote—"

"No, I didn't think you would be," he interjected.

"But I think Obama would've voted the same way if he'd been in Congress at the time."

"You really do?"

"I really do. If he'd been eyeing the White House, I should add. He just had the luxury of being able to oppose it, and now he gets to wave that around."

He fake recoiled. "So cynical!"

"You don't even know how cynical. Sorry."

His eyes narrowed slightly. "No. I think I do."

His comment made her smile and look down briefly. "So what about you?" she asked. "What do you do?"

"Obligatory D.C. party question," he observed. "Well, you're gonna laugh, because I'm a stereotype. A big old Jew lawyer for the ACLU."

"Oh, thank God!"

"Why?"

"I dunno. I thought you were going to say you did some kind of regulatory thing at OMB or SEC and I was going to have to figure out how to sidle away."

He laughed. "Oh, really?"

"Really."

"Well, you don't. I'm a big fat juicy left-wing litigator. Full of righteous passion just like our Baghdad truth teller here."

"Ha. Maybe if you're good I'll tell you one day what I was drinking the night I wrote that e-mail."

So that was how it began, and she had to admit that the last few months had been sublime, the biggest lift she'd had since getting back from Beirut three years ago, in 2004. After being suspended by the *Standard* she'd stayed in Lebanon for six months, constantly on the phone with her union rep about just how much leverage she had to fight for her job. Meanwhile, offers poured in: from a large talent agency with offices in four cities around the world, urging her to write the book-length version of her e-mail; from networks asking her to come on as a talking head about Iraq; from other papers asking her to write editorials. She had to put them all off while she fought to keep the job she'd wanted since she was in high school.

Then one day she got an e-mail from the executive director of the Foreign Affairs Foundation, which since the first Gulf War of 1991 had lobbied against U.S. military intervention in other countries in all but the most dire circumstances. Rita had quoted him often over the years.

"Wanna talk?" the e-mail had read.

"Come work with us," he'd said, once they'd gotten on the phone. "You'd be a tremendous get for us."

"I'm so honored," she replied. "But I'm still fighting for my job. I'm a journalist."

"Yeah, but when it comes to foreign policy, you've shown your colors. You can't put that genie back in the bottle."

She laughed. "That's exactly what my editor said to me, and I told him to can it with the Orientalism!"

"Pardon that, you're right. But it's true. Whatever the *Standard* is paying you, we will more than match it. And you'll have your platform to write books, do TV, whatever you want to do. If Hillary gets elected president in 2008, we'll need a prominent woman to dog her on military stuff."

"So that's what this is about?" she laughed again. "You need an anti-Hillary."

"Something a bit more suited-up than Code Pink." He was referring to the women who routinely disrupted congressional military hearings and were carried out by the Capitol Police as they screamed antiwar messages.

She chuckled. "I love those ladies, actually. I guess I'm free to say that now."

"Freedom from the *Standard* would have its upside. And we'll put you in the region a lot. We know that you're part Arab and that you speak the language. It'd be fantastic for all of us."

She was briefly quiet. "Thank you for offering. You know I can't do anything right now. But I'll keep it in mind."

"That's perfect for now."

She told her parents about it on a call home.

"Why can't the *Standard* just put you back in the office in New York or Washington?" her father asked. "No, better. They can put you in the Boston bureau. Then we'd get to see you from time to time."

The thought of being relegated by the paper to Boston was enough to make her cringe with humiliation. That was a post for a twenty-six-year-old, someone plucked from the *Boston Globe*. "I'm not sure I want to be hidden away in an office, Dad."

"You're just gonna have to take your lumps and see what they wanna do with you," said her mother—a response, Rita thought, supremely grim even by her mother's standards.

"Thanks, Mom."

Then she dared to ask what she'd been long dreading.

"Are you guys ashamed of me?"

She was asking her father, really. Her father for whom her job at the *Standard* was item number one on his list of paternal bragging points. Her mother had always more or less projected a studied indifference to her success in life.

There was a pause on the other end of the line. "All you did was tell the truth," her father finally said. "We can't be ashamed of you for that."

"That's good to hear," she said softly.

"But we need to know something," added her father.

"What?"

"Are you gonna be home for your nephew's birthday?"

"Probably. It depends on what happens with my review."

"That'd make your sister so happy," her mother said.

In her final weeks in Beirut, she turned the offer from FAF over and over in her head. She read up on the group obsessively. She desperately needed something to occupy her mind. She'd been on deadline for so long, day after day, for so many years since college, always in reporting mode, that she was climbing the walls for lack of a story to work on.

"Freelance!" insisted Salma one night as they ate fatteh together at a Kababji chain in Hamra before heading to a party. (They now laughingly referred to the e-mail incident as "Fattehgate.") "You're still in the region, and a hundred places would take your stories."

"I can't write for other places while I'm in review, per my contract."

"Use a pseudonym."

Rita laughed. "Like what?" She paused. "Fiona Fatteh?"

Now they both laughed. Being with Salma again, Rita thought, was part of the upside of having been exiled. She'd not had a girlfriend during her whole time in Iraq. She'd initially hoped it might work out that way with Asmaa, but she'd ended up feeling guilty and uncomfortable around her most of the time. And now here was Salma, newly accepted into NYU's graduate program in creative nonfiction and preparing to move to New York, having just secured her student visa. Another incentive for Rita to head home.

"Habibti," Salma continued, "you know, if you feel strongly about what you saw in Iraq, and you don't think it's right, why not take the job where you can say as much? People will listen to you! You were in the thick of it for a solid year."

"Why don't I just go write for the *Nation* or *Mother Jones* and become a completely humorless leftist with scraggly hair?"

"Because they're not offering you almost twice what you make at the *Standard*, that's why."

"Good point."

"Go to FAF and be a star! You'll be on the news every night, you'll write books, you'll be the headliner at conferences."

"I'll never be able to go back to being a real reporter again. And that's all I ever wanted to be."

Salma lit a cigarette. "It's not what it's cracked up to be. Why do you think I'm going to grad school?"

Rita stole a puff from her. "Because you want to live in Brooklyn."

Salma shrugged in concession. "I'm just sad that if you take the job, you'll be in D.C. and not New York with me."

Rita handed her back the cigarette. "Weekends, my dear."

She took the job. FAF simply wooed her too hard. She'd considered her other options: Duke it out with the paper through the union for God knows how long and then either leave with a severance or be taken back in some low-profile capacity, likely as a desk editor, so the *Standard* haters of the world couldn't squawk that an avowed antiwar ideologue was back reporting under a byline. Either that or somehow maneuver her way to one of the respectable but lesser outlets, though none of those were exactly clamoring for her.

But FAF was. And so she had to admit to herself: she'd been a big shot for too long not to continue to be treated like one, even if it meant accepting that she'd concluded her childhood dream far earlier than she'd expected. She'd always wanted to be one of those tough gals who covered war and unrest right up into their fifties or sixties. Instead, she was going to become a Beltway talking head.

She would not start the job until after Labor Day 2004, so she resolved to spend another month in Beirut, packing her things and preparing to vacate the apartment that had, with the exception of the year in Baghdad, been her home since well before 9/11. The year in Iraq had made her miss certain American things she'd never thought she'd long for, things she remembered from Cambridge, such as an efficient public transit system, ample green spaces, and orderly driving; and now even Beirut, despite its relative functionality compared with Baghdad's, put her on edge with its chaotic traffic, threadbare Internet, intermittent electricity outages, and utter lack of open space save the Corniche along the sea.

A car blasted its horn one night just as it passed her and Salma in Sodeco. "Oh my God!" Rita cried, her palms flying up over her ears. "Jesus Christ!"

Salma put a hand on her arm. "Sweetie, it's not that loud."

"That just went through me like a chain saw."

"You're having a Baghdad hangover."

Rita hadn't much considered this. "Maybe I am. I know that happens to other people who come back but I didn't think it would happen to me."

Salma reached for her bag. "Do you want a Xanax?"

Rita laughed. "No. I want a drink."

*   *   *

The last time she saw Sami was on the beach in Tyre, a week before she left. She'd gone with Salma and her old Beirut friends Sabah and Cyrile and others for an overnight trip to Lebanon's southernmost city, with its mesmerizing seaside Roman ruins, dim view of Israel in the distance, and plentiful street banners lauding the various rock stars of Hezbollah and the pan-Arab Shi'a clerical elite. They were at a beach club, lying on blankets in the sand, when Salma said, low, in her ear: "Sweetie. I think I should tell you who's here."

Rita did not even have to lift her head from the blanket. "Don't even fucking tell me," she groaned. "Is it who I think it is?"

"It is."

"That just ruined the trip for me."

"Don't let it. And I only told you because they're not that far away from us."

"*They're?*"

"Yes. He's with someone."

"A girl?"

"Yes."

Rita suddenly felt nauseated. "Can you make them disappear? Can you just pull some supernatural jinn shit on them and make them vanish, please?"

Salma laughed. "Of course, sweetheart. Ma fi moushkala."

She determined she would simply not look at them. But that lasted all of three minutes before she sat up on the blanket. "I may as well get this over with," she announced. "Where are they?"

"A little in front of us to the right," Salma said.

She scanned the beach. Sure enough, there was Sami, long hair now shorn to a sort of crew cut, his lean and hirsute body in a Speedo, lying on his stomach aside a bronzed, wraithlike white girl in a tiny white bikini, her white-blond hair, still wet from the water, atop her head in a messy knot. Sami's hand lay on the small of her back.

"She's Danish," said Cyrile. "She's here for the summer studying cooking."

Rita just stared at them, transfixed, through her opaque sunglasses. "Wow," she cracked. "He really won the Aryan prize this time."

And it was at that moment—perhaps because he heard a wisp of her voice on the breeze—that Sami jerked his head, propped himself on his elbows, and spotted her. Her first instinct was horror, to get low again, roll away from him. But she felt waves of longing and, surprising herself, took off her sunglasses and stared him plain in the face.

At which point he took off his own sunglasses and stared back. After several seconds, he cocked his head sideways, as though to be playful. Then he dared to raise a hand in greeting, wiggling a few fingers, mouthing the word *hi*.

She felt her lips curl downward. She didn't reply but held her stare. And when she felt tears rising, she put her sunglasses back on, slithered back down to the blanket, and rolled over, away from him and from her own company.

She felt Salma's hand on her back. "Chérie," Salma clucked. "That girl looks like they only give her three lentils a day."

"He is such a douche bag, Rita," Cyrile added. "You should be—you know—what's the word? Soulagée."

"Relieved," Salma translated.

"I am," Rita said flatly. "I truly am."

And then, in ten days, smack in the middle of August 2004, she was sitting on another beach, in Rye, New Hampshire, the beach she had grown up on, her family's house not one thousand paces away. Alongside her were her mother; her sister, Ally; and her four-year-old niece, Leila, and nephew, Charlie, who'd just turned two, demanding she come help with the sand castle.

"But you guys are doing such a good job yourselves," she protested, scooping them both up in her arms and smothering them with kisses and tickles, which sent them into hysterics. She'd barely seen them in the years she'd been away and now she was delighting in them. She was an aunt, with two children she could dote on and spoil for years to come, if she stayed in the States. She'd hardly considered this.

"But we need your help!" insisted Leila. "To make sure we're doing it right."

Ally and her mother laughed. "Now they think you're an engineer," Mary Jo remarked dryly, from the lawn chair in which she sat, under a floppy-brimmed Red Sox hat and gauzy white coverall, her pink face covered in white sunblock. A pulpy-looking historical romance set in Ireland sat in her lap.

"You are doing it right," Rita assured them. "I can see from here. I'll come down in a second and take a closer look, okay?"

But by now Charlie was running his tiny fingers over her face. "You look like Mommy," he observed.

Ally grabbed him and smothered him with her own set of kisses. "You know why, honey? It's because Mommy and Auntie Rita are sisters. Just like Leila is your sister."

Charlie seemed to ponder that for a blank moment before he wrested himself free and ran back down to the sand castle.

"That was more information than he could handle," Mary Jo chuckled.

Ally ignored her mother and rolled toward Rita on the blanket. "They are so excited that you are back," she said, jerking her head toward the children. "Especially Leila. You've been, like, this fantasy to her, and now you're really here. She's in awe of you."

"I'm in awe of them. Leila talks like an adult."

Ally blushed, pleased. "She's very precocious. Her teacher said she's already reading at a third-grade level." Ally jerked herself up on the blanket and twisted herself around. "Did I tell you that, Ma?"

Mary Jo had her sunblock-frosted nose in her book again. "Tell me what, honey?"

"That Leila's reading at a third-grade level already?"

"Really? Well, I'm not surprised. You and Rita both read ahead of your grades."

"I really think it's Gary," said Ally. "I swear, from about six months, there was not a night when he didn't read to her before putting her down. Same with Charlie. Nights when I was almost too tired to move."

"That is incredible," said Rita, trying to be supportive. She and her parents didn't particularly like Gary, and Ally knew it, so Rita at least made an effort to echo Ally's praise, which was more than could be expected of Mary Jo, who remained pointedly silent.

Then Mary Jo spoke: "He's comin' up after work to watch the game tonight with the rest of us?"

"He's gonna try."

"I'm a wreck," Mary Jo continued. "I'm afraid if I get my hopes up again I'll just be—what?" She fumbled for a word.

"Devastated?" Rita offered. "Destroyed? Deflated?" She and Ally both laughed.

"Exactly," said Mary Jo. "And it's not funny, either."

Their mother was obsessed with the Red Sox. Of course, Rita had returned to New England that summer to find everyone obsessed with the Red Sox, with the desperate hope that they might redeem the prior season's brutal last-minute downfall against the Yankees. You could not walk through a mall or enter a restaurant or turn on the TV or the radio without being led to believe, had you been a newly arrived alien, that the ubiquitous red-stocking icon and the big red *B* were this society's primary objects of worship. David Ortiz, Manny Ramírez, Johnny Damon, Pedro Martínez, Curt Schilling—they might as well have been members of everybody's family, they were talked about so constantly.

But now Rita had to admit that Ally's funny e-mails had been true: every unbridled expression of pride, love, and hope Mary Jo had always withheld from her children she now lavished on the Red Sox, whom she called "my boys." Her love of Johnny Damon in particular was so pronounced that Ally would say, "Stop, Ma, you're making me uncomfortable!" and their dad, George, would grumble, "Why don't you just get it over with and run away with him?"

* * *

Later, Rita and Ally left Leila and Charlie with Mary Jo back up at the house, and drove to a farm stand in Stratham to buy tomatoes, corn, and other things for dinner.

"Can I tell you something now?" Ally said, eyes on the road even as she reached across and took Rita's hand. "Now that Ma won't make fun of me?"

Rita turned to look at her sister, who had just turned forty. She was a suburban mom to the core, hair back in a simple ponytail, sunglasses she'd likely bought at a Filene's Basement, T-shirt and shorts she likely wore to yoga, tanned legs, and New Balance sneakers. The back seat of the car was filled with games, coloring books, and crayons for the kids, to keep them occupied on trips. She could not have more thoroughly embodied a life that Rita had always dreaded, and yet Rita was still as mesmerized by her green-eyed beauty as she'd been when they were kids, role-playing, and Ally was always the mother or the princess and Rita was always the vassal or the villain.

"What is it?" Rita asked.

"I am *so glad* that you are back, Reetie. So, so glad." She'd started crying, and now she wiped a tear away from her cheek with the back of her left hand as she navigated a bend in the country road with her right.

"Sweetie!" exclaimed Rita, slightly alarmed. "I'm glad I'm back, too. I mean, back with you."

"No," Ally protested, still snuffling. "I mean, I know it must be complicated for you, coming back, with everything that happened. I'm not an idiot. I get that. I'm just saying that the past few years—I've just felt like an only child with Ma and Dad, that's all."

She began crying again.

"I've wanted so badly for the kids to have an aunt and an uncle. And Gary doesn't really get it because his sister lives two towns away from us and he think she's a pain in the ass, and—"

Rita laughed. "He does?"

"Yes, and—well, anyway, I'm just saying, I'm sorry for what happened, but I'm really glad you're back."

"D.C. is so close to Boston," said Rita. "Such an easy jump. We'll see each other so much more. And you'll bring the kids to D.C."

"If Gary wants to."

"No," Rita said firmly. "If Gary doesn't want to, then you bring them anyway. We can still have a great time without Gary."

Ally turned toward her and laughed. "Okay," she said. "I will."

Then a year passed, during which the Red Sox won the World Series. Rita's entire family and everyone she'd ever known growing up went bananas, which made her relieved that she was in D.C., where her new job at FAF devoured her life. She kept meaning to properly decorate the spacious one-bedroom she rented in the elegant art deco building in Kalorama, but usually found herself at conferences on weekends, talking about pathways out of U.S. interventionism with other talking heads from like-minded groups, some of them media exiles like herself. She lived amid a few dull pieces of furniture she managed to have delivered from Crate and Barrel and some of the art she'd had sent back from Beirut.

She hated D.C. her first six months there. Because she never spent time in the poor parts of town, the city seemed impossibly pristine and airy to her, too hushed, too dull, too orderly, too manicured, too maintained, too affluent, too smug. She missed the broken-down, earth-toned mess of Baghdad—well, of the Baghdad she'd known in her first year there, before going into the street had become a deadly risk—and also of Beirut, where even the poshest sectors of Achrafieh still conveyed the snug feeling of people living on top of one another, stray cats everywhere and backyard roosters heralding the sunrise. Americans felt soulless and myopic to her, and she spent her scant free time with foreigners and Arabic-speakers or at least other Americans who had lived for long periods out of the country and didn't spend dinners discussing *Desperate Housewives* and Paris Hilton, two new cultural phenomena she found utterly emblematic of the nation's turning inward, away from the catastrophe it had caused overseas and into mindless pop cultural trivia.

She also often found her job boring, slow-paced. She'd once worked simultaneously on three stories full of multiple and conflicting sources, ever-changing facts and assumptions, her e-mail and phone abuzz, a constant adrenaline rush in which she might enjoy the ego spike of seeing her byline several times in one week. She couldn't believe the glacial pace of the policy universe. She was given so much time to write papers, even briefs, and had to wait so long for them to be reviewed and marked up by others—usually in the leaden academic language that reminded her of the Harvard-speak she'd spent years unlearning—that she lost interest in the pieces shortly after she'd begun.

And yet. And yet. She was making more money than she'd ever made before. She traveled in comfort. And as 2004 rolled into 2005, into her first D.C. spring, in which the city transformed into a lush garden of cherry blossoms, she finally allowed herself to relax into her new life, to tell herself that she was still fighting the good fight, even if now she was more of a foreign-policy scold than an excavator of hidden truths.

She was dining outdoors with colleagues one lovely night, sharing some excellent bottles of rosé and a perfectly grilled Chilean sea bass, when she surprised herself by having her first conscious moment of gratitude, rather than resentment and discomfort, for no longer being in Baghdad. No longer eating Umm Nasim's monotonous food trapped inside a joyless bunker, no longer unable to enjoy a sidewalk café on an exquisite evening, no longer surrounded by grim faces and sadness and death. She'd not thought much about how hard it had been to be cooped up daily with Nabil and Asmaa and Ali and the rest of the Iraqi drivers and guards, to absorb their fear and desperation and be able to do so little about it except to ensure their salaries. It was a relief not to have to feel that afresh, day after day.

Then, just a week after that distinctively good meal and lovely night, she read an e-mail from Rick Garza about the death of Asmaa and Ali and the departure of Nabil.

Her hands rose to her face as she read it. She stood up at her desk, closed the door to her office, locked it, then stood against it, palms still to her face, for several minutes. Slowly she sank to the floor and sobbed quietly. She had not felt such a bottomless wave of guilt for having left Iraq in a very long time.

At some point she rose, wiped her face, and called Rick's sat phone, sitting through the ringtones and the eerie crackle of the heavens between D.C. and Baghdad.

"It's Rita."

"Hi there." He sounded surprisingly nearby, but his voice was flat, hollowed out.

"I read your e-mail, and I had a brief meltdown, and now I'm calling you."

"You really got out before the worst of it."

"I know." She paused. "Do you have any idea who did it?"

Rick sighed. "I mean, Ali's family does, but, you know, there's nothing they can do about it. We told the Iraqi police and the military."

"But the families will get insurance?"

"Yep. We're in touch with Ali's family and Nabil's gonna handle it on Asmaa's end with her mother in Damascus."

"Have you heard from him?"

"Yep, he got there safely, thank God. He's with his family."

She exhaled deeply. "Thank God. I'm so glad he got out."

"If we'd lost all three—" He broke off.

"I know."

"Nabil still has the same e-mail address?" She felt that she was grilling Rick because she dreaded a pause.

"Yep. The Yahoo one. That's what he e-mailed me on to say he'd made it."

"I'll write him right now."

"Good. He'll appreciate that. You know I told him before he left, anything he needed, just reach out, we'll bust our asses to make it happen."

"He can't really work legally in Syria."

"I know. Maybe that's why we can hook him up there with a job as a stringer or a fixer. Marna's working on it. But Nabil needs a moment to breathe. Ali and Asmaa were killed and he left Baghdad all in the same day, can you believe it?"

"I'll just reach out and say that we're all here, ready to help him with whatever he wants, when he wants it."

"That's the best thing to do now."

But then they did finally lapse into a silence. "How are you guys hanging in there?" she finally asked.

"We're hanging in and that's it. Life is very grim, as you can imagine."

"Yep."

"And we miss you."

She felt tears rise again and squeezed them back. "I miss you guys, too," she said hoarsely. Self-recrimination overcame her. Why had she been stupid enough to get herself kicked out? Why couldn't she have acted differently?

"I gotta finish a piece," Rick said.

"Of course, of course. I'll let you go. Stay safe and stay in touch and give my love to everyone."

"Will do, Rita. Be well. Enjoy normality."

She sat, bereft, for several minutes before turning to her e-mail.

"Nabil," she wrote (she almost wrote *Danger Twin*, but the term of endearment suddenly felt all wrong),

> *I just talked to Rick about everything that happened. Nabil, I am sorry from the bottom of my heart. I am sitting here devastated by the news just wishing I could be with you now to hold you.*

Was that too odd? she wondered. But it was how she felt, she determined, so she let it stand.

> *I was so relieved to hear that you made it safely to Damascus and are with your family now. They must be so relieved, too. Please send me your Western Union info, I would like to send something to help you and your family get through this really difficult time.*

Rick and I know that you are probably just processing everything that's happened and getting your bearings in Damascus, but please know that when and if you need any sort of help at all in terms of a job or even applying for asylum in the U.S., we are 100 percent ready and willing to help. I am in D.C. now so I am within reach of all the pertinent offices that would handle your case.

She didn't know what else to say. Except for the things she didn't want to burden him with, such as her guilt. So she merely wrote:

Allah yusmallak [may God protect you], *my beloved Danger Twin* [she decided to write it after all].
    Rita

She received an e-mail back from Nabil within the hour:

Hello Rita, my Danger Twin!
    Thank you for your e-mail. I hope you and your family are safe and well in Boston. I am writing to you from an Internet café in the Old City in Damascus. It is not too far from Muhajirin where I live with my family and with Asmaa's mother. It is a rather lovely neighborhood running up a hill overlooking the city and we were able to afford it because of the income I accrued at the paper. Most Iraqis live farther out in Jaramana. But here we are close to our Syrian cousins who found the apartment for us.
    But of course you probably know this because I know you came to Damascus a few times when you were living in Beirut. I love Damascus. It is pretty, I love the hills, I love the trees, you can dress how you want, and it smells like jasmine everywhere! Most of all it is safe and orderly and Damascenes are so generous to the new Iraqis. They are like our cousins and they even have a picture of Assad everywhere you go which is just like it was in Iraq until the invasion. Nostalgia! Haha. :)

I am also so happy to be with my family again. It feels like a dream. Everyone is well except my teyta (remember I told you about Bibi?) who is depressed and misses Baghdad. Sometimes she fights with Asmaa's mother, who is also depressed and cries most of the time. But they still cook all day as teytas and aunties do! We wish the apartment were a bit larger but we are not complaining. We are all finding ways of staying busy while we wait to see what happens back home.

Thank you for your offers of help. I have immense gratitude for you. I am going to try to relax a bit and then figure out what to do. Rick said he would help me become a freelancer from Damascus. I think that would be very exciting but it also makes me nervous because the government is very strict here and I'm not sure it would be good for my family. So we shall see, inshallah!

Thank you for your kind letter, Rita, and I hope we stay in touch.

Fondly,
Nabil (Danger Twin)

She read the e-mail, then reread it. First, she was struck that he mentioned Asmaa only obliquely. Then she figured that he was in shock or simply didn't know how to talk about it in an e-mail. Mostly, she was relieved to hear that he was alive, reunited with his family, and happy to be out of Baghdad. *You can dress how you want,* he'd written. She pondered that. Damascus was not as liberal as Beirut, but it was far more so than Baghdad, especially in the Old City, full of Westerners and tourists.

She wrote back instantly:

I am so happy to hear back from you so fast and to know that you are safe and sound with your family and happy to be in Damascus. It is an incredibly beautiful city, isn't it? I love the Umayyad Mosque so much.

Take care of yourself and let's talk soon. Xo R (a.k.a. DT)

After that, she tried to work but couldn't. She kept picturing Asmaa coming back to the villa, worn out, and tearing off her hated abaya, throwing it aside in a ball. They would all watch her out of the corner of their eyes, and when she caught them, she would briefly come back to life and declare, "I hate this fucking thing!"

For a moment, they'd all laugh.

She rang in 2006 in New York with Salma, at the party of a friend of theirs in Fort Greene, Salma's new neighborhood in Brooklyn, where everyone toasted with champagne while Kanye West boomed from the sound system. A few days later, she was back in D.C., knee-deep in planning an April conference on "progressive realism," which aimed to articulate a post-Iraq American foreign policy that blended cold self-interest with humanitarian intervention. And in April, just three days after the exhausting conference ended and she thought she might be able to join Salma for a few days on the beach in Miami, her mother called to tell her that her cousin Bobby, whom she had not actually seen in person since Christmas of 2002, had had his leg blown off in Ramadi.

"*RAMA-dee?*" her mother asked. "Like RAMA-dan? Like the holiday?"

"It's *ra-MAH-dee*," Rita corrected her. "But, what, what? What do you know? Is he alive?"

"He's alive. And he lost his leg below the knee, thank God."

"That is a good thing." She knew that much from her time in Iraq.

"He's in the hospital in Germany."

"At Landstuhl?"

"What's that?" her mother asked.

"That's the U.S. military hospital in Germany. That's where all the serious Iraq and Afghanistan injuries are flown."

"Well, I forget where exactly your Auntie Carol said he was, but I guess that's it. She said that his commander said he got hit by a—um—oh, you have to know the term, Rita."

"I don't. Like, a grenade? An RPG?"

"Yes! Yes, I'm pretty sure that's the term Carol used. She and Uncle Terry are flying over tomorrow to be with him."

"How can they afford that?"

"We covered the tickets for them."

"Oh." Rita paused. "Jesus Christ," she finally said.

"Don't say that, Rita."

"I'm sorry, Ma. I'm just sad because I knew something like this would happen to Bobby, and now it's happened."

"I know. It's awful. But you know, your cousin felt very strongly about going off to serve his country."

Rita made a slight *tsk* over the phone. "Well, can you just confirm with Auntie Carol where he's at and his contact so I can get in touch there? Or, don't worry, I'll find out."

"I'll check again with Carol and e-mail you."

"Okay, Ma. Love you."

"You too, honey."

"My dearest cuz," she wrote later that night.

> *I don't know exactly when you'll read this—I assume you're at Landstuhl right now?—but I just wanted to let you know that we got the bad news from your mom. Oh cuz, I am so, so sorry. I don't know what to say. I worried that something exactly like that was going to happen to you.*

Was she was already veering over into berating territory? She deleted that last line.

> *I guess just that I love you and am worried about you and we are desperately awaiting word of what comes next. I'm really glad to hear Uncle Terry and Auntie Carol will be with you in Germany. You'll probably be transferred to Walter Reed, right? Do you have any idea yet of when? At least I will be able to visit you regularly.*

Well [and here she paused for a long time, at a loss], *I don't know what more to say so I'll simply say that you are in all our prayers* [she couldn't believe she wrote stuff like that to family, but she did] *and we are awaiting word and we want you back in the States so we can take care of you. Okay, you did your soldier bit, now get home!*

She almost instantly deleted that last line as well. Then she hit "send." But she did not hear back for several days, and when she did, it was from her Auntie Carol.

Hi Rita,

Uncle Terry and I are here in Landstuhl with Bobby. They had to put him in a coma for three days while they went in and cleaned out his wounds and took a little bit more bone off his leg so that the prosthesis would fit better, eventually. Bobby just came out of his coma yesterday and is in decent spirits, all things considered. He is mostly obsessed with two of his buddies who died in the blast and another one who he's not sure what happened to yet. We are trying to get word for him to settle his mind. He is on a lot of painkillers, which is good because he would probably be more agitated if he weren't.

Anyway, all this is to say that he gave me his e-mail password so I could get back to anyone (like you) who was reaching out over e-mail. We will probably be here in Germany with him for a few weeks while they do a few more operations on him. He had some damage to his hand that they are going to try to go in and fix up with titanium. It is really hard to see him this way, our brave boy. After that, they are going to fly him to a brand-new amputee facility in San Antonio, not Walter Reed, so Terry and I will probably join him out there. They have housing for the families there. That's where he'll get fitted for his prosthesis and have his rehab, learn to walk, etc.

I did let him know that you wrote and that you and the whole family back home are praying for him. Maybe once we are in San Antonio (the hospital is called Brooke Army Medical Center) you

*can come out and see him, I know that it would probably cheer him
up to see his favorite cousin.*

*Honey, I am glad you and Bobby are BOTH out of Iraq alive
and let's keep it that way! It sounds like hell on earth.*

*Please keep the prayers for Bobby coming and I'll keep you
posted.*

Love,

Auntie Carol

She did, in fact, travel one weekend with her mother to San Antonio to see him, once he'd been installed there, about five weeks after
her aunt's e-mail.

"Can you please come so I'm not alone with Ma for three days?"
she had begged her sister.

"I can't come that weekend! It's the fair at school and I'm the head
of the food."

"You can't off-load that on someone?"

"They would talk about me forever."

Rita sighed. "Honestly, Als."

"I'm sorry. I'll tell Ma to be nice to you."

"A lot of good that'll do."

She flew in from D.C., and her mother flew in from Boston, so
they met at the hotel in San Antonio.

"This is strange, to say the least," said her mother, upon opening
the door of their hotel room, the high-rise Holiday Inn alongside the
San Antonio River.

It was Rita, as usual, who initiated the obligatory hug. "Hey, Ma.
Well, we made it out here. That's the important thing."

They got lunch, then drove in Rita's rental car over to the medical
center, an ugly, 1980s-era red stone behemoth.

"You would think there'd be a place like this closer to Boston,"
Mary Jo remarked as they walked through the parking lot.

Inside, once they registered at the front desk and were directed
to Bobby's unit, they entered a universe of the limbless. They walked

through a cavernous, gleamingly new arena where hundreds of young men (and, Rita noted, but a handful of young women) of all different races, many of them muscled and tattooed, yet all of them missing at least one of four major limbs, worked alongside staffers on every manner of rehab, from sit-ups and push-ups to walking with walkers to working out on treadmills, ellipticals, and strength-training machines. A sound system played, at a tolerable volume, country-and-western music. In one corner, a man with an extremely high-tech prosthetic leg climbed a rock wall.

"Would you look at that," Mary Jo murmured, looking up. "Things have come a long way since my day. You should've seen the legs people got forty, fifty years ago."

Rita glanced at her mother, who shook her head. What little sense of wonder Mary Jo possessed emerged mostly when she talked about medicine. Modern advances never ceased to fascinate her.

She nudged her mother slightly. "Maybe it'll be Bobby up on that wall soon."

"God willing."

They found Bobby in a large, sun-filled room with his parents, lying on the bed with his back slightly to them. The football game played low on the TV overhead. Bobby was doing lifts with his stump, which had a sort of hard foam bumper over it. Rita had made herself visualize this in advance, so as to mute her reaction when she saw him, but with her first view she still gasped slightly and touched her mother's shoulder.

Auntie Carol saw them first. "Well, look who the cat dragged in from Boston!" she exclaimed, suddenly beaming.

"Don't move," Rita called out to Bobby. "We're coming around."

But as soon as he heard her, he called, "Is that my long-lost cuz?"

And in a second, everyone was embracing, and Rita was surprised, when she pulled back from the bed, to find that she had teared up because she was so grateful to see her cousin alive again, albeit looking a bit sallow from lack of fresh air and vague around the eyes from medication, with one leg gone and a splint over his right hand, but nonetheless alive, and with the same stupid grin on his face and cheekiness in his voice. He wore a tank top that revealed his biceps tattoo of the Red Sox logo with "2004" etched beneath it.

"It's so good to see you, even without a leg," she laughed.

"I can't believe ya found time to quit yakkin' about the war and come out here to see your own flesh and blood." But he was giving her a wicked smile while he said it.

"Shut up!" she laughed. "I can see you haven't changed."

"Nope!"

Mary Jo pulled up closer to the bed. "How you doin', honey? How's your pain level?"

"Honestly, Auntie MJ? The pain can be pretty intense. And the phantom limb stuff. That is a weird fuckin' sensation."

"Bobby, come on," Auntie Carol tsk-tsked at his language but without much force.

"I'm sorry," he laughed, "but it is. Especially when it wakes me up at night, and then I'm like, *Oh, there's nuthin' there*."

"That'll fade with time, though," Mary Jo said confidently. "With mirror box therapy. They got you started on that yet?"

"Oh yeah," said Bobby. "They already got me up in front of the mirror."

"The staff here is so incredible," Auntie Carol said. "I have never seen such dedication. They're like family."

"They really are something else," said Uncle Terry. It was virtually the first thing he'd said since they'd arrived. Which, Rita thought, was fitting. Uncle Terry never said much, just tended to nod or shake his head in unison with whatever everybody else was saying.

Then she turned to her mother, whose casually dropped medical knowledge never ceased to quietly impress her. "What's mirror box therapy?"

"It's when you do your rehab in front of a mirror so your brain can remap what your body looks like."

"Or in other words," added Bobby, "so you can see what a freak you look like just when you've forgotten about it."

Everyone clucked in dissent. "You look great, honey," Mary Jo said. "Hey, Rita, tell him what we just saw coming in."

"A bunch of freaks without limbs?" Bobby asked.

Rita shook her head. "You are still the worst. The absolute worst. No, cuz, we saw a guy with a below-the-knee amputation just like yours *scaling a rock wall.*"

"Oh yeah, the infamous rock wall. They say when you're finally able to climb the rock wall, then you're ready to go home."

"And how long will that be?"

Bobby shrugged.

"It depends," said Auntie Carol.

"Yeah," Bobby added. "They told me I'm probably gonna get a shitload of infections in my stump first that they're gonna have to treat. That's par for the course. Really looking forward to that. Then a ton of problems and pains and scabs and stuff once they put my prosthesis on. So who knows? Maybe the war'll end before I get out of here, and I won't even have a job to go back to."

This caught Rita up short. She even laughed briefly. "You mean you want to go *back*?"

"What else am I supposed to do? I wanna get back to my unit. They don't have to put me outside the wire. I'll find something to do."

Rita shifted her gaze silently from Bobby to her aunt and uncle.

"But we're gonna cross that bridge when we come to it," Auntie Carol said gently. "Right, Bobby?"

"Yeah, Ma," he replied flatly. "Whatever you say."

A brief silence ensued, during which Auntie Carol fluffed the pillow behind Bobby's head, and he did a few more half-hearted stump lifts.

"What about you, cuz?" he finally asked, with a faint edge that Rita remembered all too well. "How's the career shift? You miss being in hell?"

She laughed with the sharpness that he seemed to expect. "I miss it *so much*," she groaned. "Every day was a picnic, wasn't it?"

"Yeah. That's the good life all right. Blue skies and dust in your face all day and a surprise around every corner."

"We're just so glad the two of you made it back alive," Auntie Carol interjected. "You don't know the workout my mother's rosary got while you were gone."

"Don't put it down yet, Ma," said Bobby.

"But I mean," Rita was surprised to hear herself say. "I feel lousy about everyone I left behind. People I worked with who died. I feel guilty all the time."

Nobody responded. Until Bobby replied: "Now you know why I wanna go back."

She frowned at him. "I think you're crazy, but I suppose I do," she said. "But that doesn't mean you have to!"

He laughed. "We're gonna cross that bridge when we come to it. Right, Ma?"

Bobby had physical therapy at three o'clock, so Rita and her mother kissed the others good-bye, saying they'd stop in after dinner.

"You wanna do some of this River Walk that everyone here talks about?" she asked her mother as they drove back to the hotel. "It's right next to the hotel."

"I'm not sure I'm up for that."

"Okay." She wasn't surprised at the answer. Her mother seldom was up for anything. "You don't mind if I go, do you?"

"Of course not."

But when they got back to the hotel, her mother announced: "What the hell. I'll do some of the walk with you. May as well see some new sights while we're here, right?"

"Okay, great."

And so they joined other tourists in walking the path alongside the San Antonio River, which Rita found remarkably narrow, almost like a canal. She said as much to her mother, who agreed.

"What's the river you had in Baghdad again?" her mother asked. "The Tigris or the Euphrates?"

"The Tigris."

"Is it big?"

"Very wide and very winding."

"As much as the Merrimack River?"

"Wider and more winding."

"Hmm."

Her mother grew quiet as they walked. Rita wondered what she was thinking. The image of a legless Bobby sat smack in the middle of her own mind like a bruise. Eventually, they came upon a riverside café and stopped for a glass of white wine.

Mary Jo took out her cell phone. "I'm gonna call your father."

"He's probably working and won't pick up."

Rita watched while her mother awaited the call. Finally she turned to Rita and mouthed, *You're right*. Then she spoke into the phone, at what seemed to Rita a comically loud volume: "Hi, George, it's me and Rita calling you from San Antonio. We just saw Bobby at the hospital with Carol and Terry. He's doing okay. He's in early rehab but, uh, we're confident because the facility is excellent. You wouldn't believe the stuff they have in there these days. Isn't that right, Rita?"

"She's right, Dad," Rita called.

"They even had a rock wall to climb. Anyway, we're goin' back later tonight. Right now we're just having a nice drink next to the river here in San Antonio. Rita, what's this river called?"

"The San Antonio River," Rita called again.

"Oh." Mary Jo laughed. "Ha. The San Antonio River. Well, that makes sense. Okay, Georgie, anyway, that's it for now. Remember the salmon I bought for the grill or it's gonna go bad. Okay. Love you. Bye-bye."

"I knew he wouldn't pick up," Rita said.

Mary Jo shrugged. "Married to his work, that man. Always has been, always will be."

She put her phone away and turned to stare out at the river. Rita did the same, only to turn back to her mother and find a tear rolling down her cheek.

"Ma!" Rita was slightly shocked, so seldom had she seen her mother cry. "What's wrong?"

Mary Jo turned to look at her with such a nakedly needy visage that Rita almost grimaced. "I'm just so glad you're back from that place and in one piece," her mother said, with a snuffle. She extended a hand. "Promise me you're gonna stay with us."

"Ma!" Rita laughed. She leaned over and put a hand over her mother's. "I'm not goin' back, Ma. At least until it's really stable again."

"After your father and I die."

"Ma, stop it!" Rita shook her head. "Jeez, we should visit rehab centers together more often. It brings out your soft side."

Her mother slapped her hand, her eyes flashing with a familiar and, to Rita, reassuring indignation. "Why do you always have to be so fresh? Even when I'm being serious?"

Rita laughed and held her hand atop her mother's a moment longer.

And then came 2007, and all the talk in policy circles about the wisdom and particulars of the surge, the United States' last-ditch effort to set Iraq right. And then came Jonah. Only two weeks after the party at which they met they were meeting for lunch, spending weekends at each other's apartments, hiking or running through Rock Creek Park, hitting events and parties together. He was her entrée to the universe of people who worked for liberal nonprofits and advocacy groups, some of whom she'd gone to college with, people who lived in funky neighborhoods like Adams Morgan or the U Street Corridor. The Democrats had taken back Congress the year before, would likely take the White House in 2008, and the city's young professional left flank was exultant, allowing itself to dream again about finally recovering clout in D.C.

As for Jonah, he would almost salivate, Rita teased him, when he talked about his dreams for the courts in the coming years—victories he thought they'd likely achieve on immigration, campaign finance, gay rights, reproductive rights. After her years of fraternizing with journalists, who were all basically liberal but trained to evince high levels of cynicism and irony and not to betray overt bias, it was refreshing to be with someone who wore his beliefs on his sleeve, even if she sometimes found his arguments oversimplified and his reasoning stubborn. He was a lawyer, after all.

She was also madly attracted to him. She yearned for his body when she wasn't with him, for his furry chest, full lips, slender fingers, and eyes that seemed rimmed lightly in natural kohl. She also savored the relief, after Sami, of being with someone who was as busy as she was—often busier, frankly—and who harbored no sulking resentment that she lived first and foremost for public affairs and her career. It was D.C., after all, and people were their jobs, their BlackBerrys a natural extension of their brains and fingers. There was no shame in it.

Here he was now, as they sat at Busboys and Poets, the new preferred watering hole of the Beltway left, asking her to meet his family.

"In Croton-on-Hudson," she said.

"In Croton-on-Hudson, yes. My niece's bat mitzvah. Hey, it's on the river! You can swim away if it's that traumatizing."

She cocked her head at him. "So you're serious about this, then?"

He smiled and shrugged. "I don't think you have to read into it so deeply. I just thought you'd be amused to meet my big old crazy tribe."

Now she laughed. "I have one of those myself, you know."

"I do. And I hope to meet them, too."

She sipped her wine. "Enemy tribes, you know."

"I know! That's where the excitement comes in. Think of the role we can play in the peace process. We'll be like one of those summer programs where Israeli and Palestinian kids make, like, yarn art together."

"Oh my God!" she exclaimed. "There actually is a program like that!"

"Yes! I read about it in—" He paused. "Your old employer."

"Yeah, I know," she said sourly. "Marna Gelman wrote that story. Last year."

"Uh-oh!" He sipped. "Poor Marna Gelman. You really have it in for her."

"Please. I could care less anymore."

He let seconds pass before he spoke again. "So you'll come this weekend?"

"If I can subject you to my tribe next time. Absolutely. I might even take you to a mahrajan."

"A what?"

"It's a big Arabic fair where you stuff your face and then you'll have to get up and do a line dance."

He leaned over the table and laced his fingers through hers. "It's a deal."

CHAPTER ELEVEN

HABIBI

(2006)

They were glancing at each other. Nabil was sure of it.

He'd been sitting for the past thirty minutes in the Internet café in Bab Touma, Damascus's picturesque, stone-walled Christian quarter, which was filled with Westerners and tourists. He loved Bab Touma; he spent most of his days there. All his life, or at least until right before the American invasion, when journalists had flooded Baghdad, he'd seen Westerners—Europeans, Australians, Americans, with their infinite shades of blond or red or brown hair and creamy pink or tan skin—only on TV or in movies or photos. Here he saw them all the time, with their backpacks and sunglasses and Lonely Planet guidebooks, the girls respectfully covered in gauzy pants and long-sleeved blouses, some of the boys looking absolutely moronic and out of place in shorts, their tanned, furry legs, atop Birkenstocks or Nikes, drawing Nabil's eyes like a magnet, as much as he willed himself to look away.

He'd been smoking and nursing a Nescafé in a tiny plastic cup he'd bought at the counter, writing an e-mail to Rick Garza:

Hello, Rick!
I hope this finds you safe and "hanging in there" in Baghdad. It is odd to think that you are still there and I am not! I cannot believe

the high levels of sectarian killing and how the neighborhoods are becoming segregated. The country is at civil war even if America won't call it that! I cannot believe they build a giant wall around Adhamiya. I used to walk between there and Kadhimiya every day to work and back! I truly do not recognize my country anymore and I do not know if we will ever go back. It is a great sadness.

I am writing to respectfully enquire if you heard anything from Marna Gelman related to my possibility of working for you in Damascus. Most of the work here for Iraqis occurs if they can find work through another Iraqi, such as working as a business partner supplying some sort of goods from Syria to Iraq. I do have a small job that I hesitate to say what it is as it is "under the table," as are many jobs here for Iraqis. As you know we cannot get work papers. Some Syrians here have told me that I would probably get into trouble if I tried to work as a reporter here. However, I decided that I would "cross that bridge when I come to it"! I miss working! I felt useful at the bureau with my education finally putting itself to use. The days are rather long here. Thankfully my nephew and niece are in school and we are far better off than many Iraqis here. Yet still there is not much for us to do. I continue to read a great deal. Currently I am reading The Crying of Lot 49 by Thomas Pynchon. Have you ever read that, Rick? It is quite challenging for me, which I enjoy!

Well, I will not hold you further. Thank you, Rick! Please continue to take extreme precautions and please give my warmest regards to Claude and to Umm Nasim. And I will once more humbly reiterate my great desire to hear from Miss Marna Gelman if at all possible.

Yours very sincerely,
Nabil

He sent the e-mail, wondering whether he would hear back this time. Rick hadn't replied to his last e-mail, sent two weeks before, but Nabil was aware he had sent it during a particularly brutal week of Sunni-Shi'a killings in Baghdad.

He sat, sighed, finished his cigarette. He had three hours to kill before he had to be at the cell-phone shop, whose owner, Milad, had had the wherewithal to leave Baghdad in late 2003. The shop was in Muhajirin, where Nabil's family lived. The neighborhood was not quite as picturesque as Bab Touma but was still older and prettier than most Damascus districts—a dense network of small streets and warm yellow buildings that climbed their way up the lower reaches of Mount Qasioun, which towered over the city. Iraqi newcomers with some money, like his own family, lived there, sparing themselves life in the congested Iraqi refugee ghettos of Jaramana and Set Zeinab, farther from the city center.

He sat back in his chair, stretched. He'd probably pay for another hour of Internet and continue his idle research into marketing and communications career opportunities in the Gulf states.

But then he allowed himself to glance over his shoulder to the left.

He was still there. The blond boy. The kind of blond that was picture-book blond, Swiss Alps blond, California surfer blond. Blond, with blue eyes that Nabil found shocking and skin that looked as though it had been brushed in liquid sunlight, with more blond fur on his arms. A T-shirt and jeans and tennis sneakers and a backpack and a book on introductory Levantine Arabic and also a small plastic cup of Nescafé and a cigarette at his side, his e-mails opened on the screen before him.

And then, when Nabil looked back again, the boy looked at him, quickly appraised him from top to bottom, and then, ever so faintly and shyly, smiled.

Nabil darted his head back toward his own screen, horrified and delighted. Had that really just happened? Suddenly, he was trembling. Had anyone seen? Nearly every cubicle in the café at that moment was occupied, a few by other Western backpacker types, a few by young Damascene men who seemed to live here, smoking and drinking coffee and playing online video games all day, filling the café with the irritating bleeps and buzzes of points gained or lost. There was a high chance at least one of them was a member of the Mukhabarat, Assad's secret police force, who were rumored to haunt Internet cafés, looking for people who might be reading or writing anti-government material. More than once since coming here, thinking back on what Rita had whispered to him just before leaving Baghdad, Nabil had been tempted to type the terms *gay* or *LGBT* plus *asylum* and *United Nations High Commissioner for Refugees* into Google. But he didn't dare. It was an extremely frustrating feeling to know that either a lifeline or an arrest (or, worse, deportation back to Iraq) might await him just on the other side of an Internet search—a liberty that Nabil had come to take for granted back in the villa of the paper.

Now he could barely focus on the jobs page of the Abu Dhabi multinational he had been perusing.

"Afwan?" he heard someone say in a foreign accent.

He looked up. The blond boy was standing before him, his Arabic-language book in hand, that same shy half smile on his face. Nabil's stomach sloshed about. The boy's cheeks were so creamy, pinkish-tan, his lips so petulant, full.

"I speak English," Nabil managed to say.

But the boy, who was perhaps nineteen or twenty, continued to speak in his first-year Arabic, which charmed Nabil. "Min fadlek, ya akh," he continued, nodding toward his book. "Sadoony bi arabi?" *Help me with Arabic?*

Nabil smiled broadly; the request seemed so childlike, so guileless. "Ma fi moushkala," he said. *No problem.*

Now the blond boy smiled, apparently familiar with the phrase. "Isme Liam," he said, offering a hand. "Ana danmarki." *My name's Liam. I'm Danish.*

"Isme Nabil. Ana eiraqi."

Liam's eyes widened, seemingly with understanding—although, Nabil surmised, he lacked the Arabic word for *refugee*. Liam pointed toward the door. "Yalla?"

Nabil paused a moment, then nodded. Why shouldn't they go? This was the most innocent and elemental thing in the world, agreeing to help a foreigner with the language. It was the essence of hospitality, even if he himself technically wasn't a local. He closed his web browser, signed out of his stall. At the counter, he moved to pay, but Liam waved him away and handed over one hundred Syrian liras. Nabil silently acceded, feeling a kind of luxury, a letting go, wash over him. The young ponytailed guy behind the counter, intent on a soccer game on the radio, barely seemed to notice them.

They exited onto a narrow, quiet side street whose left end revealed a small portion of the old Roman stone gate of Saint Thomas, the portal to Bab Touma. "Shaqti qarib," Liam said. *My apartment is near.*

Nabil nodded okay and followed him around the corner and into the covered stretch of Straight Street that held the souk. Nervously, Nabil glanced at stall keepers tending to canaries in cages, at old ladies with bags of vegetables, but nobody seemed to be staring back at them. Liam walked slightly ahead, dispensing with small talk, which Nabil found slightly odd but intriguing and a bit exciting, as though Liam had no need for words to assert his will. They turned a corner onto another impossibly narrow side street, and then Liam turned a key in a lock in a typical Bab Touma building, where the windows of the second floor jutted out slightly over the windows of the first, as likewise did the windows of the third over the second.

They entered a courtyard, the typical sort of inner chamber of an old Damascus building, with its diamond-patterned tile floor, empty stone fountain in the center, jasmine hanging from some of the balconies. It was unpopulated at the moment, Nabil noted with relief—no neighbors to take note of them.

They trudged up two flights of stairs just half a meter wider than their own bodies, the walls smelling mysteriously of coffee, spices, and old bricks; then Liam turned a second key in a lock, and they entered a dim room not much bigger than the computer stall Nabil had been sitting in, with just enough space for a very narrow futon on the floor, covered in a mussed sheet, and a small table beside it, stacked with books and magazines. The putty walls were bare save a cluster of taped-up photos of Liam in what appeared to be various sites around Europe, some with fellow blonds whom Nabil assumed to also be Danish, some with darker sorts whom Nabil assumed to be friends he'd met along the way. There was one small window, placed high near the ceiling, which allowed a dim square of light.

They each put down their backpacks. Liam slipped out of his sneakers and sat on the futon, but Nabil just stood frozen in place, looking down on him.

Liam reached out a hand to him, laughing softly. "Anta—" he began, *You*, then "Ana la baref kalimatan." *I don't know the word.*

"Tell me in English."

"You are shaking."

Nabil felt himself blush, mortified, looking at his hand. He was, visibly. Liam sat up slightly and reached for his hand, pulling him down gently, until he gave way and sat beside him on the futon. "It's okay," Liam said softly. "Nobody saw us come up. Ma fi moushkala."

Nabil was reeling, desire and fear churning in his stomach. "Are we going to study?"

Liam laughed softly. "Do you want to help me study?"

"I need a job," he said helplessly. "I'm not allowed to work officially in Syria."

Liam seemed to sober, considering this. "I will pay you to help me with my Arabic," he finally said. His English accent was so odd! Odder than Claude's French accent. But it mesmerized Nabil. "But first may I do something?"

Nabil felt as if he had a whole lemon in his throat. "What?"

"May I kiss your eyelashes?" Liam raised a hand and lightly grazed one of Nabil's lashes with his thumb. "I saw them in the Internet café, and I thought, I have never seen such long lashes on a man. Even in the Middle East. They are so beautiful."

Nabil felt himself crumbling under the feather touch of Liam's thumb. All his life, people had commented on his lashes, telling him he looked like a girl. His lashes were a curse and, on a more secret level, a source of pride and vanity.

"So, may I kiss them?" Liam asked.

"Yes," he barely managed to croak.

Liam leaned forward and placed his lips atop Nabil's right away, expelling a sigh and a wash of warm breath over Nabil's face, grazed there a moment, then moved to his left eye. Nabil felt his right hand moving toward Liam's, until their fingers interlaced. Nabil felt a curtain falling, a scrim. He'd wondered since he was eleven, twelve, what this experience felt like, tried to conjure it when he masturbated behind a locked door or in the shower, assumed he might never find out. His heart cannonballed in his chest; his whole body was shaking now.

Liam put both his hands on Nabil's thighs. "Shhh," he whispered. "Nobody is here. And the guy next door isn't home now, but he is a student like me, from Rome. He wouldn't even care."

"I have never done this before."

"That is why you have to enjoy it." Liam's lips grazed over his nose, to the bottom of his ear, eventually to his lips.

Nabil gasped. "Oh my God," he whispered.

"Remember, I am paying you." Liam regarded him and smiled. "I command you to enjoy it." He had a mock sternness in his voice that made Nabil laugh, momentarily, relaxing him.

"Yes, master," he quipped back.

Liam laughed, a little mischievous rumble. "Much better."

When Liam pressed his lips firmly to Nabil's, when his tongue breached Nabil's teeth, and Nabil allowed himself to drop his jaw in acquiescence, a wave of terror shuddered through him. He was now officially among the people of Lot; he was defying the hadiths of Muhammad, and he would surely die for this. Briefly, his jaw froze. Liam said nothing but brought an arm around his neck and pushed in harder with his tongue until it filled Nabil's mouth, and Nabil's last wall of defense gave way with a moan he could not withhold, and his arms found their way around Liam's slim waist.

"Now I have you," Liam chuckled, satisfied.

Fifteen minutes later, Liam said, "You come first," and immediately after Nabil came, he erupted in sobs, curling over on his side, baffled while he wept as to what he was feeling or why, in that particular moment, it had overcome him so completely. And while he wept, Liam held him from behind and covered the back of his head, his neck, and his shoulders with kisses, whispering again and again, "It's okay, it's okay, Nabil, it's okay."

"It's your turn," Nabil choked.

"No, it's okay."

He wasn't sure how long he cried, but at some point he subsided and fell asleep, grasping Liam's arm around his chest as a child might. When he woke, the room was dark. He smelled cigarette smoke and turned to find Liam lying on his back, his hairless chest a line in the dimness, a cigarette resting there, a burning orange pinprick. Liam offered it to Nabil, who dragged on it, then sat up in a panic.

"I have to be at work!" He reached over Liam for his jeans, extracting his cell phone to find that he still had twenty minutes to get to Muhajirin. "Oh," he exhaled. "I'm okay."

"Come here, then." Liam pulled him back down.

"I have only three minutes."

"That's okay. Finish the cigarette with me, then go."

Nabil struggled to relax. He lay on his back, rigid. Eventually he allowed himself to glance rightward at Liam's torso, to discern, as his eyes adjusted to the dimness, the dark blond trail that ran south of his navel. Nabil reached for it until he had Liam's limp goods in his palm, stroking them and releasing another unbidden groan.

But Liam put his own hand there. "You don't have time now."

Nabil looked up at him, sheepish.

"Can you meet me tomorrow at two at the Jupiter Café? To study?"

Nabil knew the café fairly well. It was popular with Westerners. "I can," he said.

Liam reached for his own wallet and pulled out a five-hundred-lira Syrian bill, offering it to Nabil, who instantly conjured images of cab rides, groceries, cigarettes, pistachio ice cream for his nieces and nephew. "I can't take that," he said. "I haven't taught you yet."

"It's an advance." Liam sat up and tucked the note into the pocket of Nabil's jeans. "Plus, our lessons already started today."

Nabil sat up now, pulled his underpants back on. "Thank you." He was standing now, dressing quickly, anxious to descend the stairs to the street.

Liam stood now, naked, distracting Nabil with the full length of his body, the flatness of his torso, and the twin curves of his butt. Was this really happening?

"Let me kiss you good-bye before you go to work," Liam said. And in an instant, they were exactly where they had begun, Nabil reaching helplessly between Liam's legs, betraying another soft groan. "Oh my God," he whispered.

Again, Liam removed his hand. "Next time."

Nabil regarded him, exasperated.

"Ma'a assalama, habibi," murmured Liam.

This made Nabil laugh. "You know," he said, one hand still on Liam's waist, "all my life, I am wondering, what does it sound like to have a man say that to me? Not my mother or father or brother or friends, but a man, like the way you just said it."

Liam ran a finger around his lips. "And what did it sound like?"

"It sounded delectable," he said, using a word he loved. "Even with your funny accent."

Liam gasped in mock offense. "How rude! Get out of my mansion!"

Just before he opened his door, he kissed Nabil again. And then he sent Nabil clattering down the stairs, through the courtyard, and out into the street, where he heard both church bells and, farther afield, the late-afternoon call to prayer. He walked briskly past the stall keepers toward the gates of the Old City, then, feeling giddy out in the open street, he broke into a run to catch a taxi. As he ran, he shook his head in disbelief, then smiled like a madman and said to himself several times in astonishment, "Ya allah, ya allah, ya rab!" *Oh my God, oh my God, oh my Lord!*

That day was a turning point, bringing magic into his life. Before that, true, there had been the joy of seeing his family again, all of them coming to meet him at the minivan in Muhajirin, Rana and Ahmed running ahead into his arms screaming, "Ammo, Ammo!" just as he had hoped. He wept as he embraced his parents, Bibi (who had made him date cookies to eat on the way home), Amma Mariam and Ammo Adel, his brothers and sisters-in-law, his littlest niece, Mena, who was now four; and most of them wept with him, most heavily his mother. He had not thought he'd make it of Iraq out alive to see them again, and to look into their faces was his first true release since the moment he'd knelt on the garden stones to retrieve Asmaa's fallen body.

"Isn't Damascus beautiful, Ammo?" Rana had exclaimed. "It's so different from Baghdad. And a man keeps pigeons on our roof, just like in Baghdad."

"It is beautiful, aini." And it was. Of course, he had seen pictures. But he wasn't prepared for the city's breathtaking verticality, neighborhoods arrayed on hills, ancient apartments stacked atop one another, lush green trees lining the streets, the smell of jasmine everywhere, the dome and spires of the famous Umayyad Mosque, and all of it overlooked by majestic Mount Qasioun. How had they lived among such sand-colored flatness all their lives? Already, as they walked to the apartment, he saw the image of Assad posted everywhere, and he found it oddly comforting, nostalgic, as it reminded him of street life in Baghdad before the American invasion. Syrians, too, lived under a strongman and a secret police, and they understood Iraqis and had been uniquely hospitable to them, offering them schools and health care, if not work permits.

And Damascenes were also beautiful. Their beauty was often spoken of in Iraq, and as they walked, Nabil noted the profusion of piercing blue and green eyes, for which Syrians were noted. He also had a strange, uncomfortable sensation walking through open, crowded streets, unable to do so with ease, as though he should hurry his entire family along and indoors before something awful happened. When a car nearby emitted a sustained honk—Damascus was as car-choked as Baghdad had become when new-model vehicles flooded in after the lifting of sanctions—the noise sliced through his head like a cleaver.

But when they climbed the steep streets of Muhajirin and reached the well-maintained apartment, Nabil saw with his own eyes for the first time the comedown his parents had often lamented over the phone. Twelve of them were living in two adjoining apartments with a total of eight rooms, including kitchens and salons. Hardly a square meter, even in the salons, was not covered by thin mattresses, bedsheets, piles or sacks of clothes, or racks on which damp clothes dried. In Kadhimiya, both his own family and Asmaa's mother had lived in proper, spacious homes—no more than two to a bedroom—with plenty of outdoor space and the aid of a maid and a gardener. He could not fathom how they had been living this new way. They had been part of Baghdad's professional, educated middle class. "We are living like refugees," his father had told him over the phone, again and again. And Nabil had clucked, "Ya, Baba," as though to suggest he was exaggerating. But now, setting down his own bags, Nabil saw what his father had meant. How would *he* live this way? For one thing, he would share a room with elderly Ammo Adel and Ahmed—three of them on mattresses that barely left enough space to tiptoe out of the room to the toilet in the middle of the night.

In the kitchen, as everyone gathered around a homecoming meal that had been prepared for Nabil, his mother embraced him.

"Habibi," she began, stroking his face. "It's not the house in Kadhimiya, is it?" She laughed.

"It's okay, Mama. We're alive, and we're together."

She embraced him again and whispered in his ear, "You know I can't say this around Mariam, but I thank God ten times a day that you made it out alive."

"I know, Mama." He regarded her. She looked exhausted. She'd stopped coloring her hair, indifferent to the bounty of gray that now shot through the black. She'd found teaching work, for a pittance, with a small Palestinian-founded nongovernmental organization that provided classes for Iraqi and Palestinian refugee kids in the area around the Sayyidah Zeinab mosque. But Nabil's father, with no such diversion, spent his days watching TV news in the small apartment or drinking tea and smoking all afternoon with a group of similarly idle Baghdadi men at a café around the corner.

Nabil dreamed of Asmaa constantly. In half the dreams, they were in the garden or in the front room of the *Standard*'s villa, and Asmaa was usually giving him orders of some sort—he could never remember exactly what the dreams had been about—and sometimes, oddly, they were at work in the garden, the two of them on their sat phones in the garden swing. And in the other half of the dreams, they were inside a building, and Nabil was trying to keep Asmaa from going outside because something bad lurked just beyond the door, and then Asmaa would pass defiantly through the door wearing her hated abaya, and Nabil would wake in terror at the sound of a gun. And often, confusingly, the two kinds of dreams would merge so that they would be working one moment, Asmaa would die the next, and they'd be back to work the next moment. Nabil would always wake up exhausted.

During the day, he wondered how he was going to get through the rest of his life without her. He thought of how much more exciting Damascus would be, how much more optimistic he'd feel, if she were here. Asmaa would find them some kind of work. She always did. She had no shyness or hesitation to hold her back as she charged in among strangers, brimming with crisp competence as she made her inquiries, proffering her résumé and a glowing recitation of her assets. Rita had been that way, too. He'd been focused and motivated when he was with one or the other, or, especially, both, but now, on his own, he felt the old preinvasion listlessness coming back. There were days when he would wake up, old Adel to his left and his beloved, glossy-haired nephew, Ahmed, to his right, and wish to lay his head back down and sleep through the entire day straight into nightfall, simply to make it pass.

Not long after his arrival, though, he made Bab Touma his refuge. It was the most cosmopolitan place he'd ever seen, with its daily youthful mix of Damascenes with uncovered heads and fashionable clothes and tourists and students from all over the world, yearning to know at least a bit of Arabic. Surely he could set up some sort of teaching business under the table. But he feared getting caught trying to do so by the police. Asmaa would know how to set it up discreetly, he thought.

He began spending far too much money at the Internet café, obsessively reading news about Iraq. He read Rick's stories from the *Standard* that he should have been working on, read the names of leaders and clerics he'd become intimately familiar with, and he wondered whom the paper had hired as the new interpreters. (They were never credited in the stories; it was too dangerous for them.) He read that Rita had taken a fancy new job in Washington as an expert at a place the press referred to as "center-left." He e-mailed his handful of contacts throughout the Gulf to ask about job opportunities.

And he began researching the United Nations' asylum process, just in case. He wanted to read stories about how gay refugees got from Iraq or Iran or Syria or Saudi Arabia to Europe, the United States, Australia, or Canada, but he was afraid to search the terms *gay* and *LGBT*. It was widely known that Syrian intelligence monitored Internet searches for certain terms, and he did not want to get the café owner in trouble. He started to go crazy from boredom, wondering if he should have stayed in Baghdad and continued risking his life at the paper just so he had something to do all day, and colleagues to do it with.

Then he met Liam.

They fell into a pattern. Most days at two o'clock, after Liam's Arabic classes, Nabil would meet him at the Jupiter Café where, with Liam's book open and his pen poised over his notebook, they would engage in stilted conversation Arabic conversation along the lines of: *I like Damascus very much. Do you like Damascus? Yes, I like Damascus very much.* Then Nabil, nodding at a girl across the way, would continue: *She likes Damascus very much. We like Damascus very much. They like Damascus very much. Damascus is a very beautiful city.*

They would drink coffee and sometimes smoke an apple-flavored nargileh or share baklava while they practiced, and sometimes friends of Liam's from the Arabic institute would drop by their table and join them, which is how Nabil started to make a small circle of friends from Australia, Italy and the U.K., all of whom were very impressed to learn that he had worked for the *American Standard* in Baghdad, which did wonders for his self-esteem amid his current refugee malaise. And then he and Liam would get back to work, and he would wait until he felt the faint impression of Liam's sneaker against his ankle under the table. He would glance at Liam, whose lips twitched with a tiny smile, and then he would take the pen from Liam and correct his rendering of the Arabic *y*, whose particular strokes Liam seemed incapable of mastering.

"You are not watching closely when I show you this *y*," Nabil would complain. "This is the third time this week."

"I think you need to be more firm with me about it like you are now."

And Nabil would blush and force himself not to smile and not to look up at Liam as he wrote.

And then Liam would settle the bill and leave and Nabil would sit there and smoke and chip away distractedly at *The Crying of Lot 49* for another twenty minutes. But he wouldn't really be able to concentrate, as he was merely marking the minutes until he, too, would leave and walk along the few narrow alleys, then through the marketplace, his heart pounding, to Liam's apartment, to the street door that Liam left unlocked for him, through the courtyard, up the narrow stairs, and into Liam's tiny room, where Liam was usually already naked, his hands clasped behind his head, waiting for him on the futon.

"Get your clothes off, habibi," Liam would say, sidling toward the wall to make room for him on the futon.

Liam's face and body became his new world within the world. Books had always served that purpose for him, the world he slipped into amid the claustrophobia of Baghdad under Saddam, with its sanctions and limited prospects, the cheap and easy way to travel when he couldn't really travel. After the American invasion, when he was working and had no time for books, the villa of the *Standard* became that world within the world, the womb where he was safe. That had been shattered. In the minivan from Baghdad to Damascus, he was an open wound; in the first overcrowded weeks in the apartment in Muhajirin, he choked inside as even the very end of his day found him not alone with his poster of Younis Mahmoud but squeezed between his nephew and his elderly uncle on the floor.

But now, once again, he had a compartment utterly his own, and the compartment was a face with full lips and a body that felt so good against his own, so soft and warm, he would hyperventilate when he first wrapped his own limbs around it.

"Habibi, are you okay?"

Nabil would nod. "It's just you are the first body of a man I have ever felt."

"You never got with a man in Baghdad?"

"No. I wanted to but I was too scared."

"You never walked around Shaalan here and met someone in front of Byblos Bank?" Shaalan was a nearby area where Damascus homosexuals congregated, many with long, streaked hair, armloads of jewelry, and tight, embroidered jeans.

"I walked through a few times, but I wasn't attracted. They are too feminine for me. And I was scared. I don't want to get caught doing something and sent back to Iraq. I would disgrace my family, and then I would go back and be killed."

Liam kissed his eyes. "The only thing feminine about you is your eyelashes. And they are perfect. And the rest of you is a hairy, masculine Arab man. You are my dream."

Nabil blushed and squirmed a bit, both complimented and embarrassed. Liam often told him that he was his hairy, dark Arab dream, which made him laugh awkwardly. Then again, he conceded, part of his fascination with Liam was that he had only previously seen in pictures such smooth pink skin, covered only in the faintest blond down, such a sculptured nose and cheeks, such white-blond hair. Liam was studying political science in a Danish city called Arhus and intended to someday work for a large international NGO such as the World Health Organization, which is why he was spending a semester in Damascus, to acquaint himself with Middle Eastern culture and learn Arabic. He might have been the first man Nabil had been with, but the reverse certainly wasn't true. Liam knew very clearly what he wanted, which was to be fucked hard by hairy Arab men. He'd been with as many as he could find in Denmark, and that had partly spurred his desire to spend his semester abroad in the region. Nabil thought it was funny that he had mistaken Liam for being shy that first time Liam had approached him in the Internet café.

Liam wasn't shy—especially on the futon. After a few afternoons there, Nabil learned quickly that he didn't have to be gentle with Liam.

This felt a bit dangerous at first, but once Nabil was assured that Liam liked it, he allowed himself to like it as well, and once, as he strove with all his might to meet Liam's desired level of aggression, he felt a switch go off inside his own head, and he began pounding Liam with a wild rage whose depths astounded him. His eyes fixed on Liam with what felt, to him, like a strange blending of yearning and hatred. He grabbed him by the neck and whispered over and over again: "Is this what you want? Is this what you want?" Until he let loose wildly inside Liam and then collapsed atop him, heaving.

"Oh wow," Liam finally said, beaming.

Now spent, Nabil was mortified. "I don't know what happened."

"I don't either, but I hope it happens again. You were so wild, habibi. That was the best."

Afterward, they always lay there, sometimes smoking, sometimes napping, until Nabil had to get up, dress, and hurry to the cell-phone shop in Muhajirin. In Liam's arms, Nabil would feel the knots in his neck and back unlock, twitchingly, as he fell asleep, and in all of his other waking hours, he would hold on to this moment, which he thought of as perhaps even more delectable than the frantic moments that led to his sudden onrush of sleepiness. And before or after napping, they would talk.

"Habibi, listen to me," Liam said to him more than once. "You need to go to Douma and register with UNHCR. You can't stay here long-term."

Douma. Just thinking about that place, just outside Damascus, made Nabil tense up. He'd seen pictures and heard stories about the throngs of Iraqis and Palestinians waiting there for days on end just to get registered with UNHCR and be counted as refugees, never mind that a refugee's number might not come up for months or years. He was exhausted. He liked Damascus, and he didn't want to move again. He knew some sort of work would emerge. Rick Garza had finally replied, briefly but affectionately, saying that he was waiting to hear back from Marna Gelman about whether Nabil could work as a stringer from Damascus somehow.

Plus, Nabil privately added, he now had a Damascus boyfriend.

"I can't leave my family," he would tell Liam. "I need to earn for them."

"But you can't really work here. Habibi, you were a reporter for the *American Standard*."

"Not a reporter—an interpreter."

"They could not have done their jobs without you. You need to go to a country where you can do that kind of work. You are too talented to work all your life in a cell-phone shop in Damascus."

Nabil twisted around on the futon, grinning. "Oh, really, you think so? I thought I was just a hairy Arab."

Liam laughed, gripping him tightly inside his arms and legs. "You're *my* hairy Arab. Mine, mine, mine. Hamdullilah."

Their laughter blended, up through the small window near the ceiling. "You are so profane," Nabil chided. "If my grandmother could hear you."

And as for his grandmother, he had reclaimed a ritual with her that seemed to keep her alive, a reminder of their old carefree shopping trips. On Fridays, she would cloak herself completely in black, then she and Nabil would take a taxi down the steep streets of Muhajirin to the ancient Umayyad Mosque, where they would join in prayer pilgrims and tourists from all over the region, staying roughly an hour. Then the real fun for Bibi would begin: the walk to Souq Al Juma, the Friday market, where Nabil would watch her regain her old Kadhimiya gusto as she haggled with vendors over string beans, tomatoes, oranges, spices, okra, rice. Occasionally she would struggle with their Syrian accent, then she would have a laugh with the sellers over their differences in pronouncing, say, "banadoura," tomatoes, which were called "tamata" in Iraq. Nabil loved watching her; he marveled at her ability to adapt, after all she had been through, and approaching eighty.

"Have you noticed," she asked him, her arm in his as he carried her bounty, "the strange shape of the tomatoes here?"

"You think so, Bibi? They look normal to me." Produce here, in fact, seemed to him generally more bountiful, beautiful, and diverse than it ever had in Baghdad.

"No," she insisted. "They are bigger but they have a funny shape. It's not right."

He suppressed a grin. "What's the shape, Bibi?"

She glanced at him and frowned, perceiving his amusement. "It's the wrong shape," she said flatly.

"Well, you still do wonderful things with them with the green beans."

"I didn't say they tasted bad. I just said their shape was wrong."

"Okay, Bibi."

She tugged rightward on his arm, leading him toward a pistachio vendor. And as she did so, a man, oddly, cut diagonally in front of them, slowing down so that they, in turn, had to slow down to let him pass. He then stared at Nabil pointedly before passing.

"That was rude," Bibi muttered as she regained her pace. "Typical Damascus behavior. And even on the holy day!"

"That was strange," Nabil conceded.

As the pistachio vendor and Bibi negotiated, Nabil glanced gingerly over his shoulder. The man was there, about twenty meters back, now lighting a cigarette, watching them. Nabil's stomach flopped. Now he was almost certain the man was targeting them. The man was perhaps a decade older than he was, stocky, in a bland and unflattering beige open-collar shirt and unfashionable jeans, two days' growth of stubble on his broad face.

He was a typical-looking middle-class Damascene man, someone Nabil would never have noticed. But now he wondered if he'd seen him before. At the Internet café, perhaps? Had he been there, in the next cubicle, or the one opposite? Nabil's stomach flop deepened into a sicker, more ominous feeling. *Please God*, he begged silently. *No. Please, no.*

Bibi was finished, her bag of pistachios in hand, explaining to the vendor with great seriousness the particularly rich quality of the pistachios in Iraq. He nodded earnestly, indulging her—another kind Damascene who knew all too well that what had happened to Iraqis, ruled by a dictator despised by America, could just as easily happen to Syrians. Bibi bade him good-bye with her blessings and turned.

"Some Syrians aren't so bad," she allowed.

Nabil muttered in assent, but he was fixed on not making eye contact with the man as they passed him. And yet, as they did, Nabil heard him say the word aloud—not loudly but certainly loud enough that he intended Nabil, if not Bibi, to hear.

"Ya khawal." *Faggot.*

Nabil winced as he heard the word. This could not be happening. His reflex was to look back at the man, but he forced himself not to. He had to pretend he wasn't even aware of the man's presence. But inside, he felt as though his world was collapsing. Who was the man? Why had he said that? Was it merely because, to the man, Nabil looked like a khawal? Was it a random act of cruelty? Nabil could live with that. But if it was because the man knew something . . . Nabil's stomach roiled again.

"Let's get in a taxi, Bibi." He absolutely did not want the man following them to their apartment.

"The bag isn't that heavy," she protested. She loved the entire ritual of Friday, the time out of the cramped apartment, amid the bustle of the city.

"I feel as if I'm getting sick."

"What?" Now Bibi was going into a tailspin. "What's wrong with you? Is it your head? Your bowels? Eat a banana. That'll tighten you up." She reached into the bag of produce.

"No." Nabil put a hand on her arm. "It's okay. I just want to get home and lie down."

In the taxi, Bibi prattled on. "I'll boil you turnips with salt when we get home," she said. "That'll fix you in exactly one hour."

"Okay, Bibi, thank you." But he barely heard himself say it. He was staring straight ahead, terrified.

He wanted to cancel his meeting with Liam the next day, to call and say that he wasn't feeling well. But, he feared, if his calls were being tracked, he would betray that he knew something was wrong. Plus, he wasn't doing anything wrong, he thought defiantly. He had already begun telling himself that he and Liam met merely at the café, for lessons, and that the magical Part II, in the tiny room a short walk away, had never happened. He could simply will that part away.

Liam was already at the Jupiter Café, smoking and struggling to decipher *Tishreen*, the state-owned daily, when Nabil arrived. He'd gotten a haircut and looked especially handsome, which made Nabil feel uncomfortable. He sat and forced a smile.

"Anta mutakhir, habibi," Liam noted. *You're late, my love.* Of course, in Syria male friends or even acquaintances could address each other this way, meaning it affectionately but without a grain of romance. But today, hearing it nearly made Nabil recoil.

"I'm sorry." He sounded stiff to himself. "I had some things at home to take care of." Already he was scanning the café, trying to do it nonchalantly.

"I was just teasing you," Liam said in English. "Is everything okay at home?"

"Oh yes. No worries. Just something routine with the oven."

"That's good."

"Yes. So, where did we leave off? Past tense of *I like, I want, I need,* correct?"

Liam smiled, puzzled. "You are very businesslike today."

"I am?"

"Yes."

And then, with that same churn of the stomach, Nabil saw him. Sitting across the room, alone, the paper in his lap, sucking a nargileh, wearing virtually the same clothes today as the day before, looking straight at him. And when their eyes met, the man—very clearly and, Nabil was certain, with sly malice—smiled and nodded in his direction.

Nabil looked away, his whole body rigid with terror. Up until this moment, he'd been able to maintain the possibility that it had all been a fluke, but now it was apparent to him: he was being followed. Just why, he wasn't sure, but he knew it was really happening.

And yet, he felt he couldn't let on.

Liam's hand moved in the direction of his own, so he removed his into his lap.

"What's wrong, habibi?" Liam asked. "Your hand is shaking."

"Stop calling me that in public," Nabil hissed. "It is very unwise."

"Everyone here calls each other 'habibi.'"

Nabil thought he would die if Liam uttered the word again. *There is a man behind you watching us who was following me the other day*, he wanted to tell Liam. But he was afraid that the man might know English and read his lips. He had to proceed as though he didn't know he was being watched.

"Let's just begin the lesson," he said, nodding at Liam to open his notebook, to give the impression of official business taking place.

Liam did so. It was the most rigid lesson they'd ever conducted, Nabil willing himself throughout not to glance over at the man. It was an exhausting effort. Liam, thankfully, refrained from the usual foot-to-leg grazing under the table that he usually delighted in.

After about twenty minutes, Nabil couldn't take it anymore. "I think that is very good for today," he announced, once again forcing a cordial smile. "I actually have to be at the cell-phone shop a bit earlier today, so I will be getting on now." He rose to leave—and felt his entire body go weak with terror when he saw the man do the same, summoning the waiter to settle his bill.

"Nabil," Liam nearly exclaimed. "What is wrong? Don't you want to be paid?"

"Tomorrow."

"Will you be here?"

"Of course." But he was already walking toward the door, as fast as he could without attracting undue attention. Once outside, he hurried down the narrow street, staring straight ahead, toward the gate of Saint Thomas, out of the Old City and into the incessant chorus of car horns that marked every Damascus traffic jam. He had no idea where to walk. He didn't want the man following him home.

And suddenly the man was striding up alongside him. "Nabil al-Jumaili?" he asked. "Son of Uthman al-Jumaili from Kadhimiya in Baghdad?"

Nabil could stand it no longer. He stopped abruptly and turned. "Why are you following me?" He felt nearly as though he would cry.

"Come with me, please."

"Who are you?"

"The state police."

"Why should I believe you?"

The man laughed curtly. "If you disobey me, you will soon find out why you should have believed me."

"But I haven't done anything!" he protested. He tried to contain his voice, so as not to attract the attention of passersby. "I'm Iraqi, yes, but I just went back to the border to renew my guest pass. I can show it to you. I'm not violating any rules."

The man seemed unmoved. "Come with me, please."

Nabil hesitated. What if it was a hoax? He could be kidnapped, or worse. But then again—Syria wasn't lawless like Iraq had become. Assad and his police ruled with brutal absolutism. And everyone knew that Damascus was crawling with secret police, especially in the Old City, where Damascenes interacted freely with Westerners. Nabil had heard that there was one Mukhabarat agent for every one hundred Damascenes.

The man took two steps and Nabil followed. The man put a hand on his elbow, the way someone might walk with a friend, but Nabil knew it was a means of asserting control. They walked down Qasaa Street, then into an alley, where a black sedan with tinted windows was parked. The man unlocked the doors from ten meters away with his key fob and instructed Nabil to get into the passenger seat.

"I am very frightened to get into the car with you," Nabil said. "Can't we just talk here?"

Again the man emitted his short, cold laugh. "You are very difficult. I told you to get in the car."

So Nabil did, praying it wouldn't be the last time he was seen in public. Inside, the car reeked of smoke, and indeed, the first thing the man did when he got into the driver's seat was light a cigarette. This came as some relief to Nabil, who'd feared that he'd instantly drive them away, to some remote outskirts of the city.

"You know," the man began, "you are breaking the law here in Syria."

And so the cat-and-mouse game was beginning. "I am breaking no law, sir."

"You are committing sodomy with the European you were just with. I have watched you go to his apartment several times. You come to Syria seeking refuge and you become a prostitute with men?"

"That is not true, sir." Nabil could feel sweat breaking out on his face, under his shirt. "I am teaching him Arabic, that's all. I need the money for my family, sir. There are thirteen of us here."

Again, the curt, contemptuous laugh. "I'm sure you would not want them to know how you earn the money. What a dishonor to them. They would probably have to kill you just to hold their heads up with their neighbors in Muhajirin."

Nabil could not believe the man's cool gall, invoking his worst nightmare. "I am not having that kind of relations with him!" he insisted.

Now the man cocked his head and curled down his lips, almost comically. "Do you really think we are that stupid? Do you really think we don't know how to do our job?"

What could he mean? Had they bugged that room? Photographed them somehow through the tiny window up by the ceiling?

"What do you want from me?" Nabil finally asked.

The man enjoyed his last drag on his cigarette, stubbed it out in an ashtray already brimming with butts. "There is no choice. We will have to deport you back to Iraq."

"I beg you please not to do that. You know I will die if I go back there."

"Yes, because you were a spy for the CIA and it was widely known. You are probably doing the same thing here."

"I was not a spy for the CIA! I was a journalist."

The man just looked at him and shook his head, as though to chide Nabil for taking him for a fool. "If you promise to desist from your behavior and your relations with that European," he finally said, "I can let you go this time with a fine. But we will be watching you."

"How much is the fine?"

"Five thousand liras."

"*Five thousand liras?* That is nearly as much as all the money I have."

The man shrugged, shook another cigarette out of his packet.

Nabil could barely hold back tears. "Why are you doing this to me? I'm not hurting anyone, I'm not causing trouble. I just want to help my family and live in peace."

The man inhaled. "You have done this to yourself. And we are offering you a second chance here."

I don't even know if you're real, Nabil wanted to say. But he constrained himself. It didn't matter if the man wasn't the state police; he still had the power to destroy him. In Iraq, the Mukhabarat had blackmailed people all the time. All he wanted was not to be deported and not to shame his family. How could he have been so stupid as to go home with Liam that first day, behaving as though he'd escaped to Scandinavia and not just the country next door?

"I don't have the money on me now," he said. "How can I get it to you?"

"Meet me right here tomorrow at the same time."

"Can I go on in the café with the Arabic lessons? Sir, please. My family needs the money."

The man opened his mouth, as though to laugh at the brazenness of the request, then seemed to think twice. "I think you had better ask your European friend for twice as much per day. Maybe three times as much. After all, you have a family depending on you."

The words puzzled Nabil for a moment until he discerned their meaning. This was not likely to be over tomorrow.

"May I go now?"

"Go."

He exited the car back into the streets of Damascus, which he suddenly experienced in a darker cast, as though every pair of eyes he passed was watching him. In minutes, his city of refuge, his new paradise of hills and jasmine and handsome faces, had become his new nightmare.

He walked to the cell-phone shop, smoking and panicking; put in his hours; then walked around the perimeter of Muhajirin for an hour before going home, dreading to see his family. When he finally entered the apartment and saw them all—heard the ritual cries of "Ammo!" from Rana, Ahmed, and Mena; looked into the tired but loving eyes of his parents—his shame overwhelmed him. How could he have done something so haram, so forbidden, how could he have jeopardized them all? They had been living here peaceably for a year before he came and now, only a few months after his arrival, the state had marked their house—all because he had to pursue his own disgusting desires. He claimed a headache, passed up dinner, and climbed under his sheets, for once too upset to mind Ammo Adel's snoring alongside him.

The next day, he greeted Liam with the same stiff smile.

But Liam didn't smile back. "What was wrong yesterday?" he asked. "You ran away from me."

"I told you, I had to get to work early." He was willing himself to be cold, to disregard Liam's tenderness and his beauty. "And we must discuss something," he added, in English, and in as low a voice as possible.

"Shou, habibi?"

"For one thing, stop calling me that. I'm serious. For another, we meet only here from now on, and we study Arabic, and then I go. Nothing else."

Liam looked stunned. "What's happened?" he finally asked. "What did I do?"

"It's nothing you did. But it's against my religion. And I don't really like it."

Now Liam broke into a wide, sardonic smile. So wide, so radiant, in fact, that Nabil squeezed his hands into fists under the table to greet it impassively. "I find that very hard to believe!"

"I ask you please to respect my religion and my culture. It has gone on long enough."

Liam's smile faded. "You are serious."

"I am."

Nabil was then devastated to see tears pooling in Liam's eyes. *Please don't cry here*, he privately pleaded. *That will be more than I can take.* But Liam blinked once, hard, and managed to say: "Okay. I respect you. And you are still a good tutor."

"And that's something else. I will have to ask you for twice your fee, or I will have to find someone else to tutor. My family needs more money. We are really struggling here."

Liam laughed sharply. "Will the insults never stop today?"

"I am sorry. It is just a need. I am not trying to be mean."

Now it was Liam who took on a rather businesslike cast. "Well, I am sorry, I cannot afford to pay you double. I have a limited budget while I am here. I can pay you twenty-five percent more per lesson if that suits you."

He had a hard, hurt look in his eyes as he said it. Nabil kept twisting his hand around the fabric of his pants, miserable and tense. Perhaps he should just tell Liam what was really going on. The man, the so-called police agent, had at least had the decency to spare them his presence today in the café, Nabil had noted after a furtive look around the room. He opened his mouth to speak.

Then he thought of the terror he would plunge Liam into if he disclosed anything. Not only his own Damascus idyll but Liam's as well would be ruined. Of course the man had targeted the Iraqi refugee and not the Danish student who could come and go freely from his rich country! For a nanosecond, blood pounding in his head, Nabil wasn't sure whom he hated more—Liam, blithely swaggering around Damascus, his temporary playground, picking up local boys with impunity; or himself, for his miserable position on the map of the world. Suddenly, he felt like a dark, hairy Arab in the worst way. Not Lebanese or Jordanian or a Gulfie, or even Syrian, but from the most damned country in the region, one whose very name had come to be synonymous with hell. For the first time, he had a curious new feeling, something he'd not felt even in the final days in Iraq. It was a bottomless feeling, an exhausted feeling, like being in a black pit with no sense of walls or roof from which to begin plotting an exit. It was despair. Never before had he felt so of a piece with his circumstances, as though they not only challenged but utterly defined him.

Of course he wouldn't tell Liam what was going on. "Twenty-five percent more is fine, thank you," he said instead. "So let's begin."

But the lesson was joyless. There were no more of the little jokes, the double entendres, the light foot touches under the table, that had once given it the feeling of foreplay. It was hell for Nabil, who forced himself not to focus on either the new coldness between him and Liam or where he had to be in thirty minutes. The wad of liras strained against his front pocket.

"Very good for today," he finally said. "May I ask you now to pay me for yesterday and also for today at our new rate?"

Dutifully, Liam counted out the liras and handed them to him. "I paid you at the new rate for yesterday, too."

"That wasn't necessary. We hadn't discussed the new rate yet."

Liam closed his eyes briefly and sighed. "Please just take the money and stop insulting me."

A stab pierced Nabil's chest. Surely, he thought, that was his heart breaking.

"Thank you," he said, putting the money in his pocket.

"But I have to tell you something," Liam continued, in a suddenly very low voice. "I wasn't just having sex with you. I thought you were beautiful. On the outside and then, once I met you, on the inside."

"Why don't you take me back to Denmark with you, then?" Nabil was shocked to hear the words fly from his mouth.

And so, it seemed, was Liam. "But I'm not going back for another month," he finally said. "Is that what you want?"

"I want to be free. I'm dying."

The hard mask Liam had assumed for most of the lesson fell away, as though he were allowing himself to look at Nabil like a lover again. "I'm not sure I could get you in at the airport. But I could ask friends and look into it. There is domestic partnership for gay people in Denmark."

And yet, *not sure I could get you in* was the part that felt like a smack in the face, though Nabil knew Liam hadn't intended it that way. He had never felt so dirty, so unwanted, so bereft. He rose before he cried in front of Liam.

"I knew I could never get in. I was just joking with you. Anyway, I'll see you here tomorrow."

He willed himself not to look back at Liam, not to cry as he exited the café into the street, greeted by the familiar chatter of canaries in their cages. He felt a panic, a craziness churning in his stomach as he retraced his steps of the day before toward the alley. A wave of missing Asmaa overtook him, a strong and unexpected sensation of having misplaced something vital, like a limb. How utterly at a loss he felt without her—motherless, even.

You would not believe the mess I'm in! he would begin, as they sat on the garden swing, and he even laughed briefly, thinking about how crazy it would all sound as he related it, watching her eyes grow larger by the second.

The black sedan was where it had been the day before. Nabil tapped on the tinted window by the driver's side. He then heard the click of the car unlocking itself, walked around, and stepped in. Again, it was thick with smoke. The man was there, reading *Tishreen*, just as Liam had been, with a Gulf football match on the car radio.

"I have your money." And Nabil handed it over, feeling utterly powerless.

The man thumbed through it. "There's a problem," he said.

"What?"

"My superior referred me to the Syrian penal code for sodomy. The fine for the first offense is actually twice this."

Nabil absorbed this at a cynical remove. He'd been dreading exactly this.

"I don't have more to give you."

The man paused, then shrugged. "We'll have to take you to the border then and make sure you don't come back."

"Just take me then. I don't care anymore. I'm tired of living, anyway."

The man was quiet, finishing his cigarette. "It's hell in Iraq, isn't it?" he finally asked.

"What do you care?" Nabil mumbled.

More quiet from the man. "There is one other option in the state law."

What game was he going to play now? "Shou?"

"You could help the state."

"How?"

"There is a sodomy problem around Shaalan Street, as you probably know. In front of Al Madfai Park and on the steps of Byblos Bank. You are one of the community."

"I'm really not. I've never spent time there. I mind my own business and go to work and then go home."

The man smiled, as though to tell Nabil it was hardly worth lying at this point. "You go there, and you meet other khawalat, and then you give me their names and numbers."

It was all playing out, Nabil thought, like a nightmare script he might have written. Every Iraqi in Syria only wanted to avoid the government, the police. And now they owned him.

"And the state even gives you a small portion of the fines."

"Why should I believe you? I don't even know your name."

The man shrugged. "My name is Mohammed," he said, as though it were no great burden to share it. "But for security reasons, of course, I can't tell you my family name."

"Everyone is named Mohammed."

The man shrugged again, blithely ceding Nabil's point. "Well," he added, "there is your offer. You can start tonight. Pretty soon the khawalat should be coming out. You can get at least one or two names tonight. But I should add that if you don't bring me names and numbers soon, we'll take you to the border. And we will have to inform your family why."

Nabil almost marveled at the man's matter-of-factness. For how many years had he been bureaucratizing cruelty like this? It was merely a job to him. What did it matter if he did it for the state or as a free agent? He knew whom to target. And Nabil also knew that the state employed thousands of part-time secret police who were no more than paid neighborhood snitches, who had deftly parlayed Assad's wide-ranging paranoia into their own lucrative one-man shops, preying on the vulnerable of all sorts: refugees, khawalat, Christians.

"I'll go tonight and see what I can find," he said.

The man regarded him for a minute, as though parsing his sincerity. "Good," he said at length.

"How do I contact you?"

"I'll be right here at this time every day. And if you don't come around, we'll come find you."

Nabil exited the car without another word.

Children ran and played in the vast courtyard of the Umayyad Mosque. Nabil sat cross-legged on its polished floor, leaning against one of the wide columns, as the afternoon call to prayer commenced. His stomach was in knots, his next steps were uncertain. *Get on a bus to Beirut*, part of his brain urged, while the other flashed before him images of his family, of the twelve of them in the apartment, needing his income, his role as the young man of the household. *What would Asmaa do?*

He cupped his hands over his mouth, looked up at the mosque's minaret. "What would you do?" he asked, staring intently at the spire, as though expecting to see Asmaa emerge from its turret.

I would do what I had to do. Asmaa's voice came to him very clearly, as though she were right there, regarding him frankly with a look on her face that said, *Isn't it obvious?*

It's true, he thought. Asmaa would simply do what needed to be done and not fuss so much about the ethical implications. She was a pragmatist.

"It is so hard to figure things out without you," he mouthed again into his hands.

You have more capability than you think, he heard her say back. *Look! You got out of Iraq alive. Do what you have to do.*

He waited until the call to prayer ended. Then he rose and walked the thirty minutes eastward to Shaalan, where he sat on the steps in front of the imposing, contemporary Byblos Bank and pulled *The Crying of Lot 49* from his backpack. He opened it before him and passed a few token seconds pretending to read it before glancing around the area, busy with café-goers and late-afternoon shoppers, the usual din of car horns in the streets. He saw no one he thought might be homosexual.

Until, at length, an extremely slender young man, perhaps even younger than Nabil, unremarkable save his fashionably embroidered and flared jeans and black Adidas shoulder bag, passed, glanced briefly his way, then slowed and sat on the opposite end of the stairs, lighting a cigarette. The young man stared out coolly ahead for several seconds, but Nabil—just as he glanced up and rightward from his book—caught him glancing leftward, then away again.

It all seemed to be happening so easily that Nabil wondered if it was a new kind of trap, if the young man was working in concert with the so-called Mohammed. He nearly rose and walked away. Then he could say that he was the one who'd brushed off the advance—or, an even better narrative, had simply gone on with his day, oblivious to the weight of the glances, as any normal man would be.

But he thought of what he'd heard Asmaa say she would do. She would simply push through and get what she needed.

So he turned in the young man's direction and called, "Marhaba, keefak? Maak nar?" *Hey there, hi. How are you? Got a light?*

The young man regarded him blankly for a moment before reaching into his jeans pocket and gesturing with his head for Nabil to come over. Which Nabil did, seating himself a meter away from the young man and pulling out his packet of cigarettes.

"You want one?" he asked the young man.

"Thank you."

The young man lit first Nabil's cigarette, then his own. He inhaled and then expelled the smoke languorously through his nose. Nabil regarded his profile for a moment. He had an extremely delicate nose, much like his brother Rafiq's, which everyone in the family jokingly referred to as a "princess nose," khashim al amira. He also, Nabil now noted, wore a small gold cross under his shirt.

"You're Iraqi?" the young man finally asked.

Nabil nodded. "You heard my accent?"

"Yes. And I can see it in your face. There are so many Iraqis in Damascus now."

"I know." Nabil wasn't sure if he detected scorn in the young man's voice. He didn't think so. It had sounded fairly neutral—perhaps even sympathetic.

They were both silent another moment, smoking. "Is your family okay?" the young man then asked.

"Yes, hamdullilah. They are all here."

"Really? You didn't lose anyone there? You're very lucky."

Nabil could detect now a softening in the young man's eyes, a passage from wary first inquiries to a quicker engagement, and he relaxed a little into the exchange.

"Well, no, actually. I lost my cousin."

"Oh, I am sorry. What happened to her?"

"She was shot."

The young man's eyes widened in apology before he looked away. "Well," he said, after a few respectful seconds, his voice dropping a register, "it'll happen here, too, soon enough. It can't stay the way it is. This is all going to crack."

Nabil said nothing. The remark was too charged. It all could still be a trap, he told himself.

"May we all live in peace one day," he finally remarked. It felt anodyne enough.

The young man merely shrugged and laughed lightly, as though the idea were lovely but preposterous. "What did you do in—where, in Baghdad?"

"Yes, Baghdad. I was a journalist." Best to keep it at that, Nabil thought.

The young man's face brightened for the first time. "Anjad? My sister is a journalist. For an entertainment channel. She's a producer. Not on the screen."

"Anjad?" Nabil echoed politely. "That sounds interesting."

"Come home with me to dinner. We are in al-Qassa'a. We're a very welcoming family. My sister has brought Iraqi friends home."

Nabil had heard of al-Qassa'a. It was adjacent to Bab Touma, also a Christian district. The invitation seemed to be coming very quickly. Everything felt like a setup after his encounter with Mohammed. And yet, the young man's eyes—which, Nabil noticed, were that bewitching green he'd seen so often in Damascus—seemed sincere.

And then the young man laughed. "Oh! I haven't even introduced myself. Isme Michel."

Nabil managed a smile. "Isme Nabil."

Another odd silence passed, this so-called Michel turning away briefly to take his last drag before exhaling and turning back.

"How are you keeping yourself busy in Damascus?"

Nabil paused. "It's difficult," he then said. "You know, we are not allowed to work here." Too risky, he determined, to mention his cell-phone job or his tutoring.

"I know. That is a stupid rule. You should really come to dinner and meet Nadine—my sister. I bet she can help you get some work under the table. Is your English good?"

"I like to think my English is quite superb," Nabil said in English, in his flattest American accent.

Michel laughed. His laugh felt generous and light, not manufactured, thought Nabil. "That is a huge advantage," he said. Then Michel shook his head. "Brother, I'm just sorry about what's happened in your country. This whole region's going to crack soon. It's been on the brink for years. I'm surprised Lebanon's kept it together the past year, with the assassination."

He meant the assassination of Rafiq al-Hariri, a beloved political and entrepreneurial figure in Lebanon, the country's great postwar savior, who'd died in his motorcade the prior year, alongside twenty-one other hapless victims, in a spectacular bombing right on Beirut's

Corniche in the middle of a busy day. Most people assumed the bombing was engineered by Syria to keep its hold on its tiny neighbor, and for months Damascenes expected that America, Lebanon's big gorilla friend, would bomb Syria in retaliation. But peaceful mass protests in Beirut, mostly of young people, had succeeded in pressuring Syria to finally remove its military from the country—and the Levant had not fallen into chaos.

Again, Nabil would not be led down a political path. He merely shook his head, adding blandly, "There are so many complications, it is true."

The two of them sat there silently, facing out, and when Nabil glanced quickly to the right, he saw that Michel was glancing toward him, leaning toward him ever so slightly. Nabil could faintly smell a cologne he was wearing.

"So come to dinner with me!"

He had to act now. All he needed was a phone number.

"I can't tonight, unfortunately, although it is so generous of you to invite me. My family is expecting me to bring groceries home. May I have your mobile number and come another night?"

"Of course! What is your mobile number, and I will call you so you have mine."

He dreaded handing over his own number. "My phone's power has died, and I haven't memorized my new number. Can you write your number down for me?"

"Of course." Without hesitation, Michel reached for a pen and a torn-open envelope inside his bag, jotted down a number, and handed it to Nabil. "My mother and grandmother are good cooks. They'll stuff you. Do you like makdous?"

Nabil had sampled the Levantine specialty since being in Damascus—pickled eggplants stuffed with walnuts and garlic. "Yes. They are delicious. We don't have it much in Iraq."

"My grandmother makes the best makdous."

Nabil managed another wary smile. "I will definitely try to come soon. I will call or SMS you."

Michel leaned in and kissed him on one cheek, then the other, then rose. "So now you have a new friend in Damascus! This city is not so bad, right?"

"It's beautiful. I love Damascus."

"I'll ask my mother to make prayers to the Virgin for your family. Her prayers always work." Then Michel winked at him and smiled, turned, and headed in the direction he'd originally been taking. Nabil watched his bottom twitch left and right in his tight jeans as he receded.

Then he just sat there. He could not make heads or tails of the encounter. It had not felt very erotically charged, except perhaps for the first moments of eye contact. After that, Michel had behaved merely as a friendly stranger. It was not so out of the ordinary, after all, for Michel to have invited him to dinner. Syrians, like Iraqis, were hospitable. And there were plenty of fashionable young men, especially in central Damascus, who were not khawalat.

But then he heard Asmaa's voice again: *Do what you have to do.* And he had. He'd gone to the very spot Mohammed had instructed him to go to and procured a name and a phone number. All he had to do was show up at the black car the next day, hand it over, and say, "This is a homosexual." If Michel was another setup, then he, Nabil, was merely playing his prescribed part in a cat-and-mouse game. And if Michel wasn't—if he was simply a kind fellow, and whether or not he was a homosexual—then he would merely have coming to him the same cold jolt of terror that Nabil himself had already withstood. There was plenty of fear, Nabil thought bitterly, to go around.

He was numb through his shift at the cell-phone shop. Iraqis coming in and going out, topping up their minutes to talk with stressed-out relatives back in a country they dreaded having to return to once their savings ran out in Syria. Iraqis lamenting the depth of sectarian violence their country had fallen to, and Nabil lamented alongside them, emptily, thinking about what he planned to do the following day.

Back at the apartment, the sight of his nieces and nephew cheered him, as it always did. He felt closer than ever to Ahmed, his glossy-haired angel boy, now that they shared a room and together suffered through the snores and moans of Ammo Adel. The children were occupied with coloring books on the floor of the small kitchen, where his mother, Bibi, and Mariam sat at the small table, stuffing dolma and drinking tea. Egyptian pop from the 1970s, the kind of music his parents had danced to while at university together, played low on the radio.

"Where's Baba?"

"Probably at the café," his mother answered. "Will you go get him in a bit for dinner?"

"He lives there now," Bibi tacked on flatly.

It was true. His father was fading away from them—most painfully, fading away from his mother, probably too ashamed to be with her because she continued working and he did not. It killed Nabil to watch this rift grow between them, to watch them both slowly lose a joy for life, for family gatherings, that they had somehow managed to maintain through two decades under Saddam. How could he blame them? How could he blame his father for wanting to be out of the apartment all day? Nobody could turn around in those quarters without bumping into somebody else. He knew that only the unceasing production of meals kept his mother, grandmother, and aunt from devolving into outright war. The duress had actually softened Bibi, made her kinder and more solicitous toward her daughter, as though she intuited that, unlike the Kadhimiya villa, the new household simply didn't have the physical space to accommodate her theatrics.

Moments later, when his mother, a dish towel in her hand, joined him on the cushions in the salon—a rare moment with only the two of them in the room—he observed as much about Bibi.

She laughed. "We should have moved here with her long ago if we'd known it would mellow her."

His heart melted a bit, watching her smile. When she smiled, which was so rare now, he still saw that university student, that young mother and teacher—with her feathery ebony hair, large-framed glasses, slacks or A-line dresses, and stack-heeled boots, which he'd found so glamorous, so modern—in the late 1970s and the early 1980s. That had been his childhood, before even the war with Iran had much marred the idyll of daily life.

She must have detected the melancholy in his face, because she put her hand there, cupping his right cheek, as she had always done, and asked, "Habibi, are you okay? Nobody ever asks about you."

"I'm okay, Mama. I'm just sad like everyone else and worried about the future. And I miss working, even though it was dangerous. I was doing something real."

"I know." She shook her head. "It's a bad situation now, and I pray every day for some sort of answer. Much more than I ever prayed before."

"You're becoming Bibi."

She laughed. "I am! They say every woman becomes her mother eventually."

They fell silent a moment. "Habibi, there is something I wish for you so much, though. I wish you'd meet a girl, so you'd have some comfort in the middle of all this, as your brothers do. I worry about you. You're always alone."

Queasiness overtook his stomach. It was The Topic. His mother rarely brought it up anymore—it was Bibi and Farah, his annoying sister-in-law, he usually relied on to needle him about it.

"Mama, I'm okay. I have the family. I've made some friends here."

"But habibi, you're twenty-seven now. You can't go on being single your whole life."

"Mama, we're stuck in limbo here." Then annoyance pricked him. "I didn't think you were one for these old rules. You married a Sunni."

Her expression hardened and anger flashed in her eyes. "Do not talk to your mother that way. It was a different time. And I still married."

He flushed with shame. He wasn't sure if he'd ever spoken to her so harshly before. "I'm sorry, Mama."

Her eyes softened again. "I just want you to find a wonderful woman to take care of you. It makes the hard times so much easier when you have someone by your side."

He wanted to ask her if Baba was currently making her hard times so much easier. But this time he held his tongue. And then a wave of tremendous unhappiness overtook him. Why could he not simply tell her the truth? She was his mother. Nobody loved him more, knew better who he was, his temperament. Except, perhaps, Asmaa, but Asmaa was gone and he simply had to accept that.

"Mama—" he began, his eyes welling up. "It's so hard."

She held him. "I know, hayati. It's hard for all of us right now. I cry myself, when nobody's looking."

She wasn't, he realized, really understanding him. Nor did he even expect her to, because he knew that it lay beyond her comprehension. It didn't exist in this world. True, there were boys and young men who used one another silently for pleasure, even some married men who did the same. But to not just *do* that but *be* that was an abomination, a perversion, one that left even the most loving family with no choice but to preserve its honor with a gun or a blade. It didn't matter if his mother had once shown her legs, kissed his father even before the engagement party, married a man outside her sect. He could not expect her to sympathetically intuit something she would understand only, if at all, as an illness, a tragedy, a source of deep shame.

"We'll find someone for you," she continued. "A girl from an Iraqi family here who will change your life and give you children and a little bit of happiness in the middle of this mess. Have you talked to Jananne upstairs with her mother and aunties?"

"A bit." She was the sullen girl with the greasy hair who wore the same sad blue sweatshirt every day.

"She studied engineering in Baghdad, you know."

"I know."

"Talk to her more. Take her for ice cream."

"Okay, Mama."

She cupped his face in her hand one more time. "You don't have to be so lonely here, aini." Then she rose and walked back into the kitchen.

*   *   *

He was barely present through dinner. His brothers were talking at length about a deal they were trying to work out with another Iraqi in the neighborhood to join a small business this Iraqi had started with a Damascene cousin trucking electronics between Damascus and Baghdad. That was among the few ways for Iraqis in Syria to start a business, by partnering with a Syrian.

They were all there together, yet Nabil had never felt so removed from them. He found himself looking at his father and his brothers in a new light. He'd never questioned that they'd be his protectors. They were family, after all. But now he wondered whether they could ever become his tormentors. He thought about vague stories he remembered from Kadhimiya, about families with members who'd disappeared under foggy circumstances involving some kind of unspecified shame or scandal. From his brothers and male cousins he'd heard *khawal this, khawal that,* his entire life, but he'd thought of it as merely the jocular slang of men, as tossed-off and affectionate as joking that someone's sister fucked donkeys.

It made for an eerie dinner. After dinner, his nieces and nephew begged him to take them out into the neighborhood for ice cream, and he obliged them. As he watched them lick their cones—particularly Mena, whose four-year-old perfection was a salve on his wound of a life—he had an elegiac feeling, as though it were the last time he would ever witness them in this happy, mundane ritual, this hour of respite he'd been able to give the adults in the household.

His mind churned as he lay in bed, Adel and Ahmed sleeping on either side of him, Adel snoring gutturally as usual. Tonight, for some reason, he was reliving images from Baghdad he hadn't called up in quite some time: the feet that hung out of the back of the truck that morning after the invasion when his father was driving him to work, amid the looting that went on in those early days that would prove to be a mild first chapter; the severed hand reaching out in the rubble after the massive American bomb had fallen in the neighborhood in Mansour; the woman wailing on the ground for her son, who'd been pulverized beneath the wreckage.

And then he'd shift to thoughts of Liam lying alone on his futon in that room. How could he have known such happiness, such serenity in that room only a week ago, and how could it all seem so far away now, like a dream?

And then he thought of Michel's phone number. It was near midnight now, which meant he had about fifteen hours until he had to meet the black car again.

I don't think you're right this time, he told Asmaa silently in his head.

He sat up on his mattress, plotting. As quietly as he could manage, he rose; put his jeans and T-shirt back on; then—his every move glacial, to minimize sound—filled his backpack with a few more garments, a toothbrush and paste, *The Crying of Lot 49*, and his Iraqi and Syrian papers. From a seam he'd cut into his mattress, he withdrew what was left of his savings after he'd handed such a large portion over earlier in the day to the so-called Mohammed. He still had six thousand liras, or what would amount to about $120.

He crept into the dark, empty kitchen and left half of those bills on the table. He knew he should write a note, but he didn't have time. Besides, he thought, what would he say? He could call them later—which reminded him to put his mobile in his jeans pocket.

His arm was tense as he unlocked and opened the apartment door with maximum quiet, closing it behind him, locking it, then slipping the key back under the door. He slung his backpack over both shoulders and padded his way down the stairwell. Outside, the street was cool, that ubiquitous, heady Damascus jasmine scent overwhelming him. Now it seemed cruel, as though it were saying, *Time for you to leave this garden.*

The street was nearly empty save the usual cats; he saw no familiar faces. He walked to the larger street and hailed a cab to Baramkeh Station. He'd often fantasized about doing just this—about the tantalizing closeness of Beirut, that dream city, just two and a half hours, a bit more than one hundred kilometers, away. And here he was, doing it before he could even really think about it. In the taxi, he glanced out the rear window, wondering whether he was being watched or followed, or if a black car would be there to greet him at Baramkeh. It all depended on how much they wanted to extract more money from him versus how much they simply wanted him to leave. If the latter had been their true wish, they'd succeeded.

He exited in front of the taxi pool at Baramkeh Station and walked up to the first driver he saw, who was smoking a cigarette and drinking tea from a plastic cup, leaning against his car.

"Can you take me to Beirut now?"

The driver nodded indifferently. "It's five hundred liras."

He nodded back.

"Wait while I piss," the driver instructed him, flicking aside the cigarette and disappearing around a nearby corner. Nabil stood by nervously, glancing around, until he decided to simply get in the car and wait.

Back in his seat, the driver pulled out, heading northwest toward the Beirut Road. "Are you Iraqi?" he asked, in a tone that Nabil still chose to hear as general indifference.

"Yes."

"You're playing a crapshoot at the border, and if they turn us back, it's still five hundred liras."

"That's okay."

He looked out the window at the dim outline of Mount Qasioun in the distance, tiny lights glinting atop it. Not particularly caring how the driver interpreted the gesture, he pulled the envelope scrap with Michel's number out of his pocket, tore it into confetti, and liberated it swiftly from his palm into the wind outside the car window.

Amid his anxiety and a gutted, elegiac feeling as the car sped out of the city, he also felt something new. He felt that he'd stepped up to play for his own team.

CHAPTER TWELVE

LIVE FREE OR DIE

LABOR DAY WEEKEND, 2008

Before he left the house that day, he fed Auntie Bunny's bunnies. Everyone in the family said that, *Bunny's bunnies*. Auntie Bridget's nickname had been Bunny all her life, since her godfather started calling her that when she was four, and in her late fifties, after she went from full-time to part-time at the AutoZone in Nashua, she decided she wanted to keep bunnies in the backyard. So she did, three rabbits—Huey and Dewey (both mottled black-and-white) and Louie (pure white). Louie was his favorite.

He was so grateful for Auntie Bunny. When his mother had complained to her, "I can't live with that boy anymore, he's scaring me! I wish his father were still around," Bunny had said, "Tell him to come live with me; he's never given me any trouble! You just never knew how to handle him, Marie. I'll keep him in line."

If Bunny hadn't taken him in, he wasn't sure what he would have done. His twice-monthly paycheck from Target was $573.64. He might have been able to find a room in Keene for about that much, but then half his paycheck would be going toward rent. Bunny charged him only two hundred dollars a month for the room on her top floor with its own bath, and he knew most of that went to the food she bought him, because he ate like a horse compared with her. If Bunny made a lasagna on the weekends, she'd joke that she had to set a third of it aside for herself, to take to work for lunch in her Tupperware, or she knew she'd wake up Monday morning to find most of it gone, her nephew having eaten it at two in the morning, in those hours when Bunny slept, but he stayed up on the Internet, reading, reading, reading. He loved to read online, especially late at night when the world was quiet except for the chorus of crickets in the yard. He felt that everything he ever wanted to know was right there at his fingertips, in the glow of Bunny's big Dell computer, and if he stayed up all night, he maybe could learn it all.

Out at the bunny hutch, he reached in and caressed the trio, those precious mounds, each with two black eyes pressed into a plush head. They were so damn cute, they could have been stuffed animals if they weren't actually alive, he often thought. From its corners, he folded up the newspaper covered in bunny poop and mostly chewed food pellets, wrapped it tightly, extracted it, laid down fresh pages from the *Union Leader*, scattered atop that fresh pellets, then, finally, topped up the bunnies' water bottle. Instantly, the trio began feasting on the pellets, which made him grin with satisfaction.

Inside, he took his Wellbutrin and his Adderall. He would have remembered anyway, but Bunny had left the pills in the middle of the kitchen table, right alongside *Woman's Day* and those other magazines she loved, with a big note that read DON'T FORGET! alongside a smiley face.

Bunny was at work. Bunny was the only woman he'd ever known who knew so damn much about cars, who could hear a noise underneath his 1992 Civic and say, "Honey, you gotta get your exhaust system looked at." She'd never so much as gotten under a car. She'd learned all this in eleven years at the AutoZone.

He'd given this a lot of thought in the past few months. That sharpness was from the high-quality Scotch Irish stock on his mother's side of the family. How else to explain how a woman with no real car training could assimilate all that technical knowledge? You couldn't expect that of everyone. And yet he was shocked to find out that Bunny wasn't making much more an hour than the Dominican guy from Lawton she worked with, even though she'd been there two years longer and had had to train him.

"That's not fair," he'd told her.

"Honey, they *asked* me if I wanted to move into management, and I said no. Working fifty hours a week? Forget it. I like my free time."

"But that's exactly what I mean."

"Mean about what?"

"About paying the Dominican guy the same as you. He don't have your experience."

"Luis, you mean?" She waved her hand in the air. "He's fine. He knows what he's doing. The one before him barely spoke English. *That* was a pain in my ass. Luis is fine."

He was troubled by his aunt's equanimity. "It still ain't right. He's probably not even a citizen. Taking jobs away."

She looked up from her magazine and rolled her eyes. "He's not taking away nobody's job. We were shorthanded before we hired him. Luis is fine. He's my buddy." She smiled slightly, as though recalling some joke she and Luis shared at work.

But he kept staring at his aunt. In a second, she looked up again from her magazine, then scowled. "Ah, jeez, honey, you're not still on your whole obsession, are you?"

This hurt him. "It's not an obsession. It's science."

"It's not science, honey. Come on." She sounded deeply disappointed in him. He'd offered to print stuff out for her, and she'd declined. "You gotta drop that stuff. It's really—" she searched for the word. "It's gonna get you in trouble. And don't get in trouble when you're living with me. Please? Don't let your mother say *I told you so* to me. We're trying to show her, right?"

He continued to stare at her, deeply uncomfortable.

"I know you're a good boy," she said, softer. "So just let it go. There's hardly any minorities up here anyway. They're all in Massachusetts where the benefits are better." She cackled.

"Except the next president." He said this as evenly and unblinkingly as possible, enunciating, so she would see it was coming from reason, that he wasn't being illogical or making shit up. What greater evidence did he need to prove his point—that they were taking over?

She laughed sharply. "Ha! Well, you might be right. So you better get used to it." She stood up, picked up her magazine. "Hey, I'm ready to give him a chance."

It pained him deeply to hear this. It wasn't the first time Bunny had suggested as much. "Really? He ain't even a citizen, probably."

"Aw, come on, honey, that's BS." Again, she sounded not so much angry at him as disappointed, which hurt. He needed Bunny's approval.

"I'm jumping in the shower," she announced. "Be a good boy. You working today?"

"At three."

She murmured a response and padded toward the bathroom. Once he heard the shower start and knew she'd be occupied for a while, he sat down before the computer in the den. *Obama* and *birth certificate*, he began to type, just enough that the search window brought the words up themselves—he'd searched them so many times. He looked at the scan of the so-called real birth certificate that TeamKenya, as they were called online—he himself was fond of calling them by this moniker on his chat threads—had posted to try to prove that KenyaBorn was actually born in Hawaii. He looked carefully at the watermark that several of his favorite and most trusted websites had magnified many times, showing that it had been photoshopped. He wondered if he should show this to Bunny when she came down from her shower.

He strongly needed to show her. He hated that she would think he'd been hoodwinked. He knew it might upset her before she went to work, but it was probably worth it.

He sat very upright before the website, afraid to click elsewhere lest he somehow lose the image, and made himself stare at the fake document, committing its every detail to memory, until he could feel his blood boiling. He could not believe that KenyaBorn had been leading in the polls all summer against a man of such strong English and Scotch

Irish stock, a war hero. Something more had to emerge between now and November. KenyaBorn had spent time not far away in Cambridge, in the late 1980s, in law school. He had days off. He could drive down there, talk to people, find something that hadn't been uncovered yet. He worried that he might not act fast enough. He'd planned other missions for himself on his free days. His heart pounded, panicked.

"I'm takin' off, honey," Bunny called from the kitchen.

"Come see something," he called back.

"I ain't got time!"

"Just real fast."

He heard Bunny padding into the den. "What is it?"

"Look here," he said, as she leaned over his shoulder toward the monitor. "Can you see how the watermark's a fake?"

"What is this?" Then she realized. "Aw, Jesus, B.D., I told you I thought this was bullshit!"

He turned around and looked at her. Her face was set in a scowl, two angry lines popping between her brows. How could she be mad at him when he was trying to point something out that the TV news just wouldn't cover, since all the liberals there were too scared of being politically incorrect? Shouldn't she want to know the truth?

"Please find something useful to do today instead of sitting here reading this crap." She was nearly yelling at him, something she never did. "Clean the bunny hutch, for God's sake. Mow the lawn. Go to the Y and play some ball or something."

Her words pierced him. This was like being yelled at by his own mother. Bunny even looked a bit like his mother when she was angry, with that same contemptuous grimace.

"I'm sorry, Auntie Bunny." His voice was a hoarse whisper.

Then her face softened. "Come on now, B.D." She took his chin between her thumb and index finger. "I just don't want you glued to this thing all day."

"Okay."

"Promise?"

"Promise."

He watched from the window as she drove away in her Toyota, waving to Cathy Vinci, the neighbor, as she did so. Cathy was married to a Sicilian, Carmelo Vinci, a man so dark he might as well have been Dominican himself, but she herself was Scotch Irish like Bunny. He wondered if Cathy had ever thought about the fact that she was essentially married to a nonwhite man, and if she'd ever thought about how dark her own children might be if she had them. And when he saw Carmelo, he wanted to ask him if he was ever mistaken for a Puerto Rican, a Dominican, or an Arab, and if that bothered him. Yet he refrained from that question as well.

Arabs. They were his greatest concern. Hispanics might be taking jobs and living on welfare and shooting one another over drug deals in Lawton, just over the state border. He followed the news avidly to see whether Michael Addison, a black gang thug who'd shot a cop in Manchester, would get the death penalty. With some other folks he'd met online, he was prepared to protest in front of the courthouse if he did not.

But still. Blacks and Hispanics were not as cold-blooded as Arabs. They did not have a whole religious ideology motivating them to kill as many people as possible at the same time. Admittedly, like many, he had not given Arabs or Muslims a great deal of thought before 9/11. He'd known that John Sununu, the governor in the 1980s, was an Arab, but apparently he was Christian, which did not fully make sense to him. He also knew that Jeanne Shaheen, who'd also been the governor and was running for the Senate, was married to an Arab. This nettled him, in the way that Cathy Vinci and Carmelo did.

His greatest source of outrage, though, was the fact that Muslims were actually building a mosque in Manchester. He found this beyond comprehension. It was bad enough that there were enough of them to already gather on Fridays in a makeshift mosque, above a dance studio in a mall. How had even a few hundred Muslims found their way to the Granite State, of all places? But now they were building their own mosque out of an old, octagonal brick building in a remote, hilly part of the city where they could plan and plot right under everybody's nose?

Every day, he followed news of the mosque on a website called Granite Gabber, written by a true live-free-or-die patriot named Dick Lefferts who shared his disgust. "How many mosques have been used within the Islamic region as weapon storages and hideaways for homicidal thugs?" the blogger wrote.

That prompted him to write his first online comment. "This so called place of worship must be stopped at any cost," he typed underneath the article. "These things are like ants or magots. If you see 1 or 2, if you don't exterminate proptly, pretty soon you gotta deal with a whole infestation. Thank you Dick for continusly alerting us to the terror in our own backyards."

Now, today, he typed "Arab" and "southern New Hampshire." He did this every day. It was his monitoring project.

A new article he hadn't yet seen came up: "St. Jude Church to Hold Annual Middle Eastern Festival."

> *Friday through Sunday of Labor Day weekend, St. Jude Maronite Church in Lawton, Mass., will hold its 48th annual "Mahra-jan" Middle Eastern festival featuring traditional regional food, music, games and dancing. American fare will also be served and all are welcome, according to St. Jude's Father Jean-Paul "Gene" Saab.*

What the hell was this? Why was the church hosting this? Forty-eighth annual? They hadn't had the good sense to stop this after 9/11? Granted, it was in Lawton, over the border—but still so close, only a half hour from Derry. Muslims in Manchester, a "Middle East" festival in Lawton—they were coming in from all sides.

He went to write something in the comments underneath the article, only to find there was no comments section. So he copied the URL for the article and pasted it into the comments section below the latest update on the mosque on Granite Gabber. "Now look at this," he wrote. "This is just getting worse and worse. I wonder if there is a link hear."

* * *

It all sent him to work in a bad mood. He was in electronics that evening, and no sooner was he opening a new shipment of USB cords with a box cutter than he fumbled and sliced an eighth-inch cut deep into the top of his left index finger, right over the knuckle.

"Goddamnit!" he shouted, watching a crimson line emerge and bubble.

Ana came hustling around the corner. "What is it?" she called, then saw his finger. "Oh, B.D.!" she exclaimed. "Come on." She grabbed his other hand and walked him into the break room, where she tore a paper towel from the roll and wrapped it around his finger. "Sit," she said. "I'll get the first-aid kit."

She returned and sat opposite him, daubing the cut with Neosporin, then applying a thick Band-Aid. He watched her as she administered to him. Ana was always nice to him like this, motherly. He hated that he had the feelings about her that he did, that the first thing he thought when he saw her on every shift was *Dominican*. But why did she have to come here in the first place and take jobs away? She lived in Lawton, of course, with her two teenage sons, who sometimes came to pick her up and looked like gang members with their twisted ball caps and jeans falling halfway down their underpants. Puerto Ricans, at least, were part of the U.S.A.

Then again, he thought, that's why Dominicans worked harder, because they couldn't get handouts like the P.R.s. Looking at Ana, he felt sad. He knew she was nice, and he wanted to make an exception for her, but he couldn't.

She looked up. "What?" She smiled.

He tensed. Had she read his mind?

"Well, you probably know what I was thinking," he replied.

"No. Does it still hurt?"

He stood up. He would not be moved. "Do you wish it did?" he asked.

She laughed. "What? No! What are you talking about?" She put the Neosporin and Band-Aids back into the first-aid kit. "B.D., I never know what's going on in there." She tapped his head lightly with her finger and walked away, shaking her head. "Nobody do."

He went back out onto the floor. *She should be lucky I didn't tell her about her sons*, he thought.

His anger mounted in the next few days as he watched the TV news coverage of the Democratic convention. He could not escape KenyaBorn! He was everywhere. Thinking he was some kind of preacher, some kind of great savior. He admitted that the man was a good speaker. Yet he could not believe he had come this far, so close to the presidency, with no incontrovertible proof that he was a citizen. What was about to happen was a grave breach of justice.

Labor Day weekend approached. As a kid, he'd always hated it. It meant he would be leaving the safe enclosure of his family and walking back into school, where it was always open season on him, with shoves and taunts in the hallway. And his sensitivity to noise and crowds of any sort was increasing, and even in the classroom he was unable to sit at a remove. The week before Labor Day had a feeling, in the humid air and the smell of cut grass and the sound of crickets at night, the chime of the ice-cream truck, that was like a death knell to him. That week was the feeling of danger closing in.

He wasn't scheduled to work that Saturday. The night before, driving home from work, he'd slowed the car on the way, turned off the highway and onto a country road where the Morans lived, in a single-wide on a desolate stretch, keeping three goats in a pen in the backyard. The sky had darkened, and he pulled the car over, noting that the Morans seemed not to be home. He stared for several seconds at his glove compartment, eventually put a palm against it, and sighed deeply.

He exited the car and walked across the Morans' small plot of land to stand outside the wood-and-wire fence that encircled the goats. In the gloom, he thought, inhaling their warm scent of hay and poop, they didn't look so different from dogs. And that thought bothered him. Why did the Morans keep *goats*?

He crossed his arms and stood there for several more seconds, his heart pounding, wondering what to do. He thought of the glove compartment again, his right leg twitching as he considered going back to the car, unlatching it. But perhaps it was too soon. He paced, looking down, until he found a rock the size and shape of a strawberry. He threw the rock as hard as he could at the goats, hitting one of them in the neck. It winced and emitted a short, sharp bleat, stunned for just three seconds before it began head-butting the other goat, business as usual.

Was it even a *goat*? Something about its dim reaction had seemed electronic. Had the Morans put a robot goat in with the two real goats to monitor them?

And if they had, why would they do that? How far was the electronic goat's range of perception? Since he was a boy, Mrs. Moran had been very nice to him, waving him up into the single-wide for a moon pie and a glass of milk—alongside her own girls, Brittany and Brianna, with whom he'd sit uncomfortably while they watched *Beverly Hills, 90210* or *The Simpsons*—whenever he was visiting Bunny. Now, anger and betrayal crept through him. If this goat was an electronic surveillance system, they would know what he was looking at online, and they'd also know about the contents of the glove compartment.

Well, if ever there were a time to disable their intelligence, it was now, when they apparently weren't home—and not only their house but the entire street was dark. He knew the time had come.

Five weeks had passed since he'd bought the used Glock for $250 at the gun store on Route 28 in Salem, only two weeks since he'd last practiced at the firing range. In his car, it whispered to him from behind the glove compartment door as he drove. He'd had it for thirty-seven days. On day one, he'd posted in an online thread on one of his favorite websites, Digital Patriots: "Starting today, these parts up here will be defended. Not tollerating any parisites." And his friends on the thread had replied: "Way to go, LiveFree22!!!!!"

Back in the car, he unlocked the glove compartment door with the little key on his key chain, giddy and dizzy when he saw it there. The sky was so dark, the stars were so abundant, the street was so quiet! He always feared a rush of cops, of sirens and *Come out of the car with your hands up!* the moment he opened the glove compartment—evidence they'd been tracking him all along.

But the darkness and the silence persisted. The burly, good-natured ex-marine at the gun shop had not reported him after observing his nervous handshake or the catch in his voice. In fact, he now remembered, the ex-marine, watching him hold the gun, feel its weight in his hands, had smiled fraternally and said, "Amazing, right? I love watching newbies right about now. You're never gonna be scared again."

"There's so many shitheads out there," he'd replied, suddenly also feeling fraternal with the bruiser, which was a wonderful new feeling for him, because there'd seldom been a man he'd felt that way with.

He thought it would be hard, his hands would fail him, when he finally loaded the Glock outside the firing range. But doing just that right now, in the dimness of the car, wasn't hard at all. Every slide, every click, felt satisfying. That feeling he'd had at the range came back, which was that the world in the radius of his weapon felt ordered, something he could mark out and contain, not a slippery pool of confusion and noise.

Back in the gloom of the Morans' backyard, no light but the moon, he struggled to remember which goat was the robot. If he killed a live goat but failed to disable the surveillance robot, he would be devastated. So he stood there, the gun at his side, observing the nuzzling, head-butting trio until he determined that the movements of one of them were jerkier, less spontaneous than those of the other two. He raised the Glock and struggled to establish, through the dimness, his front sight, then his flash-sight picture.

Then he fired, feeling the barrel jerk up smartly between his hands, hearing the shot rip through the whining of crickets. One of the goats crumpled to the ground while the other two went berserk, bleating and running wildly around the pen.

Had he taken down the robot? He thought so, but he wasn't sure. His heart pounded. If he hadn't, it would track him as he walked away. Goddamnit. Well, here was his first lesson in the stoicism of the defender, the ugly choices that had to be made without sentiment.

He waited until the two surviving goats quieted and slowed, reduced to baffled, bereft bleating, then circled their way back to the fallen third, trying to nudge it back to life.

One shot, then another. Front sight, then flash-sight picture, once, then again. He'd gotten them both. Now there were only the crickets and the waning echo of his shots. That computer was dead, no doubt. Then a new thought seized him. What if it had been connected to a mainframe in the house? What if it all had been captured?

He ran down his options. He could tear open the disabled computer and pull out the wires, the chip. He could breach the house and shoot into the mainframe, if he could find it. His heart began to pound. *You're being crazy*, he told himself. *Vacate, vacate.*

Dizzy, he walked back to the car, unloaded the gun, put both it and the magazine back into the glove compartment, locked it, and drove away. When he neared the corner, he thought he saw a light go on in one of the windows of the Morans' house as it receded in his rearview mirror.

By the time he pulled up in Bunny's driveway alongside her Toyota, he felt no longer alarmed but grimly confident. He had known the time would come. And now he knew he could do it. Rage coursed through him as he contemplated just how long, for how many years, the Morans, whom as a child he'd thought of as good people, had been harvesting data on the community, all under the cover of selling goat's milk and cheese. There were evil people everywhere; that much was clear. But he'd done something for the town, and they could not know this, for the time being, and hence could not thank him, but that was the kind of work he'd signed up for.

Bunny was in the den, lying on the couch, still in her work clothes, watching the Red Sox and drinking a beer. He stood in the doorway.

"Hey, Annie Bunny." He'd always dropped the "t."

"Hey, honey," she purred. "How was work?"

"Okay. How's the game?"

She sighed. "Boring. I want 'em to win but not this easy. Save it till the final innings."

He laughed. Her banalities soothed him, always had. "Yeah," he said.

His eyes twitched toward the Dell computer on the desk in the corner. He desperately wanted to go to it. He had to tell his compatriots what had gone down, in coded language. Its dark green screen called to him, like the glove compartment. But he could not go on it in front of Bunny—not with the fight they'd had about it earlier.

"Well, I'm goin' up," he announced, trying to sound matter-of-fact, because of course she couldn't possibly know she was enjoying her first night at home without surveillance. It was hard not sharing this with someone—and this was why he had to put out some sort of code to his colleagues.

"Okay, hon." She yawned. "Me too, soon. Gotta be back at work in the morning. What about you?"

"I'm on tomorrow, too."

She twisted on the couch, looked up at him fondly. "Fun life for us, eh?"

"Yeah."

Trudging up the stairs, he felt crappy. He'd seldom lied to Bunny—at least about anything major. But he thought it better that she think he'd be at work the next day. He was paving a path.

He'd stashed combat and survivalist magazines away in his room, which was really his cousin Brandon's room, so he flipped through them until he heard Bunny go to bed in the room next door, then he padded into the den and clicked on the Dell.

"1st mission sucessfully accomplished tonight," he wrote on his Digital Patriots thread. "A major hurdle out of the way. Ready to send a message about the surveillance systems."

The box on the screen flashed and bleeped. "Nice going, Live-Free22! Gotta be fearless."

Another flash: "We gotta restore order."

Similar kudos followed. He'd been hoping he'd get this kind of support from his DP buddies, who—he was proud to say—were from all over the country, while he was the group's sole New England ambassador.

Another flash. Someone posted a link to a story about the guy in Pennsylvania, the former deputy attorney general named Berg, who'd filed a lawsuit to keep KenyaBorn out of the election.

"Good luck w/that," one of the DPs wrote. "That train has left the station."

"Hey, check your negative attitude," another wrote.

He found Bunny drinking coffee in the kitchen, WMUR on the TV, at nine the next morning, back in her work clothes, smelling good, like the body wash she used in the shower.

"You know the Morans?" she asked.

"Yeah?" Oh God. He'd thought he might wake up to this.

"Someone shot their goats! When they were at the movies last night. They came back and found all three of them just lying there dead. They were just on the news."

His heart pounded. Was he arranging his face in the right expression of surprise, dismay?

"That's terrible. Why would somebody do that?"

"And not with a hunting rifle either, but a handgun. They could tell from the bullets."

Was Bunny peering at him oddly? Suspiciously? "That's gotta be someone from Manchester," he said. "Or Lawton."

She didn't even bother to frown at his comment, she seemed so upset by the news.

She shook her head, as though to clear it. "I gotta get out of here. I'm running late." She retrieved her purse and car keys from the tabletop. "When you gotta be at work?"

"Eleven."

"You wanna do me a favor? You wanna stop by the Morans on your way and see if they're okay? Tell 'em I'll come by tomorrow, on my day off?"

"Sure."

"Poor Linda." That was Mrs. Moran. "What an awful thing." She pulled her sneakers on by the screen door and blew him a kiss. "I bought you Honey Nut Cheerios." She pointed to the top of the fridge.

He stepped over, kissed her good-bye. "Thanks, Annie Bunny."

"*Lock* the door when you leave for work." Usually, they didn't bother locking the doors. "I almost feel like we should bring the bunnies in."

"Well, they're not really visible the way the goats were. They're in the hutch."

She sighed. "I know. I'm just freaked out, that's all. I can't believe someone would be that much of a sicko."

"I know."

"I mean, what did they get out of that?"

"I don't know."

He questioned his conviction of the night before. Something—his cold, hard certainty—had dissipated in his sleep. What if there'd been no mainframe?

"Questioning my intel today," he wrote on his chat thread.

But the thread was quiet. He sat there, staring at what he'd written, waiting for a reply, but none came.

"But nows not the time to chicken out," he wrote.

After several seconds, one of the DPs wrote back: "You know what you have to do, LiveFree22!"

"You'll see the fruits of my labors very soon," he wrote back.

He carried each of the three bunnies in both hands, three trips in all, from the rabbit hutch to the basement, where he let them wander freely amid the old bicycles and the storage crates.

Upstairs, he fixed a bowl of Cheerios, brought it back down to the basement, where he plucked a few of the soggy rings out of the milk and put them on the concrete floor for the bunnies, one of which quickly approached and ate them all. Delighted, he used his spoon to put down more amid a small pool of milk. Eventually, all three bunnies partook. He sat back down on the couch, enjoying his cereal alongside them.

But he'd begun to wonder: *If one of the three bunnies was a computer, which would it be?*

Don't ask yourself that, he told himself.

But it was too late. He could not unthink the thought once he'd thought it. And after he scrutinized them for several seconds, he determined that it was Huey, always most likely to be hunched alone in a corner while Dewey and Louie gamboled. Now he wondered why he hadn't noticed this long before.

He put down his cereal bowl on the wide arm of the couch and put his hands to his head. "Goddamn!" he exclaimed. All his thoughts were running together.

It bothered him that he'd brought the bunnies inside, that their wireless rays were inside with him, not out in the yard where they might weaken before reaching the house. He had to will himself not to think about where he planned to go, for fear that the bunnies would latch onto his thought waves.

When he finally stood up, he had to search for the bunnies, which he found napping in a bundle of three behind the couch. He needed to find an impermeable container for them before he left the house. He scanned the dim and musty space. Finally, he opened the lower door, into the freezer compartment, of the old fridge that Bunny kept in the basement to store food she couldn't fit upstairs. He transferred the contents of the freezer to the fridge, then unplugged the fridge—reaching back into the filthy space between the fridge and the cellar wall—and, one by one, transferred the bunnies into the freezer. Inside, they whined and stomped their back feet. Humanely, he left the freezer door ajar and walked away, but then, halfway up the stairs, he turned around, walked back down, and closed the freezer door on the bunnies, who were by then huddling together frantically, still whimpering.

"If I can't figure out which one of you cuties it is, then you all are gonna have to stay in there," he said.

Before he left the house, he put on his Patriots sweatshirt, the one with "2005" emblazoned on it, which his mother had bought him after they'd won the Super Bowl. That was before she gave up on him, he thought, briefly and bitterly, but he still cherished the sweatshirt, which had taken on new meaning for him in the six months since he had started thinking about his own role as a patriot.

In the car, after he set his GPS, he bypassed the country road that led to the Morans' place. A dim buzz commenced between his ears, intensifying to something like a crackle, the sound the bunnies had made in the fridge, as he took the exit off 495 into Lawton. He opened the car window to clear his head, but the air, the indolent thickness of the heat, tasted on his face like the weekend before the first day of school, stabbing him with sadness and even more anxiety, so he closed the window and blasted the A/C instead. The radio was set to the hits station, and on top of the roar of the A/C came "Tonight" by those Jonas Brothers, full of exciting guitar riffs that he assumed were meant to pump him up. He sat up straighter in his seat and gripped the wheel, alert for more surveillance robots.

As he drove into downtown Lawton, it became Spanish-land. Spanish stores, Spanish restaurants, Spanish signs, Spanish music coming out of cars so loudly he could hear it even through his own closed windows and over the Jonas Brothers. Dominicans and Puerto Ricans everywhere. His stomach churned sickly. How could they have done this, taken over? This wasn't even America anymore. Then his mind flashed to the night before, Ana bandaging his finger, and he made himself quell his disgust over Spanish-land and remember why he'd come here.

On the right, you have reached your destination, said the approving female voice of the GPS. It was the church, a modern, tan-colored building, and outside, looped to the gate leading into a full parking lot, was a sign, red and green type with a white border, like Christmas colors, reading: MIDDLE EASTERN FESTIVAL, "MAHRAJAN," FRIDAY–SUNDAY, FOOD/GAMES/DANCING, ALL WELCOME, TODOS BIENVENIDOS. Little green fir trees were in the four corners of the sign.

He turned off his motor and could then hear the music, a throbbing, rhythmic kind that sounded like the snake-charmer music he'd heard in cartoons, coming from the far side of the church, beyond where the cars were parked.

Well, he thought, this was it. He assumed all the computers were tracking him now and that he had only a slim window of time before they converted their incoming data to whatever they'd send to the police, or the FBI, or wherever they sent it. He opened the glove compartment, took out the Glock and the magazine, snapped the magazine into place. He'd thought he might fumble with nerves at this point, but the series of actions seemed easy and familiar from the night before. How, he wondered briefly, would his colleagues on Digital Patriots know he had carried out his mission if he did not return alive? He knew that was a possibility. He had to trust, he concluded, as he pulled the slide back on the Glock, that the media would put out the word, which would make it to the thread. *LiveFree22 actually did it!* they would write—perhaps with some awe, because he would be, to his knowledge, the first patriot on the thread who actually ever carried out a mission.

In the parking lot, he walked straight toward a woman about Bunny's age, in a pink jersey T-shirt, cargo shorts, and those flip-flops with a small wedge heel that only women wore, clicking her car keys toward a Honda CR-V, balancing a foil tray of some sort of food in her other hand, on an open, upturned palm. She glanced at him, glanced away, glanced again, then froze briefly in terror as she saw the object in his hand, and gasped, "Oh no."

He raised the gun. She dropped the foil tray and ran toward her car, but he expertly brought her down, just four feet from the driver's-side door. Briefly, he stood and regarded her still form on the pavement. There, he thought. He had done it. Goats last night, people today. Once they were shot, they were all quiet.

The snake-charmer music throbbed on. Apparently nobody had heard the shot. He walked toward the music, this time with the good sense to put the Glock in the baggy lower pocket of his cargo shorts.

With that, his head finally full of simple purpose, the music growing louder as he approached it, he walked straight toward a long line of fucking Arabs doing a kind of snake dance, right here on American soil, as though they had a right to be here.

He pushed right through two of them until he was standing in the middle of a large circle of dancers, then he turned to face them, pulled out the Glock, shot first a woman, stood there briefly mesmerized as she went down, then shot a man next to her, who also went down, and became paralyzed as adrenaline and a surge of accomplishment shot through him.

Then he went down himself as some giant weight slammed against his back, knocking the Glock out of his hand, pinning him entirely to the ground, the left side of his face smashed into the pavement by what he knew was a man's meaty hand.

"Don't touch the gun!" he heard the man call. "Just back off and call the police, call the EMTs. Rip off some clothes to tie up those wounds. I need backup here from some big men to keep him down."

Around him, there were screams and moans, children sobbing in terror, the agonized calling of names that meant nothing to him. For only a second or two, he tried to throw off the weight atop him, then he relented, went slack with indifference. He'd completed his mission and would get the respect he deserved from the thread, and now everything else was out of his hands, and all the computers in the world tracking him didn't matter anymore.

CHAPTER THIRTEEN

WITHOUT YOU

(2008)

Rita was a zombie. She might as well have died herself.

She would wake up in her childhood bedroom, briefly disoriented. Why was she here? And then it would all come crashing down on her again, morning after morning, and she would smash her head down into the pillow, and murmur, "Oh God, no, please just kill me now."

She could not imagine that the nightmare, the double blow of loss, could ever end. Exhausted at the end of the day, exhausted all the time, and numbed out on pills, she nevertheless began dreading going to sleep, because it meant only bad dreams, then waking to realize that they weren't bad dreams after all. It was real, it had happened, and within seconds of the oblivion of waking, she had to relive it over and over and over, with no power to bring either of them back.

It had been immortalized on video, seen around the country and the world. Joey Hajjar, a sales-force team leader from Tewksbury, had been videotaping while he was dancing, one arm around his wife, the other holding the camcorder, and everything had happened so fast that he had simply stood stock-still for several seconds while he kept recording, saying aloud, repeatedly, "God help us."

And so he had captured how Brian David ("B.D.") Zajac, twenty-four, of Derry, New Hampshire, a part-time employee at the Target in Nashua, had shot dead with a Glock 26 first Allison Khoury-Lanouette, thirty-nine, of Mendhem, Massachusetts, a health-care executive, wife, and mother of two (Leila, eight, and Charlie, six); and then Jonah Gross, also thirty-nine, of Washington, D.C., counsel, American Civil Liberties Union. And he then had captured how Rita Khoury, thirty-seven, senior analyst at the Foreign Affairs Foundation, sister to Allison and girlfriend to Jonah, also of Washington, D.C., had thrown herself over her niece and nephew and forced them to the ground, in a bid to protect them from bullets, screaming, "Ally! Jonah! Get help!"

And finally, he had captured Robert "Bobby" Coughlin, thirty-four an Iraq War veteran with a below-the-knee prosthetic leg, sprinting up behind the gunman, who was tall but reedy, springing into the air like a panther, and body-slamming him to the ground with a tremendous holler, propelling the Glock out of the gunman's hands and onto the ground four feet ahead of them, whereupon everyone within its vicinity recoiled from it as though it were a hand grenade.

"Don't touch the gun!" Bobby was heard to shout on the tape. "Just back off and call the police, call the EMTs."

And that was the point where Joey Hajjar had turned off his camcorder and embraced his wife. Upon the arrival of the Lawton police—as they handcuffed the gunman, whom Bobby and three other youngish men had kept pinned down, his face on the concrete floor—Joey Hajjar had walked up to one of the cops and said, "Here, here. I got it all on tape."

And the cops, three days later, had released the tape to the press, which broadcast it with various degrees of redaction for the sake of decency, and that is how those seconds of horror had been seen (or at least heard) by millions all over the world, and how Rita attained recognition beyond those who followed the foreign-policy talking heads on the Sunday morning talk shows, and also how Bobby became an American hero for stopping a madman who still had fourteen rounds left in his magazine. He was a former soldier who had gone off to fight terrorism but had not succeeded in stopping a real terrorist until he'd come home.

Not caught on the video, of course, was the murder of Celeste Daher, a woman of Sicilian ancestry from nearby Dracut, who had married into a large Lebanese family, the Dahers of Haverhill, and who had been leaving the mahrajan earlier than her husband, her two twenty-something boys, and her mother-in-law—a still warm foil tray of stuffed cabbage and zucchini in her hands—so she could meet her sister to help her shop for a mother-of-the-bride dress.

After the tragedy, those who had been in attendance divided into those who had heard the shot from the parking lot and those who had not, and those who had heard it divided further into those who had thought it was firecrackers and those who had been absolutely certain it was gunfire but assumed it was coming from beyond the gated perimeter of the church property. It was the cops, upon driving into the parking lot with their sirens blaring, who had first spotted the lifeless body of Celeste Daher, lying on the ground alongside the foil tray, whose white cardboard top, oddly, had remained sealed.

"There's a woman down in the parking lot," one of the cops had shouted as he and six others pushed their way into the mayhem under the tent. Upon hearing this, Eli Daher and his two boys, Tony and Zack, leaving their bewildered matriarch behind in a folding chair, had run out of the tent and into the parking lot, where the boys screamed their mother's name and fell, howling, to the pavement before her.

"Ma! Ma!" they screamed, "Wake up, Ma!"

The EMTs came rushing in next. But by that point a doctor, named Peter Saab, had already come over and, feeling the wrists and necks of both Ally and Jonah, had looked at Rita, his eyes welling up, and said, "I'm so sorry, honey, they're both gone."

She had snapped. Clutching Jonah's hand with her own left hand and her sister's with her right, she had begun screaming like a wild woman, full of a rage that made her feel like a beast, not a person, and a desire to beat her own head so hard against the concrete that she, too, in moments, would be dead alongside her boyfriend and her sister. And were it not for what felt like a dozen arms holding her back, she would have succeeded.

"Let me go! Let me do it!" she screamed. But then, as she thrashed, she caught, from the corner of her eye, her niece and nephew, Leila and Charlie, clinging to her mother, all three of them sobbing, and she had risen from the bodies and stumbled over and joined them, and the four of them held one another as they let out great choking wails.

It all came out in the local and national news about B.D. Zajac, the shooter. He'd had various diagnoses of depression, bipolar disorder, autism spectrum, and ADHD all his life and had been taking Adderall and Wellbutrin at the time of the shooting. This news, in turn, prompted a spate of commentary from doctors and activists in various patient groups, especially those for autism, insisting there was no categorical link between any of those diagnoses and violent or pathological behavior.

When B.D. was twelve, his father had fled to Florida, and in recent months, his own mother, scared of his outbursts at home, had asked her older sister, Bridget McLeish of Derry—a jovial woman known as "Bunny" to customers of the AutoZone in Nashua—if she wouldn't mind temporarily putting up B.D., who everyone simply assumed would never be able to maintain his own apartment and pay his own rent. And Bridget had agreed and it appeared that, overall, the arrangement had worked out okay.

"He was a good kid," Bridget told WMUR, even after a bullet match made it fairly clear that B.D. had been the mysterious shooter of the Morans' goats, the night before what came to be called the Saint Jude shootings. It was the biggest shooting in Massachusetts since 2000, when a man who thought he was a Nazi hunter had walked into a tech facility in Wakefield and killed seven coworkers with three different guns, including an AK-47.

But Bridget said she hadn't known that, as was revealed by an FBI search of the browser on her Dell computer, her nephew was an active member of a white supremacist website, where, both the day before and the day of the shootings, he'd spoken cryptically of his plans. She said he hadn't mentioned this Arab festival that he'd been reading up on.

"I'd go to bed, and he'd be up on the computer, and that was his time," she said. "I saw him playing solitaire once, so I figured that's what he did, or he was reading the news. It's true, he'd say things that I really didn't like about blacks and Hispanics and Arabs," she said. "And I'd say to him, 'B.D., cut it out. That talk's gonna get you in trouble at work. There's good and bad in everyone and that's the end of the story.'"

Ana Polanco, whom he'd worked with at the Target in Nashua, said that she'd often caught him staring at her broodingly, but then, once she'd smiled and said hello, he'd seem to soften up and make small talk with her about something or other, perhaps about the Red Sox, which she'd learned in her seven years in the Merrimack Valley was the fastest way to warm people up.

B.D. had bought the Glock legally. He'd shown his driver's license at the gun store on Route 28 in Salem, New Hampshire, and he'd honestly answered "no" on the background-check form to questions asking whether he had a felony, an alcohol or drug problem, a discharge from the military, or a restraining order against him. Bridget was shocked to learn that he'd been able to buy a weapon so easily; as she said, nobody who knew B.D. and his mental history would have vouched for him.

Once Bridget had realized that B.D. was the shooter, she'd of course embarked on a frantic chain of communications involving lawyers, B.D.'s mother, the Massachusetts state police and investigators, reporters (because B.D.'s mother wanted nothing to do with them whatsoever), and other parties. No wonder she'd forgotten about her bunnies.

But when she opened the hutch to find them gone, she did not—by that point—hesitate for a moment in assuming that B.D. had killed them. It was only a matter of wondering what he'd done with them.

"You were a helluva lot sicker than we thought, B.D.," she said aloud. Then, in the late-summer dusk, she leaned back against the hutch and allowed herself to cry for the very first time in the past twenty-four hours.

She did not go to the basement fridge for almost another week—a week in which she slept and ate little, at the end of which she padded downstairs to retrieve a frozen meal from the freezer, to force nourishment on herself. She screamed when she opened the freezer door, her nose assaulted by the smell.

The Khourys were all in the house in Mendhem in the week following, huddling together: Rita (back in her old room); her parents; and Gary and the kids, Leila and Charlie. They were a family of sleepwalkers, sobbers, nightmare sufferers who cried out in their sleep, insomniacs who barely slept at all but instead pored through photo albums into the wee hours, looking at pictures of Ally. Elementary-school princess Ally, straight-A good-girl high-school Ally, track-and-field college Ally, young mother Ally, camping-trip family-vacation Ally. They climbed into one another's beds and held one another and wept; they forced themselves and one another to eat bits of the food brought over by relatives and friends; they rebuffed phone calls and even a few brazen front-step visits from reporters; they gathered around the kitchen table and muddled through the details of the funeral together.

Rita's phone rang.

"My sweetheart?"

It was Salma.

Rita wept when she heard her voice. She wept for quite a long time, a full minute perhaps, while Salma cooed, "I know, sweetheart. I know. It's so awful."

"Are you in New York?" Rita finally managed to ask.

"No, chérie. I'm at an inn in a pretty town on the water called Newburyport just a few miles from you, and I'm here when you need me. When is the funeral?"

"You're kidding me! You're in Newburyport?"

"Yes, chérie, I'm really here."

"Don't stay there. Come here, come stay with me. Please?"

"Won't I be in the way of your family?"

"No, you won't. They love you. And I need you now."

An hour later, when Salma pulled up, Rita flew from the front door of the house and threw her arms around her friend as soon as she stepped out of her cherry-red rental car.

Ally's funeral would be Friday, Jonah's shiva the following Tuesday, in Westchester, with his stricken family. If only one of them had died, Rita thought, she could cope. The loss of Ally was all around her, constant and bone deep, but then suddenly she'd remember that she'd lost her boyfriend, the man she might have eventually married and had children with, the man who'd shown her kindness, admiration for her mind and values, who'd respected her sharpness and knew how to shrug it off, too.

Then she'd feel a new and sickening wave of emptiness, followed by the endless if-only scenarios she'd run through her head. If only she'd brought Jonah home some other weekend. If only the family had planned to go to the mahrajan on Sunday, not Saturday. If only they'd not gotten up to dance. If only Ally and Jonah had not been hand in hand, next to each other. She was terrified of seeing the Gross family at the funeral. She couldn't help feeling that his death was completely her fault, she told Salma over and over again.

"That's ridiculous," Salma replied. The two of them were always out behind the house now, sitting on the old picnic table and smoking. "This was random. Look, this could have happened when you went to see his family, a crazy anti-Semitic person with a gun. The problem is this fucking crazy country that lets anybody buy these horrible guns."

Intellectually, Rita understood Salma. But this provided little comfort. "It's hard not to feel like there's almost something karmic about it."

"How?" Salma peered at her skeptically.

"Don't you think it's weird that not one but two people there that day had been in Iraq? One who went there to kill people and one just to observe it all?"

"You weren't there to kill people."

"I mean my cousin. Bobby. The one who jumped the guy with the gun and brought him down."

"Oh, right." Salma exhaled. "No, sweetheart. I think you're just having normal guilt feelings. If there were real karma in this country about Iraq, you and your family would not be the victims. You know it would be Bush. Cheney. Condoleezza Rice. Definitely something terrible would happen to her, like she would at least fall from, maybe, a third- or fourth-story window. Not so high that she would die, but high enough to lose some major bodily function for the rest of her life."

Rita laughed with some force for nearly the first time since before the shootings. "You are a sicko."

"Come on, you know you would like to see it."

"To all of them, though. Not just Condi."

"Exactly. Something really horrible where they would have to live in extreme pain for the rest of their lives."

Bobby came by the next day with Aunt Carol and, to Rita's surprise, Cheryl, the woman he had broken off with a few months earlier. She was a bombshell by Merrimack Valley standards: swingy blond hair, tan, makeup, a Pilates body encased in a fitted baby-blue hoodie and sweatpants, matching baby-blue Nikes. She held Bobby by one elbow as they came up the walk, steadying him. He limped.

"Are you hurt?" Rita called from the door.

He nodded as he made his way slowly up the stairs. "That jump fucked up my fitting."

"Bobby—" Aunt Carol scolded.

"Sorry, Ma. Messed up my fitting. I gotta go into Boston next week after the funeral and get looked at."

She hugged him. "Does it hurt?"

"Nothing I'm not used to. I just pop ibuprofen all day."

"You gotta take food with that, babe, or you'll wreck your stomach," Cheryl said.

Bobby looked Rita in the eyes. "You holdin' up okay, cuz?"

"Not really. It's like waking up to a bad dream every morning."

"You're gonna have trauma, you know," he said bluntly. "Maybe more than from Iraq. You know you gotta get help."

They all moved into the kitchen.

"We already have a woman coming to the house with Father Gene," Rita said. "A grief counselor."

"Yeah," Bobby persisted, "but you're not gonna feel the worst of it until later."

"That's enough, Bobby," Aunt Carol said loudly. "Let everyone go through this one day at a time."

Everybody else came down to the kitchen. Cheryl began slicing a still warm lasagna she'd brought, passing around plates. It was the first time everyone had seen Bobby since the day of the shooting.

Gary, chalky and unshaven, embraced him. "Thank you, man," he said.

"I'm sorry I couldn't do more."

Gary nodded soberly. Then, slowly, standing in the middle of the kitchen, one hand to his forehead, he began to cry. Leila and Charlie rushed to him, and he knelt down, took them both in his arms, and continued crying. Then Charlie cried while Leila stroked his back.

The others just sat there, their lasagna untouched, utterly silent, exchanging brief looks, some shaking their heads in dazed chagrin. Finally Gary snorted, wiped his face almost violently with his palms, kissed both his kids on their foreheads, stood up, and said, brightly, "Okay, sorry about that! Let's eat! Who made this amazing lasagna?"

On day five, the day before Ally's funeral, Rita finally braced herself and sat down before her e-mail. She skimmed a flood of condolences, opened none of them. She didn't have the stamina to read them, let alone graciously respond to them. She was looking for an e-mail from her boss at the Foreign Affairs Foundation—and she found it.

I hope I didn't call too early yesterday. I just want to reiterate what I said in my voice mail yesterday, which is that everything is off the table for you and on ice until you're ready to reengage. Whether that's in a few weeks or several months. You know you're invaluable to us and we've got nothing but prayers and love here for you and your family. Please know that we are here to help you in any way.

I will be checking in on you regularly whether you like it or not! Please take care of yourself in this horrible time.

Take care of yourself. The grief counselor had told them the same thing, several times. *It's so important right now to care for yourselves and for each other.*

What did that even mean, Rita thought bitterly. She was a broken person, as were her parents, her brother-in-law, her niece and nephew, and the entire Gross family. What was the point of trying to take care of oneself?

Amid the e-mails she had no stomach to read, her eye caught one from Nabil al-Jumaili.

Nabil. The name hurtled toward her like an old bad dream crashing down into the middle of a new one. It also pricked her with guilt. She'd not been good about keeping up with him. The last she knew, he'd fled to Syria to join up with his family after Asmaa had been killed.

Gingerly, she clicked the e-mail.

Rita,

Rick told me the terrible news about your family. I send my sincerest condolences. My prayers are with you.

Nabil

But she noticed that he'd forwarded the e-mail from one he'd sent eight months prior, which read:

Rita,

I hope this e-mail finds you very well and finding satisfaction in your new position. I cannot believe those nights in the villa have passed, they seem like yesterday!

Do you remember some advice you once gave me? After I reunited with my family in Damascus, I decided to act on it. I am now living in Beirut as I go through the asylum process with UNHCR, putting together my case as a sexual minority. May I burden you by asking if you would write a letter of recommendation and attestation on my behalf? Perhaps you might say that you were the first to suggest I do this?

I imagine you are very busy in your new position so I understand completely if you cannot find the time for this. Rick has been helping me as well.

I wish you the very best and hope to see you again one day soon!
Sincerely,
Your Danger Twin

She leaned slowly back from the screen, her hand over her mouth. How could she have missed this e-mail? Had it gone to her spam folder? Panic and guilt shot through her.

She retrieved her cell phone in the other room and called Rick, who was in D.C. on a six-week leave from Baghdad.

"It's Rita."

"What's going on? Can I do anything for you before I see you Friday?" He was coming up from D.C. for the funeral.

"No, no, all that is fine. Or as fine as it can be. It's something else. I'm so horrified. I just saw an e-mail that Nabil sent me eight months ago from Beirut asking if I'd help with his asylum, and I never saw this e-mail and I'm—I'm horrified. Did you know about this?"

"Of course, I helped him through the whole thing. You don't remember me e-mailing you that he was doing it and was going to send a note your way?"

Her brow furrowed. Did she? Eight months ago, she'd just started her new post with the Foreign Affairs Foundation and had plunged into a flurry of research, papers, conferences, and travel. She'd allowed herself to breathe a bit once she started dating Jonah, but before that—she later admitted to herself—she'd been obsessed. She was transitioning to a new career after being disgraced in her old one, and she'd wanted to embark flawlessly.

"I don't remember that," she admitted.

"I definitely sent it to you. You think you didn't get it?"

"Hang on." She searched back in her e-mails, found one from Rick answering some general questions she'd asked about the state of the surge. The addendum about Nabil was at the bottom.

"I just found it," she said. "At the bottom of this e-mail we had about the surge."

"Ah. I should have sent it under separate cover."

"And goddamn it," she said as she typed. "I just found the original e-mail from Nabil. I hate myself, Rick."

"Well, you can breathe easy. Because our friend just arrived in San Diego. To stay."

"What?"

"That's right. Just three weeks ago."

"*What?*"

"I helped him get a job as a junior reporter at the *Union-Tribune*. I was talking to a friend there and, you know, there's a huge Iraqi refugee population there. A lot of Yazidis but not just. Christians, too, also Shi'a and Sunni. All living in this one little town outside San Diego. It's like Baghdad on the Pacific. With pretty much the same weather."

"I think I remember reading that."

"Right. Well, I told my friend, I have the perfect staff addition for you. He's fluent in Arabic and English, and he knows how to report. And he's a sweetheart of a guy. So Nabil's not going to be getting rich, but at least he'll be gainfully and usefully employed. And safe."

"I can't believe this. I can't believe he's here in the United States and I didn't even know. What is wrong with me?"

Rick was quiet momentarily on the other end. "Honey, nothing's wrong with you. You're in the middle of something really horrible."

"You don't even know. I mean . . ." She slowed, reaching for words to put to unformed thoughts that had been plaguing her during the past five days. "All those deaths we wrote about. I had no idea. I thought I did, you know, nodding my head with what I hoped was a caring look. But I really didn't. I feel like I was so—" She searched for the word.

"You weren't," he said, before she found it. "Or even if you were—I mean, if we were, and still are sometimes—you were just doing your job."

The phrase sounded intensely cold to her. She thought about the reporters and network-branded news vans that had plagued her and her family for the past few days, jostling toward their suffering to get that perfect quote. Rita had thought they were horrifying, vultures. But then again: they were just doing their jobs.

"Now just promise me to take care of yourself and your family for the time being," Rick said. "Nabil is safe and sound, and you can go see him soon enough."

She smudged her eyes with the back of her hand. "This is the only good news I've had. Wait—where is his family?"

"They're still in Damascus, but they're probably going to go back to Baghdad soon, now that it's a little more stable. They can't make a living in Syria."

"Do you think he'll try to bring them here?"

"I think it's too early for him to decide. I also think our friend needs a moment to process the past few years and to find out who he really is."

She was silent briefly. "I whispered that to him once. He got so angry. I never mentioned it again."

"Well, I think it lit a spark. He had quite a run-in about it in Damascus."

"What? Was he hurt?"

"No. Look, I can't go into it all now. I have to prep for a phoner in five minutes. I'll tell you soon, or he can. Just do what you need to do right now."

"This is the first thing that's pulled me out of it, and it felt so good."

"Well, just remember everyone who loves you."

After they hung up, she replied to Nabil:

Nabil,

Thank you for the condolence. I appreciate it.

I also owe you a huge apology. I missed your original e-mail and I missed one from Rick about the same issue. I am so sorry. I just talked to Rick and he told me you are now in San Diego and working for the paper there. I am so relieved to hear that and so proud of you for getting through that long, hard process. They are VERY lucky to have you at the paper.

Please let me get through this terrible time and then I'll come out and see you. I am so relieved to know you are safe.

Love,

Your Danger Twin

The morning of the funeral, they woke to one of those perfect early-September days. The local newscasts rolled tape of the sun shimmering over Boston Harbor during the weather segment. It was what Rita called "September eleventh weather," because that 2001 morning, too, had been perfect, and in her first thoughts upon waking, as she sat up in her childhood bed and braced for the events of the day, she thought grimly that it was better to wake up depressed on such a day, already well into the journey of grief, than to wake up happy and not know what horrors the day held in store. The morning of the mahrajan, she and Jonah had woken up, their bodies enlaced, in a three-star roadside chain hotel in central Connecticut, having traveled halfway from D.C. the night before, and one of her first thoughts had been to wonder, with a thrill, what her sister would make of her funny and sweet new boyfriend.

The proceedings in the Mendhem house that morning were brisk and purposeful—a string of showers; hurrying about for clothes and shoes, purses and ties; coffee and various nibbles in the kitchen—but joyless and dazed. The black SUV with the funeral flags flapping from either side of its hood pulled up for them at 9:15 a.m., to get them to Saint Jude's for the funeral Mass at ten.

Rita double-checked her purse before they left the house to make sure she had the notes she'd written, then put her arms around Leila and Charlie, telling them how grown-up they looked and how their mama would be proud of them, and walked them out to the vehicle, an arm around each child's shoulders.

The church—where two armed Lawton cops stood outside, and the news vans were parked just beyond the perimeter—was filled past what the pews could handle. Family in the front rows; friends and colleagues of Gary, Ally, and the kids behind them; Saint Jude's parishioners—many of whom had been at the mahrajan—farther back.

The Mass began. "A great, great tragedy has fallen on our community," Father Jean-Paul commenced. "A tragedy that is something like the tragedies known by our parents, grandparents, and great-grandparents, such as war, senseless killing, famine, and pestilence."

He's taking it all the way back to the mountains, Rita thought. If Ally had been sitting by her side, she'd have leaned over and whispered as much, and Ally would have constrained her laughter and slapped her remonstratively on the thigh. They had grown up together whispering impieties in church, earning outraged glares from their sittu, which had only made them want to laugh more.

Rita closed her eyes. *I cannot believe you're not here*, she thought. *Ally, Ally, Ally. The rest of life is going to be so lonely without you.*

Then, as had been the case multiple times a day the past week, her grief flickered to rage at the shooter. *That disgusting, stupid mound of white trash from New Hampshire.* He had targeted them because they were Arabs. It was unthinkable. Catholic Lebanese had almost never been objects of hate in the Merrimack Valley; they had merely married and blended their way into the larger Catholic populace, as much a part of the local fabric as Sicilians or Greeks.

Then she would remember that he was mentally ill. Bipolar or autistic or—it wasn't even clear what. Then her rage would shift to *stupid fucking New Hampshire*, where pretty much anyone could walk into a gun store and walk out a few minutes later with a killing machine—no license, no screening required.

The entire cycle of rage, of whom or what to blame, was exhausting.

The entirety of the Mass, then the cemetery, then, for just family and the closest friends, the mercy meal at Salaam's, the buffet of Arabic food—lemony salad and hot, fresh pita bread and kibbe and stuffed peppers and stuffed cabbage and hummus and bowls of cold homemade yogurt—with some bland American options as well, baked scrod and grilled chicken. Rita could not have imagined stranger dynamics, the presence of so many people who also might have died that day were it not for Bobby, who received a hero's reception after the Mass, Cheryl clinging to his arm.

"I just did what I was trained to do," Rita heard Bobby say again and again. "I wasn't carrying, so I had to think fast and figure out how to take him down. I knew the other guys would back me up as soon as I got him down and got the gun out of his hand."

Rita came over to him at one point and put her arm around him. "You're the action hero today. The Maronites might canonize you and make a shrine to you up in the mountains in the old country."

He put his arm around her. "You jealous of me, cuz?" The same wicked grin.

But she didn't take the age-old bait. "I'm proud of you," she said quietly. "You were a hero that day."

"See?" Cheryl, standing at Bobby's other side, piped up. "Babe, I told you she felt that way."

Rita glanced from one to the other. "What'd I miss?" she asked.

Cheryl put her arm through Bobby's, rubbed his back. "He just takes your opinion of him very seriously," she told Rita.

Bobby blushed deeply. "Ah, Cher, come on," he whined. "Jesus."

Rita glanced at Bobby, who was staring at the floor. She smiled at Cheryl and hugged Bobby, then pulled back to look him in the eyes. "You are my hero," she enunciated slowly.

He wouldn't look at her. "Get the fuck outta here. You're embarrassing me."

She allowed herself a rare, sharp laugh.

Later, after everyone had bade them final condolences and left, the family made its way out of the banquet hall. Rita, emerging from the bathroom, found her mother briefly alone in the foyer, her arms crossed over her chest, in front of the easel that showcased the collage of Ally's photos she'd spent the past two nights assembling. Rita stole up silently and put an arm around her.

"Where is everyone?" Rita asked.

"In the parking lot, waiting." Her mother sounded aloof, vaguely indifferent to the delay.

"You did a great job with this," Rita said.

"Hmph." Then, turning to her, her nose wrinkled, her mother said, "You know what I've realized the past few days, Rita?"

"What, Ma?"

"There's no God." She said it in a tone of everyday disgust, as though she'd just caught on to a scam at a car dealership or in a government agency. "There's love, sure. But there's no God. That's a lie we were fed."

Rita said nothing. She'd long held that opinion. But she well knew her mother had not, and to look into her cornflower-blue eyes now was excruciating—not because they were glassy with tears but because they were not.

Rita laid her head briefly on Mary Jo's shoulder. "Come on, Ma," she then said. "Let's go." They stepped out into the nearly empty parking lot and, exactly in time, raised their hands to their foreheads to shield themselves from the assault of sunshine in their eyes.

CHAPTER FOURTEEN

HOPE AND CHANGE

(FEBRUARY 2009)

Jack McCourt was enjoying a ratings surge since Obama's election. Perhaps that's why he seemed particularly chipper that night, his face lacquered in so much stage makeup that it almost looked, to the naked eye unmediated by lights and cameras, like a Kabuki mask.

"Good to have you back," he said to Rita moments before they went live. "I'm very sorry for all you've been through the past few months."

"Thanks, Jack. But you won't mention that on the air, right?"

"Of course not. How are you doing?"

She wished he hadn't brought up the topic at all, right before they aired. "I'm hanging in there."

"You're tough."

She smiled wanly. "Thanks."

They were interrupted by Jack's punchy, bombastic theme music, which straightened him up in his seat, cued him to put the signature "skeptical" arch back into his right eyebrow.

"And we're back, people," he commenced. "President Obama, today at Camp Lejeune, North Carolina, announcing before a packed house that he'll have all combat troops out of Iraq by August 2010, all remaining troops out by December 2011. He said, and I quote, 'We will complete this transition to Iraqi control responsibly, and we will bring our troops home with the honor that they have earned.' This after six years of American presence in the country, more than $650 billion spent and more than four thousand American lives lost.

"Rita Khoury, Foreign Affairs Foundation, always good to have you with us. Always an unshellacked take on Iraq from you. So: Is this feasible?"

She took a deep, sharp breath, mindful of her own posture. "Thanks, Jack, and I want to add something crucial to your numbers, which is that, according to the independent Iraq Body Count project, the current figure on Iraqi lives lost is slightly over one hundred thousand."

Jack paused only briefly before: "Absolutely, thank you. Massive losses on the Iraqi side. Which have plunged since the surge last year, yes?"

"Well, they've come down from being in the thousands per month to being in the hundreds."

"Duly noted. So Obama today—"

She was surprised to hear herself interrupt him. "I just think it's important that we remember what we've done in Iraq so far as we talk about what we're going to do going forward. We never see those bodies on American TV, Jack. One hundred percent never."

Another brief, mildly vexed pause from Jack. "Absolutely. So much loss. Incredible suffering among Iraqis. Can we be out of there in two years, like our new president today promised?"

"We have a Gordian knot here, Jack, that we tied ourselves. The reason we've seen more stability in Iraq the past year is because we put more boots on the ground, street by street, and we forced order out of a chaos that, frankly, we brought on Iraq when we didn't nail down security when we invaded. We created the conditions for the chaos, and now, in the past year, we've tamped it down, thankfully."

She allowed herself a small sip of breath before continuing: "And we're also seeing factors align that are very key to preserving sustained stability for Iraq, like the so-called Sunni Awakening of the past two years, where Sunni tribal leaders have determined it was more strategic to align with the United States than with the extremists of al-Qaeda. But my main point is that, if we don't have clear evidence of genuine autonomous Iraqi governing and police cohesion and stability every step of the way of this phaseout that President Obama is talking about, we're just opening up the vacuum again."

"Irresponsible of the president to promise a hard exit by 2011, then?"

She paused and sighed. "Well, I think he chose his words carefully. But he's going to get military pushback from the top, from Petraeus and Ray Odierno, if he tries to do this faster than he should just because he's keeping an eye on reelection come 2012. And as well they should push back. I've said this before on your show, Jack, but we made a mess we never should have made, and you can't just walk away from it because it's unpopular over here in the States."

"No end in sight, then?"

"I didn't say that." She'd almost snapped it, startling herself. Usually she was very good at modulating her tone on air. "I'm just saying that we have to proceed from what's happening on the ground, not our own wishful-thinking timetable."

"Be realists about this."

"Right." He was always punching her meaning back at her.

"Obama on foreign policy so far: Go."

"Whoa!" she laughed. "That's a big one. Well, he's saying the right things so far, about modulating our presence in the world, but we'll see how it plays out. He's already ordered his first drone strike—three days into office."

"Not wasting any time."

"Sadly, no."

"Rita Khoury, Foreign Affairs Foundation, thank you so much and wishing the very best for you."

"Thanks, Jack, you too."

She was cross in the taxi on the way home from the TV studio to her apartment in Kalorama. It was one thing to have played the Debbie Downer role on Iraq in the Bush years, but it was tougher playing it under Obama, who'd never supported the war. Everyone was rooting for Obama. Nobody would like someone who was taking him to task right out of the gate.

Washington sped by outside the taxi window—the broad nighttime streets and the obelisk illuminated in the distance. The city was full of new energy, filling up with the Northeastern neoliberal and progressive eggheads she'd gone to high school and college with, the boys (and precious few girls) she'd sparred with on the debate team over issues like foreign trade and humanitarian aid.

She'd returned to town just after the holidays—which, as everyone in the family had expected, were awful, instantly transformed from a season of joy into a grim ordeal to be endured, with the bare minimum of acknowledging gestures, such as a few gifts and arranging a Santa visit for Leila and Charlie. Everyone had cried the whole time, and Rita didn't even have Salma there anymore. Salma had flown back to Beirut to spend the holidays with her own family.

Rita had thought it would feel good to be back in D.C., to throw herself back into work and start the slow process of going on with life. Four months had passed since Day Zero of the nightmare—that, she had told herself, was a proper period of acute mourning. Grief would follow, she assumed, but it would be manageable. The contours of normal life would slip back into place.

But, after six weeks back in D.C., she knew it wasn't happening. She took Ambien to sleep, to block out the bad dreams she'd have otherwise, but never slept well. She woke each morning with a chemical hangover and a burning resentment that she actually had to get out of bed, make herself presentable, and construct some sort of day for herself.

She felt haunted. She had terrifying moments on the street or in the office when her surroundings were suddenly alien to her, she lost all sense of where she was, and, her legs suddenly like jelly, she would have to sit down, dizzy, her heart pounding, sweat dampening the inside of her blouse. She'd not been a fool, of course. As soon as she'd come back to D.C., she'd started seeing a psychotherapist, one well known in foreign-correspondent circles, who specialized in post-traumatic experience.

"You're having depersonalization," the therapist explained. "A very, very common post-traumatic symptom. Do you feel like you've never been where you are, suddenly, or that you are watching a film of yourself?"

"Exactly. And it comes on so fast. I mean, actually, I feel a low-level version of it all the time, and then suddenly sometimes it's like someone just turned up the dial, and it's really bad."

"Did you get any treatment after coming back from Iraq?" The therapist's own husband had been a correspondent in Vietnam, and the therapist had published a book about how to live with and love someone with post-traumatic stress disorder.

Rita shook her head. "I don't think I had many symptoms, except I'd jump at loud noises and I had a hard time not being on edge for about three months."

"I think what you might be experiencing now," said the therapist, "is the two experiences, Iraq and your family, kind of commingling and having a synergistic effect. Are the meds helping since you started them a month ago?"

She ignored the question. "Iraq was so mild compared to what happened with my family," she said. Then she laughed in self-disdain. "I can't believe I just said that."

"No, no," assured the therapist. "I know what you mean. You didn't sustain an acute trauma in Iraq."

"But people I know did. My interpreter did. He nearly died, and he watched his cousin die, and, Ann, I never reached out to him about it. Not really the proper way I should have. I was back in D.C., and I just went on with my life. I hate myself so much when I think about it now."

The therapist, Ann, shook her head. "Well, now you're in the circle of loss, and you've realized a really awful thing, which is that everyone outside the circle just goes on with their life."

"I spend all my time and energy now trying not to hate well-meaning people who are just going about their lives."

"It's why you have to spend at least some of your time with other people in the circle with you."

* * *

She had once loved her deco-era apartment with the arched doorways and the sunken living room, but now she dreaded closing the door behind her at night and being alone with her thoughts. In the weeks before the mahrajan, Jonah had all but moved in. It had been her first time living with a man since Sami in Beirut, and she'd loved picking up groceries and wine on the way home from work, planning to make dinner, or to arrive home finding that he'd done the same.

Weekends, after sleeping in and sex, it was bagels and the *Washington Post*, and then maybe a run in Rock Creek Park, then a nap together back in the air-conditioning, then dinner with friends at Coppi's on U Street.

She thought of his niece's bat mitzvah in July, meeting his family, feeling they were so much like hers, their sprawl and their teasing closeness, their deep catalog of family in-jokes. Sometimes, to Salma or other friends, or merely to herself, she would shake her head, dazed, and realize that she'd managed to find not only a fellow egghead and political obsessive whom she couldn't keep her hands off but a kind person as well, someone who actually wanted the best for her. After Sami, she'd wondered if something was wrong with her, if maybe she should go to therapy to find out why she'd been drawn to someone who continually poked fun at her ambition and her work ethic and ultimately sabotaged both. Not until Jonah did she realize that Sami had been merely a bad call.

She had come back to the apartment to find Jonah's remains: his T-shirts, his briefs, his ties, his books, his curve-brimmed, sweat-stained Yankees cap, his copies of the *New Yorker* and the *Economist*, his work notes scrawled on a pad on the kitchen table, his toothbrush (its bristles splayed outward) alongside hers in the bathroom, the clippers for grooming the facial scruff he'd been cultivating. These inanimate objects now seemed to whisper and weep. She scolded herself for not having asked a friend, or even the building's super, to come in first and clear them out. Then she picked up his Yankees cap and a white Calvin Klein T-shirt, with a faint splatter of what she imagined was hoisin sauce on the front, and a pair of his running shorts, gathered them to her chest, and lay down on the bed, smelled the clothes, and wept.

She'd thought that coming back to the city amid the whirl of inaugural parties, the infusion of new energy, would boost her spirits. She'd been wrong. It had all been too much to take, and she'd ended up declining most invitations at the last minute and staying home in her sweatpants and Jonah's ACLU sweatshirt, barely eating, drinking red wine, knowing it wasn't a smart mix with her antidepressants but still appreciating the warm fuzz it wrapped her in, how it smudged away the hard edges of her gloom.

Claude, the French photographer from the villa in Baghdad, came into town for a few days to cover the inauguration. He'd been out of Iraq since 2007, shooting for the *Standard* in and around New York, where he was living with his girlfriend, Céline, whose ad agency had placed her there.

When Rita walked toward him in the restaurant in Columbia Heights, where he sat waiting for her at the bar, she noted that he'd lost the modest gut he'd accumulated in Baghdad, where exercise was nearly impossible and each day ended in whiskey.

"You are a sight for sore eyes," she said as they embraced.

"No, you are."

She pulled back to look at him again. "It is so strange seeing you here after all the nights we spent together over there. It's almost not quite real."

"I was just thinking the same thing. Was that the dream or is this the dream?"

They were seated at a table. Rita could not stop studying his face. It was thinner than when she'd last seen it, but she also felt, uncomfortably, that the new thing in it she couldn't place was more than that.

"How are you doing, Rita? I didn't think you'd come back to work so soon."

He wasn't the only person who'd remarked as much since she'd been back in D.C.

She shrugged. "I had a job I needed to get back to. Life has to go on. Doesn't it?"

"Oh, no, of course, of course." He sounded hurried and apologetic. "Actually, you know, it doesn't surprise me you handled it that way. Like in Baghdad, even on the worst days. You always pushed through."

She shrugged again, unsure of his meaning.

"You were strong."

"I guess I cracked in my own way, though. On the keyboard at two in the morning."

He grinned. "Well, look. That e-mail was the start of a whole new career where you get to say exactly what you want. And now you do—on the TV, in the papers."

She smiled back mirthlessly. "I guess that's one way to look at it." She was desperate to change the subject. "What about you, Claude? From a Parisian to a Baghdadi to a New Yorker in, what, five years?"

"Aha, yes." He poured for them both from the bottle of wine they'd carried over from the bar. "A magic carpet ride."

"Do you and Céline love New York?"

He held his glass aloft, considering. "Céline loves it," he finally said. "It makes a long time that she wants to live in New York. You know, all Parisians dream to move to New York and vice versa." He laughed quickly. "Such a cliché."

"What about you?"

He put down his glass. "Rita, honestly? I know I can tell you this. I am angry all the time." He began counting off on his fingers. "Angry. Irritated. Depressed. I always want to be back inside the apartment. I pretend to enjoy everything for Céline, because she waited for me when I was away. This is supposed to be our time now, maybe to have a baby soon."

"Do you hate noises and crowds?" she asked.

"I can't stand them. I just want to get back inside. I clench my teeth walking in the streets with Céline. I can only make it go away when I'm working because I go into a different . . ." He trailed off, pointing to his head. "A different zone. Like a cocoon. But I can't relax."

"Yep." She clinked her glass against his in a mock toast. "Jonah knew, when we were together, that I'd never sit in the front of a restaurant. He knew a stupid boom sound on the street would make me jump. And that was all before—" She shrugged.

"Yes, I know what you mean."

"Anyone moving toward me on the street a little too quickly freaks me out."

"Right," he said.

"I don't really even want to leave the apartment, to be honest."

They both sat there silently while the server arrived to put down olives and a cheese board, for which they murmured thank-yous.

"Can I tell you?" Claude continued, ignoring the food. "I dream about Asmaa and Ali over and over again. Like we are still in the house, working together. But it always ends bad, like I hear Asmaa cry out in the next room, and then I can't get into the room. The door's locked."

Rita ignored the food, too. So Claude was going there with the conversation, she thought. She resented it on one level, welcomed it on a deeper one.

"I flaked on Nabil when I got back," she said, looking Claude straight in the eye. "I mean, not intentionally. But I was angling for this new job, and I missed an e-mail from him asking for help with his asylum process—for a reference letter. And I was the one who told him to try to get asylum the day I left Baghdad."

Claude cocked his head forgivingly. "Well, it worked out okay for Nabil. Rick and I wrote letters and made calls for him."

"I know, but he was *my* interpreter. I should have been writing those letters and making those calls."

"I didn't say that to make you feel bad. Just to say, it terminated okay. We talk and we e-mail all the time. He's making a new life."

"I'm going to go out and see him."

"Me, too."

"We should go together."

Claude nodded. Then they fell into silence again, began picking at the olives and cheese.

"But Umm Nasim made it out," she finally added.

"I know. A few months before I left. Her sons got her to Bahrain."

"Hamdullilah," Rita said, and they both laughed a bit.

"They had to take her out in the trunk of a car, just like Nabil. I thought she was going to have a heart attack before she got away from Baghdad."

Rita shook her head. Then she gestured broadly at their setting: pulsing, low-volume house music that sounded like easy listening, dim amber lamps, small candles flickering on tables, mid-century chairs, and a sleek, slate bar. Diversely photogenic, expensively educated twenty- and thirtysomethings laughing around them, jacked up for the new administration, trading Beltway gossip.

"I can't make sense of all this after we were there," she said.

"It was the same for me in Paris and now New York. People so happy with no idea. Just going on like it's not even happening."

"And the hardest part for me—can I tell you, Claude?"

He nodded.

"All that death, and I didn't even witness an actual death before my eyes until I came home. That's the strangest part."

After Jack McCourt's show, after she'd returned to her apartment, torn off her work clothes, pulled her sweatpants and Jonah's sweatshirt back on, poured herself a glass of wine, and collapsed on the couch, she called home.

"We watched you on TV tonight, honey," her father said. "You were great."

Just hearing his voice stabbed her heart. "Thanks, Dad. Nobody wants to hear Obama critiques this early in the game, though. I felt like the spoilsport who's not giving him a chance."

"Well," he continued uncertainly. "You were doing your job, right? Saying what you know."

"I guess so." The quality of his voice, the fact that she could hear him but not see him or put her arms around him and hold him close—her father, whom she was so insanely lucky not to have lost, who lived! Who lived! Just like her mother and her niece and nephew—tore at her, put a burr in her voice when she spoke again. "How is everyone?"

He sighed. "We're surviving. I've gone back to the office a few times. Your mother's been going to church every morning."

"It doesn't bother her to go there?"

"She says it doesn't. She has coffee with Father Gene after. She talks to him a lot."

"Is she with you right now?"

"Nope, I'm watching TV in the den, and she's upstairs going through pictures."

Rita began to tremble. "How are Gary and the kids?"

"They're having a hard time. They spend a lot of time talking to the grief counselor lady."

She was silent briefly. "And the trial's coming up soon," she finally said.

"I know."

She heard her mother in the background.

"Hold on, honey," her father said.

Then he came back on the line: "Your mother just handed me this picture of you and Ally when we went to the Flume in New Hampshire. I think you had to be about four in this picture. This was the summer before Carter was elected. Do you remember how wet we got on that trip?"

"Vaguely," she said, her voice thick. She pictured her mother in the upstairs study, her reading glasses on, going through boxes of pictures. It's what she did most nights now. She was "organizing" them, she told everyone.

She heard her mother in the background. "Your mother wants to talk to you," her father said. "She wants to ask you about another picture."

"Dad, wait," she interjected. "Before I talk to her. I wanna tell you. I'm coming home again." As soon as she said it, she cried tears of relief.

"Sweetheart—" her father began. "You don't have to do that. We're okay."

"*I'm* not okay. *I'm* not. I came back too soon. And I don't want to be here. I want to be with Leila and Charlie." She wept freely now. "I just want to hold my nephew and my niece in my arms and—" She caught her breath. "I just don't want to be here all by myself. I can come home, right?"

"Habibti," her father said. "Of course you can come home."

The weekend after the next one—after she spoke at one final day-long conference in the capital, after she negotiated with the Foreign Affairs Foundation to work remotely, after she'd found a friend of a friend to sublet her apartment, after she'd said good-bye to her circle of D.C. friends, after she packed her laptop and a few suitcases of clothes to see her through the Massachusetts winter and early spring, along with all of Jonah's things in a box she marked "J," save for his Yankees cap and ACLU sweatshirt, which she wore—after all that, she took a flight from D.C. to Logan, where her father picked her up. She held him longer than she'd ever held him, grateful for the smell of the aftershave cream he'd used since the 1970s, and then he drove her to her sister's house, where—upon seeing their car pull up out front—Leila and Charlie, heedless of the frigid February day, ran out of the front door across the dead grass of the lawn without their coats, shouting "Auntie Rita! Auntie Rita!" and throwing themselves into her arms.

"I missed you guys so much!" she exclaimed.

Charlie stroked her face as though she were a long-lost pet who'd returned. "Are you really gonna stay?" he asked.

She smothered him, then Leila, with kisses, ravenous with love for them. "I'm really gonna stay. For good."

Her brother-in-law, Gary, walked across the lawn, also coatless. She stood to meet him. He held his arms out, embraced her, and murmured, "Thank you."

CHAPTER FIFTEEN

THE NEW WORLD: RITA

(SPRING 2009)

It was not the home she had been expecting.

When Nabil had texted her his address in Encinitas, a beach town about twenty-five miles north of San Diego, she'd pictured a modest apartment complex, that kind of sand-colored, single-story affair, resembling a motor inn, perhaps with a swimming pool in the center of the parking lot. The kind of building she'd passed multiple times in her rental car on the way from LAX to West Hollywood, from which she'd spent the past two hours driving south amid relentless sunshine, rugged hills, and stunning intermittent views of the Pacific, below the bluffs, off to the right.

She knew Nabil was gainfully employed at the *Union-Tribune*, yes, but, she'd assumed, at a modest salary, perhaps forty or fifty thousand dollars. In an expensive city like San Diego, that wouldn't allow for much more than a convenience apartment.

And yet here she was, only a few blocks above the beach, pulling up in front of an impeccably maintained 1920s Craftsman home, painted slate blue with cream trim, set before a small front yard charmingly landscaped with palm trees, cacti, and jasmine. An American flag hung from the porch, where bright red twin rockers sat, angled gently toward each other.

She double-checked the address in Nabil's text, wondering if she'd misread it. She'd spent the whole trip in a bit of a daze, she knew that much. It had been her first plane trip since Day Zero, which was now exactly 196 days ago. She could not believe that they, the family, had not suffocated and perished under the heartbreak—that they had survived. And yet they had. They had just made it through Easter. Which meant that they had made it through their first round of the winter holidays, Easter, and even Ally's late-February birthday, without Ally. Only Mother's Day, in a month, remained to be gotten through.

After Rita had moved back from D.C. and taken up residence once again in her childhood room while she shopped for an apartment, she would get in the car every afternoon and pick up Leila and Charlie from school. Sitting in a queue of Subarus and Volvos, she would peer keenly through the car window until she saw them, bundled in winter coats and hats, straining under their enormous backpacks, trudging toward her.

It was, every afternoon, her first moment of not just genuine happiness but relief. Then sometimes there would be that funny interval of low-level dread as they walked the distance to the car. Would they make it?

Then they would make it, they would be clambering in, their cold cheeks against her own, Charlie unleashing a rapid-fire narration of the day's events, and she would ask, "What's the reward today, guys?"

They had decided that they should have a small reward every day of this school year, just because it was a school year like no other, a nightmare of a school year, a very hard year in which to expect two suddenly motherless children to go to class every day and concentrate, focus, work hard. And most days the reward was a drive to the Friendly's in downtown Mendhem, where Leila and Charlie would each have a small sundae, and Rita would have a coffee but would draw eye-rolling complaints from Charlie by picking up her spoon three or four times and helping herself from his dish.

But some days the reward was a movie, like *Coraline* or *Monsters vs. Aliens*, and once it was a trip to the mall to buy spring Nikes, and once it was a drive to Charlie's personal mecca, the Comic Book Palace. And sometimes Rita would glance at her BlackBerry and then would marvel that she was able to answer e-mails about matters of foreign policy while still having her niece and nephew at her side. She'd had no regrets about coming home. She would not stay forever, but she still considered it nearly the most important thing she'd ever done, and even though she did not really believe in an afterlife or the sentience of the deceased, there was rarely an afternoon with Leila and Charlie when she did not fervently wish for some sort of reassurance that Ally could see them together.

After the daily reward, she would bring them home, sometimes picking up dinner en route and hanging around, making calls or tapping on her laptop, until Gary arrived home around six or seven, at which point she might have a tea with him, each debriefing the other on the day, before leaving him to supper with his kids. He smothered them with hugs and kisses when he saw them, his eyes sometimes welling up. Rita saw, for the first time, the large-hearted, dependable man her sister had fallen in love with, and she felt shame for having, over so many years, dismissed him as a Merrimack Valley dullard.

At her parents' house, she usually cooked dinner—either that or she would bring something home. And then, after her parents had gone to bed, she would recline before her laptop, ostensibly working, but inevitably she would begin to click through her trove of photos from her fourteen months with Jonah. That period—which she defined as beginning at that Capitol Hill town-house party, where they had discussed candidate Hillary's war vote, and ending in the motel in Connecticut where they had spent their last night together—had taken on a magical quality for her.

"I think my family was punished because two of us were in Iraq," she'd once confided to Carol Bradstreet, the family grief counselor brought to them by Father Gene, as she'd earlier confided to Salma. Rita found comfort in Carol's kind, hazel eyes and her sensible nature, that of a Pilgrim wife carrying on with cheer and humility amid the austere conditions of the early seventeenth century. Rita had gone so far as to drop in at the meeting of the antiwar group Carol chaired at the

Unitarian Universalist church in Mendhem—where, to her embarrassment, she was greeted as a celebrity and ended up reluctantly playing
the role of guest speaker.

So Rita felt she could tell Carol something like that—an idea her
own family would find preposterous, if not offensive. And Carol had
not dismissed the idea out of hand.

Instead, after a pause, Carol had asked, "Punished by whom?"

"Well," Rita had answered, "if not by God, exactly, then by karma."

Carol considered more. "I hate the word *punished*," she finally said.
"I don't want to see the world that way."

"I know." Rita laughed. "I guess you can take the girl out of the
Catholic Church, but . . ." she trailed off.

"But if you were going to talk about karma, which I do believe in,"
Carol continued. "Rita, I think it's so much bigger than you and your
family. Look at the damage of these boys coming back from Iraq and
Afghanistan. And women, too, I guess. Look at the depression and the
domestic violence, the suicides. Look at the man who sold B.D. Zajac the
gun. What did he do when he got back from the marines? He opened
a gun store."

"I know," Rita said.

"And B.D. Zajac didn't know that you had been in Iraq. He said
himself that he targeted the festival because it was Arab."

It was true. During the trial, B.D. Zajac, who was sentenced to three
life terms in state prison, one for each of the three people he had killed,
had said he didn't believe that there really could be Arab Christians, that
they had to be Muslims who were trying to fly under the radar, to pass.

Rita had thought that she would not be able to get through the
trial without wanting to stand up and murder B.D. herself. But she'd
ended up sitting there for much of it regarding him with a strange sort
of detachment, a quietly stunned horror. He was mentally troubled, it
was so clear. Just watching his incessant hand and leg twitches, listening
to his nonlinear, disjointed syntax as he spoke, was proof of that. He'd
expressed racist ideas, but he hadn't invented them. Instead, his bent
mind had seized on them and magnified them into obsessions.

After the trial, she'd called the woman who'd previously called her from the national gun violence victims group. And she told the woman that, yes, she would join them that spring in D.C. with survivors of massacres in DeKalb, Illinois (five killed just the week before); Omaha, Nebraska (eight killed last December); Virginia Tech (thirty-two killed last April); Salt Lake City (five killed last February); Nickel Mines, Pennsylvania (five killed in October 2006); and about eighteen other incidents, stretching all the way back to 1984.

"It means so much to us that you are coming," the woman had said. "You have name recognition in front of Congress."

"Do you think that'll change anything? It hasn't so far."

"Nothing will change until a group of little children or elderly people are shot, I hate to say," the woman had replied.

She would be meeting some of these other victims and their advocates in Los Angeles and San Diego. That was partially why she'd decided to go out. That, and because she was speaking on a panel at a foreign policy conference at UCLA's Burkle Center. She was forcing herself to do public appearances again, even though big spaces, full of people, in buildings with unlocked doors and entryways without metal detectors made her extremely nervous.

And now she was sitting in the car in front of this slate-blue bungalow with the palm trees, cacti, and jasmine out front, the southern California sun bearing down. She pulled out her phone to make sure she had the right address and only then saw a text from Nabil: *I'm delayed one hour at the office. Jorge will be there to greet you.*

She had no idea who Jorge was. She stepped out of the car, but was not halfway up the walkway when a tall, brown-skinned, forty- or early-fiftysomething man in a T-shirt and shorts, incredibly well built and with silver shot through his crew cut, stepped out onto the porch to greet her, two identical cocker spaniels following him.

"Rick?" she called, squinting in the sun. It was Rick Garza! She laughed in delight. "What are you doing here? Is this a reunion?"

But then, as she got closer, she discerned that it wasn't Rick at all.

The man, jovial, laughed. "Nabil predicted it!" he called out. "He said he knew you were going to think I was Rick. And you did!"

She stood there, half-dazed. "I'm so sorry. It's just that the resemblance is uncanny."

"That's the first thing Nabil said to me when we met. He said, 'You look just like my boss when I worked for the *Standard*.'" The man then held out his large hand. "I'm Jorge. I'm Nabil's partner."

She failed to take his hand, she was so surprised. She laughed again. "Really? He didn't tell me."

"I think he wanted to surprise you."

"Well," and she finally remembered her manners and shook his hand. "He succeeded. Hi, I'm Rita. It's nice to meet you."

He smiled. His teeth, she noticed, were perfect. Gleamingly white and almost unnervingly straight. And his eyes had the sympathetic squint that Rick's had. "Nabil's told me a lot about you."

"Uh-oh."

"Only good things. And all about your crazy adventures together. The Danger Twins, huh?"

"Wow, he *has* told you a lot."

"And here we have," he said, crouching down and scooping the dogs up in his rather huge arms, "Bo and Luke."

She knelt down and scratched them behind the ears. "Hi, guys." She looked up at him. "They're very cute. And your house and yard are beautiful."

"Thank you. Nabil knows I'm a little OCD when it comes to the landscaping. Come inside. Nabil should be here soon."

The house was charming on the inside as well, the rooms filled with mid-century furniture, the sand-colored walls hung with Mexican rugs and bright abstract art. As they walked through a hallway, Rita noticed an array of photographs hanging, formal groupings of people in the red-trimmed dress blues of the marines; in a few of them she discerned slightly younger versions of the very man leading her through the house.

A kitchen whose shelves were laden with terra-cotta pots and bowls opened out directly onto a garden with a firepit and a stone waterfall that gurgled into a small man-made pond.

"Go sit," Jorge commanded. "What can I bring you? Let's see, we have beer, white wine, lemonade, fizzy water, Diet Coke. Ummm, let's see." He opened the refrigerator. "What else?"

"Fizzy water is good," she said. She stepped outside, followed by the dogs, and sat in a chaise, where one of them—she wasn't sure if it was Bo or Luke—jumped up and joined her. She looked around. The small yard was a little paradise of palm trees and flowers. There were koi darting about in the miniature pond, she noticed. She was having a hard time picturing Nabil amid all this—having a hard time picturing him anywhere, in fact, except in the drab bunker of the villa where they had spent most of their time. Her feeling of unreality, which had been blessedly muted for most of this California trip, surged.

Rick stepped out with two glasses, a bottle of Perrier, and a terra-cotta bowl of chips with guacamole in a smaller bowl built into its center.

"How has your trip been?" he asked, sitting down in a chaise angled toward hers.

"It's been good." She reached forward, accepted the glass of Perrier he poured her. "It's my first trip since—well, I don't know if Nabil told you—"

"He did," Jorge interrupted, soberly, sparing her more. "I'm very sorry."

"Thank you." All her life, she thought, she would have to endure these *I'm sorrys*. "And so—yes, well, my first trip, and I think, given the circumstances, a pretty decent trip. I didn't have a total meltdown when I was in crowds at the airport." She laughed.

And he joined her. "That's a good thing."

"And I'm very excited to see Nabil."

"He's excited to see you too."

"It's all a bit surreal," she admitted. "I didn't expect—" She gestured about her.

Now he laughed. "Me? Well, I didn't expect Nabil."

"Can you tell me—how you met?"

He leaned back with his drink. "You know a restaurant and bar named Urban Mo's?"

"No."

"It's a gay bar in the city where you can go on Sundays and have a few beers, nachos, watch the game. And I was there on a Sunday afternoon about six months ago with some friends from the base—"

"What's the base? You mean Camp Pendleton?"

"Exactly. I'm a lieutenant colonel in the Marine Corps. A field officer."

Rita nodded. "I thought you might be. I saw the pictures on the way in. Were you in Iraq? Or Afghanistan?"

"I was in Iraq the first time, the Gulf War. At the very end, winter 1991. I was twenty-two at the time."

"Ah, okay. Well, go on, I'm sorry."

"Well." He leaned back again, sipped at his seltzer, absently massaged his enormous biceps. "I was there with some buddies watching the game, and I saw a handsome young guy with big eyebrows and long lashes standing off in the corner all by himself, smoking—which, by the way, I got him to quit. Mostly."

Rita smiled. "That's great."

"And one thing led to another, and we got talking and had a laugh," Jorge continued, "and that's how it started. I ended up buying us both a beer and kind of blowing off my friends for the night, and, you know, he told me his whole story, and I told him mine. I'm from San Antonio."

"There we go again," Rita smiled. "Just like Rick. Oh, no, wait, Rick is from El Paso."

He shrugged. "Well, close enough. Maybe I'll meet this Rick someday. My double."

"Maybe! And so then . . ." Rita paused. "Nabil just moved in?"

"Well, not that night. Come on, we're not lesbians. No, I'd say he started staying over most nights, and then he moved in about a month later. He was living in a pretty sad room in El Cajon. That's where a lot of the Iraqis here live."

"I've heard."

"And he doesn't make that much at the paper, so I told him this way he could save, send more money back to his family, and also share the co-parenting duties of these two."

He pointed to the two dogs, who had settled around Rita's feet. "Nabil's a great doggie mommy. And I haven't had someone in this house with me since my breakup three years ago—so it worked out great."

Rita took all this in. "Things really turned out okay for him," she finally said. "I'm so happy."

Jorge raised an eyebrow. "Weeeelll," he drawled. "I'm making him go to therapy."

He glanced back inside toward the kitchen, to be sure that Nabil had not returned yet. Then, back to Rita, "He cries every night in his sleep. Literally, almost every single night. Crying out, crying. I hold him, and I say, 'Hey, habibi'—did I say it right?"

She smiled, touched. "You did."

"I say, 'Hey, habibi, it's okay, you're not there, you're here. You're safe. I won't let anything happen to you. Shh, go back to sleep.'"

"He's lucky he found you," she said.

"Well, vice versa, too." He shrugged, then added: "He carries this picture of her everywhere."

Rita was briefly lost. "Ah," she then said. "You mean Asmaa?"

Jorge nodded. "His cousin. I think that's the hardest loss for him. Even more than leaving his family."

Then came the slam of the screen door in the front of the house, the two dogs bounding back inside in reply.

"He's home," said Jorge, standing. Then, calling into the house: "We're out here, habibi."

But then he proceeded back into the kitchen to greet Nabil, so Rita followed.

And there he was. Her Danger Twin, whom she hadn't laid eyes on in five years, since her shame-filled morning in 2004, when an armored car sped her away from the villa toward the Baghdad Airport. She thought she detected flecks of age and fatigue in his face, in the bit of gray hair at his temples. How old was he now—thirty? He'd put on some healthy weight, stopped gelling his hair, cultivated facial scruff, looked American and urban contemporary in his slim black jeans, Nikes, and fitted plaid short-sleeved button-down shirt, a backpack slung over one shoulder.

She stood before him and put both hands over her face, overwhelmed.

"Oh my God," she exclaimed and then, crying, embraced him. She held him close, like an intimate part of her own self.

CHAPTER SIXTEEN

THE NEW WORLD: NABIL

Nabil held her in turn. "I can't believe it's you, Rita. I can't believe it's you."

Jorge, he noticed, had slipped back out into the yard to play with the dogs but really, Nabil knew, to leave them alone for a moment. After they embraced, Nabil led her to the couch in the living room, where they sat and began the halting process of fitting together the pieces of all that had happened since they'd last seen each other. As they did, as Jorge silently brought her drink in from the backyard and put another drink down before Nabil, massaging his right shoulder briefly before he left the room, Nabil studied Rita's face.

The intense eyes, the prominent nose, the faint blush of olive in her skin, the curly dark hair that was now lightly shot through with gray—it all brought back a rush of memories from a circumscribed but explosive segment of his life. The chaos of the early months of the invasion, but also, in retrospect, the innocence of not knowing what was to come, how much worse it would get. And also, right or wrong, the excitement, the sense of purpose, skill, and competence he had felt out there on the streets translating with her, in those first months when it was still safe enough to do so.

"Do you like your job here?" she asked him, studying his face minutely as well, and he answered yes, that once again he was able to use those skills from the *Standard* days in his job, now in San Diego, after a depressing eighteen months in Damascus and Beirut when he'd really had very little to do except for a bit of work as a paid-under-the-table stringer in Beirut for various Western journalists to whom Rick Garza and Marna Gelman had connected him.

Yet he also found now that he could not look into Rita's face without thinking of Asmaa—seeing Asmaa, in fact. They had always borne a dim resemblance to each other, and at some point in that brief year before Rita was sent away, when they had all worked together, the two had blurred in his head in various ways. Excepting Umm Nasim, they were the only two women in the villa, equally matched in their work ethic and occasionally their intimidating temper. There had been times, when one or both arrived back at the villa and had yet to take off the polyester abaya, when he wasn't totally sure who was who.

But he also saw something new in Rita's eyes—the hollowed-out, wounded look, which resided deep in the pupils, of those who've lost a loved one abruptly or violently. He had not even known that this effect existed until he'd gotten away from Iraq, until he noticed an unbothered simplicity in the eyes of many Damascenes. And then in Beirut, he noticed that lightness among younger Beirutis, and particularly among Europeans and Americans, but also the gutted look in the eyes of older Beirutis who'd lived out the civil war there in the 1970s and '80s.

It was in America, however, that the disparity was most vivid. Americans, he soon noted, had the lightest and brightest look in their eyes, the look of never having seen injury or untimely death occur, of never fearing that their state would not keep them safe. White Americans mostly, he meant—he was learning, in his job, that many black Americans and other minorities did not feel this way—but he could not entirely attach this brightness to white people alone, because truly there were so many kinds and colors of Americans in the San Diego area, such a profusion of races in one place, the likes of which Nabil had previously been unable to imagine, that ultimately one had to simply call them all Americans. They smiled and said, "Hi there! How are you today?" in big, loud voices, with a sunny oblivion in their eyes that perceived him not as someone who had observed mutilated, charred bodies and nearly died himself, not even as someone coming from a broken land whose very name evoked pity, discomfort, and shame for Americans, but as merely the next customer in line, and did he have a points card, or did he want to add to his purchase a one-dollar donation to help children with a certain ailment, or did he want whole, skim, soy, or almond milk in his latte?

And it all played out under a sun and a blue sky as reliably unrelenting as Baghdad's, with nights that also became suddenly cool after sunset. The landscape was different from Iraq's flatness, though, quite rugged, an endless marvel of hills covered in a kind of desert scrub and wildflowers and cut up forever by freeways.

And then there was that mesmerizing ocean, just a short walk from Jorge's house in Encinitas. Proximity to the sea was a terrifying novelty to him. Many empty, soul-piercingly lonely days in Beirut, he had walked the Corniche and stared out at the Mediterranean, trying to fathom how it could not be infinite, how it would eventually give way to other ports: Cyprus, Antalya, Alexandria, Athens, eventually Barcelona, and Marseille.

But the still waters of the Mediterranean could hardly have prepared him for the hypnotic force of the Pacific's waves, that endless, rhythmic roar of water cresting and then falling, spilling itself over and over again onto the sand. He would sit on the beach far, far from the water, Jorge's large arm around him—a sensation he willed himself not to resist but to relax into, even though everything he had ever known previously told him that they were making themselves targets for harm—and he would watch the surfers in their wetsuits, shaking his head, wondering how it was that those monstrous waves did not entirely swallow them up, submerge them into oblivion.

He was shell-shocked, disoriented, those first weeks in San Diego, stumbling through a dream that was too bright. He had a room in a small apartment that he shared with a middle-aged couple, Chaldean Catholics who'd fled from Iraq to Syria, then to the United States, a few years before the U.S. invasion. The apartment was in El Cajon, a town some fifteen miles inland from San Diego that, for a few decades (Nabil had been astonished to discover), had been absorbing layer after layer of Iraqi refugees—first Christians and Yazidis, religious minorities who had never felt safe in Iraq; then Kurds and Shi'a seeking sanctuary from the vengeful wrath of Saddam after the Gulf War; then, in very recent years, both Shi'a and Sunni escaping the sectarian hell, the kidnappings and revenge killings, that had emerged after the invasion.

Nabil could not in a million years have imagined such a strange place: a town where all the buildings were low-slung and sand-colored, much as in Iraq, but where Iraqis from every corner of the country, from every ethnicity, religion, and tribe, had to coexist in an area the size of Kadhimiya, crossing paths daily with Mexicans, Guatemalans, and Hondurans, not to mention Anglos. On Main Street, over which arched a sign that read "El Cajon: 1912," an Iraqi grocery sat across the street from a taqueria, an Iraqi gold vendor a few doors down from a store selling fluffy white Disney-princess dresses for quinceañeras. The most familiar things, he marveled, amid a landscape, a nation, that could not feel more otherworldly.

And on top of all that, he was working again. He was the only reporter from the Middle East at the *Union-Tribune*, and, to his near-shock, his colleagues had made a ceremony of welcoming him, expressing something approaching awe at his résumé and previous travails. He was put on a team with two young reporters: Elliot, a half-black, half-Jewish boy who had recently graduated from the Columbia School of Journalism in New York City, which everyone assured Nabil was very prestigious; and Jessica, a very short, cheerful Mexican American girl who had just graduated from the University of Southern California and spoke flawless Spanish. Together, the three of them would do stories on the various immigrant communities, including the Iraqis, around San Diego.

Elliot and Jessica ended up being not only his colleagues but his lifelines: They taught him how to drive according to American rules, helped him get his license, and assisted him in procuring, via Craigslist, a battered 1998 Honda Civic for seventeen hundred dollars. They introduced him to the complexities of Facebook and invited him to dinner and to parties on weekends.

And one weekend, late on a Sunday afternoon when he was not thus engaged, he dared himself to put on a dress shirt and some cologne and make the short drive from El Cajon, where homosexuality among Iraqis was nearly nonexistent, as it had been in Iraq, to Hillcrest, the part of San Diego that Elliot and Jessica called "the gayborhood," lined with trendy restaurants, shops, and cafés. He parked and walked (trembling) into a bar called Urban Mo's, where patrons, men and women, drank and guffawed while half the video screens showed the Padres game and the other half showed the singer Rihanna, whose "Don't Stop the Music" throbbed over the speakers. He had known of a gay bar or two in Beirut, but he had been terrified to set foot in one after what had happened in Damascus and had stoically resigned himself to celibacy while he was there.

So now he approached the bar, his whole body shaking, assaulted by the pounding music; ordered a beer; and retreated with it into a corner, where he lit a cigarette. Elliot and Jessica frowned upon his smoking— journalists here did not suck down cigarettes all day, as everyone had done in Iraq—but he had no idea how he would stop, even with the various patches, pills, and programs his colleagues had told him were available to him. He was nervous, wound up, all the time, and for as long as he could remember, lighting a cigarette provided his only relief, however brief.

What was Rick Garza doing here? That had been his first discombobulated thought upon spying at the bar, several yards away, a well-built Mexican man with graying temples, laughing with friends. But then, as the man caught his stare, only to look away but then keep glancing back every few seconds, Nabil realized it wasn't Rick at all. The man's eyes were set wider, his shoulders were broader, his nose was less aquiline.

But the resemblance was still uncanny, and as he drank his beer, Nabil fell into a reverie about how sometimes, back in Baghdad, he and Rick would work at the laptop side by side, their shoulders touching, Rick talking in his scratchy voice, and Nabil would feel an exquisite calm course through his whole body.

Then the Rick look-alike was walking toward him, an amused, curious smile around his eyes, and the first baritone words out of his mouth as he reached Nabil had been, "Someone as young and handsome as you shouldn't be smoking."

And that was how it began. Jorge had told him that very first night at the bar that he was in the marines—that he was, in fact, there with some buddies from his base, Pendleton, where he was a field officer, which meant overseeing recruits in a vast field, which aimed to mimic the rough, desertlike terrain of faraway lands, as the recruits learned to eat, sleep, and survive, "in the rough," was how Jorge put it, while they fought Iraqis or Afghanis.

And as he amiably related all this, Nabil could not help thinking that this good-looking, friendly man, who also happened to be gay, was part of the vast American machine that taught soldiers to shoot wildly into crowds of Iraqis or to blow a fully occupied Iraqi family car to pieces if they felt the least bit threatened. The machine that had often dropped bombs in the wrong places.

Nabil was so confused as Jorge kept telling him all this. How could he, Nabil, be here, now, finally on the other side of the American machine, where it seemed so friendly and relaxed and welcoming, hardly the apparatus of terror and death it had been in Iraq? As Jorge spoke, one part of Nabil wanted to kill him, he was so enraged. How could he stand here and talk so sunnily about training men to go kill Arabs and Afghanis? But the other part of Nabil wanted to wrap his arms around Jorge's wide torso and feel Jorge's large hand stroke his head as he laid it on Jorge's chest.

Technically, gays—Jorge was explaining to him in that same affable twang—were still not allowed to serve in the military. But, he added, his closest colleagues had known he was gay for years now, had not cared, and had even met and socialized with his former partner. And moreover, he added, with sober confidence, the ban was going to come down before the end of the commander in chief's first term.

"President Obama, I mean," he added. "That fact is well established on the gay military grapevine," he told Nabil. "And meanwhile, I'm not gonna live in hiding when I'm off duty."

Nabil finally smiled, still feeling that prick of hostility. "And meanwhile, Mister Marine, do you know where I'm from?"

"At first I thought maybe you had an Armenian background," Jorge replied, "but now that I've heard you talk—I'd say Iraq, right? I remember that accent. I was there during the Gulf War. I love the Iraqi people. We got plenty of them around here." He sipped his beer. "Iraqis are good, hospitable people. They don't deserve what they've had done to them."

Nabil laughed, flabbergasted. "But *you* did it to them! To us. *Your* country. *Your* military."

"Weeeeelll," Jorge began slowly. "It's a little more complicated than that, isn't it? The original bad guy here was Saddam. And as for the American intervention, the intention was correct. It's the execution that was flawed."

"The intention was not correct!" Nabil said it so loudly, with such an off-key stab of anger in the high-spirited bar, that some people turned to regard him, which embarrassed him. "Not correct at all," he repeated, more subdued. Then he looked away, self-conscious and angry. He drew on his cigarette and willed himself not to look back at Jorge.

"Hey, hey," Jorge finally said. Nabil felt a hand on his shoulder. "Let's table this one for another night, huh? It's distracting me from my main agenda when I came over here, which was to ask where you got those killer eyebrows."

Nabil allowed himself to exhale a laugh, shaking his head. "From my Uncle Saddam," he said, proud of his quick wit. "I even once had the mustache to match."

Jorge ran a thick index finger over his upper lip. "I'd like to see that," he said.

Nabil's first instinct was to brush away Jorge's hand, lest anyone see them. Then he remembered where he was, tried to make himself relax.

He surrendered to Jorge. There was no other way to put it. In the ensuing days and weeks, Jorge made it clear that he wanted to be with Nabil, make life easier for him, take him under his wing, introduce him to his friends and family, and Nabil let it happen.

It was not only because he was strongly attracted to Jorge. It was also because, in this sunny new paradise where everything was alien and surreal, laced through with strange new rules and values, it was simply nicer to have someone who made everything easier. It was nicer and easier, at the end of the workday, to go to Jorge's pretty, comfortable house near the beach, to play with his sweet dogs while Jorge grilled them fish or made them chilaquiles rojos for dinner, to relent later when Jorge pulled Nabil away from his laptop and into his big arms in bed, than it was to go back to the small, grim apartment in El Cajon with the older Chaldean couple. They were forever sad, dispossessed, the wife always crying, the walls occupied only by tacked-up pictures of an even sadder-looking Jesus.

To some extent, they reminded him of the parents he had left behind in Damascus.

He had called them from Beirut the morning he arrived.

"We woke up and couldn't find you!" his mother had screamed at him through the phone. "How could you scare us like this when we are already so anxious?"

"I had to come here to find work," he pleaded. "I have more contacts here. There's nothing better for me in Damascus than working in a cell-phone shop a few hours a week."

"But you just left without saying good-bye? What's wrong with you?"

"I left you almost all the money I had. And I will be sending you money again soon."

That had turned out to be far from true. He'd just barely paid rent in expensive Beirut with his meager savings and money from odd jobs as a stringer for journalists, the very same ones who always picked up the checks in cafés or bars and invited him to their homes for dinner, thereby reducing his food costs. He had only recently begun wiring his family a small portion of his *Union-Tribune* check—about the same amount monthly he paid to the U.S. government on the standard loan, arranged through the International Organization for Migration, for plane fare from Beirut to San Diego, via London.

"But when are you coming back?" his mother had demanded.

"I don't know."

He hadn't told her then that he planned never to come back. And he did not tell her for another eighteen months, from the spring of 2006 until the fall of 2007, through the entire grueling UNHCR asylum process, through the shock of Hezbollah's brief summer war with Israel, until he got his final approval and flight date. And even then, he waited until his offer from the *Union-Tribune*, brokered through Rick Garza acting as his UNHCR sponsor and facilitated by numerous Skype interviews across many time zones, was firm.

And then he had Skyped his family in Damascus to tell them he was not coming back—that he had earned refugee status and that he was going to California.

He had braced himself for the wailing, the tears, on the other end of the connection. But when it erupted, it still sliced through his heart, particularly the looks on the faces of Ahmed and Rana, who began pleading, "Ammo, you're not coming back? You're never coming back?"

"Of course I will come back," he insisted. "Someday I might even be able to sponsor you to come live there, too."

"We can really come live with you in America?" Rana exclaimed.

"Maybe, habibti. We will see. I have to get settled in my life here first."

After he had all but moved in with Jorge he would Skype his family from Jorge's house, from the large marble-topped counter floating in the middle of the kitchen. (This, he now knew, was what Americans called an "island.") And after a few minutes, Jorge would come sit beside him, crowding alongside Nabil into the screen that his family saw seventy-five hundred miles and ten hours away.

"This is my friend Jorge," Nabil would explain. "I'm at his house."

"Marhaba, Jorge!" everyone would call, and Jorge would call back, "Marhaba!" Then, to Nabil, he would say, "Tell them I'm taking good care of you." And Nabil would say to his family, instead, in Arabic: "He cooks very good Mexican food."

After that call, Jorge had asked him brightly, "So does that mean you want tacos tonight?" And Nabil, still sitting at the island, staring at the blank screen, had experienced a strange moment of blackout in which he did not hear the question. Then came a wave of grief so sudden and powerful, underscored by a frightening nausea, that he broke out not only in sobs but in ghastly wails, his head in his arms on the marble countertop. Terrified that he would never again lay eyes on his parents or any of his family, he wailed, "Ya, Mama, ya, Baba," again and again, like a madman, and Jorge guided him to the sofa in the other room and held him, stroking his back. He wailed until he lay motionless and exhausted in Jorge's arms, as though he'd wailed out his insides. And Jorge did not, in fact, make tacos that night but merely lay there with him until they both fell asleep, waking in the wee hours, starved, to revisit the countertop for bowls of cereal before heading up to bed.

Why did Jorge love him? He often asked himself this. His teeth needed work, he chain-smoked, he did not (he soon realized) dress fashionably, he was not able to invite Jorge to his home, he made a modest salary. He was in San Diego only by the grace of the United States' cooperation with an international aid program for the world's most unfortunate. This last fact nagged at him every day.

One night he asked Jorge this, after they had had sex, which was always so wonderful for Nabil but after which he would lie, mute, too many large and overwhelming feelings ricocheting wildly through his mind. On this one occasion, full to bursting with discomfort, he had turned back to Jorge, in Jorge's large, luxurious sleigh bed, and asked, "Why do you like me?"

"Why shouldn't I like you?" Jorge replied.

"You're a big successful military American man, like out of an action movie, with many nice things, and I'm a refugee."

And Jorge had pulled him in toward him with one arm and brought the other hand to Nabil's face. "For one thing, you're not just a refugee—you're a journalist. And to answer your question, I like you because of this right here," he had said, gently tracing his index finger around Nabil's eyes. "Because I saw everything I needed to know about you right here that first night."

"What did you see?" They were lying close in bed now, their noses only inches apart.

"I saw someone who'd been scared to death but who wasn't giving up."

It had never occurred to Nabil to see himself this way before. But as he mulled it over in Jorge's arms, he decided he liked the sound of it. It was something he had been looking for but hadn't realized: a frame through which to look at his whole life, at everything that had happened so far, and what was happening now, and what might happen next. And it was, in fact—he could say with confidence and pride—the truth.

The morning after his reunion with Rita, Nabil pulled up outside the DoubleTree where she was staying in Hotel Circle, a vast complex of chain lodgings off I-8, and waited until she emerged, behind dark sunglasses and wearing jeans, sneakers, and a men's-style white button-down shirt, much like the shirt she'd worn the day they'd first worked together. She pulled her wheeled suitcase behind her. He got out of his car to retrieve it from her and put it in the trunk.

"Good morning," he called.

"Good morning and thank you." She embraced him lightly. "The weather here is perfect every single day, isn't it?"

"It's a lot like Baghdad weather, right?"

"It is. Minus the sandstorms, I suppose."

"That is true."

He got back on the highway and headed east, into the usual endless expanse of blue sky, palm trees, and scrubby hills. "Did you eat breakfast?" he asked.

"I never do. I have no appetite until noon, usually."

"So you are okay that we just wait until lunch, and we can have some food in El Cajon that will be very familiar to you?"

"Sure." She paused. "Why is it called 'The Drawer'?"

"Excuse me?"

"El Cajon means *the drawer* in Spanish."

"I thought to live in America I would just need your help from our English lessons in Baghdad, but now here you are teaching me Spanish, too!"

"Ha!" she laughed. "But don't expect too much. It's rusty. My Arabic's getting rusty too, now that I haven't been in the region so long." She paused again. "It's like a piece of your mind or your memory that starts to fade away."

He listened, twisting his mouth. "I want parts of it to fade away. Most of it, actually."

He now could feel her staring at him protractedly, and glanced briefly her way to confirm that, yes, behind her sunglasses, she was regarding him.

"What is it?" he asked.

"Nothing. I just got lost in my thoughts for a minute."

He was driving into El Cajon now, that flat, sunbaked expanse of strip malls and modest homes. He pulled onto Main Street, a vast, boxy beige corridor of stores, and parked.

She turned to him again in her seat. "So what are you reporting today?"

"I am meeting a woman named Huda Chalabi. She is an Iraqi Shi'a lady who came here after the Gulf War, and she started a nonprofit that helps new refugees adjust to life here. But specifically she helps husbands and wives learn to communicate and talk things out, because men can't just hit their wives here when they get stressed."

He watched Rita sit up, her eyes sparkling. "That sounds like a great story," she said.

He recognized an old posture in her, that hyperalertness she would always assume right before she plunged into a group of strangers in Baghdad, ready to engage. "Help me with the story," he said. "Ask what you want."

She smiled, shook her head. "You don't need me. My Iraqi is so rusty, anyway."

"If you have a question, just ask."

She shrugged.

He led her a long block down Main Street before signaling her to cross with him. Everywhere, they passed Iraqis. Women in hijabs or abayas, women without hijabs wearing gold crosses around their necks, old men in the drab workaday dress shirts and slacks of the Iraqi middle class, old men in dishdashas carrying prayer beads, teens in sweatpants or jeans or soccer shorts walking in groups, blending with friends who were also Latino or Asian or black. Iraqis coming into and out of grocery stores with signs in the window advertising deals on masgouf, zaytoon, laban and lahmabajin Iraqis looking at gold jewelry mounted on black velvet busts in shopwindows latticed by security grates.

Nabil glanced at Rita, who was looking all around, mouth agape. "This is unreal," she finally said. "Even just hearing that accent again."

"But you knew about this place, right?"

"I knew about it, but I didn't think it would be so obviously Iraqi everywhere you look. When did this start again?"

"Many years before the war, but the Iraqi population has really gone up in the past few years."

He walked Rita over to a storefront with both an Iraqi and an American flag in the window and a sign reading in Arabic, "Alem Jadid."

"New World," read Rita.

"This is the nonprofit," he said. "The New World Association."

Inside, before laptops at desks in the back, sat Huda, in a head scarf, long-sleeved blouse, jeans, and Nikes, alongside two other women, their heads uncovered. When Huda saw Nabil, she broke into a wide smile, rose, and walked toward him.

"Nabil! Marhaba, habibi, salaam alaikum. You look good, hayati." She extended a hand, which he shook briefly.

"Wa alaikum salaam," he replied. Then, continuing in Arabic: "This is Rita Khoury, the foreign-policy expert I told you I was bringing. We were journalists together in Iraq."

Huda trained her smile on Rita. "Hello, Rita, nice to meet you," she said in English, touching her lightly at the elbows and kissing her on either cheek. "Welcome to our little Baghdad in California."

"She knows Iraqi Arabic," Nabil said. "And she's Lebanese, too."

Huda beamed at Rita. "Ah, inti taarfeen arabi? Wa inti lubnaniya? Kolish zen!"

Nabil watched Rita blush. "Arabiti shway taabeneh." *My Arabic is a little rusty.*

"La, la!" Huda insisted. "Kolish zen, kolish zen." *Very good, very good.*

Nabil adored Huda, who was in her early forties and had two kids and a husband who was often away in the Gulf states working as a cultural liaison for large American companies. She reminded him of his mother before the final years of Saddam and the invasion had beaten her down—her energy, her optimism, her modernism, and her habit of always pointing out the best in others.

"Come, come," Huda beckoned them both in English. "Come sit." She pointed to chairs arranged before her own desk, on which were propped photos of her husband, kids, and various other family members. She turned to one of the other women and asked if she would make their guests tea.

Nabil pulled out his notebook and his recorder. He was very proud of the genuine reporter's notebooks, with their spiral bindings at the narrow top, that the *Union-Tribune* had furnished him with, and he hoped that Rita noticed that he took notes in the fashion he'd learned from her, which was to flip the notebook so that he had notes running straight down two pages, top and bottom, then to flip the bottom page and continue writing on the reverse, so that when he later typed from his notes he could look at two whole pages at a time and easily riffle through the pages as he worked.

"What do you think of El Cajon?" Huda asked Rita, now in English.

"I'm very amazed," Rita answered in Arabic—quick, confident Arabic, Nabil noted. She didn't sound that rusty to him after all. "I knew there were many Iraqis here, but I didn't expect it to feel like a street in Baghdad."

Huda laughed. "It's true. It's like Baghdad except a lot of the old men, instead of sitting at a chaikhana, sit all day outside the Starbucks just down the street." Then she turned to Nabil. "Okay, habibi, what do you want to talk about today for your article?"

"My editor wants a story on how you work against domestic violence in the Iraqi community here."

"Okay," said Huda, leaning forward, clasping her hands together. "Well, to start, the funny thing"—and she alternated her gaze between him and Rita—"I started the agency ten years ago to address domestic violence only, but it turns out, basically, we"—and she gestured at the two other women nearby—"me, Dilkhwaz and Zeinab—basically we end up doing everything, because you can't address domestic violence in a vacuum. The whole experience of moving here after enduring difficulties in Iraq is so, so . . ."

She paused, searching for the word. "Really, it's so violent, so disorienting. You must have felt that, Nabil, yes? Even with your excellent English."

He nodded. "I am still feeling it." He was aware of Rita regarding him keenly, her brow furrowed.

Huda beamed. "Exactly! So, you know, the people in our community here, especially when they first arrive, they need help with everything. Where to sign up for health care, services, how to get their kids in school, what is and isn't legal here compared with Iraq, how to get your license for the ones who need to drive, how to drive American-style. I mean, there is so much to adjust to. So even though we keep domestic violence at our center, basically we've become the only game in town"—she laughed self-consciously at her own Americanism—"when it comes to the transition process."

Nabil scribbled frantically as she spoke. "So, the domestic violence. How—how does it present itself?" He poised his pen, hoping that Rita thought he was sufficiently incisive.

Huda sighed. "Oh wow. Well, think about the context. You know, I left Najaf in 1993, because Saddam was slaughtering Shi'a left and right, and I just could not take it anymore. So I've been in the United States for sixteen years, and I've had a—what's the word—a big learning curve for what women's rights are, domestic rights. But think of someone who doesn't know this and just arrives here. Man or woman, you are coming from a culture of patriarchy. Not to say there isn't a culture of patriarchy in the United States, but you know what I mean. It exhibits itself differently."

She paused, sipped the tea that one of the other women, Zeinab, had brought them, Iraqi-style, in small glass cups with matching saucers.

"So here, we talk to husbands and wives, or we talk to parents with children, and we say, 'Here, when you are angry, you cannot just hit, slap.' We show them how to use words. You have to say, 'I am very angry because you did this or you said that.' And then you have to let the other person say, 'I am'—well, you know, whatever it is, very angry or sad or stressed-out—'because of this.' And then we ask them to work it out with words, and if any of them are so angry that they can't, we show them how to call a time-out, leave the house and take a walk, go have a tea with a friend. Or if it's really bad, come to our office so we can mediate."

Nabil scrawled notes to catch up to her words. She was talking in English, likely to be polite to Rita, and he was far from the point where listening and writing simultaneously came as easily to him in English as it did in Arabic.

"And so—" he asked, when he finally caught up, "when they do talk, the couples or the families, what do they say?"

Huda smiled. "Well, that's interesting, and I think that's where the breakthrough comes in. Because when they come in here, and we really explore where this anger or this stress is coming from—"

She paused.

"Sometimes it's the first time that they acknowledge the ordeal they've been through, you know? All those years living under Saddam and maybe losing relatives, and then the upheaval of the invasion and the violence, then leaving their homes they've known all their lives, being able to bring only a few things to Syria, Turkey, Jordan, Lebanon, you know? Wherever they fled to first before enrolling with UNHCR and making it here. And sometimes it's actually beautiful, because they sit here in front of me and cry, and they end up taking hands, because they finally realize what they've been through together. That they're just sad, they're exhausted, they're angry. And they finally see it as something that they survived together, that they're not each other's enemies, that actually, they are both victims of this—"

"Trauma."

Nabil turned. It was actually the first word Rita had said since the interview had properly begun.

"Trauma, yes, exactly," Huda continued. "We try to introduce them to that concept, and it reframes their relationship, whether it's husband and wife or parent and child. Because they see themselves as bonded in this difficult experience, and it brings out a much gentler side of them. We give them permission to forgive themselves and forgive each other because of this larger thing they've gone through."

She paused again, sipping. "It's really quite beautiful, actually. When it works!" she laughed.

Nabil scrawled, then looked up. "Is there someone I can talk to?" he asked. "I don't need to use their full name if they don't want."

"I have someone for you right here," Huda said, in a low voice, in English. Then she turned and, in Arabic, said to the woman Zeinab, who had brought them tea, "Habibti, you still feel comfortable talking to Nabil, the journalist?"

Zeinab looked up from her computer. She was a middle-aged woman—about fifty, Nabil guessed—plump, her shoulder-length hair, obviously dyed brown, judging from its faint gray roots, brushed back from her face, drugstore reading glasses propped low on her nose. She looked a bit to him like the twenty-five-years-prior version of Mariam, Asmaa's mother.

"Yes," the woman answered. "I am very happy to help."

"I don't have to use your family name," Nabil said.

"No," answered the woman. "It is okay. My name is Zeinab al-Jubouri and I am forty-eight years old. I am from Adhamiya and my husband's name is Mazen al-Jubouri, and we have two children, Mazen and Amina, who go to the high school here. We have been here two years."

Nabil smiled as he scribbled. "I am from Kadhimiya," he said.

The woman smiled, her eyes crinkling. "Then you remember the time we would go freely between those two beautiful neighborhoods over the bridge," she said.

"I do."

"The Al-Aimmah Bridge," Rita noted.

"Yes, exactly," said the woman.

"May I ask," Nabil continued, "what your two years in America have been like?"

Again, the woman smiled, shaking her head, as though at a loss where to begin. "Very, very hard years," she said. "Of course, we are safe here, which is the main point. And my children love the school, and they have many friends, so, you know, my husband and I, we say that we are living for them now, for their future, because we will never be happy here."

She then glanced at Huda, who regarded her gently.

"Of course, I am very, very happy to have met Huda and to be able to work with her," she continued. "She has helped us with everything. And the fact that I can love this Shi'a woman like my own sister, with no fear, that reminds me of Baghdad before the invasion and all the ugliness and killing that came after."

Huda nodded soberly, reached out, and put a hand briefly over Zeinab's. "Hamdullilah, we can be friends here, as it was meant to be, habibti," she said.

"Yes, it's true," the woman continued. "But, no. This is all for our children. For me, you know, I will always just remember the Iraq of my childhood, before Saddam, when it was a paradise. It looked like a postcard. That's where I live—" she paused, then tapped her finger against her temple. "In here." She smiled again, the same rueful crinkle around her eyes.

"I know what you mean," Nabil said.

"You know where I go in my head?" the woman continued, her voice perking up a bit.

"Where is that?" Nabil asked.

"You know Pig's Island in the Tigris?"

"Of course."

"I go there," she said. "When I was young, our uncle would take my little brother and me there on very hot days in his motorboat. We would bring watermelon and dolma and lemonade and cards to play, and my uncle would smoke a cigar and drink arak, while my brother and I played in the water just off the island. My uncle would bring a radio and sing along to Abdel Halim Hafez while we swam. You know," and the woman, her eyes watering, began to sing. "Ahwak, wa atmana law ansak—"

Nabil smiled. It was truly one of the region's most famous old songs, the Egyptian legend's "I Love You." So he briefly joined her: "Ansa rohy wayak . . ." *I love you, and I wish if I ever forget you . . .*

"Ahhh!" cried Huda, joining in the next line: "Wen dalet teba fadat . . ." *That I also forget my own soul as well.*

The three of them faded out, laughed self-consciously. Nabil glanced at Rita, who was smiling but quiet.

"Well, so," continued Zeinab, dabbing her eyes with a tissue from a powder-blue box on her desk, "that's where I go in my head. The feel of the sun on my skin, the green water up to our knees, my hands sticky from the watermelon, the smell of my uncle's cigar in the air, and the sound of the music coming out of his little radio. With his motorboat pulled up on the sand just a few feet away. And I remember those beautiful swirls of water in the river farther out from where we were wading. Those whirlpools. Our uncle always told us to stay away from them, that if we were caught in one of them, we would never get out, and the river would carry us all the through Iraq right into the Persian Gulf!" She laughed. "But I was always so—so fascinated by them. They were so beautiful to watch under the sun."

Nabil scrawled, looked up. The woman tapped her own head again. "That's how I get through the sadness. I live in the past."

"Is your brother here, too?" Nabil asked.

The joy that had briefly animated the woman's face drained away. She shook her head. "No. He's gone."

"He's dead?"

"Habibti," interjected Huda. "You don't have to talk about it if you don't want to."

"No, no," the woman insisted. "I can. You showed me, Huda, that I can talk about it and still be okay." She turned again to Nabil: "A Shi'a militia kidnapped him three years ago. He was missing for six days, then we woke up one morning and found his body with his hands and feet cut off outside our garden gate. With a note pinned on him, 'Get out before it happens to you and your children.' Signed in the name of one of the militias."

She paused to shrug. "And so we arranged his burial, and we left Iraq for Syria the next day, and that was the start of what brought us here."

As Nabil scribbled, he caught, from the corner of his eye, Rita, as she rose, quietly said, "Excuse me," and walked out of the office.

His scribbling completed, he looked up at the woman. "They did the same thing to my cousin," he said. "I'm not sure if it was Shi'a or Sunni or both. But they shot her in front of me, and she died in my arms. We were on our way to work one morning, just rushing to the car."

The woman nodded, regarding him. "So I have a little place in my head where I go to keep from going crazy," she said, then laughed. "Is that so bad?"

"That's not bad at all, habibti," Huda assured her. "Whatever works for you is good."

"And we live here now," the woman continued, "because at least we are safe. I mean, yes, of course, we know there are some people here who don't like us, but not really that many. We know it is nothing like Iraq. This is a normal country, like Iraq in the sixties and seventies. Again, it's all for our children now. My life is over."

"What about the work you do here with me?" Huda asked. "Isn't that an important life?"

The woman considered a moment. "I mean my happiness is over. My personal happiness."

Nabil looked up at the woman. "I know what you mean," he said. He was thinking not so much of himself as of his mother.

But she mistook his meaning. "You're younger than I am," she said. "You'll have a good life and take the best from this country. Look at you now. Sahafi!" *A journalist!*

He put down his pen for a moment. "I am grateful I have work here." Then he rose. He'd wondered where Rita had gone. Had she needed the bathroom, she could have merely used the one in the adjacent room, clearly marked. "Would you excuse me a moment to find my friend?" he asked.

Huda waved him away affably. "Of course, habibi. Go. We will be right here."

He stepped back out onto the sidewalk, into the sun, which briefly blinded him. He looked up Main Street, then down, but Rita was nowhere to be seen. He walked to the corner—where, peering down the side street, he saw her leaning against a parked car, sobbing, her shoulders shaking, one arm crossed over her chest, the other hand raised to cover her face. Even from several yards away, he could hear the choked, oddly high-pitched hiccupping sound she made, almost like a laugh.

He stood there, silent, just watching her a moment, mesmerized. Rita crying was an alien and upsetting sight, so utterly out of character. The only other occasion he could remember her crying in all of their time together in the villa was that bizarre moment, right before she left, when he was extolling to her the virtues of his Bibi's bamia, her okra stew, and she had abruptly burst into tears and run out of the kitchen, baffling him.

He turned, began walking back toward the New World office, resolved not to embarrass her, but, after a few steps, stopped again. Slowly, he turned, retraced his steps, and, rounding the corner, walked to her, whereupon he put a hand on her shoulder from behind.

She started briefly, but, seeming to sense it was him, did not raise her head from her hand or stop crying. He had no idea what to say to her, so he merely began rubbing her back, gently, as his own mother had done to him when he was a very small, crying boy.

Wordlessly, after a moment, she embraced him and continued crying into his shoulder.

"It's okay," he murmured, for lack of anything else to say.

"I'm so sorry," she gasped as she wept.

"What are you sorry for?"

"That I forgot you."

"When did you forget me?"

"When you were trying to get out of Iraq."

Oh, he thought. When he'd e-mailed asking her for help with his UNHCR case and he'd not heard back. And he remembered that, as no reply came from her after days, then weeks, he had been hurt, only because she'd promised him before she'd left that she would be there if he ever needed her. But then he had just chalked her silence up to her being American. She'd moved on. Had he really expected more?

By now she'd pulled back from him and was wiping her face with the back of her hand, one arm still on his shoulder. She looked vulnerable and childlike, he thought, as though she'd just cried out all the usual hardness in her face, that reflexive half smirk.

"Well, I still made it." He tried to put some cheer into his voice.

"I'm glad you did."

"I'm glad you're here, too."

He actually was. She was, he realized, the only person he'd been with on American soil who'd ever known Asmaa.

He gestured backward. "I should go back in and finish."

She nodded. "I'll go work at that Starbucks just down the street." Then she regarded him. "You've become such a good reporter."

He'd been hoping she'd say something to that effect. "You really think so?"

She nodded again. "You make me miss it."

"You can do it again."

"Probably not."

"You can write for someplace else. The *American Standard* isn't the be-all and end-all, you know."

She laughed, surprised. "Where'd you learn that expression?"

"I pick up a lot from Jorge."

"He's a great guy. He's crazy about you, too."

She turned and walked up the street, in the direction of the Starbucks.

* * *

An hour later, after he'd walked up and down Main Street talking to people and gathering more quotes for his story, Nabil found Rita sitting at a table outside the Starbucks, frowning over her laptop, not far from a group of old Iraqi men playing dominoes.

"Hello, hello," he called.

She looked up. "Well, hello. Did you get more good stuff?"

He sat. "I did. But I'm done for the day. It's Friday, and they told me I don't have to file until Monday."

"You're not on this weekend?"

"Not until Sunday morning."

She nodded. "Nice."

He mimicked her nod. "But," he added, "would you be okay to go straight back to Encinitas for lunch? I have had enough Iraqi intensity today. Jorge will cook for us."

She made some final clicks on her laptop, then closed it, rose. "Absolutely. I nibbled on something here anyway."

When they arrived at the house, they found Jorge putting away groceries. "You two feel like branzino tonight?" he asked, approaching Nabil, lacing both arms around his waist and planting a kiss on his lips. Nabil felt his entire body flush. He still had not learned to let Jorge touch him in front of others without seizing with fear and self-consciousness. "I'll grill the fish outside."

"That sounds amazing," Rita said. "Are you sure it's not a burden if I stay?"

Jorge gestured around his kitchen. "Doesn't this beat a sad room on Hotel Circle?"

"It does," she said.

"Good." Then he turned to Nabil. "Hey! You should take Rita to Moonlight Beach."

Nabil laughed. "To help me get over my beach fear?"

"Unfair!" Jorge protested. "I didn't say that, baby. I just thought that it might be nice to take a beach walk with Rita before we eat."

"Can you believe," Rita said now, "I've never swum in the Pacific? Can we do it?"

"I do it," said Jorge. "It's cold as fuck, but I love it. In and out in one big plunge. Ask Nabil."

"He does it," Nabil confirmed. "He is crazy."

"I grew up swimming off the coast of New Hampshire," said Rita. "In June. Cold water doesn't faze me."

"All the better," said Jorge.

"But I forgot a bathing suit."

"You can wear the suit my sister leaves here."

In ten minutes, he and Rita were walking, in flip-flops pulled from a basket Jorge kept by the cellar door, down the hill, past the bungalows with their yards set with cacti and jasmine bushes. Nabil still gawked at the near-nudity of San Diego beach life. His life up to this point, he thought, had been increasing levels of public undress, from women's bare arms in Baghdad, then barer arms and bare legs in Damascus, to the sports bras of Beirut's Corniche and the shockingly tiny dresses of its nightlife, to this just-like-American-TV landscape of sixteen-year-old girls walking around, looking eternally bored, licking ice cream cones in bikinis no bigger than three cocktail napkins held up with string, of boys with surf shorts half falling off their waists, exposing pelvises that disappeared in a V in the front.

And here he was, self-conscious in red board shorts borrowed from Jorge and a *Union-Tribune* T-shirt he'd been given in a package of goods on his first day at work. Pretending at, performing, Americanness, as though he were actually laid-back, oblivious to darkness.

The beach was not crowded despite the piercing heat and sun of two o'clock. They passed the parking lots, the snack bar, the showers, the volleyball courts. That otherworldly roar of the waves breaking on the sand filled his ears.

They laid down a blanket and sat side by side, their arms hooked around their knees. Rita, Nabil noted, was transfixed by the water, by the surfers in their wetsuits, who bobbed and lolled, waiting for the next big wave.

"I think I need to just do this and get it over with," she finally said, rising, pulling off her T-shirt. She stood over him in her one-piece—her legs and armpits stubbly, Nabil noticed, her dark corkscrew curls, with their gray dusting, pulled back in a bun. "I'm going to take a plunge for my sister. We always tried to do the first and last swim of the year together."

"You are brave," he said.

"Are you coming?"

"No way. I'll watch you the way I used to watch Asmaa jump in the pool."

She looked, for a moment, he thought, as though she were about to scold or tease him for his cowardice. Then she knelt down and kissed him on the cheek.

"Wish me luck," she said, before running down to the water, her buttocks jiggling in the too-tight suit Jorge had given her, her thighs pumping, arms cocked and up by her chest.

She stopped briefly when her feet touched the water, shouted back at him, "Oh my *God! Oh my God!*" She was hugging herself, laughing, hopping from foot to foot. Then she looked back one more time and pushed forth, flinging herself into a wave just as it crested and broke.

Nabil stood, concerned. She was not surfacing. He walked briskly down to where the sand became damp, where he felt the first blush of cold shoot up through his legs. The sun dazzled on the roiling surface of the water; gulls cawed overhead. He craned his neck forward, alarmed.

Just then, she surfaced, whooping, sounding uncannily like Jorge.

"Oh my God!" she called. She'd never sounded so unpinned from herself, Nabil thought, so wild. "Nabil, come in, it's amazing!" The sun played on her face, so that she was clear to him one moment, opaque the next, just a silhouette.

"I can't!" he shouted.

"I know you can swim," she shouted back. "Jump in! You won't regret it."

So this was the new world. He thought he'd already found it, but it turned out that there was a world beyond that world, and then another beyond that, and even then at least the creator's intimation of other worlds. They unfolded eternally, as in a hall of black mirrors in which only the crystalline image of himself, running hard for his very life, was the constant, the bridge that lifted him from one world to the next, at once less and more of himself than he'd been a world before.

He pulled off his T-shirt, shouted to her, "Get ready!" and plunged in.

ACKNOWLEDGMENTS

For the second time in a few years, I thank Susan Golomb (and, this time, Mariah Stovall) at Writers House and Peter Blackstock, Morgan Entrekin, Deb Seager, John Mark Boling, Emily Burns, Christopher Moisan, and everyone at Grove Atlantic for working with me to bring this book into the world. I could not have a better bunch of folks on my side.

A great pleasure of writing *Correspondents* was reading so many other wonderful books as part of the research, including (but not limited to) *Bread and Roses: Mills, Migrants and the Struggle for the American Dream* by Bruce Watson; *Children of the Roojme: A Family's Journey from Lebanon* by Elmaz Abinader; *Naked in Baghdad: The Iraq War and the Aftermath as Seen by NPR's Correspondent Anne Garrels; The Unraveling: High Hopes and Missed Opportunities in Iraq* by Emma Sky; *The Forever War* by Dexter Filkins; *The Fall of Baghdad* by Jon Lee Anderson; *Newtown: An American Tragedy* by Matthew Lysiak; *The Bread of Angels: A Journey to Love and Faith* by Stephanie Saldaña; *We Crossed a Bridge and It Trembled: Voices from Syria* by Wendy Pearlman; *Collateral Damage: America's War Against Iraqi Civilians* by Chris Hedges and Laila Al-Arian; *Operation Homecoming: Iraq, Afghanistan and the Home Front, in the Words of U.S. Troops and Their Families* by Andrew Carroll; *Waiting for an Ordinary Day: The Unraveling of Life in Iraq* by Farnaz Fassihi; *Between Two Worlds: Escape from Tyranny: Growing Up in the Shadow of Saddam* by Zainab Salbi; and *Night Draws Near: Iraq's People in the Shadow of America's War* by Anthony Shadid. I am also indebted to the documentary *Homeland (Iraq Year Zero)* by Abbas Fahdel (watchable on Netflix).

Also warm thanks to Amita Kiley at the Lawrence History Center in Lawrence, Mass.; John A. Ryan, Jr., MD; Hospital Corpsman Third Class Jeremy Butler; Mike Ackil; Hadi Kebbeh; Shirine Saad; Cara Buckley; Dan Murphy; Mo Mustelidae; Dahlia Tucker; Myriam Fizazi-Hawkins; Nabil Canaan; Reem Niyazi; everyone at the Levantine Institute in Tripoli, Lebanon, particularly Nadia Zreik Adhami and Manal Masry; and Shatha and Aya Alboosi.

I reserve the most gratitude for two very special people. In El Cajon, California, the unstoppable and compassionate Dilkhwaz Ahmed opened up her home and her community to me, introducing and translating to show me how recent Iraqi refugees in the United States were coping with the jarring transition to American life after undergoing stress and upheaval in Iraq. Her nonprofit licensetofreedom.org does amazing, crucial work helping people make this adjustment, and if you were at all moved by this story, I humbly urge you to consider supporting it.

Finally, I am not sure I could have confidently written *Correspondents* without some early conversations I had with my fact-checker turned friend Yasir Dhannoon, who then put his eyes upon every line of the book that takes place in Iraq, Damascus, and the Iraqi community in El Cajon. Please consider supporting thesyriafund.org, whose board Yasir sits on; it does important work in the Middle East for Iraqi and Syrian refugees.

My maternal grandfather, Peter Ackarey, emigrated from Syria (in what is now Akkar, Lebanon) in the early twentieth century to a United States that has long provided not just safety but a thrilling blank slate of opportunity and hope to so many immigrants like himself. The United States, which has blithely visited so much misery on other parts of the world, has always been far from perfect. But its open arms and its un-rivaled cosmopolitanism are among the ways in which it has been, and remains, truly great. As I write this, that aspect of American greatness faces, not for the first time, severe challenges. My final acknowledgment in these vexed times is to everyone—U.S. born or immigrant, documented or not, finely skilled or with nothing to offer but industry and optimism—who continues to fight for this expansive vision of the troubled, divided country that I still dearly love.